"I heard a rumor yesterday that you have a daughter." Ben chuckled. "Is it true?"

Rebecca placed one hand on the stainless steel counter, trying to stop the quiver as it ran up and down her body. *Her daughter.* How much did he know? *She'd wanted to be the one to tell him.*

"Yeah, I'm a mom now," she said, struggling to keep her voice steady and her breathing even. "To Lexie."

"Lexie," he repeated the name, the word on his lips sending another wave of worry down her back. "And who's the lucky man?"

"Man?" she asked.

"Your husband?"

Gulp. Husband. *Hmm.* "I...ah...well, there is no lucky someone. It's just me and Lexie."

"You mean some man left you, after you'd had his child? That why you didn't stay in touch with me? Because you knew I'd hunt him down?"

She did *not* like where this was going. Hmm, what did she say? *Yes, Ben, and that man was you? That's exactly why I stopped returning your e_____t, becaus_____a secret.*

HIS UNEXPECTED
BABY BOMBSHELL

BY
SORAYA LANE

Published in Great Britain 2015
by Mills & Boon, an imprint of Harlequin (UK) Limited,
Eton House, 18-24 Paradise Road, Richmond, Surrey, TW9 1SR

© 2015 Soraya Lane

ISBN: 978-0-263-25140-1

23-0615

Harlequin (UK) Limited's policy is to use papers that are natural, renewable and recyclable products and made from wood grown in sustainable forests. The logging and manufacturing processes conform to the legal environmental regulations of the country of origin.

Printed and bound in Spain
by CPI, Barcelona

As a child, **Soraya Lane** dreamed of becoming an author. Fast forward a few years, and Soraya is now living her dream! She describes being an author as "the best job in the world." She lives with her own real-life hero and two young sons on a small farm in New Zealand, surrounded by animals, with an office overlooking a field where their horses graze.

For more information about Soraya, her books and her writing life, visit www.sorayalane.com.

For Carly and Kathryn. I truly feel as though I hit the editor jackpot with the two of you! Thank you for all your wonderful ideas, and for making my books so much stronger.

CHAPTER ONE

REBECCA STEWART GULPED as the door to the restaurant opened. *Ben McFarlane.* It had been almost four years, but she'd have known him anywhere. Dark blond hair cropped short, broad shoulders stretching the material of his T-shirt and a stare that still managed to make her heart beat too fast. He was exactly as she remembered him and then some.

"Long time no see."

His gaze softened as he came closer, the corners of his mouth turning upward into a smile, but she could tell he was angry. Those eyes had caused her heart to break and heal all over again so many years ago, the last night they'd had together still burned into her memory as if it was yesterday. *She knew every expression he had.*

Rebecca swallowed, smiled back, her stomach flip-flopping. *He didn't know. Couldn't* know. That angry gaze, determined stride…she'd thought he was coming in with a purpose when she'd first recognized him. That he knew about his daughter.

She pushed those thoughts away and tried to remind herself of how they'd been before that night, back when they'd been best friends and nothing more.

"Hey, stranger," she said. "I had no idea you were back."

Rebecca moved out from around the counter, hands smoothing the soft cotton of her apron. She didn't know what to do—whether to embrace him, touch him. What did you do to a man, formerly your best friend, once your lover, who you hadn't seen or heard from in years?

"Hey." His voice was surprisingly gruff.

Rebecca stepped into his arms when he opened them, gingerly at first, until he pulled her in, giving her an awkward kind of bear hug. She tried to relax, focusing on breathing in and out. *They were just friends.* But after all this time he still had that effect on her. The smell of his cologne, the strength of his body, everything about him took her back to that night, when a decade of friendship had turned into something more. The night before he'd left and she'd encouraged him to leave her behind even though it had shattered her heart into a million pieces.

"How are you, Bec? Haven't heard from you in a while."

Ouch. The hug must have been a formality.

She took a step back, his hands falling from her waist. It was warm but she shivered, wrapping one arm about her body, the other hanging awkwardly at her side.

"I've been good, Ben. Really good," she said, forcing a big smile, avoiding the question. It wasn't as if he'd emailed her lately, either.

"Your folks?"

Rebecca smiled. Her parents would love to know that Ben was back in town.

"They're great." This time she didn't have to force the grin. "Very busy, enjoying their retirement, so I'm running this place on my own most of the time."

She looked over her shoulder, catching a glimpse of commotion in the kitchen. When she turned back to Ben she noticed he was watching, taking everything in. He'd known her parents' Italian restaurant just as well as she had when they were teenagers. They'd both worked waiting tables over their last summer break, before he'd had the opportunity of a lifetime and left for Argentina.

"Anyway, how about you? What brings you back?"

Ben jammed both hands into his jeans pockets, eyes down before he looked up and met her stare. She knew something was wrong. Why was he even back here?

"Has something happened to your grandfather?" Rebecca heard the falter in her own voice.

"He's not doing great, even though he'd hate me telling you that." He squared his shoulders and pushed his feet out wider. "It was time to come home anyway. I've done my time overseas, for now."

"Really? It's not like you were getting too old to play." She ran her eyes over his superfit frame. He was all muscle, *all athlete*. It wasn't like polo players had a use-by date, so long as they were still performing, and she'd never expected him to give up his career voluntarily. Not for anything.

That made him laugh. "I'm not too old, and I'm fit as hell, so don't go feeling sorry for me." His voice was dry. "I just decided I'd been away for long enough, and Gus needs the help. Argentina was fun, but I missed the old fella."

Oh. She tried to digest his words. It sent a cold streak down her spine. "So you're back for good?"

"Yeah, for the time being, anyway," he said. "If you'd been better at emailing me back, I might have given you a heads-up."

Ouch again. "Ben, I just got busy and there was so much happening. I'm sorry." She knew it sounded like a cop-out, and it was. But he hadn't emailed for a long time, so it wasn't all her fault.

He looked up, gave her a long, hard stare before training his eyes past her head.

"So tell me, how long have you been back? What are your plans?" she asked.

"I'm just playing it by ear. I'll see how it goes, how much I can do around the farm."

Rebecca tried not to react, digested the information as if it meant nothing to her. Polo had always been his life, his dream to play as a career, and now he'd just given it up like that? As if it wasn't the single most important thing to him after years of being desperate to make it happen?

"So that's it. You're just not going to play anymore?" she asked.

A shrug of his shoulders told her he was uncertain. Ben always pushed them up, then hunched them when he was uncomfortable.

"Things change, Bec. You know how it is."

Yeah, she did. Only she was pretty certain that he hadn't just had a change of heart—something else had to be going on. If he was doing it for Gus, she completely understood, but she smelled a rat.

"Anyway, I've only just arrived back in. I'm still going to be training horses, I'm just taking time out from playing." He smiled. "I'm heading for Geelong in the morning."

Rebecca turned and walked back toward the counter, trying to ignore the rising heat in her cheeks. Her pulse had started hammering hard at her temple. *Geelong.* The place where his grandfather's horse training establishment was. The place she'd spent every school vacation and weekend, hanging out with Ben and dreaming about their future. Only she hadn't realized how much of a man's sport polo was—she'd ended up bravely waving Ben off while she stayed behind. It had been tough for him to make it, and even tougher for her to try to make a career out of it. But they'd only been friends, it wasn't as if he'd left his girlfriend behind.

"My granddad turned eighty last week, and I know the cancer's probably worse than he's letting on. I'm heading there to learn everything I can and slowly take the reins from him. Excuse the pun."

"He must be so happy to have you back," Rebecca said, refusing to think about what-ifs just because Ben was back in town and standing before her. It wouldn't have mattered if he'd stayed or not, they'd both wanted different things, and their one night together had been the result of too much to drink. He hadn't owed her anything. She took a deep breath. "You're going to love being home."

He smiled, but his eyes told a different story. He was annoyed with her, and she didn't know what to say to him except sorry for not staying in touch. But she hadn't been able to keep emailing him and not mention what was going on in her life, which meant that losing contact with him had been the only option. She'd always sworn that if he came back she'd tell him, but the guys he played polo with had become his family, he'd always said he loved what he did and wouldn't give it up for anything.

"It was what we always talked about, huh? The two of us playing polo overseas then coming back to run a horse stud together."

"Yeah," she said softly, not wanting to go back in time because thinking about the past only hurt. "Yeah, it was."

"But, anyway, tell me about you? I heard a terrible rumor yesterday that you have a daughter." He chuckled. "Is it true?"

Rebecca placed one hand on the stainless steel counter, trying to stop the quiver as it ran up and down her body. *Her daughter.* How much did he know? *She'd wanted to be the one to tell him.*

"Yeah, I'm a mom now," she said, struggling to keep her voice steady and her breathing even. "To Lexie."

"Lexie," he repeated the name, the word on his lips sending another wave of worry down her back. "And who's the lucky man?"

"Man?" she asked.

"Your husband?"

Gulp. Husband. *Hmm.* "I, ah, well, there is no lucky someone. It's just me and Lexie."

"You mean some bastard left you, after you'd had his child? That why you didn't stay in touch with me? Because you knew I'd hunt him down?"

She did *not* like where this was going. Mmm, what did she say. *Yes, Ben, and that bastard was you? That's exactly why I stopped returning your emails.* But she didn't think of him like that, because she'd made the decision to keep Lexie a secret, to protect both of them, but mainly to make sure she wasn't the one responsible for clipping his wings.

"Let's just say I was better off bringing her up on my own, at least for the time being," Rebecca said, being careful with her words. "My folks have been great and she's a happy little girl, so it's all worked out okay."

The look on Ben's face told her he was unconvinced.

"And your dad didn't try to do something about it? Or your brother, for that matter?"

Rebecca needed to change the subject. Fast. She needed time to think about how she was going to tell Ben, how she was going to break it to him. "They weren't thrilled about the whole thing, but sometimes life throws a curve ball and you just have to deal with it."

He opened his mouth, looked grumpy as hell and about to say something else about her solo parenting situation so she quickly interrupted him.

"Do you want something to eat?" she asked. "We can still rustle up your favorite seafood linguine if you like?"

The frown on Ben's face almost instantly spun upward into a smile. "You still do it?"

"We still *can* do it," she said with a laugh. "It's an oldie but a goodie, that one. Not officially on the lunch menu, but a version of it's still a dinner favorite so we have the ingredients."

This time when he looked at her he didn't break the stare, not for a second. His eyes were locked on hers, his dark brown irises flecked with gold in the bright light.

"I have to go, but how about I take you up on that offer another day? Maybe when you're not so busy and you can join me?"

She forced herself to keep breathing, which felt like the most unnatural thing in the world all of a sudden with Ben standing in front of her. The last thing she needed was to sit down and have lunch with him.

"Sounds good. It would be nice to catch up."

Someone in the kitchen called out her name, giving her an excuse to break away, to finally glance away from the eyes that had been holding her captive.

"I'll see you around, Bec." Ben held his hand up in

the air and took a few steps backward before turning and heading for the door.

Rebecca watched him, didn't move a muscle until he'd disappeared from sight, ignoring the chaos behind her. Her heart was thumping with what she knew was excitement, but the rest of her was a quivering mess of nerves, ready to slip into a puddle on the floor. Because there was no part of Ben being back that was okay, none at all.

Ben stuffed his hands deep into his pockets and walked down the street, through the crowded lunchtime buzz of inner city Melbourne. He loved Australia, loved being back on home turf and knowing he was where he belonged. Living overseas had been a blast, but the idea of dividing his time between the city and his granddad's farm was what he wanted now, and he knew he'd made the right decision coming home. As hard as it was leaving his polo family behind, he couldn't stay away from Gus any longer.

And seeing Bec? *Wow.* He'd only been home one day and it had been a fight not to turn up at the restaurant that first night, just to lay eyes on her again. The girl who'd waved him goodbye, his best friend, and then slowly disappeared from his life. But who could blame her? He hadn't exactly been the best at staying in touch, but then she'd been downright terrible.

And then she'd met some other guy and had a kid? Little Bec all grown up and a *mom*? Now, that he hadn't been expecting. In his mind he'd imagined her life on hold, expected he could come home and somehow he'd be able to convince her that their night together had been a good thing, that they were supposed to be more than just friends. He'd been a fool, naive at best, and after seeing her today he knew he'd waited too long, that she'd moved on and he'd missed his chance.

Because even though he'd had the time of his life away, ridden some of the best polo ponies in the world and traveled to the most incredible countries, he'd never stopped thinking about Rebecca. Not for a moment. At the time, he'd been so desperate to belong, loved being part of a big extended polo family, when in reality he'd had a little family here with Gus and Rebecca all along, only it had taken being away so long for him to realize it. It wasn't until his granddad had finally admitted how sick he was that it had really hit home.

Rebecca's soft, smiling face, pillowy lips and shining eyes had been the memory he'd clung on to, and almost four years on, he was darn pleased she didn't have a husband. He could never stay angry with her and seeing her today had proved it. He'd gone in all tough guy, wanting to demand why she'd lost touch. *But he hadn't.* And they might have been drunk that night together, but he hadn't forgotten a moment of what had happened between them.

He'd kill the guy who'd left her, on her own and with a child, and he'd bet her parents would be happy to help him find him. Rebecca had been his best friend, and for one night she'd been his lover. Ben grimaced as he jumped behind the wheel of his car. *And that one night had ruined everything between them.*

Rebecca strolled in to the preschool center and locked eyes on her daughter. Lexie was running around the room at high speed, arms spread out as if she was flying, her little lips bouncing off one another to make a noise like a plane. Her heart fluttered and she turned away, not wanting Lexie to see her yet. Her little girl was clingy enough as it was, and she loved seeing her play with the other kids.

"Hey there."

Bec turned to find Julia, one of the teachers, behind her. She was holding out a colorful, smudged sheet of paper.

"Lexie painted this today and insisted I put it somewhere safe for Mommy."

The grin that followed made her smile, and she reached out to take it. "She has quite a talent, don't you think?"

Both women laughed then as Bec held out the painting and squinted, trying to decipher exactly what it was. "A house covered in green slime?" she guessed.

"Day at the beach?"

A little voice interrupted them. "Mommy!"

Bec turned and scooped up her girl, planting a kiss on her shiny blond head. "Hey, sunshine."

"Do you like my painting?"

"Of course!"

"It's me on a horse. A horse, Mommy!"

"Mmm." She tried not to grin as she looked back at her. The teacher had to walk away to keep from laughing. "We were just saying what a lovely horse it is."

"It's a polo horse." She fought to stand on the ground. "Me on a polo pony."

Rebecca's smile fell from her face, until she realized Lexie was still watching her. She forced her panic away. A polo pony? How did she even know about polo ponies?

"Let's go, sweetheart. Grab your bag and say goodbye to Julia."

She watched as her daughter darted away, reached a hand to push back her hair as she stared at the picture.

Lexie had never even been around horses, let alone ridden one, but she'd been obsessed about them since she could say the word. *Just like someone else she knew.* As much as she didn't want to admit it, Lexie was more like her dad than she'd let herself believe.

"Mommy?"

She dropped to her knees, taking the bag from her daughter and zipping it up. "Yes, sweetheart."

"Granddad says you used to ride horses. That you used to ride *polo ponies*."

"Did he now?" She would kill him for even talking to Lexie about her riding. That was a part of her life she'd left behind. She'd never even been near a horse since Ben had left, and she'd long since given up any dreams of making a career out of the sport she'd loved since she was fourteen. The last horse she'd had…she didn't even want to think about the accident.

"He said you were real good, too, until you fell off one day. Did it hurt?"

"And when was Granddad telling you all this?" she asked.

"Yesterday."

Lexie skipped off toward the door, waiting for her, her hand outstretched.

"Can *we* go horse riding?" she asked.

"Maybe."

"Why maybe?"

"I don't know anyone who owns a horse." It was a lie, but what else was she going to say?

"Could *we* get a horse, then?" Lexie asked.

"Get in the car."

She closed the door after her and stood on the sidewalk for a few seconds, eyes closed, taking a deep breath to calm her nerves. Once upon a time she would have done anything to spend her life around horses, but that was in the past, and that was exactly how she wanted to keep it. She had to tell Ben, she knew that, but she still didn't want to go back.

CHAPTER TWO

BEN SMILED AT his granddad and walked over to the young colt. The animal's nostrils were flared, body rigid as he approached him.

"Keep your hands down. Don't touch him until he touches you first."

Ben listened to him, and followed his instructions. More and more he was realizing that his grandfather's instincts were always right. He'd argued with the trainers he worked with overseas until he was blue in the face, and he'd been tired of their old-fashioned attitudes. Some trainers liked to force horses into submission, but that wasn't something they did at McFarlane Stables. Just because half the polo trainers out there thought they were crazy for practicing natural horsemanship didn't mean he was going to change their approach. And it was one of the reasons he'd finally had enough of being overseas, one of the reasons he'd finally broken ties with the guys he'd loved working alongside for so long to come home.

"Good. Once he turns his head in, pat him and then move the rope over his neck."

Ben did as he was told. The horse responded to him, moving quietly, but all hell broke loose once the rope was over.

"Keep hold, even if he goes right out to the end."

A damp line of sweat graced his forehead, but he kept hold. This was the only rough part of the exercise and he hated it, but if he got it right this time, it wouldn't need to be done again. Because *animals* and *force* were not two words he liked used in the same sentence.

The horse stopped bucking and rearing and came to a halt, eyeing him cautiously from a small distance.

"Good boy." He said the words softly before approaching him again. "What a good fella."

"Give him a pat and then put the halter on him," his granddad called out.

Ben moved forward, smiling at the horse as he stood calmly. He gave him a scratch behind the ear and then lifted the halter, rubbing his sweet spots as he did so.

Nice and gentle, Ben reminded himself, reaching up and folding the leather strap over the horse's nose and behind his pricked ears. The horse stood still, ears flickering as he listened to him, accepting what was happening.

Ben stood back and grinned. Working with his grandfather for just one morning was worth having come home for.

"Good job, son. Well done."

He gave the horse one final pat and then opened up the gate out of the yard, letting him canter off over to the other young stock. Ben moved toward his granddad, pleased to see the smile on his weathered face.

"It's in your blood, always has been, always will be."

His granddad's voice was strong and deep, but the slap he gave Ben on his shoulder wasn't as powerful as it used to be; his gnarled, weathered hands failing him after years of hard work. Gus McFarlane was a strong man, the kind of man who was used to commanding attention when he wanted it, but he was deteriorating fast. There was something the old man wasn't telling him, he just knew it.

"So have you been coping okay? On your own I mean?"

Gus used a cane, walking slowly over the grass. Mind as sharp as a tack, but the body just not keeping up. Guilt washed over Ben—he'd been so desperate to leave Australia and follow his own dreams, but now that he was back he was seriously regretting leaving his granddad for so long.

"You ever hear from the Stewart girl?"

Ben's body went rigid. "Rebecca? Yeah, well, sort of. I mean, I went to see her when I got back." He tried to sound nonchalant. "Yesterday, actually."

"Great girl that one. You should have married her, you know that, right?"

Yeah, he knew. But Bec was…well, *Bec*. It was never that he hadn't been attracted to her, or that he hadn't wanted her, but he'd always known he could never give her enough and he still couldn't. Settling down with a nice girl just hadn't been part of his plan, what he'd imagined for himself, because he'd always been focused on what he wanted. And now that he didn't have polo, he was at more of a loss about what he wanted from life than he'd ever been.

"She gave up returning my emails a long time ago, Granddad." He wasn't going to let Rebecca off the hook, not when he was getting *the look* from the old man. The fact their friendship had fallen by the wayside was as much her fault as it was his. "And we were only friends, you know that. Nothing more." His granddad didn't need to know they'd spent a night together, and that's all it had been—one night, not a relationship.

"Great little rider, that one. Hard worker and a good seat in the saddle. Not to mention darn nice to look at."

"Yup," Ben agreed.

"Bring her out here sometime. I've a filly that needs to be ridden by a woman, and there ain't none of them out here anymore."

Ben thought about Bec, about having her out here again. Would she even come if he asked her to? Four years hadn't quelled his desire for her, but things had changed, heck, *she'd* changed.

"She won't have ridden in a long time." He doubted she'd make the trip. "And I'm not sure we're on the best terms." It had been awkward between them the other day, even if he had enjoyed seeing her again.

Gus stopped then, resting heavily on his cane.

"Don't matter how long it's been, because a woman like her? She's a natural, just like you." He chuckled. "And unless she's already married, don't be a quitter, son. You don't give up on her if she's what you want."

Ben cleared his throat. His grandfather was unbelievable—he'd only been home a few days and already he was giving him advice on his love life.

"I haven't got long now, doc said maybe only six months. I'm not gonna beat the cancer this time, son." He shrugged. "Tell Rebecca I want to see her. What kind of girl would say no to a dying old man, huh?"

It was his turn to give Gus a slap on the shoulder. Thinking about his granddad dying was not something Ben wanted to give in to, and if the old man wanted Rebecca, then who was he to say no?

"We'll be right, Granddad. Cancer won't beat you."
But it would and they both knew it.

* * *

"Table six! No menus yet."

Rebecca hurried to the kitchen as the bell dinged. She hated keeping her customers waiting, especially the regulars she saw seated at her tables every week.

"Phone for you, Bec."

"Take a message," she hollered back.

"Sure?"

She gave the young waiter a hard stare and he shrugged. Who the hell would be calling her during a lunch shift?

She placed the empty plates down and hurried out back.

"It wasn't about Lexie was it?" She regretted her sharp tone and gave the young guy a smile.

"Nah, someone called Ben. Said you'd know how to get in touch."

The name hit her like a thump to her lungs. *Ben.* Why was he calling here? She glanced around, saw that everything was under control and stepped back from the counter. "I'm taking ten," she called out, heading out the back door, suddenly desperately in need of fresh air and sunlight.

She ignored the noise of the city, the streets filled with all kinds of people rushing back and forward, and took a deep breath, pulling her mobile from her pocket. She should have ignored his call, stopped thinking about what she'd had with Ben before he left, but it was an impossible task and she knew it.

Seeing Ben had reminded her, what they were both missing out on, of how nice it would be to have a man around. *Not just any man, but a Ben kind of man.* But she'd made the decision to let him go without saying anything about how she felt, and no amount of regrets was going to change that.

And now she had to decide whether to return his call or not. *And at the same time figure out what the hell I'm going to do about telling him he has a daughter.*

She bit down hard on her lower lip and dialed the number, quickly as if the speed was going to make a difference. The number was still ingrained in her memory, digits that she had never, ever forgotten. Hell, it had once been her favorite number, and not just for Ben being at the other end of it. Because Gus had been as much her lifeline back then as Ben had. When he'd offer her a ride it had been like a junkie getting a fix.

She kept repeating the number in her mind, silently, lips barely moving as it rung.

"McFarlane Stables."

Phew. It wasn't Ben.

"Gus!" At least she didn't have to hide her excitement with him. "I've missed you so much."

"I don't have many young ladies call me, so I'm guessing that's you, Rebecca."

His voice was strong, but it crackled more than it used to. Those soft, kind tones that had soothed her and taught her when she was a girl—he'd been the grandfather she'd always wished was her own.

"How did you guess?"

His laughter rumbled down the line. "Something to do with me telling that grandson of mine to get you out here before I kick the bucket."

"Gus! Don't talk like that."

"Ah, but it's true, love."

"*Gus,*" she said, not knowing what else to say to the man she still cared so much about.

"Let's not talk morbid. Just promise me you're coming to see us."

The silence was all her doing this time. She hadn't expected an invitation to McFarlane's, in fact, she hadn't even considered the possibility of going back there. But it was tempting, just the thought of taking a step back in the past even if it was just for a few hours.

"So, are you coming or not?" He never had been one to waste words.

"I, ah…" She'd kept her secret for so long, the last thing she needed was for it to all unravel now before she had time to figure everything out and deal with it properly, and she'd have to ask her folks to look after Lexie.

"Rebecca?"

A tightness in her throat made it hard for her to say *anything.* "Well…" She paused. "Yes."

"Yes?"

"How about I come down this Saturday?" she asked.

"Bring your bag, love. I want you to enjoy the weekend here. Got a horse that needs your help."

She choked. The thought of going back in time, of horses, of Gus…*it was hard.* Exciting, thrilling, terrifying …but still hard.

"I'll tell the boy you're coming."

Uh-oh. The silver-tongued old fox had talked her into a weekend away, all without a hint of protest from her, and she'd forgotten about the reality of Ben. About the fact that it wasn't just going to be her and Gus reminiscing, that it wasn't about being old friends and catching up. *Just like old times.* That's what he'd said, but there was no way anything between her and Ben was like it used to be.

At least she had nothing to feel guilty about where Lexie was concerned—she spent every Saturday night with her grandparents anyway, but still…she usually didn't feel bad about having Saturday night off from parenting each week because she worked, but having an evening to herself seemed wrong somehow. Even though she'd never done it once in her daughter's three years before.

But she deserved one weekend to herself, and she just couldn't risk taking her with her.

A butterfly-soft shiver ran the length of her spine. But this was Ben, this was a step back into the past for one night, and the idea of seeing him again… She shook her head as if it would somehow push her worries away.

She was going to do it. And then she'd figure out how to break the news to him, because now he was home, and if he was home for good, then all the reasons she had for keeping Lexie from him were gone.

CHAPTER THREE

THIS WAS HARDER than she'd thought. Just the idea of seeing Ben had her stomach turning, twisting into a cavalcade of knots. She focused on the road and gripped the wheel tighter, pulling over just near the turnoff and trying to slow her breathing, trying to stop her hands from trembling, too. If she could only still them enough to smudge some gloss over her dry lips, run her fingers through her hair and press a smidge of perfume to her neck, she'd be fine.

The driveway loomed ahead; as immaculate as she'd remembered it. Gus was an old man now, but his standards hadn't slipped, and she found herself hoping the stables and house were unchanged, too. Her memories were so vivid, colorful in her mind as if she'd been here merely months ago, instead of years.

She pushed the lever down into Drive again, satisfied that she looked passable in the mirror, and pulled slowly into the driveway. Gravel crunched under the tires and trees softly waved against the metal of the vehicle as if welcoming her. Bec took a deep breath and found emotions getting the better of her. Up until a week ago, she'd never expected to see this place again, but it was so good to be back.

Up ahead she could just see the house, a triple brick, beautiful residence that was as immaculate as the drive. Roses were neatly clipped, windows thrown wide, one of the most gorgeous houses she'd ever seen. Her own family home was nice, better than modest, but this place was something else. And then her eyes settled on her once favorite part of the property—the row of stables, in an L-shape, to the left of the house.

She slowed the car to a crawl as she surveyed the place, looking for any sign of life and seeing none. There were no horses in sight, but then at this time of day it wasn't to be expected. Apart from a ginger cat stretched out in the sun, it was as good as deserted. In a way she was glad, it gave her time to walk around and reminisce before figuring out what to say to Ben.

She pushed open the car door and let it shut behind her as she stretched her legs. The sun was warm on her bare arms and she moved toward the stables, eyes wandering everywhere. What she loved about this place was the privacy, with only the side of the stables visible. Bec had heard there were fewer horses here than ever now that Gus had slowed down, but as soon as she rounded the building it became obvious that reduced numbers for him were still impressive.

The property had been purpose built with horse rearing and polo playing in mind. The old stables had been meticulously cared for and maintained over the years, and Rebecca stopped to look. The stables stretched in a long line, flanked by larger, box stalls tying up bays. The wooden structures were faded yet clean, the white and navy colors still vivid in her mind from years ago. Wisteria curled down over the edges, pots of bright flowers infusing color into the well-kept area. The door to the tack room was wide-open, and Rebecca could smell the aroma of saddle soap and sweaty horse blankets. It was a blast from the past that made her smile.

She continued on, stopping to rub a nose poking out from one of the boxes. The smell of hay, the sight of horseflesh, it sent a shiver of both excitement and worry through her body. The same kind of feeling she got thinking about Ben.

Rebecca looked ahead to the land before her. The most sheltered field was still kept for young stock, and from the looks of them, recently weaned fillies and colts. Frisky-looking babies who were having a ball of a time, playing and scolding one another in the safe, well-fenced environment. Working with the young stock had been something she and Ben had both enjoyed. Teaching them their manners, how to respect humans, all without needing to use a firm hand. Back then, she and Ben had always had their heads buried in a Monty Roberts book, the legendary horse whisperer who flaunted industry-standard horse breaking rules.

Rebecca walked on and let her eyes wander, taking in the sights, but it was the noise out to her right that had the blood pumping that little bit faster in her veins, that had a smile turning her mouth upward.

She could just make out someone, who she presumed was Gus, excitedly waving what looked to be a cane as some young guys trained. At least six horses rushed past in a blur, hooves pounding hard on the ground as they thundered fast alongside each other. Her feet picked up speed and she rushed toward them, desperately wanting to watch the game as the horses and riders galloped around the polo field.

She didn't want to disturb Gus, so she approached

quietly once she was close, watching the riders compete for the ball, heading toward the goal. From her vantage point, she snuck a quick glance at the old man before her and felt sad, it was like he'd shrunk a little and aged so quickly, but it was unmistakably the same kind person who had been so good to her for so many years.

"Go, go, go!" She jumped as Gus screamed, waving his stick again.

As one of the players made a goal he threw his stick, one hand pumping up in a fist. She couldn't help but laugh.

"Gus." Her voice was soft but he turned immediately on the spot, his eyes meeting hers.

Gus looked her over for a moment before a big smile spread out wide over his face.

"Rebecca! Well, look at you."

He held out his arms and she reached him in no time, embracing him fondly.

"It's so good to be back here, to see you," she mumbled, holding him tight.

He smiled at her as she stepped back, his eyes shining.

"Just look at you. Look at you, huh? All grown-up."

She beamed, embarrassed yet flattered. Before she could answer a voice interrupted them, sending her almost a foot in the air with fright.

"Becca."

Ben. She would recognize that voice anywhere. Deep, rich and delicious. He sat astride a blowing, sweaty polo pony that was now dancing very close to her.

"Good goal, son. I'll walk him back for you."

Ben jumped to the ground and passed Gus the reins.

"You sure you're okay taking him?"

The older man just looked skyward, eyes rolling. Bec

knew it would take more than a highly strung horse to keep him from where the action was, walking cane or not.

Bec stole a glance at Ben while his attention was still directed at the horse before looking away. If only he wasn't so handsome, so charming, so...*not available*. Or possibly available, she had no idea if he had a girlfriend or not, but not available to her. She was all about no complications, being a mother, nothing else. *Nothing else*, she repeated inside her head just in case her body was thinking of disagreeing. She'd been happy being friends with him for so long, but ever since that night...

"Hey."

He was talking to her. *Damn it!* And there she was away in fairyland.

"You looked good out there." It was all she could think to say, but the truth was she hadn't even realized he was the one in the saddle.

"Yeah, well, I'm happy to be home, but I'm still craving some saddle time." He grinned at her and pulled his helmet off, turning toward the field where some of the guys were still training, and ran a hand through his short hair. "You ever think about getting back up again?"

It had been a long time for her, a dream she'd long since given up, and now she was a mom she was way more cautious than she'd once been. The allure of the polo field now was more about watching than actually doing. And besides, that fall had almost broken her. It had taken everything away from her; her dreams, her future. And Ben.

"Maybe," she lied. Or maybe it wasn't a lie. Being back here was giving her all sorts of mixed emotions, making her question everything. "It's not something I've really thought about, to be honest."

Ben turned to her then and reached out a hand, touching her arm so lightly she almost wondered if she was imagining it.

"It's great to have you here, Bec."

She struggled for words, her skin tingling where he'd touched her. They'd been best friends for years, before one night had changed everything, and now she could hardly look at him without thinking about the fact she'd seen him naked. *And how darn good he'd looked.*

"It feels good being back here." She hardly trusted her voice.

He started to walk and she followed his lead, his long legs eating up the ground.

"There's something about this place, Bec. It's good for the soul."

He stopped then, turning to face her, pulling her hands into his and holding them tight. He studied her with such intensity she didn't know where to look or what to say.

"I'm sorry, Bec, for expecting you to stay in touch after what happened, for leaving you in the first place," he said, his voice low. "I never stopped thinking about you, but it all just got so complicated. So much for best friends, huh?"

Until we ruined it. They were the unspoken words hanging between them.

Bec gulped, her eyes burning with tears. Their friendship? Was that all he wanted from her? Lexie's beautiful little face flashed before her and she almost told him, so wanted to tell him that he was the father of her beautiful daughter, but she didn't. Couldn't yet, even though she knew she had to. Because she also knew that he never wanted children—he'd told her since they were in high school that he wasn't ever going to be a dad after what he'd been through—and she knew nothing would ever change his mind. But she couldn't deny him the chance, couldn't keep this from him any longer.

"I've missed you, Ben. But things change, and I guess we just grew apart, right?"

"Maybe we should have both stuck to our plan. Gone to the UK together and both played."

"It would have been good, huh?" Only the reality was that Ben had been picked up by a team in Argentina, and she hadn't, and instead of telling him the truth, she'd made out like she couldn't leave her family. That it wasn't what she wanted. Maybe if he'd asked her to go as more than friends, maybe if her confidence hadn't been shattered after the fall and she'd not been such a mess over everything. Maybe then things could or would have been different.

His eyes were as sad as hers as he watched her. "Come on, let's show you around. There's something I want you to see."

Her eyebrows dragged together as he turned and started to walk again, tugging her along with him.

"Well, more like Gus wants you to see it. Just come and take a look."

Her curiosity was piqued, and she hurried to keep up with him. Make her hair longer, she thought, take away the soft crinkles around his eyes and they could have gone back five or so years. To a time when everything had seemed possible, when they were both in charge of their own destinies, before fate and life had intervened. Before she'd fallen pregnant to a man she'd loved with all her heart, and instead of asking him to stay behind because she loved him, she'd let him go. She couldn't help but wonder if he would have left and not come home, had she told him how she really felt. If she'd called him and told him that she was pregnant. But then deep down she knew the answer to that.

Ben would *never* have left her, not if he knew how she felt, if he knew that she was carrying his baby. And that was precisely why she'd lied, told him they'd made a mistake that night, that they were better as friends. Because she didn't believe in clipping the wings of a bird to keep it at home, and Ben had been like an eagle ready to soar through the sky. And she never wanted to be responsible for ruining Ben's life, and seeing him repeat the same mistakes his mother had.

CHAPTER FOUR

"SHE'S BEAUTIFUL."

Rebecca ran her eyes over every inch of the horse. It wasn't hard to act interested—the filly was one of the most beautiful animals she had ever seen. Endless black legs, four white socks and a silky long tail. Her face was framed by a wide white blaze, stretching all the way to her nostrils; dark brown eyes like pools of trust, following every movement she and Ben made.

He didn't say anything, just watched the horse, arms slung over the corral fence, one foot resting on the lowest tread of timber.

"So, what's the deal with her?"

Ben shrugged, broad shoulders moving under his shirt. She was glad to have the distraction of the horse, because she was finding it almost impossible not to stare at him.

"She's had all the guys on, doesn't seem to like them."

"How about you?" Rebecca asked. "Does she like you?"

He laughed. "Nope, not particularly."

They looked at one another. They were both thinking the same thing, Rebecca could tell by the look in his eyes. There had always been the odd horse that had worked better for one of them or the other, it was about personalities, the rider clicking with beast. But there had been one very special mare who'd only ever worked for Rebecca, to the point where Gus had decided the horse was useless for anyone else, and had given her over to Bec. It had all worked well, her dream come true to own such an amazing mare, until the accident. She'd lost her nerve, and her will to ride, and her beautiful mare had lost her life. The memory flash made her skin prickle. And then she'd lost her best friend, all in the course of a couple of months, as well as her dreams of making it big in the polo world. She'd never gotten over that period in her life, had always just pushed it from her mind, but her pain was still raw.

Ben let out a big breath of air and gave her a smile— a slow rise of his mouth, followed by a gentle wink. It was as if he had put his arm around her, comforted her, just by looking at her. No one else had ever made her feel quite like Ben could. Embraced, comforted, cared for, all in a single look. Pity it had taken her so many years to figure out that she was in love with him. When they'd finally taken that step, he was gone, and then she went from losing a friend to nursing a broken heart. Ben had never said anything, never told her that he thought of her as any more than a friend, and so she'd just kept her mouth shut and let him get on with his life.

"So what do you think?"

Rebecca raised her eyes. *What did she think*? Her mind was racing, took her a moment to remember what they were even talking about. And then she glanced at the filly before them.

Ben was watching her, waiting for her answer. But here, back on a horse again, after all this time?

"I, ah, don't think so."

Ben stepped up onto the railing and hauled himself into the corral. "If I persist long enough, she'll let me catch her, but she's wild when anyone tries to get near her."

"And you expect me to do what you guys can't?"

Ben walked backward until his back was pressed against the wooden rails, before climbing up to sit on the fence.

"You know you can do it, Bec."

Rebecca stayed on the other side of the fence, close to Ben but not quite touching. It was tempting, she could admit that, but there was no way she was up to it. No way she could summon the courage to climb on a spirited horse and stay calm enough and confident enough to be in control. Not after all this time.

"What's her name?"

Ben turned and smiled. "That mean you're ready to give it a go?"

She laughed, shaking her head as she looked back at the horse. No, all it meant was she was trying to change the subject.

"Missy," he told her. "Her name's Missy."

Rebecca kept watching the horse. *Missy.* She played the name through her mind. It was a pretty name, but it didn't make any difference. She wasn't going near her.

"What do you say?"

"Just give me some time." The words came out before she could think longer. And she wasn't even sure she was still talking about horses.

Ben jumped off the fence and landed on the hard packed dirt, his feet falling inches away from hers. Rebecca had a funny feeling she would live to regret that comment. There was no way he was going to let her leave at the end of this weekend without trying her luck with that horse, and the very idea terrified her. She didn't know if it was simply losing her nerve or just the years of not riding catching up on her, but she couldn't even comprehend climbing back into the saddle, with or without Ben egging her on.

He stood close to her, too close, and their eyes met for just a second. It was long enough to feel like one second too long, though. Neither of them knew what to say. Ben because he wasn't the type to just come out and say something, and her because she had too much to hide. Too much at stake. Just being with him was a risk, or at least it was until she was ready to come clean and tell him what she'd done. It wasn't that she was going to keep it from him, she just wanted to do it right, to break it to him the right way, if that was even possible.

Rebecca walked beside Ben. She was listening to him but her eyes were floating around their surroundings, drinking in the familiar sights she had gone so long without seeing.

"What do you think?"

She turned her attention back to Ben. She had no idea what he was talking about. *Again.*

Gus appeared ahead of them and saved her from having to answer. He leaned against the corner of the stable block, resting a leg, but he was smiling. Rebecca guessed that he was probably feeling worse than he let on, but this was his life. The alternative was to cart him off to hospital, or a rest home, and what good would that do him? He deserved to be here till his last day, doing what he loved.

"So when are you two going off for a ride?"

Rebecca laughed and glanced at Ben. She hoped that

he hadn't put his grandfather up to it. "I'm not sure I'll be riding at all this weekend. These days I prefer my feet firmly on the ground."

"Do you remember Willy?" Gus asked

She nodded. "Who could forget him?" Although as she said it, she was wondering if it was a trick question. "He must be, what? Twenty...twenty-two years old now?" He'd been Gus's horse when she was a teenager. The most reliable, safe, sweet horse she'd ever come across, and he'd been Gus's pride and joy.

"Sure is. I can't ride anymore and he's going to waste just sitting around. Thought he could do with a walk around the farm. What do you say?"

Rebecca took a step backward and walked straight smack bang into Ben. He must have stopped right behind her, his large frame preventing her from making a getaway. She lurched forward and felt trapped. Backward meant into Ben and forward meant the horse. She didn't know what scared her more. Her heart was hammering, although the idea of falling back into the warmth of Ben's body was sounding like the more attractive option right now.

"I, ah, I don't know, Gus. Really, I..."

"Are you telling me you came all the way here without your riding gear?"

Gulp. He had her there. Yes, she had brought it, but with no intention of actually *putting it on*. She eyed up the horse some more and felt a lump of genuine terror knot in her throat, but at least riding would give her a distraction aside from Ben.

"How about it, Bec?"

Ben placed his hands on either side of her arms, still standing behind her. It was nothing more than a gentle press of his skin against hers, but it sent a butterfly-soft shiver down her back. He was too close and it was only making her feel more guilty about everything, like a traitor for even being there.

Gus was watching her, Ben was touching her, even the horse seemed to be staring at her, waiting for her answer.

"Okay fine, I'll do it."

Maybe it was the pressure, the sun making her giddy, hell, it might have even been the way Ben was looking at her, but she felt her resolve buckle. But all of a sudden going for a trail ride didn't seem like the stupidest idea in the world.

"Okay?" Ben seemed doubtful, and Gus winked before leaving them to it.

"Don't sound so surprised," she muttered.

She knew this was only the start of it, or maybe it wasn't. Because once she told Ben the truth he'd never forgive her, and then she'd never be invited back ever again.

"Do you want to go get changed?" Ben asked.

He looked her up and down, and Rebecca tried not to laugh as a smile kicked the corners of her mouth up. "I've never ridden in a sundress and sandals before, and I'm not about to start."

She turned and headed back to the car as Ben laughed, wanting to look back at him but not letting herself. There was something about Ben, there always had been; a quiet strength about him that she'd been drawn to when they were both only at school, and that confidence had translated into a super sexy guy. There was nothing arrogant about him even though he'd played with the best polo players in the world, and his manner with animals? That had always set him apart from any man she'd ever met

before. *And it was why he'd be such a darn good father.*
She swallowed hard and tried not to think about what-
ifs—Ben had made it clear he wasn't ever going to have
a family of his own, that he wouldn't ever repeat the mistakes his own mom had made, and she knew that his hurt
ran so deep that nothing, *nothing*, was capable of changing his mind. Which was why she'd kept her secret all
this time. But now it was time for him to decide, for him
to be the one to make that choice.

She tugged the car door open and grabbed her bag.
All of her other belongings were in a small suitcase, but
her riding clothes were in the same bag they'd always
been in. She pulled back the zip and just looked at them
for a moment, before sucking up all her jitters and swallowing them away.

She looked around to check she was alone, then took
off her sandals and replaced them with socks and pulled
her jodhpurs over her ankles and up her thighs. The material stretched tight, but she was pleased to be able to
do the waist up. Years on, not to mention one child later,
and she could still fit into the tight breeches—it was a
good feeling.

Rebecca tugged her dress over her shoulders and
placed it on the backseat, before grabbing her former
favorite faded gray Pearl Jam T-shirt she had once worn
on a daily basis. She searched for a tie in the glove box
and then yanked her hair into a plait, before grabbing her
helmet and gloves and closing the car door.

This was it. It was now or never.

Ben emerged from around the side of the stables, sitting astride a striking chestnut horse, and leading Willy
on his left. She drew in a big breath of air and marched
onward, trying hard to keep her smile from faltering.

"You look good."

His words made her smile, even if she didn't believe him for a second. "Liar liar pants on fire," she joked. "But thanks for the compliment."

"Need a hand getting on?" he asked.

"Nah, I'm fine." She was lying, but she'd rather struggle on without any assistance from Ben. His hands anywhere near her body right now was not a good idea.

She took the reins and lifted her left leg, hopping on one foot as she tried to get it high enough to get her left one through the stirrup.

"Not quite as flexible as you used to be, huh?"

Ben dismounted and moved to help her. Heat flooded Rebecca's face as he touched her shoulder, laughing softly.

"If it makes you feel any better, some of the guys I rode with in Argentina spent half their lives on horseback and could only mount if they were standing on a fence."

Rebecca grimaced. She hadn't realized that getting *on* the horse would be the tough part.

"Here."

Ben cupped his hands and indicated for her to put her knee up. She did, his strong palms closing around her leg, sending spasms of warmth through her body.

"Thanks," she said. "On three."

She bounced three times before Ben sprang her into the air, and straight on to Willy's back. She landed with a soft thump and felt that all too familiar turmoil in her stomach. The accident hit her memory bank like it was yesterday.

She was about to jump straight off when Ben placed a hand to her thigh, almost sending her flying off the other side. All those years they had touched, slept side by side in sleeping bags, sat close, and there had never been a re-action like that. It was as if that one night all those years ago was still pulling them together; their skin still reactive to the pressure of one another's touch. His hand felt hot, heating through the fabric of her jodhpurs, and she knew he felt it, too.

"You're okay," he soothed, never taking his eyes off her.

She swallowed a lump that felt as big as a rock and nodded. Suddenly the horse seemed like the safe bet.

Ben raised his other hand to shield his eyes from the sun, gave her one of his sexy-as-heck winks and then turned back to his horse.

"You'll be just fine."

All of a sudden she knew she was right. It wasn't the horse she needed to be scared of. Danger had just looked her straight in the eye and she'd managed to survive it. For now.

CHAPTER FIVE

REBECCA FINALLY STARTED to relax. Her back had been rigid, legs clammy and neck stiff. She wondered if she'd even been breathing for fear of falling off.

"I guess this is why they say to get straight back in the saddle after a fall."

Ben was riding slightly ahead of her but he reined back to match her horse's stride.

"Sometimes that's easier said than done," he said.

"I've kept something from you all this time, Ben," she admitted. It was almost impossible preparing to confess this, let alone telling him her big secret. *Baby steps*, she just needed to take baby steps.

He turned to watch her, eyebrows raised in question.

Rebecca sighed, looking away from him. She'd told him at the time that she'd turned down the offer she'd been made, that she'd decided she just didn't want to leave her family and live overseas anymore. "I lied to you," she said simply. "I was never offered a position on the women's team, but I didn't want to hold you back, and then after my fall, I didn't even know if I wanted to play anymore."

When he never replied, the only sound their horses' hooves echoing on the dirt, she braved a glance at him.

From side on his jaw looked like it was cut from steel, his entire face like stone.

"You shouldn't have done that." His voice was deep and gravelly. "I wouldn't have just left you like that if I'd…"

"And that's why I did it. I wasn't going to make you second-guess what you wanted. We were only friends, right?" Just saying it hurt her. "It wasn't like you were walking out on your girlfriend."

"So you lied and told me you couldn't leave your family? That staying behind was what you wanted? That we just didn't share the same dreams anymore?" He grunted. "And we might not have been dating, Bec, but we were damn good friends. We'd always planned on going together."

She knew he was angry, but she'd needed to tell him.

"I just wanted you to know the truth, Ben. It was a long time ago, but still."

He made a grunting noise again, his shoulders bunched. "You still shouldn't have lied to me."

"I was a mess after everything that happened," she said. "I was still dreaming of making a team when in reality I was terrified at the idea of even getting on a horse and playing a game again. And then you…" She let her voice trail off, not really wanting to open up to him about how she'd felt. "I lost everything. My confidence was shattered and I was a mess."

"I would have tried to help you, Bec. I wouldn't have just walked away if I'd known the truth."

And that's why she hadn't told him. She hadn't wanted to clip his wings, would never have done that to him, but there had also been a little voice in her head telling her that after everything that had happened, she hadn't been good enough for him anymore. That he wouldn't want her if she couldn't even muster the courage to get back in the saddle and try to make another team.

They rode in silence, Rebecca staring straight ahead, her nerves about being on horseback slowly disappearing. It was a strange feeling being nervous about a sport that had once been her life.

"So how do you feel right now?" Ben asked.

Bec relaxed her grip on the reins and sat deep in the saddle, actually loving how good it felt. The start of a smile was tugging at the corners of her mouth and she couldn't resist the pull. Maybe he was going to let bygones be bygones, which meant that she had to do the same.

"You know what?" She grinned over at him, trying to push the past out of her mind, at least for the afternoon. "Now that I'm not hanging on for dear life, it feels kinda good."

"How about a canter down to the creek?"

Ben was sitting straight-backed, comfortable in the saddle, his broad shoulders stretched wide. There was something about seeing him in his white T-shirt, jeans and baseball cap that sent her back years in her mind. He probably felt the same looking at her.

She sucked up her courage and shortened her reins. "Just remember that I'm not the rider I used to be."

She clucked Willy first into a trot and then into his rocking horse canter. Rebecca moved back and forth, feeling her legs stretch out, calf muscles groaning with the movement. There was nothing particularly easy about riding all over again, but it was a bit like the old bike theory. Once you knew how, it was something you never truly forgot.

"Doing good, *cowgirl*, doing good," called Ben with a cowboy drawl.

Rebecca stayed focused, still expecting Willy to do something out of the ordinary, but he behaved like a complete gentleman.

Ben pulled back to a walk and Rebecca followed his lead, her chest rising rapidly with the burst of exercise.

"It's just up there." He pointed.

"Uh-huh." Her lungs were screaming for more air—she wasn't capable of saying anything else.

They rode in silence the rest of the way, and Rebecca felt those darn butterflies ignite in her stomach again. Ben was gorgeous and charming and so easy to be around, and he hadn't even given her that much of a grilling over the whole lie. He deserved to know about Lexie, too, once she figured out how to break it to him, then her. She just needed to make sure he was certain about staying, that he wasn't going to end up sacrificing his life simply to act out of duty and stay for his daughter. *Or her.* That was why she'd let him go in the first place.

"You coming?"

Ben's voice from up ahead spurred her back in to action. She urged Willy into a trot and shook her head to rid her mind of its worries.

Ben chanced a glance over his shoulder. Rebecca was sitting so elegantly on the horse it looked as though she was right at home, but he knew it had taken a lot of courage for her to get back in the saddle and open up to him. It was a weird feeling, being back out here with Rebecca. He wasn't quite sure what to do, how to act, what to say. Did he behave like they were just old friends reunited, or was he meant to factor in *that* night? Maybe it was because he'd become used to casual relationships with women; women he'd meet after a polo game, drink champagne with and then realize he had absolutely zero things in common with them. Whereas with Bec…seeing her again was like finding a favorite something that he'd missed for years, then realizing it still fit like a glove. But they were only friends, had been *only* friends for years.

He stopped at the creek's edge, no more than a trickle of water flowing down beneath some overhanging trees. It had been their spot, the place they'd always come to talk, when they needed to be alone. Parent troubles, friends, horse issues—it had been their place to figure life out.

It didn't look any different now than it had then. Ben dismounted and tied his horse loosely to a blue gum tree. He turned back around to Rebecca. She had her feet out of the stirrups, stretching her ankles, and the grimace on her face was hard to ignore.

"Every single part of my body is protesting right now," she explained.

"Want a hand down?"

Rebecca looked at him gratefully. "Oh, yeah."

He tried his hardest not to look, not to feel, but it was impossible. She swung her far leg over and came down toward him, and Ben put both hands up, catching her around the waist and guiding her to the ground. She landed with a tiny thump.

His palms were pressed against the flimsy material of her T-shirt, he could feel her taut skin beneath his hands. Despite his best intentions he didn't let go, not straight away, their bodies only inches apart. It wasn't until Rebecca cleared her throat that he stepped back, hands falling away.

Ben was about to apologize, but she turned, her dark blue eyes smiling in his direction. There was nothing to be said. The attraction that had started the night before he'd left was still there, he knew it and she knew it. But things had changed. She was a mom now, and he couldn't be a dad, not even a stepdad. And with Bec? If anything happened between them, it wasn't going to be a casual night of sex again—she meant too much for him to treat her like that. Which left him wondering what the hell *could* happen between them. If he had to consider the possibility of getting close to someone's else's kid.

"I should be saying thank you, Bec," he said, searching for the right words. "You shouldn't have lied to me, but the fact that you let me follow my dreams? You were an awesome friend. It was the best thing I've ever done and I don't regret it for a second."

She nodded, her eyes leaving his as if she was nervous about something. "I wasn't that great a friend."

He chuckled. "Believe me, you were." She hadn't brought up that night and he wasn't going to, either, because the last thing he needed was for her to be embarrassed when things were starting to feel easy between them again. "When my mom left, there wasn't a day that went past that I didn't feel guilty. Knowing that she'd sacrificed everything she'd ever wanted to have me, it made me feel like crap. But then I guess you already know all that, right?"

Rebecca reached out, her fingers brushing his arm in the softest caress as she met his gaze again. "She had no right to make you feel that way."

Ben shrugged. "Maybe. But when you're eight years old and you find out that your mom never wanted you? It's not exactly an easy pill to swallow. No kid deserves that."

"Maybe she regretted telling you that," Rebecca said.

He ground his teeth together, trying to keep his anger at bay. "If she regretted it she'd have come back. She made it pretty clear that her career was more important than I was."

Rebecca's hand fell away, her smile sad. "You deserved better, Ben. We both know that."

"Hey, I'm a big boy now, the past is in the past and all that," he said, brushing it off as if it meant nothing to him, even though there wasn't a day that passed that he didn't wonder how a mother could do that to her son. "All I was trying to say was I'm not angry with you, for lying to me. You let me go, and I should be thanking you instead of being so angry. You were never the kind of person to hold someone back and that makes you special."

He saw a flicker of something in her face, something he couldn't put his finger on, but he didn't call her out on it. It'd been a long time since they'd been together, so maybe he was wrong.

"Just tell me it was worth it?" she asked. "That you had the time of your life."

He bumped shoulders with her, grinning. "It was incredible. You would have loved it over there."

She laughed. "You mean the playing and the horses, or the champagne and the parties?"

"Both. Although the latter was definitely the highlight." He laughed. "Seriously, the money over there is incredible. The champagne and top-shelf liquor flows like it's soda, and the clothes and the diamonds, the cars and horseflesh, it's like nothing I'd ever seen before. I never got used to it, even after all that time, and I'm sure as hell pleased I never tried to keep up with those lifestyles."

"Sounds tough. You must have been so miserable," she joked.

"Yeah, it was such a bore riding hundred-thousand-dollar horses and swilling Veuve Clicquot."

"Hmm, I'm sure."

This was what he'd missed, just hanging out with someone he actually had a connection with. Playing overseas had been fun, but this was real life, and it was reality that he'd yearned for. Telling stories about his time was fun, but in truth it had been superficial, and he was happy to have his feet back on Australian soil, even if he still missed his teammates like crazy.

"So tell me all about it. Was it as amazing as we always thought it would be? Parties aside?"

Rebecca toyed with the frayed hem of her T-shirt and watched Ben skim stones across the water. He was lying down, propped up by one elbow, while she sat cross-legged beside him. Telling him the truth had been tough, but after hearing him say she'd done the right thing, listening to him talk about his mom again, she was feeling better about what she'd kept from him. He was still going to be furious when she told him everything, but at least they'd made some headway.

"Yeah. But the guys are rough." He grimaced. "As in rough with their horses. It's just the way things are with polo, but you know how I am. I love the sport, but I missed home." Ben looked off into the distance. "I gotta say that it was the first time I'd ever felt like part of a real family, though, so that was good. I mean, Gus always remained the most important person in my life, but feeling like I had a whole team of brothers was pretty cool. We traveled in the owner's private jets around the world to play. He even jetted the horses rather than keep different stables. The money he had was surreal."

She wondered if he'd missed her, or if he was just referring to Gus. Or maybe he meant the red Australian dirt and she was being way too sentimental. Either way, what he'd experienced sounded incredible.

"You know, it was like, every day over there was a way to prove to myself that I was worth something. I wanted to show Gus that I could dream big and achieve what I'd always talked about, but maybe it was a way to prove to the rest of the world that I didn't deserve to be orphaned by my parents."

Rebecca nodded. "I get it." She'd always known he was running from demons, because she'd always been the one he opened up to.

"And how about you? You pleased you stayed behind in the end?" He shook his head. "Or did you regret what had happened?"

"I should have told you I didn't make the team."

"Yeah, but the question is did you actually want to go or not?" he asked, his expression serious. "Was it still what you wanted?"

"To start with, yes. But after my fall? It killed my confidence, Ben. I wanted to go away, but I couldn't just head off and expect to tag along with you if I wasn't playing or working. I needed to figure out what the hell I was going to do with my life, find something that I could actually make a go of." He kept flicking the stones, listening but not saying anything, so she continued. "I should have been better at emailing, but then I had Lexie and…" She didn't know what else to say.

"I get it. You were busy, times changed. It wasn't like we were together or anything." He angled his body so he was facing her, a frown dragging his mouth down. "But what happened that night, it was a long time coming, right?"

She sucked in a breath. "Um, yeah." Rebecca glanced at Ben, his expression serious. "But we always said we'd never ruin things, didn't we? That our friendship was what mattered."

A slow smile spread across Ben's face. "Maybe we were stupid. Maybe we should have just followed our instincts from the start."

"I thought our instincts were to be friends and not complicate things," she said drily.

"Yeah, well look how well that turned out." Ben reached out and touched her hand, a gesture that shouldn't have rattled her but did. "And then you went and met someone else and had a baby."

Her heart started to pound, as if it was about to beat right out of her chest.

"You okay?"

She nodded. "Just thinking about Lexie. I only ever leave her if I have to go to work, so I'm feeling a bit guilty."

"She's with your parents, though?"

"Yeah. They adore her and she has them wrapped around her little finger." Bec laughed. "She probably has more fun with them than she has with me, but I still don't like leaving her."

She looked across into a pair of deep brown eyes that were hauntingly, yet comfortingly, the exact same as her daughter's, the gold fleck unmistakable.

"You sure you're not going to tell me who the guy was? Because if he's someone I know…"

Rebecca gave Ben a smile that could have won her an

acting award, a practiced smile to stop him from worrying. She'd been using the same one on her dad for years. "How about we pretend like we've gone back in time for the rest of the afternoon?"

He grunted. "I just wish I'd been here for you, that's all. You shouldn't have had to go through that alone."

"As my friend?" she asked, pulse hammering again. "You wish you were here for me as my friend or something else?"

He looked confused. "Of course. That's what we were, right?"

His words hurt. Like a fist to her gut. He might not have thought they were together, that they'd become anything more than good friends, but that night they had spent together had changed everything for her. She'd fallen in love with him, and if she was honest, it wasn't as though she'd ever fallen back out of love. Not once in all these years, even after meeting plenty of nice guys through the restaurant. But even if he'd stayed, they may have just gone back to being friends, to nothing more. Unless of course she'd told him about her being pregnant, then he'd have probably proposed to her because of his sense of duty. And the only thing worse than wishing they were together would have been knowing they were together because he thought they had to be.

"We *were* friends," she said, sucking back a burst of emotion that he would probably never understand. "But I was fine, Ben. I was absolutely fine."

"I guess being a mom kept you pretty busy. I just hope you were happy and busy."

Ben said it with a smile but all Rebecca felt was a lump of dread knot in her throat. Lexie. Her daughter. *Their daughter.* She needed to change the subject before they broached into even more dangerous territory, or before Ben started to figure out the timeline.

"Bec?"

Ben looked worried. She closed her eyes for a moment and felt the sun trickle through the branches above her. Her feet were hot inside her boots, but the rest of her felt great. Bare arms in the sun, the sticky air brushing past her skin, and nothing but the sound of birds cawing in the trees. She owed it to herself to relax, and if she stopped worrying, then maybe it wouldn't be so hard to change the subject and just enjoy being with Ben as she tried to figure everything out.

"You know what?" she said, her eyes lazily popping open. "Let's just lie here a bit longer. I never get to sit and do nothing anymore."

A little part of her might feel like the world's worst mother for being here and leaving Lexie at home, but it was once in more than three years, and if she kept working at the pace she did every day for another year, she'd probably end up in hospital with exhaustion.

"Fine by me," said Ben, pulling his cap lower over his eyes and reclining back.

They were side by side now, so close to touching, but achingly far apart. Rebecca had closed her eyes again, but her body was far from relaxed. She wanted to tell Ben how good this felt, to be here with him again, to forget about everything else. She wanted to tell him she'd missed him, that she wanted to be part of his life again, but she knew it was impossible. She wished she could explain why she'd done what she'd done, how she hadn't felt worthy of him, how she hadn't wanted to hold him back from his dreams, but nothing sounded quite right when she practiced it in her mind.

If she was truly honest with herself, she knew that coming here had been a mistake. She had known it from the day Gus had asked her to make the trip. But if she hadn't come, she would always have been wondering what if. What if Ben wanted to see her for a reason? What if Gus died and she felt guilty forever for not making the effort to see him? The list in her mind just went on and on.

And now that she was here, it was intoxicating. The smell, feel, touch of horses beneath her hands and around her were enough to lull her back in time. The same with Ben. The house. Gus, too. It was like being transported back to enjoy a time where everything seemed fine, where anything she dreamed was possible, where being with Ben was a possibility.

As if he knew she was thinking about him, Ben nudged his hat back and propped himself up on his elbow again. Rebecca had opened her eyes as soon as he had moved, but she stayed lying on her back.

"You ever think what would have happened if I hadn't gone away?"

Rebecca let out a low lungful of air and looked over at him. He seemed to have moved closer but she knew he hadn't. Ben was plucking at some long shoots of grass, but she could tell he was off balance, that he wasn't entirely comfortable talking to her about the past, although she guessed he'd been sitting on that question awhile.

"Yeah, I do." She took a slow, deep breath. "Or at least I used to. A lot."

They stayed silent for a moment, both looking at his hands, watching his fingers pull at each blade. Rebecca's mouth was dry, as if she'd just consumed a ball of cotton wool. He had no idea how much she wished he'd stayed, how often she thought of how different life would be. For starters, she wouldn't be a single mom, because she'd have told him right from the start. The *only* reason she'd kept it from him was so she wasn't the one responsible for killing his dream because she hadn't wanted him to resent her or her child. *Especially not their child.*

"So what was your conclusion?"

Rebecca felt her cheeks flush hot. What had her thoughts been?

"I think we'd have made it," he said, not waiting for her to reply. "If we'd just admitted how we felt instead of pretending like it meant nothing. If we'd been together instead of pretending like we were only supposed to be friends when we both know that was crap."

Ben maneuvered the single blade of grass between forefinger and thumb, before lifting it to run it over her bare arm. She couldn't stop her eyes from closing, the tiny hairs on her arm rising with the touch, her breath coming in short pants. It felt as though he was caressing her, skin to skin, even though no part of him was actually touching her, the grass doing all the skimming across her arm.

Her eyes popped open again when he spoke, but she was feeling drowsy and excited all at once. Her mind roaring, stomach turning.

"Why did it take us so long to realize?" he asked, voice sexy and low.

She knew exactly what he meant. After all those years of being buddies, friends only, why had it taken an alcohol-fueled night and him leaving to draw them together? When they could have had so long having fun instead of pretending like they both just wanted to be platonic.

But the very next day they'd gone on like *nothing* had happened.

"We could have been great," she croaked, still entranced by the grass-to-skin thing he was doing to her.

He stopped then, and their eyes met. She leaned in, her gaze falling from his mouth back to his eyes. Was he trying to tell her he still wanted her? Was he trying to tell her that their night together hadn't been one big mistake?

"Rebecca, I…"

She watched him expectantly, desperate for him to close the gap between them and move forward. Aching to taste his kiss. After all this time of wishing he was with her, that he would come home for her, and now he was so close.

Ben looked at her long and hard before reaching one hand into her hair, cupping the back of her skull and drawing her close. He crushed her lips so softly against his, the light touch of his skin sending ripples of pleasure down her spine. It should have felt wrong, but if felt so, so right.

Ben ran his hand down the length of her hair, before pulling back and looking at her, his smile crinkling his eyes in that delicious way it always did. The Ben she'd said goodbye to had had no little fine wrinkles, hardly any stubble on his jaw, but she liked him ever better this way than before. There was a maturity there that she found achingly attractive, shorter hair and a covering of barely there facial hair.

How was it that some men just got more and more delicious with age? He'd been handsome as a teen, all the women had liked him in his early twenties, especially in his polo getup, but now he was a man. Grown-up. Strong. *Real*. The kind of man you knew could protect you and rescue you, like a modern-day warrior who looked after those close to him. She could look into those dark brown eyes all day long and never tire of the view. And those lips...*mmm*, she loved those lips.

"I've really missed you, Bec. And I don't just mean that I've missed my friend. I've wanted you ever since that night."

She nodded, biting down on her lower lip. And she could spend all day listening to words like that.

He gave her a heartbreaking smile, then lay back again, his eyes toward the sky. She loved that about him, too. The way he could say something like that and not worry about hearing the words back. Confident enough in himself to say what he thought and leave it at that.

She watched him lying there and wondered what he was thinking about. Things had changed from old friends reunited to something more, and despite loving every second of that kiss, she was terrified. Alarm bells she should have been listening to were trying their hardest to signal, but she pushed them away. The bubble was going to burst soon, she was only delaying the inevitable, because as much as Ben was saying he liked her as a whole lot more than just friends now, when he found out what she'd kept from him he'd never forgive her. *Never*.

CHAPTER SIX

"How are you feeling?"

Rebecca cast her eye over Ben. She would be feeling a whole lot better if she wasn't staring at his lips and wishing he was kissing her all over again.

"I think I'll be stiff tomorrow."

He laughed, a deep chuckle that made Rebecca tingle all over.

"Maybe dinner will make you feel better?"

Dinner? "You mean just here?"

He adjusted his baseball cap, one hand on the reins. "Gus thought we'd go out for dinner, just somewhere local, nothing fancy."

She nodded. If it was the three of them, then she had nothing to worry about.

"I've missed good Australian food. Prawns, Moreton Bay bugs, baramundi…" Ben blew out a whistle. "Man, I'm starving just thinking about all that seafood."

"I eat at our restaurant all the time, but I'm usually just standing out back having a few mouthfuls when I get a chance."

"So you don't get out much?"

"Nope." She grinned. "My girl is my life, and unless

it's a burger or somewhere with a playground we tend to stay at home unless it's work."

Ben was riding close to her, but the horses didn't seem to mind. Rebecca was worried about bumping knees or stirrups. Kind of the same worry she remembered as a teen anticipating her first kiss, not wanting to knock teeth and knowing it was going to happen anyway.

"You're a great mom, Bec," Ben said with a smile. "But you deserve a night out and I need the company."

She could tell by the look on his face that he wasn't just saying it.

"How would you know that I'm any good as a mom?"

"Because I can see it in you. You've always been so caring, so gentle, I just know you'd be fantastic." He laughed. "Maybe that's why I knew we'd never work out, because I need to find some troubled woman who's as screwed up as me about kids. You were always going to make a great mom."

She looked down, but when she eventually raised her eyes he was still watching her. His eyes flickered from the track they were riding to sideways, catching her as they passed. Every time he said something like that, every little comment where he was trying to flatter her or just plain make up for the fact that nothing had happened between them, it just made her resolve to tell him waver.

"So you're still sure about that? That you'll never be a father?" The words were almost impossible to push out, but she did it. "I always thought you'd, I don't know, grow out of it or something."

"Hell yes, I'm still sure," he said straight back, not missing a beat. "I'm not dad material. Never have been, never will be."

"But you're so different to your mom, you're…"

"Not going to be a dad." His tone was final, determined. "I can't be. I like being around kids, but I can't be the dad."

Rebecca shrugged. "I just know you'd be amazing, that's all."

"Well don't eye me up as your next baby daddy, okay?" he said with a chuckle. "Because it's never gonna happen. I'll be the fun uncle to your little one and that's as close as I'll get."

Ben was laughing but Rebecca could hardly breathe, let alone joke back. Her head was pounding as loud as her heart now.

"Bec?"

She forced a smile.

"Man, I'm sorry. I didn't mean that, you know, like you'd want another baby with a different guy…"

"Ben, it's fine, you were just joking around," she said. "Now tell me where we're going for dinner."

"Everything okay at home?"

Ben reached out to touch Bec's arm, realizing he'd frightened her. She'd jumped the minute he'd spoken.

"Yeah, everything's fine."

"So you're not about to run off back to the city on me?" he asked.

"Ha, not yet. But I've never actually been away from her before, not properly, so I might bail on you in the night. I'm usually back from the restaurant by 1 a.m. and then I crash wherever she is."

They both laughed, but Ben guessed she was telling the truth. "So I have this crazy feeling that your dating pool must be pretty limited."

The shock on Bec's face was palpable. "Yeah, I guess you could say that."

"Sorry, none of my business. I just mean that between working the hours you do and being a mom…" He ran a hand through his hair, wishing he'd just kept his mouth shut. "Sorry, just forget I said anything. I seem to be getting pretty good at putting my foot in it."

Bec sighed, her chest visibly rising as she took a big breath to fill her lungs again. "Since I had Lexie, I haven't really dated at all. The last few years have just flown past, one blur to another."

Ben watched her face, tried to read whether he'd offended her or not, and got the feeling it was definitely the latter. "I guess what I'm trying to ask is whether you're seeing anyone right now."

The question hung between them, the silence almost painful as she stared at him, her mouth open but not moving.

"Ah, no. No I'm not," she stammered.

"Good." He grinned, moving closer to her, every part of him focused on every single part of her, her skin warm beneath his touch as he circled his fingers around her wrist, his other hand rising to her face. "Then you won't mind if I do this again."

Bec was still silent, but she hadn't tried to move away, either, so he followed his instincts and did what he should have done over a decade ago when they'd first met. He'd always been so conscious of not ruining their friendship, of not pushing her and waiting to let her make the first move if she wanted things to change between them, but not now. Now he knew exactly what he wanted, and tonight that something was Bec. All thoughts aside, he wanted Rebecca.

When they'd been together last time, they'd been drunk. Right now, it was still daylight, he could see every expression on her face. Ben didn't hesitate any longer; he cupped her cheek and kissed her, lips closing over hers gently at first, testing the waters, then more firmly as she leaned into him. He kissed her just like he'd wanted to kiss her the four years he'd been away, stroking her hair, inhaling the feminine scent of her perfume. Her lips were warm and pliable, so soft that he forced himself to slow down, to tease her and be gentle with her.

Ben stifled a groan as she placed her hands on his chest, pushing him back ever so slightly, but enough that their lips parted. He stared down into eyes the most beautiful shade of blue, watched as her breath came in short, ragged pants.

"Slow down, cowboy," she murmured.

"Slow down?" He chuckled and leaned in, pressing another kiss to her lips even as she tried to push him away. "I've been waiting a real long time to do that again, so I'm kinda keen to speed things up."

Rebecca laughed, eyes locked on his as they stood still. It was as though everything else had disappeared and it was just the two of them—Ben wanted her, he always had. The only trouble now was that he had to make it clear to her that he wasn't looking for a role as stepdad of the year.

"I'm not sure we should be doing this," she muttered.

Ben shrugged. "Why not?"

"Because we've already made this mistake once."

"Maybe it wasn't a mistake," he said simply. "Are you sure it wasn't the right thing, only we did it at the wrong time?"

Rebecca looked unsure. "I can't commit to anything, Ben. It's just not that simple for me anymore."

"Then let's just keep it simple," he said. The thought of being around her daughter wasn't something he was sure about, only because he didn't know what to do around kids, but he missed Bec, and he wanted his friend back.

"What are you suggesting?" she asked, eyes wide as she clutched the front of his T-shirt.

"How about we take it one night at a time." Ben wanted her so badly—in his arms, in his bed, hell, he just wanted Bec back in his life again. He knew things were never going to be the same, but still.

"What about if it was just for tonight?" she asked.

Ben hated the thought of only having her for one night, but one night might lead to more and…to hell with it. One night was better than nothing, and he had plenty of time to convince her otherwise.

"Whatever you want, Bec." Ben ran his hands up and down her arms, his body humming with anticipation. "You set the rules and I'll follow."

She smiled up at him. "Slow. Just keep it slow, and you won't hear any complaints from me."

He laughed. "Okay, well in the interests of keeping things slow, I'm gonna go do a few jobs before we head out. You okay here?"

Rebecca nodded, taking a step back, her arms folded across her chest. They stood, watching each other for a moment; a moment where Ben could have said to hell with it and stormed back toward her again, but he didn't. Because he didn't want to scare Bec off, not before their night together had even started.

Rebecca wasn't sure if she was being fobbed off, or if he actually had some things to do, but she didn't mind. Still obsessing about *the kiss*, but fine. She was bound to find something to keep her entertained for the next while. With foals to watch and horses being trained, there wasn't any shortage of things to do. And it would at least keep her thoughts pure. No more sizing Ben up as if he was a juicy steak waiting to be consumed. Or maybe that's exactly what she needed to do—get him out of her system once and for all. Although maybe that's essentially what she'd just agreed to.

"I'll take your bag up to the house and leave it just inside the door. Make yourself at home, okay?" Ben called over his shoulder.

"Sounds good. Thanks." It was as if they hadn't just had that whole awkward conversation, as if things were back to normal again.

She'd dropped her small case to the ground and Ben bent to retrieve it. Rebecca almost reached out to touch his hair—as thick as Lexie's and almost the same color.

"I'll see you soon."

Ben nodded, his mouth twisted into a smile, and turned, her bag in his hand. She just stood there, watching him go, and wondered what the hell she was doing playing along as if nothing had changed. But despite wanting to look away, Rebecca's eyes were locked on the way his jeans hung from his wry hips, his tanned arms seemingly chocolate against his white T, and the way his stride ate up the dirt as he walked.

She was in way over her head just being back at McFarlane's, but she was damned if she was going to do anything about it until at least the morning. Lexie was safe, she was enjoying herself, or at least trying to, and the surroundings were breathtaking. Not to mention she wanted a good catch-up with Gus, too. *And maybe a repeat evening with Ben.*

Once Ben disappeared around the corner, so she knew there was no chance of being caught, she wandered back over to the yards. It was as if the filly was beckoning her, only she knew it was plain stupid to even think like that. The horse was probably just grazing, minding her own business, but Rebecca felt a pull toward the yard. She reasoned with herself that it was perhaps just because she felt confident after the ride, but there was something else there. She wanted to prove that she still had it, that after submerging herself in motherhood, and everything else life had thrown her way, that she could still change, go back in time. Be the one person to make a difference and connect with an animal and develop their trust. The only problem was that she wanted to find out alone, without the pressure of anyone watching. She hadn't lied to Ben when she'd said her fall and everything that had happened had broken her—her confidence had been in tatters and it had taken a long time for her to claw back from her despair.

Her feet walked her over in the right direction but her mind was screaming out to just head back to the house and read a book. Anything but put herself in a position of potential danger with a half-wild horse. Something about being here was making her feel like the fifteen-year-old who'd first visited the farm, full of confidence and not planning on letting anything stop her from fulfilling her dreams.

Missy was watching her, although she was pretending not to. Her head was bent down, but one eye was focused on Rebecca's progress. She ignored the horse, keeping her gaze focused on a spot to the side, not wanting to threaten her. This was about the animal deciding to trust her, and direct eye contact established nothing but dominance.

Rebecca looked over each shoulder but no one was around. She walked slowly until she reached the corral, then cautiously bent to maneuver through the railings. She was still wondering what the hell she was doing but she was in there now.

The horse looked incredibly beautiful. The sunlight was bouncing off her shiny black coat, brown dapples ever so delicately showing through. Everything about the filly was immaculate, from her trimmed tail to her glossy mane, and it made Rebecca think she had to be pretty special. There was a reason Gus wanted to persist with her.

"Hey, girl," she called, keeping her voice soft. It was hard not to sound nervous but she was trying her best. She knew the horse would have already picked up on her heartbeat, and she needed to slow down.

The horse snorted but kept grazing, unworried. Rebecca felt a familiar static in her stomach but forced herself to keep on going. This was her chance to see if she still had it. She seriously doubted it.

"You and me," she half whispered, "we're going to be good friends."

Rebecca stopped and waited. The horse still didn't look up. She decided to change her tactic.

Missy was still watching her, but Rebecca didn't acknowledge it. Instead, she sat down, careful to move slowly, crossing her legs and keeping her head down. She kept her eyes focused on the ground. Looking up, even slightly, would break the connection, break the trust, and make the horse look at her as a predator rather than a nonthreatening being. Now it was time to wait.

Sure enough, it was only minutes before the horse decided to investigate. Rebecca stayed still. It seemed dangerous, but she knew that so long as she was non-threatening and didn't spook her, there was little chance of injury.

It was nerve-racking, sitting so still, but she did it. Missy had her head low to the ground, looking at Rebecca, snorting. She moved forward slowly, inquisitively, and soon her muzzle was touching Rebecca. Just gently, her whiskers skimming the very top of her head, moving her hair ever so, blowing through her nostrils close to Rebecca's skin.

And then she sniffed at her face, tentatively, and Rebecca couldn't help but smile. It had taken this incredibly untrusting horse just minutes to come close, and now she was standing, unworried, beside her. A horse Ben claimed hadn't developed a bond with any of the men, not even him.

Rebecca raised her eyes, still not making direct contact. A flutter ran through her veins. *She still had it.* Like clockwork, the horse stayed calm, brought her nose close to Rebecca's, and Bec slowly reached out one hand. It was magical, as if there was an element of witchcraft, but Rebecca knew that sometimes a horse just needed a gentle approach, and sometimes preferred a woman over a man.

She touched her gently, then drew her feet up beneath her, until she was in a squat position.

"You're a good girl, Missy," she clucked. "A real good girl."

The horse had her ears pricked, listening. But she was no longer nervous, or afraid.

Rebecca reluctantly pulled up to her full height, one hand still resting on Missy's shoulder.

"I think you and I are going to get along just fine."

Now she was standing beside the horse, running her hand rhythmically back and forward along her soft coat. Rebecca loved the senses of being back around horses. The smell, touch, feel, everything just took her on a path back in time. It didn't mean she felt confident about getting *on* them, but maybe handling them was different. She still felt an element of control that she hadn't realized she'd still have.

"Well done."

Gus's croaky tone took her by surprise. She stayed still, not letting it break her bond with the horse.

She eventually turned around, keeping one hand on Missy, and was surprised to see Gus and Ben both standing nearby, watching her. Her face flooded with heat, embarrassed that they'd been there when she'd thought she was alone.

"Nice work," said Ben.

Rebecca could tell from the look on his face that he was pleased with her. His eyes were shining, a big smile stretching his face wide.

"I knew you had it in you still," said Gus, his focus on the filly. "I knew."

Rebecca looked between the two men. Ben was like a replica of his granddad—just a young, stronger version. They both had the same magnetism, the same aura about them, and she loved them both dearly, no matter how much she tried to pretend otherwise.

"You set me up." She said her words in an even, calm voice to avoid alarming the horse. "You guys knew I wouldn't be able to resist her and I walked straight into the trap."

The two men looked at one another and smiled. The kind of coconspirator type of smile she remembered only too well. She had been prey to their duping plenty of times as a gullible teenager.

"Maybe," Ben called out. "But I bet you feel damn good for doing it."

She tried to look angry and failed miserably, not really caring what they'd done. They'd been right—it made her feel good for proving to herself that she could still do it, because lately all she did was work in the restaurant. And if she wasn't working she was caring for Lexie. It was nice to know she was still good at something else.

"I'd say you really owe me that dinner now," she said.

Gus hobbled off with his cane, whistling a familiar tune. She knew he was pleased with himself. He wouldn't have doubted for a moment that she could resist the filly, but then he hadn't known how low she'd been, what had really happened.

Ben grinned at her and Rebecca almost felt she'd be safer staying in the round pen than being beside him. He was definitely more mature than she remembered him, and with that came a certain confidence that she didn't recall. The way he looked at her, it made her feel wanted, that he appreciated her. For two people who were meant to be friends, it was most unnerving. But then hadn't they just agreed that they both wanted to be more than just platonic, for tonight anyway?

"I'm looking forward to it," she muttered, more to herself than for anyone else's ears.

She watched his eyes as they danced over her. A delicious, deep brown that was dangerous yet kind. This was a man she trusted, that she had loved and still did, but every time she looked at him, there was an echo of guilt that she couldn't truly shake. If he ever found out what she'd kept from him, she knew he'd never look at her that way again. Which was why she had to let herself have this one night with him before she sent everything into free fall. Her telling the truth wasn't just going to affect Ben, it was going to impact on her own family, and Gus. She'd lied to them all, and after keeping her secret for so long...it wasn't even worth thinking about what might happen.

Ben was still watching her and she shook away the worries and focused on the filly again. She could enjoy the next day and night; beyond that she had no idea what was going to happen.

CHAPTER SEVEN

BEN SAT ON the wide veranda that stretched around three sides of the big old house, beer in hand, mind a million miles away. The low early evening sun drifted in through the thick wisteria, and he closed his eyes, basking in the quiet peacefulness of his surroundings.

There was something about Australia, something he couldn't explain, but being back was better than good, it felt right. He thought he'd never come back, but after a few years it was all he'd wanted. He'd always craved a family; even though he had Gus it hadn't been like growing up with parents and siblings, and his polo family had given him a team load of brothers to live and travel with. But now…now he wanted to be home, was ready to be home. And the only thing he wanted more was Rebecca. His only trouble was exactly *what* he wanted from her. One second he thought he knew, and the next he was questioning himself all over again.

Ben took another pull of beer and lazily opened his eyes. Rebecca was upstairs getting ready for dinner and he was just biding his time waiting for her. His grandfather had told him with a big grin that he was tired and turning in early, which he knew was rubbish, but he wasn't going to argue with him. He wanted some time alone with Bec, just the two of them. He only wished he had his head in the right place first. All he knew was he wanted her, and beyond that he didn't have a clue what he was going to do.

He heard a noise and finished his beer, jumped up and opened the side door that led back into the house. And then he saw Rebecca, making her way down the stairs, wearing tight jeans that showed off every inch of her super long legs, and a sparkly sequined top that seemed to make her eyes shine an even brighter shade of blue when she came closer. She was a knockout, pure and simple. All the women put together from the fancy polo days couldn't hold a candle to her.

"Wow," said Ben, realizing she was staring at him. "You look great." *She looked better than great, she looked freaking amazing.*

Rebecca's cheeks flushed. "Thanks."

He glanced up and down her body again, quickly, hoping she wouldn't notice. All this time he'd wondered if he was imagining how beautiful she was, but his answer was right there in front of him.

"No, seriously, Bec, you look stunning."

She looked self-conscious, slipping her jacket on and covering up far too much skin for his liking.

"So where are we going? You still haven't told me."

Ben glanced down at his shirt with the sleeves rolled up and his worn pair of jeans. Maybe he should have gotten more dressed up.

"Somewhere good. Let's go."

"What about Gus?"

"He's missing in action." Ben laughed. "Looks like he set us both up. Crazy old fool made the booking the day you said you were coming, then scurried off to bed just before as if he had the whole thing planned from the beginning."

He liked the fact that Rebecca still blushed. She might be all grown-up and a mom, but she was still shy when it came to anything happening beyond friends between them and it was an endearing quality. Espccially after how bold so many of the women he'd met overseas had been, how brazen they'd been about wanting to bed any of the guys in his team.

"So it's just the two of us, then?"

"That okay with you?" he asked.

"Just two old friends catching up, right?"

Ben caught hcr wink and gave her a quiet smile straight back. He owed Gus a huge thank-you for giving him some alone time with Bec, and he wasn't going to waste a minute.

"You ready?"

"As I'll ever be. Let's go."

Ben grabbed his keys off thc hall stand and checked he had his wallet in his back pocket, before touching his hand to Rebecca's back and guiding her toward the front door.

They pulled up outside Ruby's restaurant and Rebecca ran her hands over her jeans and gave herself a mental pep talk. She only had a moment alone before Ben moved around to open her door. It was funny, she never expected men to be quite so chivalrous when it came to everyday things like that, but opening doors was just the kind of thing Ben had always done.

"Not quite like our old haunt."

Ben had laughter in his eyes and Bec grinned.

"Nothing like it," she affirmed. They'd had a favorite burger place back in the day, when they'd been able to eat as much grease as they wanted and still be skinny as racehorses.

"You sure you don't want to jump back in the car and get a burger? Maybe some fries drowned in ketchup?"

Rebecca shook her head and felt relieved that she'd loosened up a little. It had been silly worrying, there was nothing to feel concerned about. Whatever happened, happened. She could worry about everything else another day. She needed to give herself a break, even if it was for only a few hours.

"I think this place looks like exactly where we should be headed. It'll be nice to be waited on for once."

Ben walked beside her as they crossed the short distance to the restaurant. It was nothing too fancy, not like some of the Melbourne restaurants she encountered in the city, but it was fresh and modern, and the food smelled great. She liked that she could partially see into the kitchen at the other end of the restaurant—she loved seeing the hustle and bustle of where her food was being prepared.

There was a lovely community feeling in Geelong, and it was something Rebecca missed in the city. It wasn't for everyone, but she kind of liked that if you lived here you would more than likely know a handful of the people dining. That the waiters would know you by name because this was your favorite local dinner spot.

As if on cue a waiter appeared, dressed in black with a smart white half apron tied at his waist.

"Ben," said the man, nodding. "Nice to see you back again so soon."

Rebecca felt her back bristle and wished it away, wondering if Ben had been here with a date already since he'd been home.

"The food was too good to bother going anywhere else," Ben replied politely.

The waiter motioned for them to follow, menus in hand, and Ben placed his open palm lightly to her back again. It wasn't any less surprising than the first time he'd done it, but she managed to gulp down her nerves.

She glanced around the room, seeing mostly couples and a few bigger tables. It was nice—intimate but not fussy, just how she liked it. And it was only early so the place wasn't too busy yet.

The waiter stopped and placed the menus on a table overlooking the water, one of only a few in the restaurant. Either Ben had fluked a good spot, or that crafty old grandfather of his had planned the whole night! She was pretty sure there was no luck involved, which only made her nervous all over again.

"I'll be back to take your drink order soon."

Ben waited for Rebecca to sit before taking his jacket off and settling down across from her. He cleared his throat. Rebecca raised her eyes from the water glass she'd been focused on, trying to quell the nerves jingling like chimes in her belly. It was stupid to feel so unsure, they had way too much history for her to even think about being uncomfortable just chatting and sharing a meal with him, but she couldn't help the way she felt.

"I, ah, didn't exactly plan this," Ben said, eyebrows drawn together as if he was trying to figure out how to explain the fact they had the most romantic table in the house.

"Oh, don't worry!" Rebecca tried to take her voice down a decibel from the high-pitched soprano it had altered to. "This is fine. It's lovely. Maybe Gus did it just to embarrass you."

The waiter reappeared and Ben selected a white wine from the famous Barossa Valley. Rebecca felt like chugging a whole bottle just to calm herself, although thankfully she had the menu to scan now, which meant she had something to look at other than Ben or the gorgeous view.

"What are you going to have?" Ben had placed his down on the table and was watching her.

"Me, ah, well...maybe fish of the day. I love the sound of the king prawns that come with it."

He nodded. "Hmm, good choice. I've been hanging out for seafood so I'm thinking the Moreton Bay bugs and prawns."

They ordered and Rebecca was left with no other option but to look back at Ben. It terrified her. Apart from the similarity of those eyes to Lexie's, she was scared of the intensity of his stare, of the way his eyes looked at her as if they could see right to her soul. Maybe that was why she'd never been attracted to another man since Ben had left. Once she'd had those eyes on her, no other pair ever lived up to it.

"You never did tell me what your parents are up to. What about your brother?"

Phew, she was happy talking family. Safe topic. She was just pleased Ben hadn't run into her brother himself, because then they'd have bonded over their mutual desire to know who Lexie's father was, which would only make the whole situation worse when she did finally come clean.

"Mum and Dad are great, they're making the most of retirement," she said, gratefully taking a gulp of wine. "They spend a bit of time traveling, and I'm happy running the restaurant. It means I can spend lots of time with

Lexie, but it does make juggling things tough when they head away on one of their cruises."

Ben nodded and leaned back in his chair. Rebecca almost felt the tiny bit of extra distance made it easier for her to relax, and at least she knew Ben was genuinely interested in her family. It had almost broken her own mom's heart when he'd left—she'd absolutely loved him and the feeling had been mutual, even more so probably because Ben had zero relationship with his own mother.

"My brother, well, he's a dad now, another on the way. Met a great girl through work and they've been together and happy ever since. But they have twins, so Lexie is always trying to compete with them and keep up with their adventures."

"What about you?" Ben asked, leaning forward. "Have you been okay, really? I mean, I know you love your daughter, but it must have been pretty tough doing it alone. Growing up so quick like that, aside from all the other stuff you went through."

Rebecca felt a mist cloud her eyes but she expertly blinked it away. She didn't cry, it just wasn't what she did. And this was no exception, just because someone had actually asked her that question and genuinely cared about the answer. She wished she could just tell him, that she could open up about what had happened and he'd open his arms wide and tell her she had nothing to worry about, that everything would miraculously be okay. But she was a realist, and she knew there was no amount of wishing that could turn what had happened into them being a happy little white-picket-fence family. If that was the case, she'd have told him right at the start when she'd first found out; if she had even a niggle of doubt that he was interested in being with her and

playing happy families, then she would have told him a
thousand times over.

"It's been hard, I'm not going to lie," she admitted.
"But honestly? I love my girl and I like being in the restaurant, so life's pretty good. I might have given you
a different answer when I was sleep deprived and exhausted a year or so ago, but I've found my rhythm now."

She knew what he wanted to know, though. Whether
she'd had a man in her life, if she'd been alone all this
time. There was a steely glint in his eye, a determined
edge to his smile that told her he wanted to dig deeper.

"And Lexie's dad? He's never helped you out? Never
been a part of her life at all?"

Rebecca reached for her wine again. This was not a
conversation that she wanted to have right now. Not saying anything was one thing, but lying was something entirely different and she wasn't comfortable with it, not
for a second. If she could just find the words to tell him,
the right way to break it to him…

"How about you?" she asked, drawing on all her
strength, not ready, not prepared enough to come out
and say it yet. "You sure you don't have some gorgeous
Argentinian woman packing her things as we speak to
come live the good life in Australia with you?"

Their dinner arrived then and Rebecca smiled her
thanks at the waiter, pleased for the distraction. Any
break in the intensity of talking like this with Ben was
a welcome one.

"You know what? You're the only person I've seen
since coming home, other than Gus really." Ben took a
mouthful and waited till he'd finished before continuing.
"I just feel like I've missed out on so much time with
Gus, and any time I miss out on now seems wasted." He

cleared his throat, glancing up at the same time as one side of his mouth kicked out into a smile. "And no, there's no special someone. You think I would have kissed you if there was?"

Rebecca was pleased she'd already swallowed, otherwise she'd have choked. "Ah, well..." Talk about stunning her into speechlessness. "I guess not."

"Which means we're both single."

"I guess you're right." She had control of her voice now, her nerves settling into a more sedate ball than the writhing one they'd leaped into before.

"So back to Gus," she said, refocusing on her food and cutting the fish into a more manageable bite. "Have the doctors said how long?" she asked gently.

Ben toyed with his fork, the humor that had been in his gaze fading. "Maybe six months, maybe longer, but there's nothing they can do for him. He kept it pretty quiet, but I knew when he finally came out and told me that we were on borrowed time."

"He was great to us, wasn't he?" said Rebecca, smiling at Ben even though she knew it probably hurt like hell for him to talk about his granddad like this. "I don't think either of us would have turned out the same without him. He's a one in a million kind of man."

Ben smiled back at her, his eyes locking on hers, not giving her a moment to look away. She knew he felt the same—hell, his granddad had been the only stable thing in his life, the one person who'd unconditionally loved him from the day he was born.

"He's definitely one in a million," Ben said, grinning as he watched her. "And I'm gonna spend every damn minute I can with him so he knows it."

"Well, good." She ate another mouthful, looking out

at the water as she chewed. It was a beautiful balmy Melbourne night, and with the water twinkling under the soft lights, she could have been anywhere in the world. Ben might terrify her, but she also felt a pull toward him that was impossible to deny.

"Rebecca, the way I left, the way things went down between us before…"

"Don't," she said softly, interrupting him. "We don't need to talk about it. We've already been there."

He shook his head and reached for her hand, his fingers closing over hers in a touch so gentle, so caring, it made the tiny hairs on her arm stand on end. He squeezed, forcing her to look up instead of stare at where their skin was connected, his brown eyes focused on hers.

"I don't want you to think it was because I didn't care about you," he said simply. "What happened between us was years of pent-up attraction I reckon, and maybe if I hadn't been about to fly out it would never have happened. Maybe we never would have made that leap into dangerous territory."

"Yeah," she agreed. "It was like as soon as we knew you were going, all bets were off."

He touched her cheek, his palm so soft to her face it made her sigh. "I wanted you for so long, Bec. You have no idea how hard it was for me to just keep things between us as friends. But I always knew I'd rather have you as my friend than lose you completely, so I never pushed it."

She laughed, shaking her head. "Oh, I know."

He arched an eyebrow and only made her laugh louder. "Then why the hell did we decide we weren't allowed to take things any further? That we had to remain platonic friends?"

Rebecca shrugged. "I think it was just an unwritten rule, neither of us wanting to ruin what we had. I felt the same." She was numb just having this conversation, knowing that if she'd only said something, if they'd only... *it isn't worth thinking about the past like that.* Her heart didn't need to be damaged any more than it already was.

"I say to hell with rules, then." Ben's voice was softer now, but it packed an even greater punch than before. "Whenever you want to take things further, how about you just tell me this time around, huh?"

She cleared her throat. "I can't deal with complications, Ben, which is why I've kind of avoided getting involved with anyone." It was a lie—she hadn't let anyone close because no one had ever measured up to him, and because she didn't want to introduce Lexie to a man.

"How about we take this one day at a time and don't put any labels on what we are?" he asked. "We're friends, nothing's going to change that, but if you want more, well, then, what'd be wrong with that?"

Rebecca opened her mouth to reply, needing to set the record straight and say something, when her phone sounded out, its shrill ring almost sending her off her chair.

"Shivers!" she gasped, grabbing it and pushing a side button to mute the loud volume.

Ben picked up his fork and started to eat again, as if they'd been having a conversation about food instead of sex.

"Oh, it's home," she said by way of explanation, reading the screen. "Sorry, I'll have to take it."

Rebecca put her hand over her mouth and spoke quietly into the mouthpiece.

"Hey, Mom. Don't tell me, she's trying to convince you to give her ice cream in bed?" She laughed into the phone but her smile faded when she was greeted with a big sob.

"Bec, oh, I…" Her mom sobbed down the line at her. "We're at the hospital."

Rebecca felt an ice-cold shiver pierce her spine. This could not be happening. *The hospital?*

"Slow down. Talk me through it. Tell me what's happened."

Ben dropped his fork to his plate, worried eyes meeting hers. She shook her head and reached for her purse.

"I thought she was just coming down with a cold, but then her temperature spiked. About an hour after going to bed she went all floppy and the alarm went off on the thermometer and…" Her mom sobbed again. "I'm so sorry to bother you, Bec, when you're finally taking some time to yourself."

Rebecca was trying to keep her voice calm but tears had welled in her eyes like huge stones, her voice choking at the thought of something happening to her little girl. "Is she okay now?" She stood and indicated to Ben with a nod of her head toward the door that they had to go. He jumped up straight away, throwing his napkin down and pulling out his wallet.

"She's doing fine, but she's asking for you."

"I'm coming now," she said, sounding more confident than she was. If there was one thing she'd always been good at it was staying calm in an emergency. "Just tell her I love her and that I'll be there soon."

She watched as Ben quickly paid the bill, racing back to her and walking with her to the door. When she hung up, she took a big, shuddering breath and pushed her phone into her pocket. Tears filled her eyes, burned like fire as she thought about Lexie without her.

"Bec?"

She glanced across at Ben, let him take her hand when he reached for it, linking their fingers. "It's Lexie," she managed, her breath coming in short pants as she tried to stay calm. She needed to tell him now but the words were choking her.

"Whatever it is, she'll be fine, okay?" Ben reassured, forcing her to stop and holding her hand tight as he looked down at her. "I'll drive you wherever we need to go, and we'll get there fast. So don't worry." His eyes were determined, strong, sexy all rolled into one.

"Thanks," Rebecca muttered, keeping hold of his hand. Her heart was hammering, mouth dry as she tried to swallow. All she cared about was getting to Lexie, but if Ben insisted on coming into the hospital with her? Then tonight was going to get a whole lot tougher than it already was.

He ran ahead of her when they were close to the car, unlocking it and flinging open her door before running around to the other side. She jumped in and fixed her seat belt.

"I know she'll be okay but…" Rebecca took a deep breath. "What if it's something more serious? What if it's…?"

"Let's just take this one step at a time, okay?"

Rebecca nodded and sunk as deep into the seat as she could, wishing she'd just stayed home. Wishing she'd never said yes to seeing Ben, wishing she'd just come straight out and told him the day he'd walked into her restaurant.

"We'll be there in less than an hour, Bec. Just hold tight and we'll be there before you know it."

"I'm sorry about dinner," she murmured, wondering how things had gone from seeming so perfect to being so, so awful in such a short time.

"Dinner? Are you kidding me?" Ben made a sort of grunting sound. "You have nothing to apologize for. This is your little girl we're talking about."

The car traveled fast, gravel spitting out behind them as they left the small side road and hit the main highway back to Melbourne city. Once they were cruising fast, the road dark except for a handful of cars up ahead or passing them, he reached for her, his hand clasping hers again and settling on her thigh.

Ben glanced at her, but she couldn't look back. Tears stung her eyes again, a pain in her chest that she'd only ever felt before when she'd waved Ben goodbye at the airport and believed she'd never see him again.

"Hey," he said softly.

She took a deep, shuddering breath, then angled her body slightly so she could see his face.

"Everything's going to be just fine, Bec. I promise."

She braved a smile, but she didn't believe him for a second. He had no idea whether everything was going to be okay or not. And even worse than that? She knew, in her heart, that she'd never stopped loving him. Not for a second. Only before, she'd imagined that when he did come home one day, he'd have a glamorous wife on his arm; a wife who was happy not having children, who just wanted to be the fun-loving, polo-wife party girl. In that scenario she believed they'd never have even had a chance to rekindle what they might have had. *Never* in a million years had she thought he'd come home single.

Instead, Ben had come back the same rugged, down-to-earth guy she'd always loved. Single, strong and even more handsome than ever. And so instead of resenting him or knowing she'd been right in not telling him what had happened after their night together, she was thinking all sorts of dangerous what-ifs. And those kinds of thoughts were capable of breaking a girl's heart, if the slow, painful shattering of hers was anything to go by.

And it wasn't *her* little girl she was worried about. *It was theirs.*

CHAPTER EIGHT

BEN FELT UTTERLY HELPLESS. He had no idea how to comfort Bec, didn't even know where to start, but what he could do was drive fast and get her into the hospital before her little girl had a chance to get really upset about her mom not being there. He slowed to turn into the hospital, gripping the steering wheel tight beneath his fingers.

"We're here," he said, scanning for the nearest park and pulling into the space.

He looked across at Bec; she was white as a sheet and her hands were trembling.

"Come on, I'll take you in." He hadn't planned on going in with her, thought she'd rather just be with her family, but she looked like she needed some help.

It was as though she'd been jolted from a dream then, lurching into action and pushing her door open, eyes suddenly flashing as she glanced over at him.

"You don't have to come," she said as she hurried toward the front entrance, breaking into a jog. "I'll be fine."

He grunted, catching up to her. "I'll get you to your daughter and then go." Ben didn't say anything, but just in case they were somehow at the wrong place or they'd already gone home, he wanted to be able to drive her.

Bec reached for him and he took her hand, both of them hurrying through the entrance.

"Thanks," she said as they waited at the elevator, her eyes meeting his.

"Bec, I'd never leave you when you needed me. It's no problem."

She gulped and took her hand back, folding them tight across her chest. He frowned as he watched her fidget, wondering if he'd somehow said the wrong thing. But that was being stupid. She was a mom scared about the health of her daughter; now was not the time to go reading into her body language.

They stepped into the elevator and headed to the right floor, with Bec checking her phone for the hundredth time to reread the text from her mom.

"We're here," Ben said as the doors opened and they rushed out. "I'll go find out where to..."

"Lexie!" Bec's high-pitched call echoed straight through his ear. "Lexie!"

Bec pushed past him, running fast in her heels and then dropping to her knees and throwing her arms around a little girl. Her hair was dark brown with streaks of blond through it, her arms wrapped tight around her mom's neck.

Ben stood back, not needing to be part of it. And then Bec's mom saw him and a smile broke out on her face, the worried frown lines disappearing when she locked eyes with him. He slowly made his way over, opened his arms and gave her a warm hug.

"Ben! What a lovely surprise."

He kissed her cheek before letting her go. "Sorry I stole your daughter away for the evening."

She pursed her lips. "Rebecca? Don't be silly. That

girl needed some time to herself. Between the restaurant and her little one, she doesn't exactly take any time off."

"Her daughter?" Ben asked.

"Is going to be fine. The doctor said there's some nasty viruses going around, probably something she picked up in preschool. They said she was better off going home and having a good sleep in her own bed now that her fever has broken. The worst has long passed."

Bec stood up then, her daughter in her arms. "Ben, you can't drive all the way back to Geelong again tonight."

He laughed. "It's only an hour. I'll be fine."

"Stay with Rebecca," her mom said, patting his shoulder before moving toward her daughter and kissing her granddaughter. "Granddad's gone to bring the car around front. Why don't you meet us at Rebecca's?"

Ben looked at Bec, didn't want to do anything that would make her uncomfortable, but all she seemed worried about was her daughter.

"Are you sure?" he asked, eyes never leaving Bec's.

"You drove me all this way and we ran out on dinner. Having you back to my place is the least I can do."

"Well that's settled, then," her mom said, looking pleased with herself and striding off ahead of them.

"If we just change Lexie's seat into your car, we can go straight to my place and let my folks go home."

He nodded and followed. It should have been awkward tagging along with her family, but they'd been part of each other's lives for so many years that it just didn't. He blew out a sigh of relief as the elevator dinged and they all stepped in, watching Bec with her girl tucked tight into her arms. It was a dose of reality seeing her in mom mode, told him that he had to tread carefully, but it didn't scare him. Not yet. Because he wanted Rebecca. *He needed Rebecca.* And he doubted anything was going to change that, little girl or not.

Rebecca shut the door and padded quietly back to the lounge. Ben was sitting back on the sofa, eyes shut, and she hoped he wasn't actually asleep.

"Ben?" she whispered once she was standing in front of him.

His eyes popped open, a slow smile breaking out on his face when he saw her.

"Hey. Is she asleep?"

"Snoring her little head off already," Rebecca said. "I was going to snuggle her up in my bed, but she went happily into her own. Her temperature's fine and she seemed happy enough."

He nodded, his eyes on hers. She took a deep breath, staring at him, wishing she could just ignore the way she felt for him and carry on like she had been these past few years. But she couldn't. The one man she'd ever loved was sitting on her sofa, looking back at her, and there was no way she could resist him, even if it was under false pretenses.

Rebecca moved fast, not wanting to give herself time to doubt; one moment she was standing in front of him, the next she was straddling him, her thighs on either side of his.

Ben didn't question, he just went with it, hands on her hips as she dipped her head and kissed him, lips over his, tasting him, doing what she'd only dreamed about doing for so long. His mouth was warm against hers, his hands skimming up her body, fingers tangling in her hair.

She pushed back for a second, trying to catch her

breath, wondering what the hell she was doing. She'd resisted him for so many years, always determined never to be the one to make the first move, but after the night they'd just had...

"You okay?" Ben asked, one hand stroking her face as he gazed up at her.

"You said to tell you if I wanted this," she murmured, moistening her dry lips with her tongue.

He chuckled. "I did."

"Well, this is what I want," she said, refusing to give in to her insecurities. "Just tonight. Just once."

He nodded, his palm cupped to her cheek as he guided her back forward. "Your wish," he muttered, "is my command."

Rebecca relaxed into his touch, sighed into his mouth as he kissed her so gently, his lips soft to start with, then rougher, more insistent as his hands explored under her top, skimming across her skin. Her body hummed, every part of her on edge, reactive to his fingertips, to his mouth, to *anything* he did to her. She should have made him a bed on the sofa and gone to her own room alone, but she couldn't. Because she needed Ben like she'd never needed anything in her life before.

She worked the buttons of his shirt, undoing them slowly one by one, moaning as he took his lips off hers and started plucking gentle kisses down her neck, inching toward her collarbone. There was an urgency to his touch, to the way she was touching him, just like their first and only ever night together.

Just one night. She just needed one night with Ben. No questions, no thinking about the past. Just one selfish night of being with him.

She could worry about the rest in the morning.

* * *

Ben cradled Bec in his arms, wishing he could just carry her to her room and keep her tight against him for the rest of the evening. But they weren't just two single people anymore; she had a daughter to worry about, which meant he couldn't exactly be naked in her bed come morning.

"I don't want you to think I'm running out on you, because I'd like nothing better than to spend the next twenty-four hours exploring every inch of you, but I think I'll head home."

Her eyes popped open. She'd been curled against him like a cat who couldn't get enough of being petted, and now she was pushed back and staring at him.

"You want to go already?"

He dropped a kiss to lips plump from all the attention his mouth had been giving them. "I don't want to, but it might be easier. You know, with Lexie."

She sighed and dropped her head to his chest again. "You're right. You're absolutely right."

"You going to the polo next weekend?" he asked.

Rebecca nodded against him. "Half for fun, half for work. I need to oversee catering to one of the corporate areas."

He stroked her hair, the golden blond strands like silk against his fingers. "It'll be the first time I've ever gone for fun, although I have offered to play if they need me."

She ran her hand down his arm. "We never missed a year, did we?"

"No, we didn't." He tucked his fingers under her chin, tilted her face up to him so he could kiss her again and look into her blue eyes. "So I'll see you on Saturday?"

She nodded. "Yes."

"It's a date, then."

Rebecca shook her head. "This was a one-time thing, Ben."

"So says you," he joked straight back.

"I'm serious. We can't do this again."

He laughed at her solemn expression. "We'll see."

She stayed silent, but she didn't pull away until a noise down the hall sent her scrambling for her clothes.

"I think that's my cue," he said.

Rebecca paused and bent down, her lips seeking out his in one long, slow kiss. "Drive safely."

He watched as she hurried toward her daughter's room, waiting until she'd disappeared from sight before reaching for his jeans. Their lives had changed, hell, everything had changed, but now that he'd had her once, he wasn't going to give her up again without a fight.

CHAPTER NINE

THE CROWD WAS BUZZING. Women dressed in tiny dresses and super-high heels were drinking champagne, most of them completely ignoring what was happening on the field, their male counterparts swilling imported beer and looking more interested in the horses galloping past toward the goalposts. It was amazing being part of the event here, but she could only imagine what it was like in the exclusive areas of the Argentinian or London polo scenes.

Bec wiggled her toes, wishing she hadn't worn brand-new shoes. They were bright yellow stilettos and they looked fabulous, but her feet were protesting big-time.

"Hey, gorgeous."

A shiver ran through her body. Suddenly her feet were the least of her worries. Rebecca slowly turned, recognizing Ben's deep, sexy voice. She'd avoided his calls during the week, not wanting to talk about their night together because then she'd have to feel guilty all over again. But she'd known he'd find her today; the only question had been when.

"Hey," she said, his gaze filled with enough heat to set her on fire.

"You enjoying the game?"

Bec laughed. "Probably more than you are. I bet you'd rather be playing than watching."

He shrugged. "Hey, what's one year watching? I'll be back on the team before I know it."

"Confident, much?" she said with a laugh.

He took a step closer to her and her resolve died. So much for telling him that she couldn't be anything more than friends with him, for swallowing her fears and breaking the news to him that she'd kept something from him and couldn't go on not telling him the truth today.

"Are you all done with work?" he asked, brushing back one of her curls that had separated from the others.

She swallowed, stuck in the web of his gaze. "Almost."

"You look beautiful today," he said, looking her up and down, his smile taking her breath away.

Rebecca stayed silent. She'd be lying if she said she hadn't made a massive effort on her appearance because she'd known he was going to be there, because she knew she'd end up spending time with him. She'd brought a new dress and heels to wear, showing off more skin than she ever usually would, her hair set in soft curls that made her feel all '50s pinup with her bright red lipstick.

"We have plenty of food if you're hungry and…"

Ben laughed and reached for her hand. "In case you haven't noticed I've been trying to get hold of you this week. It's not your food that I'm interested in."

Rebecca wanted to flirt with him, to let him tug her toward the polo field so they could watch the final chukker, hear more about his time away and what it was like, so they could reminisce and have fun. But she couldn't lie to him any longer, the weight of what she'd kept from him burning into her conscience.

"Ben, we need to talk."

He laughed, linking his fingers with hers. "How about we talk later and play now."

It broke her heart to see him like this. This was the old Ben, the Ben she'd had fun with all her life, the Ben she'd always remembered. She wanted to keep this version of him committed to memory, because when he heard what she had to say...

Ben frowned. "Okay, come on. Let's go sit by the field and you can tell me whatever's worrying you so much."

She grabbed a glass of champagne from a passing waiter, taking a few sips to calm her nerves. Ben kept hold of her other hand and she followed him through the crowd, wishing they were just two people having fun, that she could let her hair down and pretend like nothing had changed between them. But she'd already done that. Now it was time for the truth.

"So what is it that you're so desperate to tell me?" he asked, sitting down beside Bec and facing the field. He was reluctant to admit it but he was kind of enjoying being on the sidelines, for one day anyway. His granddad was out there somewhere, close to the action, watching horses he'd trained and sold thunder around the field, and Ben was just happy to be back at the famous Melbourne Polo in the City.

"Ben, I don't think there's an easy way to tell you this, so I'm just going to come out and say it."

He frowned. The expression on her face had him worried, her eyes filled with what looked to be...tears? What the hell was she upset about?

"Bec, what's wrong?"

"You're her father, Ben. I know I should have told you

sooner, that I shouldn't have kept it from you, but Lexie's your daughter."

Ben froze. No part of his body moved, not so much as a quiver as he stared at her. The smile had long disappeared from Bec's mouth, and now his did, too.

"*What*?" He must have misheard her. She'd said he was...

"I know it's probably hard for you to make sense of right now, but Lexie's your daughter. I just couldn't..."

"Hold on a minute." He pushed back his chair, needing to put distance between them, to just stare at Rebecca for a moment and try to figure out what the hell she was trying to explain to him. "You're saying that our one night together, that I..." Ben jumped up, running his hand hard through his hair and grinding his teeth together. "I'm her *father*?"

He turned back to Rebecca to see tears sliding down her cheeks. She wasn't making a noise, silently crying.

"I'm sorry."

"Damn right you should be sorry!" he hissed. "I've been back here all this time, we've been with each other, and you never thought this should be the first thing you tell me?" His head was pounding, fury building inside him. "You had no right to keep this from me."

She nodded but he didn't care how upset she was. He'd come back desperate to see her again, to spend time with the one and only woman he'd ever trusted, and she'd blindsided him with this. How the hell could he be a father? He'd thought she was different, that after all the fake women more interested in fame and money he'd been surrounded with, that Bec was different. That he'd never have to worry about her not being honest. And now—he swallowed. Hard.

"Ben, I…"

"Mommy!"

The high-pitched voice calling out shattered every thought in his mind. He turned slowly, seeing a blond-haired little girl running fast, arms pumping as she made her way toward Rebecca. She flew into her mother's arms as he just stared on, watching in disbelief.

"She was so excited about coming." Ben stayed still as he listened to Rebecca's mother calling out. "Is she okay with you now?"

"Yes, she's fine," Rebecca called back.

Ben couldn't take his eyes off the girl. *Off his daughter.* All this time he'd been furious that some jerk had left Rebecca to be a solo parent, without ever guessing that that someone could have been him. And now that he looked at her…every part of him ached, with anger or resentment or disbelief; he had no idea which.

And now that she was here, he had to suck up every bit of anger that he wanted to hurl at Rebecca and save it for later. Because he wouldn't lose his temper in front of a child, and he sure as hell wouldn't do it in front of *his* child.

It was time for them to leave, and he wasn't going to let Rebecca get away without explaining everything to him. He wanted answers now and he wasn't taking no for an answer.

CHAPTER TEN

"WE'RE GOING BACK to Geelong." His words were meant as a statement, not a question. He stood staring at her, his height advantage suddenly daunting as he stood too close. "And Lexie's coming with us."

Rebecca stood her ground, refusing to be intimidated. She might have done the wrong thing in lying to him all this time, but she'd done it to protect her daughter and she'd do anything to keep her protected and in her safe little cocoon forever if she had to. She folded her arms across her chest, not giving in to the tremor of fear running through her body.

"I think we're best to just head back to my place."

Ben smiled at Lexie, touching her shoulder before moving to stand closer to Rebecca, his eyes burning into her with none of the kindness in his gaze that he'd just shown Lexie.

"We've got a lot to talk about, Rebecca," he said. "We'll go by your place and get Lexie's things, then we're heading to Geelong."

"You need to understand why I…"

"Enough," he said, his voice so low it was only just audible. "There's nothing you can say right now, Rebecca, so just don't."

When Ben finally turned away she let out a big breath she hadn't even realized she was holding. He bent to say something to Lexie, made her smile, then walked off. His long legs ate up the ground as she watched him, at the same time as she almost collapsed from fear.

"Mommy?"

Lexie's little voice was like an injection of energy to her body. She picked herself up and fixed a smile, bending down and holding out an arm to her.

"We're going on an adventure tonight. What do you think about going to visit Ben's farm?"

"Yay!"

Rebecca scooped her up and waved goodbye to her staff as she passed by where they were still working. They were almost done packing up and there was nothing left for her to do, and besides, there was no point in delaying the inevitable.

"Can we go now?"

Rebecca nodded and pressed a kiss to Lexie's forehead. "We sure can."

A fresh wave of fear washed through her, but she forced it away. There was no point in fearing the unknown. Trouble was, when it involved her little girl's future, it was impossible not to worry.

Rebecca turned and looked back at her daughter. She'd fallen asleep. They weren't even ten minutes out of the city and she had already succumbed to slumber. Her get out of jail free card was snoozing, which meant the interrogation was just about to start.

"She's asleep," she said, moving back to her sitting position as far away from Ben as possible. If she could have put a bigger gap between them in the car then she would have—in fact she'd prefer him on a plane heading back to Argentina if she had a choice right now. It might be her car they were driving in, but it felt like she was a prisoner.

He didn't answer. Rebecca glanced over and saw the tight clench of his jaw. She wasn't looking forward to this at all.

"What were you even thinking keeping this from me?" he demanded, his voice low. "You've had every opportunity to tell me, Rebecca."

She sighed and looked out the window. At the buildings blurring past, the inky-black sky, other cars whizzing by. All this time she'd wondered how it would happen. Whether Lexie would be a child or an adult, and now here she was, about to explain why she'd kept a secret that was going to ruin their friendship forever.

"Well?"

He clearly wasn't going to let her get away with staying silent, not now that Lexie was asleep.

"I don't know where to begin," she said honestly, her thoughts a jumble.

"How about starting with the part where you forgot to tell me I was a father." His voice was like ice, so cold he could have turned her to stone.

Rebecca knew he had every right to hate her, to be angry with her, but the steel-edged ring to his tone scared her. She had acted how she thought best at the time. Yes, it was flawed, but if it were to happen all over again, she'd probably do the same. She hadn't done it to hurt him, she'd done it because she cared enough about him to let him go.

"I found out when I was two months pregnant," she started, digging her fingernails deep into her palm to force pain other than what she was feeling in her heart. It had hurt at the time; the hurt had been so bad she'd been curled into a ball on the floor, cradling her belly, wishing she could make everything right and go back in time, her tears a puddle on the bathroom tiles beneath her. But this pain was stabbing, relentlessly washing over her in thick waves. She'd been so broken, so damaged already over everything, and then there had been Lexie. And from the day she'd been born, everything had changed; she'd had someone to love and pour all her energy into, and she'd never wished her baby away or resented her for a moment.

There was silence as she waited for Ben to do the math. She knew he would.

"So when I came home for that week, before I flew back for my first pro game in Europe, you knew then?"

His voice was incredulous and she swallowed down tears. A show of emotion now would only make her look pathetic, and it was Ben who should be upset and angry, not her. This was his time to be hurt, not hers.

"I'd just found out. When you came home I was so pleased to see you but, damn it, Ben! You had your whole future planned and there was no way I was going to ruin your life, to clip your wings and hold you back. I wasn't going to let history repeat itself."

"Don't..." He lowered his voice. "Don't give me that. I had a right to know. You can't put this on me when I never had the chance to be a part of our child's life, when you never let it be my choice."

She took a deep, slow breath. "What's the one thing you've always told me? The one thing you were always so sure about your future?"

Rebecca could see how tight his grip on the steering

wheel was, his body rigid as he glowered at the road. "Don't you turn this around on me, don't you dare."

"You said you never wanted to be a dad," she continued, undeterred. Now she'd started she couldn't stop. "You said you never wanted to be a parent because of your mom, because of what she did to you. That you never wanted to have a child and ever let them think they'd held you back from doing what you wanted to do with your life." She shook her head and turned to stare at him. "Tell me I'm wrong, Ben. Tell me I'm not saying the exact words you said to me so many times, that that wouldn't have been exactly what would have happened."

He was silent. The only noise was the tires on the road and it only made her mouth dryer, the pounding in her head louder.

"Ben…"

"Don't you dare put words in my mouth," he growled out, slamming one palm against the steering wheel. "Whatever the hell I said had nothing to do with *our kid*. Hell, Bec, I know what it was like to grow up without my parents. I would never do that to a child, to our…" His voice trailed off, as if he had no idea what to say next.

"I didn't even know if I was going to go through with it when you were back," she said in a low voice. "I was alone, I knew my family would be devastated, and I just needed the time to get my head around it all. To deal with…*me*."

Ben looked over at her. "What changed your mind?"

"You." She said the word simply, without hesitation.

"Me?" His focus was entirely back on the road now, but his laugh was low and cynical. "You kept it from me, but somehow *I* helped to change your mind."

"I loved you, Ben. I couldn't terminate what we'd

made." She quickly brushed stray tears away as they trickled down her cheek. "You have to believe me, that I wanted to do right by you, that I would never have kept it from you if I hadn't known you would resent me or her. Because I know you, I knew you better than you probably even knew yourself back then, and that meant I knew you'd stay with me, *with us*, out of duty."

He didn't respond and she squirmed, wishing she could get out of the car. It was starting to feel very claustrophobic and if she didn't have Lexie curled up in the backseat she'd have demanded he stop the car and let her the hell out.

"I didn't want to hold you back. I knew you'd feel obliged to do the honorable thing, and I didn't want to stand in the way of your future." She bit back a sob. "Look at your mom, what that did to you knowing that she'd compromised her medical career to have you. You forget that I was there for you when you tried to reconnect with her, that I saw how much she hurt you. I didn't want you to end up making the same mistakes as she did, when you didn't even have a choice in the matter."

"I still had a right to know." He punched out each word. "No matter what you thought or what I'd said or what we'd been through, I still had a right to know."

"I know you did," she whispered. "I know."

Rebecca felt dreadful, but she deserved it.

"I'm sorry, Ben, but I did what seemed best at the time," she said, needing him to at least understand why she'd done what she'd done. "It may have been the wrong decision, but I was young, scared and alone."

"I would have been there for you, Bec," he responded, his voice back to his soft, understated tone. "I would have stood by you. *Damn it*! You know I would have."

She let out a heaving breath.

"And that's exactly why I didn't tell you."

Lexie moaned in her sleep as Ben pulled her up into his arms. It was the first time they'd touched, other than when he'd dropped his hand to her shoulder earlier in the day. Shadows played across the girl's face as he carried her up to the house, and Ben watched each one. The way the light fell over his daughter's skin did something to him, hurt him somehow, and it took all his strength not to pass her to Rebecca. The last thing he wanted was to hold her, to be close to her when…hell, he didn't even know what to think.

He could hear Rebecca following behind, but he didn't acknowledge her. She could follow them upstairs, and when they got to the guest room she could take over. As much as he wanted to not be close to Lexie, something else was making him want to keep her close forever, to know what it was like to hold a child that was his own flesh and blood.

"She can sleep in bed with me," Rebecca whispered to him.

Ben nodded and kept walking. Lexie stirred but didn't wake, and Ben waited until Rebecca had rearranged the bedding before placing her on the mattress. He pulled the sheet and covers up under her chin and watched her long and hard before turning away. Rebecca was staring at him but he went straight past her and back downstairs.

Only hours ago, he'd been ready to ask Rebecca for something more, to apologize for leaving her behind in the first place and ask if they could be something more. If he was honest with himself he knew something had been wrong, that there had been more going on than her simply not wanting to leave her family, but he'd been desperate to get away and he'd decided not to ask questions. It had been Argentina, playing polo for one of the best teams in the world, or staying home and hoping that the girl who'd been his best friend for years might want something more. By the time they'd spent the night together, he'd already signed on the dotted line and cashed his first check from the team, and his flight was booked to go. It had been too late to change his mind even if he'd wanted to.

He was so angry with her his blood was boiling, but as much as he wanted to hate her and put all the blame on her, it wasn't all her fault. Maybe he was just tired, shell-shocked, but he could barely wrap his head around the whole situation. *A daughter.* She looked like him—her eyes were the same deep shade of brown, beautiful against golden hair the same color as her mom's. And from the desperation, the anguish he'd seen on Rebecca's face earlier, he knew there was no point in asking if she was sure about the girl's paternity. She was his; as true as the fact the sun would rise every morning, Lexie was his daughter.

Ben tripped his way down the stairs, his brain on the verge of exploding. Just when he'd thought life was going to get simpler, that things were going to be easy back home and he might have a chance of connecting with the woman he'd left behind, he was faced with this. With a daughter. A child of his own when he'd never even considered the fact that he might be a father in his lifetime, when he'd just gotten his head around the idea of being a fun kind of uncle to the girl if he and Bec did finally become more permanently involved.

A noise upstairs told him that Rebecca was on her way

down, which meant this was all about to become very real, very fast. He stifled the bellow he felt like roaring and reasoned with himself that a drink was what he needed. A very, very strong one. Or two. *Or three.*

Rebecca found Ben sitting at the kitchen table. He had a tumbler in front of him and she watched as he took a sharp swig of the golden brown liquid as she walked into the room. Unless he'd changed his habits since leaving, Rebecca knew that Ben wasn't much of a drinker. He'd always liked the odd beer, but definitely not spirits and certainly not straight. It made her eyes water just looking at straight whiskey.

"Want one?" Ben asked, raising his eyes.

She nodded. Rebecca had never drunk straight spirits before, not once, but she didn't think that now was the right time to say no.

Ben downed what was left in his tumbler before going into the kitchen, dropping a few ice cubes into his glass and into a fresh one, then pouring a small portion of whiskey into each.

"Jack Daniel's on the rocks," he announced, his glare still cold as ice.

She took a tiny sip and felt her eyes well with tears as she swallowed. Her throat was on fire as the liquid traced a fiery path right to her belly, then ignited all over again.

"It gets better," he said, downing another quick gulp. "Just keep drinking."

Rebecca didn't recall ever feeling quite this awkward, and especially not with the one person in the world she'd always been able to be herself around. She took another hesitant sip. It still tasted awful but not as bad as the first, and if it helped her feel a bit less anxious about the whole situation, then maybe it would be worth it.

"So where to from here?" Ben asked. "What the hell are we going to do?"

He was staring at her, which was worse than just seeing his angry side profile in the car, although maybe the alcohol was starting to numb her system a little because he didn't seem quite as irate.

"I know you hate me for what I've done," she said. "But I am sorry, Ben, more sorry than you'll ever understand. And I need you to get that I didn't do this to hurt you. The last few years have been rough, but no matter how tough it got I didn't want to be the one to shatter your dreams. Then as time passed, I didn't want it to be Lexie you resented." She shrugged. "*Me*, sure, but the idea that you could blame my gorgeous little girl?"

"*Our*," he corrected. "*Our* gorgeous little girl, Bec. The fact that she's ours is why it wasn't your secret to keep. Why you should have let me decide if I wanted to come home for her, if she was more important to me than my career."

"I'm sorry. There's nothing more I can say." Rebecca wrapped one arm tight around herself. "I'm sorry a thousand times over, Ben, and I need you to believe me." She bit her lip hard to stop the tears from falling.

"What if I'd not come back for another few years, though? What if we'd never bumped into one another? Would you have ever told me? Would I still be walking around not knowing that I had a beautiful little girl out there in the world?"

Rebecca realized there was no point in lying, because she wasn't going to hold back now that Ben knew. "No. I wouldn't have sought you out to tell you, if that's what you're asking. Not if you hadn't come home of your own free will."

He glared at her and took another long sip of his drink, draining the glass.

"Just because you're her mom doesn't mean you have a right to keep your daughter's father from her," Ben snapped. "I could understand a mother protecting her child from a violent person, from a drug addict, from some lowlife they're better off not knowing. But hell, Rebecca, did you really think I'd be *that bad* a parent? That I couldn't man the hell up and deal with the consequences of what had happened between us, of what we'd made?"

"No!" she almost yelled the word. "I wanted you to live the life you wanted to live, not come back here for me. For a baby you didn't choose to have." She bit back a sob, a torrent of emotion that choked her. "Don't you see, Ben? I know what a great dad you'd be, but you didn't want a child. You wanted to travel the world playing polo with the best players in the world, and that's exactly what I wanted you to do."

"I would have, though," he said, his stare unrelenting. "I would have dropped everything to look after you. I would have stayed." Ben shook his head. "Or I would have taken you with me. Either way I wouldn't have just left you. If you'd even just told me how you felt about me, not insisted that you wanted us to just be friends, this all could have changed."

"If you came home for me, I wanted it to be because you loved me, wanted me, not because you felt obliged to." She forced a smile. "I have always wanted a family, Ben, you've always known that. There was no way I could ever see us working long term because we wanted different things, which is why I wanted to stay friends.

And that was before I knew I was pregnant. Loving you wasn't enough."

"But *I did love you.*"

He said the words so softly, so honestly that it was like a sucker punch straight to her stomach. He was lying, he was… She bit back a sob, shaking her head as she balled her fists. She'd waited so long to hear those words, and now she had, it was too late. Because he already hated her. Because she'd already ruined everything. But it still didn't change the fact that they'd always wanted different things.

"But was I wrong? Did you want the same as me?"

"No." He shook his head. "I loved you because you were you, because I thought you would never lie to me, never betray me." He shook his head. "I thought I knew you."

"Ben, please don't…" His words were like a knife piercing her skin, the pain so intense she could hardly stand it.

Ben watched her long and hard before standing. "If you'd been honest with me, everything would have been different. *Everything.*"

He walked his now-empty glass back into the kitchen and slammed his hand down hard on the counter, his fury so fierce her hands started to tremble just watching him. She stayed silent, watching, listening, waiting. Ben didn't talk until he returned to the room, his eyes finally meeting hers, the storm in his gaze like a cyclone. She watched as he leaned against the wall, his big frame rigid with tension. She saw her daughter in him as she studied his face, in the line of his mouth and the slant of his eyes. That was how Lexie looked when she was cross with her, when Rebecca didn't give her what she wanted. Only Lexie's minor temper tantrums had nothing on the fierce stare and angry-bear hulk facing her now who looked as though he was capable of crushing anything in his path with his bare hands.

"Do your parents know?" His voice was low and husky, so deep it tugged every single one of her heartstrings.

She swallowed and dipped her head. "Nobody knows. Just me."

He raised his eyebrows in question. She knew she'd just sunk even lower in his opinion than she already had.

"I told them that I had a one-night stand, that it was some jerk I never saw again." She paused and looked up at him before going back to picking at her nails. "They had no reason not to believe me, aside from the fact that I've always been Ms. Responsible. The difficult part would have been believing I'd actually had random sex, not the fact the guy had bailed."

"And you're telling me no one ever put two and two together?" His glare was cool again, his entire face frosty.

"I guess you see what you want to see. You'd been gone a long time before she started to look like you, and thankfully no one ever made the connection." She sighed. "It's one of the reasons I never came to see Gus again, because I didn't want to lie to his face. And besides, no one knew about what happened between us, did they? As far as everybody else was concerned we'd just parted as friends."

"What would have happened if I hadn't gone, Bec?"

"We would never have spent the night together," she said simply. "We would have stayed as friends, we wouldn't be having this conversation."

"You're sure about that?" he asked. "I never thought

I was good enough for you, Bec. I knew that I couldn't give you what you wanted, but maybe we still would have ended up in bed together eventually."

"*You* not good enough for *me*?" She almost laughed. "That's the stupidest thing I've ever heard."

"I'm going to bed," he announced.

Rebecca merely nodded and stayed seated. She watched as he walked away. His shoulders were slumped, head down, hands jammed into his pockets. This wasn't the Ben McFarlane she knew. There was anger seething through his veins, she knew that, but she also guessed he was heartbroken. He would have thought he could always trust her, with the history they had behind them, and she knew he was probably as upset about her deception as he was about what she'd kept from him.

A painful tickle of concern played down her back, leaving her aching and worried. She could go and get Lexie and run, head back to her place since it was her car they'd brought, but that would only be delaying the inevitable. Besides, Ben would find them wherever they were. There had been a look in his eyes that said he was not going to be giving his girl up, and that frightened her more than anything.

"Ben!" she called out, jumping up and chasing after him.

He stopped, his hand on the bannister, about to walk up the stairs. He didn't say anything, but he didn't move, either.

"Ben, I want you to know that I loved you, too," she told him. "I loved you so bad it hurt, and if there was any way I thought we could have made it work, as a family, I'd have made that choice in a heartbeat."

He turned, slowly, his stormy gaze catching hers as he

stared, jaw locked hard. "Yeah? Well that ship has sailed, Bec. A long, long time ago."

She swallowed a wave of emotion, a tide of hurt and sadness exploding through her body. "Ben," she whispered. He turned and started to walk again, his back like a brick wall between them. "Ben!" she begged, louder this time, her voice full of unshed tears.

But he never turned back. She'd lost him. From the moment she'd told him, she'd lost him, and he'd just made his intentions very, very clear. It was over. Any little dreams she'd ever entertained about them reuniting, any fantasies she'd had about a perfect little family…that's all they were. Broken dreams and fantasies.

Ben was right. They were done.

There was no chance of finding sleep. Ben kept his eyes trained on the ceiling. Even in the dark he didn't feel tired. Exhausted in plenty of ways but not tired enough for sleep to seek him out. After the day he'd had he should be shattered, but he wasn't.

He was so angry with Rebecca the fury was consuming him; his body was on fire with a rage he'd never felt before. Which is why he'd walked away from her before he said something he'd regret forever. His grandfather had more patience than a handful of men put together, and he'd remembered that when he'd left Bec standing downstairs alone. He would have rather yelled at her, called her all sorts of names and slammed his fist through a wall; but he hadn't.

He had a daughter. *A daughter.* A little girl who was probably too young yet to have worried about not having a father, but he knew those thoughts would come soon. By the time he'd started school and seen all the other kids with both parents visiting on sports day and at science fairs, he'd realized he was the odd one out. Hardly any of the other kids had come from single parent homes back then. Add to that a mother who resented the time she'd had to spend with him, and he'd had a pretty lousy time when it came to parents. If it hadn't been for his grand-dad… He shook his head. He didn't even want to think about it. And now here he was, finding out that he was a dad, and no matter how furious he was with Rebecca, nothing changed the fact that he had a kid.

Ben lay another few moments, eyes shut, before getting up and pulling on his jeans, leaving his chest bare. He needed to talk to someone about this, someone other than Rebecca. Gus would be sound asleep by now, having left the game before them, but considering they might only have months left together, he doubted the old man would mind being woken. This affected both of them. Gus was now officially a great-grandfather, and Ben needed his advice. *Fast.*

There was a part of him that wanted to listen to Rebecca, that wanted to forgive her, but it just didn't seem possible. Not now. After all they'd gone through together, all the ups and downs over so many years, nothing changed the fact that she'd lied to him. Or omitted to tell him—no matter how he put it the fact didn't change. But he'd asked her about Lexie's father, that first time at the restaurant and then when they were out riding, which meant she'd had every opportunity to tell him.

He still would have been angry, hell, nothing could change how he felt, but to wait all this time?

There was nothing to like about what had happened, or how he'd found out, but he had to deal with the fact that he did have a daughter. That there were consequences to the night he and Rebecca had shared. The trouble was, he'd never have shut his own flesh and blood out of his life, never would have walked away. He'd never wanted to repeat his own mother's mistakes, and then he'd gone and done exactly that without even knowing.

He walked straight past the room Rebecca and Lexie were in and resisted the urge to push it open, not to seek Rebecca out, but to catch a glimpse of his daughter. When he looked at her, he knew he was a dad, could feel that the child who looked back was part of him. But the thought of living up to the title terrified him, just the idea of being around her or touching her, talking to her even, scaring him now that he knew he was her dad.

Ben gritted his teeth and kept moving, not stopping until he reached the other end of the long hall, tapping on his grandfather's door. He might not have had a dad growing up, but he'd had a darn good male role model. All this time he'd been scared of being a father because he didn't have his own to show him the ropes, hadn't had a parent to depend on, but he'd had Gus, and now that he was faced with being a dad to Lexie, he realized that he would know instinctively what to do, if he let himself. Because everything good in him, he'd learned from Gus. And no one could ever take that away from him.

CHAPTER ELEVEN

THERE WAS NO way to explain how she felt. Her entire body was aching, Lexie was jammed up hard against her, one arm slung over her face, and she was dead tired. Rebecca guessed that being caught out after years of hiding the truth wasn't meant to be easy, but she was exhausted. All night she'd writhed around on the sheets, trying not to disturb Lexie but desperately craving sleep—anything to give her some relief from reliving the conversations she'd had with Ben. He probably felt the same, racked with guilt and anger for different reasons. *And coming to terms with the fact that he had a daughter.*

Rebecca listened out but could hear no noise in the house. Both men had always been early risers, but given that it was Sunday she expected they might be a little later out of bed. Besides, she was desperate for a coffee to kick-start the morning. Running into Ben was a risk she'd have to take, and at the end of the day she was going to have to face him sometime. They were going to have to sort things out one way or another. To think that the last time they'd been together had been like heaven on earth, and now they were barely talking.

Once she'd pried herself out from her daughter's oc-topus-like grasp, she ran a quick brush through her hair, pulled it up into a ponytail and rummaged for a T-shirt. She looked down at her legs and left them bare—the T was superlong and she didn't have anything on show.

A quick glance back at Lexie reassured her she wasn't going to wake up while her mother was gone, and she slipped out the door, stopping in the hallway to listen out. She couldn't hear a thing. She tiptoed down the stairs, cringing when she hit a squeaky board and hurrying the rest of the way down. She padded across the timber floor to the kitchen, smiled when she inhaled the faint smell of coffee wafting around her. Gus must have made a pot last night; unless Ben had gotten back up from bed, she guessed the old man had been up, unable to sleep. Rebecca deposited the remains into the bin and scooped fresh granules from the container, just like old times. She'd always tried to be up first when she'd stayed over, making coffee and gulping down her first cup before Ben was awake, buzzed about training the polo ponies with him. By sunrise they'd always been galloping down the beach—Geelong was famous for being horse country, and the proximity to the beach for training was one of the reasons it was so popular.

The smell of fresh coffee made her smile. She could almost taste the strong flavor of black, sugary syrup just from inhaling it. A complete contradiction to her usually obsessive compulsive healthy, organic choice in whatever she put into her body, but it was a habit she'd never been able to break. No tea, herbal concoction, *nothing* could make her feel like coffee did, particularly in the morning.

She took a slow sip, inhaled the aroma and shut her eyes for a second. With her eyes closed, she could be anywhere, drinking coffee at home, at the restaurant—hell, she could be at a resort in Fiji. Then she opened them, and looked straight out the window to the yellowed green grass fields beyond the house. But she wasn't *anywhere*. She was at the McFarlanes' place, she was with Ben, and she was guessing that at some stage today she was going to have to tell Lexie that she had a dad.

Ben stopped dead. He smelled the coffee, it had lulled him down from his bedroom, but he thought Gus had just got down before him like usual, when reality couldn't have been farther from the truth. Nothing could prepare him for what he found.

Rebecca had her back turned. She was fussing over what he presumed was the coffee press, and as far as he was concerned, she could do it all morning. He couldn't see much of her upper half, with the exception of the nape of her neck, which was exposed from her hair being pulled back. But her lower half. *Wow.* He'd never seen anything so sexy.

He hoped she had nothing on at all beyond that T-shirt, but he remembered she had always been fond of boy shorts. He'd hassled her about it for years, when she'd always laughed at other girls' obsessions with G-strings, but he guessed the boy shorts had become rather brief from what he could see of her bent forward. Because all he could see was an endless expanse of tanned, toned, slim legs, stretching up to what was an incredibly firm bottom. Hmm. It was starting to be a rather uncomfortable viewing experience.

Every single piece of him was furious with her still, even after talking to Gus late into the night, but the woman looked like something out of a men's magazine and he couldn't take his eyes off her.

Then she turned around. He didn't know what to do so

he just stared back at her. The reality was, he wanted to shock her, take action instead of just standing there staring at her. He wanted to kiss the surprised pout straight off her lips. Rip her shirt off to take his mind off the fact that she'd completely thrown him.

But hell, her front profile was even more tempting than the rear. She clearly had nothing on beneath the T-shirt, and it clung gently to her breasts. With her face free from makeup she looked more like the teenage Rebecca. Lips pillowy from sleep still, eyes slightly puffy, cheeks flushed.

"Morning." He wished he'd just turned and gone back to bed the minute he'd seen her down there.

She gave him a tight smile. Hardly the come-hither look his male organs were wishing for, even if he was angry with her.

"Hey," she replied.

"You're up early." He kept his distance as he moved into the kitchen and reached for a cup, not wanting to get anywhere close to her bare skin.

Rebecca shrugged. "Didn't get much sleep. But then I'm guessing you probably had a rough night, too."

Ben poured himself coffee and went straight back out to the adjoining living room. He could still see her but it was far less arousing than being within a few feet of her. She even smelled amazing, which hadn't helped the fact that he was trying to ignore her.

They were both silent, sipping away soundlessly on their coffees, so much hanging between them that needed to be said. Had to be said. They shared a daughter, and that meant they had a lot to work out. No matter how he felt about her right now, they had to find a way to get past it enough to talk.

"Lexie's still asleep?"

Rebecca nodded. "She usually sleeps in a little after a late night."

Ben frowned and took another sip of his coffee. How the hell could they go from being strangers to friends again after so long, and then feel more like strangers than ever again, so fast? It made him furious and no matter how bad he wanted to be the better person here, he couldn't.

"Ben, I think we need—"

A noise stopped her midsentence and the same noise made Ben put down his coffee. Lexie's little voice echoed out down the hall just before a blur rushed past Ben, hurtling at high speed toward Rebecca.

"Oh. Hey, honey." He watched as Bec scooped her up for a cuddle, but the little girl was wriggling again soon, running back in the same direction she'd come from and reappearing with Gus by her side. He had his cane in one hand and the other resting on Lexie's shoulder.

"Mommy, this is Gus."

Once they were both in the room she sidled back over to her mom, grinning at Gus as she held on to Rebecca's leg.

No, he's your great-granddad. Ben was on the verge of exploding, angry all over again, but one look at the sweet, innocent expression on the little girl's face pacified him.

"You okay, sweetie?" He listened to Rebecca talk to her, watched as she kissed her cheek. There was no mistaking they were mother and daughter, and the way Lexie gazed at her? It told him that no matter how much he hated what she'd done to him, what she'd kept from him, his daughter had been cared for by someone who adored her. There was no way a child could look at a mother like that unless she meant the world to her.

Lexie tucked her head against her mom's chest, peeking over at him. "I didn't know where you were."

Rebecca kissed her again before putting her to her feet. "I shouldn't have left you. Sorry, sweetheart."

"Then *he* found me," Lexie said, sticking her thumb out at Gus. "And he told me all about the horses he has. *Horses*, Mommy. *Horses*."

Ben stifled a smile. He guessed the old saying was true—the apple never did fall far from the tree.

"Gus does have some pretty special horses."

Rebecca looked up at Gus as she spoke. He was smiling, but he was also giving her a look. She could feel Ben behind her, still keeping his distance, but close enough to know that he was there. *Gus knew.* It was obvious from the way he was looking at them, and from the way he was going back and forth with his eyes from father to daughter as if he was putting two and two together. She forced a smile. It was tough to see them like this, to know that she'd caused so much hurt, especially if it meant losing the love and respect of two men who'd always meant so much to her.

"Lexie, Gus is Ben's granddaddy," she continued, trying to stop her voice from shaking. "Mr. McFarlane was very special to me when I was…younger."

Lexie smiled coyly at Gus.

"None of this Mr. McFarlane business," said Gus, swatting his hand through the air. Lexie giggled and put her head hard against Rebecca's chest. "We had a good old chat on the way downstairs, didn't we?"

Rebecca turned her body around so Lexie was facing Ben.

"You remember Ben from last night? Mommy's friend?"

"Yup," she said, smiling as Ben held his hand up in hello, his grin all for his daughter, his eyes lighting up in a way they'd used to do for her.

"Well, let's go get us changed shall we, miss? Then we can have some breakfast."

She carried Lexie back toward the stairs, the little girl still light enough to carry on her hip.

"Who's G-Gus?" Lexie got a bit stuck on the "G" sound and made Rebecca laugh.

"I told you," she said, pulling a T-shirt over her daughter's arms and harder over her head once they were in the bedroom. When she tugged it past her ears, she shook her head and grinned up at her. "He's Ben's granddad," she repeated, just in case she had actually forgotten, despite having told her twice already.

"Where's his dad?"

She suddenly didn't like the way this conversation was heading at all. Any conversation right now that involved daddy talk seemed dangerous.

"Ben's daddy? I'm not sure."

"What about my daddy? Why don't I have a daddy?"

Rebecca had walked straight into that one.

"Let's go back down for breakfast, huh?"

She had talked about her dad before. Or at least made up a father figure and stuck with the story. He was a very busy man and might never come home, all sorts of things, but as Lexie got older she had known it wasn't a question that could be so easily shirked, especially when she was trying to make sure her daughter felt loved even if she did have only one parent. And the lies no longer sounded convincing, not as she became older and understood so much more.

Lexie jumped up and grabbed her hand and Rebecca followed her out the door. She would have liked to spend some more time on her makeup but if this got her out of talking about daddies, then she was up for it.

"So, do you go to kindergarten or anything?"

Lexie nodded, a mischievous smile on her face. Ben was all out of ideas—there was only so much he could think to talk about with a three-year-old, but school seemed like a safe topic. He watched as his daughter munched on rice bubbles. Lucky Rebecca had thought to bring a stash, because they didn't have anything like that here.

He noticed Rebecca was taking a painstakingly long time to eat her toast. She was staring at the marmalade as if it was dangerous, not taking her eyes from it, nibbling delicately around the edges. Gus had gone out to do his rounds; hell, they were like some dysfunctional family, sitting together but not communicating.

"So I'm guessing you like horses," Ben said, refusing to give up on the conversation stakes just yet, even though he was as good as terrified just sitting here with her.

Lexie's reaction told him he'd finally hit the jackpot. Her eyes were wide, bright, and she slurped milk down her chin in her excitement.

"Have you ever ridden a horse?" Ben asked

"No." Phew, for a while there he'd wondered if he was ever going to come up with something they could talk about.

"You want to go for a ride with me today, then?"

"Like on a real horse?" Lexie had knocked her bowl forward and sent milk sloshing, but Ben couldn't have cared less. He finally felt like he was making some headway.

He chuckled. "Yeah, on a real horse. What do you say?"

"Let's go!"

"Ahem." Rebecca cleared her throat and smiled tightly at Ben. "Mommy needs to talk to Ben for a second, Lexie. You go and find your shoes."

Lexie sprinted off back toward the stairs and Ben glared at Rebecca.

"I'm not so sure about her riding," she said.

"She's coming riding with me today." Even if he had no idea how to talk to her or what to do, she was his and he needed to deal with it in his own way.

There was no chance he was negotiating on this. He'd gone all Lexie's life without making decisions, without having the chance to do things with her, and today that was going to change. He was a father, and that meant manning up and taking responsibility.

"Ben..." she protested again.

"No!" He thumped his mug down and pushed to his feet. "*No.* You had it your way, now it's my turn."

She cast her eyes down and Ben wished he hadn't spoken to her so harshly. He'd never spoken to her like that before and he didn't need to start now, no matter what had gone on between them. She was *Rebecca.* They had way too much history for him to be acting like a complete idiot. And besides, even though she'd lied to him, he still wanted her.. No matter how he'd like to pretend otherwise, his desire for Rebecca went beyond anything he was capable of controlling.

He wanted to hate her for keeping this kind of secret from him. He thought deep down that part of him did hate her, but it wasn't something he was enjoying. He didn't want to feel like that about her. She'd betrayed him, *hurt him* like nothing in his life had before, and although he knew it would be almost impossible to completely trust her again, damn it but he wanted to try.

The urge to yell and curse had passed, Gus had seen to that when they'd talked, but anger wasn't something that could just be forgotten. But it was starting to fade, more a dull ache now than a bone-deep fury. And part of him knew that he had to take some of the blame. He *had* always made his thoughts on parenthood blatantly obvious. He had left her behind and moved on with his life, even though he'd known there was more between them than just friendship. But then deep down he'd never really thought he was good enough for her. He'd grown up since then, realized what kind of man he was and what he wanted, but back then he hadn't.

His mind was a jumble of thoughts and he needed to get outside. *Outside with my horses, and away from Rebecca.*

Lexie appeared behind her mother and Ben forced the smile back on his face. He didn't want their daughter to see them arguing, not when it was the first time he'd actually spent time with the kid.

"You ready?" Ben asked.

Lexie looked down at her feet and shrugged. Ben stifled a laugh and bent down, putting the girl's hand on his shoulder to balance her, then removing each shoe and putting it on the correct foot, hands shaking. He laced them up, wishing just the simple act of helping her on with her shoes didn't put the fear of God in him.

He knew Rebecca was watching them, and as Lexie reached for his hand, he closed his eyes. His daughter had just felt comfortable enough to put her small hand in his, and her skin was warm and sticky, probably still covered in some of her breakfast. Soft and innocent in a way that an adult's skin just wasn't anymore—hell, his probably felt rough as anything to her. It took every inch of his willpower not to tug his hand out, because nothing about holding on to her felt any kind of natural.

Ben turned back to Rebecca. Tears welled in her eyes that he didn't want to acknowledge. He didn't want to dig the knife deeper, he *wanted* to let go, but a familiar pool of anger was beginning to form behind his eyes again, and he just couldn't help himself.

"I don't know why you kept this from me, Rebecca," he said, voice low, barely more than a whisper. "Honestly, I just don't understand." Lexie wouldn't know what they were talking about, he wasn't saying anything that would upset the girl, but he needed Rebecca to know. She'd hurt him badly, and it wasn't something he could just take on board and move on from that easily.

Rebecca was watching them, tears soundlessly streaming down her cheeks as she stared at Lexie holding his hand. "I'm sorry," she said. "I'm sorry a thousand times over."

Something changed in Ben then, something that he hadn't even known he was capable of. Because he knew. He knew then, without a doubt, from the emotion written all over her face and the pain in her eyes, that it wasn't because she'd wanted to hurt him that she'd done what she'd done. That when she'd told him she was trying to protect him, and do the best for their daughter, that without a shadow of doubt she'd meant it. But he'd had a right to know, to make his own decision about being involved in Lexie's life, and what he wanted was his daughter, to be her dad. Right now it was the only clear thing in his seriously screwed-up thoughts. But then maybe if he hadn't had the time away, hadn't had the chance to grow and follow his dreams, he wouldn't be feeling like this.

Lexie must have heard the catch in her mother's voice and turned, dropping Ben's hand when she realized her mom was crying.

"Mommy, what's wrong?"

Rebecca wiped at her eyes and braved a smile. Lexie stood in front of her, her eyebrows pulled together, worried about her mom. Rebecca gave her a quick hug before pressing their foreheads together, eyes on hers as she gave her a look that seemed to reassure her that everything was okay.

"I'm just excited about you going out to see the horses, that's all."

"Really?" Lexie asked, clearly not entirely convinced.

"Yes, really. You go for it, cowgirl."

As Lexie scooted toward the door she squared her shoulders and stood, taking a few steps toward Ben. The look on her face was different now; she wiped her tears away and took a visibly deep breath as he watched her.

"I did what I thought was right, Ben," she said, wrapping her arms around herself as she stared straight into his eyes. "I know now that it wasn't, and when I said last night that I'd do the same thing all over again? That I wouldn't change anything? I was lying. I'd tell you in a heartbeat, Ben." She forced her lip to stop quivering. "As soon as I saw you with her, I knew it was the wrong thing. That you needed to be the one to make that decision. But at the time all I could think about was protecting her and not holding you back."

"You're a great mom," he said, staring straight at her, wanting to wrap her into a big hug and tug her hard against him. "But you're one hell of a lousy friend."

Rebecca sighed. "Yeah. I was. And for the record, you would have been a great dad."

He didn't like the past tense. "I'll make up for it," he said, surprised by how deep and raspy his voice was. "She ain't growing up without a dad, not anymore." What he needed was to know when they were going to tell her, but he didn't want to argue. They could take it one step at a time. *Starting now.* Which would give him the chance to figure out how to act naturally around her, how to just be himself and not be scared of her as if she was some fragile doll that he could break.

He was home, and now he had a daughter, and that meant he had to grow the hell up and accept his responsibilities. He wasn't ever going to make the same mistakes his mother had; his child was going to come first, there was no other option acceptable to him.

Ben walked out the door and found Lexie standing on the porch, her eyes trained on his, excitement just about bursting from her.

"Come on, Ben!"

He grinned and took her hand, letting her enthusiasm rub off on him. He'd always been terrified of being a dad, but suddenly being with Lexie, having her hand in his, was the most exhilarated he'd felt in ages. *Except for having Bec in his arms the other night.* He still had no idea what to do with her, how to act, but he was darn well going to try.

CHAPTER TWELVE

BEN PROPPED LEXIE up on the side of the corral and laughed at the serious look on her face. The kid was so excited she looked as if she could hardly breathe.

"You sit there, darlin'," he told her, putting one hand on either side of Lexie's legs and bending to look her in the eye. "I'm gonna bring Willy around so you can have a ride."

Lexie's eyes were open so wide they were about to pop. Ben gave her a wink and spun around to go get the horse.

"No running away, okay?" he called.

She was cute—shy but quietly determined. He liked that about her.

He caught Willy and gave the horse a scratch as they walked, watching Lexie as she kicked her legs against the timber she was sitting on.

"Lexie, I'd like you to meet Willy."

She looked nervous, her bottom lip grabbing under her top teeth. He hesitated then reached out for her when he saw her wobble, not sure how to touch her. She was so tiny and cute, he just didn't know what to do.

"Have you ever patted a horse before, Lexie?"

She shook her head and Ben tried not to freeze when

she looped an arm around his neck so he could swing her down, just tried to behave as naturally as she was. She kept her legs firmly locked around his hips so he couldn't let her go, taking the initiative. It was reassuring to know he could just follow her lead.

"He's a real sweetheart, this one. And he loves to be stroked just here," Ben said, laughing when she gave him a superfast touch to the nose. "You know, your mom rode Willy just the other day."

Lexie turned to look at Ben, her brown eyes so innocently turned upward in question, as though she didn't believe that her mom had ever ridden a horse, let alone this one. Then she went back to tentatively touching Willy's nose, before letting her hand drift a little higher to touch the horse on the forehead.

"I thought you and I could go for a ride together on Willy. You can sit up front and we can go for a wander around the farm."

"Okay." Her voice was so quiet it was almost a whisper.

Ben popped her back up on the fence, tied Willy up a little bit farther away and hurriedly put on the horse's saddle and bridle. He'd worry about brushing him down later. He gave him a quick pat and untied his rope, turning back to Lexie.

"So I'm gonna lift you up nice and slow, then I'll hop up behind you."

He went to scoop Lexie up but received a quivering-lipped look that told him he was about to have a crash course in how to deal with tears if he didn't do something fast. He stared at her, trying to figure out what the heck he was supposed to do.

"Ah, how about I hop on first then lift you up?"

Lexie nodded and Ben quickly did exactly that, mounting, then reaching down for her. He hauled her up so her tiny body fitted snugly against his. She tucked back tightly against him, resting her head against his chest as he kept one hand pressed firmly to her, the other looped through the reins.

"You okay, sweetheart?"

She nodded, the movement gentle against his chest. "Uh-huh."

Ben bent his head to talk into his daughter's ear, tried to just do what felt natural to him. He so desperately wanted to whisper to her, to tell her he was her dad, that she had a father who loved her, but he didn't. *Couldn't.* No matter how angry he was with Rebecca, he wanted it to be right. *He wanted to get this right.* Finding out she had a dad was special, and it wasn't something he wanted to muck up. Although finding out he had a dad who wanted him would have been a bonus no matter how it had happened where he was concerned. He'd spent the latter half of his teens desperate to find his father, and when he had finally tracked down the guy who was biologically related to him, it had been the worst thing he'd ever done. His mom was lousy, but his father didn't even want to acknowledge he existed.

"Lexie, riding's all about relaxing," he told her. "Sit back against me, feel every step the horse takes. I want you to feel safe up here. There's nothing to fear."

He felt Lexie's body soften slightly. Her head knocked back again to rest on Ben's chest, which sent his heart thumping overtime. They rode like that for a few minutes, just circling around the large round pen.

"You feeling it?"

"Yup."

"You sure?" he asked, starting to relax himself, no longer so worried about having her body against his, being in charge of someone so tiny.

"Yeah, Ben," she said, wriggling against him. "I'm feelin' it."

He chuckled and pulled her closer to him, before steering Willy out of the yard so they could ride out over the farm. He was pretty sure he'd just fallen head over heels in love.

Rebecca was shaking, her entire body as nervous as a bunch of keys jangling. She'd decided there was nothing more terrifying than seeing her daughter sit on a horse, followed very closely by the terror of knowing her little girl was sitting with her father. Would Ben tell her? How would Lexie react? She knew her daughter would be thrilled to have a dad, but what did it mean for them? Would Ben ever trust her or want to be around her again? Would he go for joint custody? Her body shuddered as she took a deep, worried breath.

She'd started out watching them from a distance, standing on the porch, on the one hand nostalgic about what could have been, on the other so scared of what was going to happen next. She and Ben had been so close, almost as if they were on the cusp of reuniting, living in a fantasy world where she didn't have some massive lie she was keeping from him. And the night they'd had? She groaned just thinking about it.

When she thought of Ben, her mind was full of memories, all of them good except for the way she'd hurt him the day before. Riding, yes, but so many other things, too. They'd had so many first times together: a stolen pack of cigarettes from Gus they'd smoked till they were blue in the face—to her knowledge neither of them had touched a cigarette since, but she remembered that day with a smile; they'd gotten drunk together for the first time; learned how to play polo, how to start a horse under saddle. The point was, they had been together every one of those times.

She and Ben went back so far. Sticky fingers from cola and hotdogs at the local fair, red faces from nasty sunburn, sitting out by the river talking, star-fished on the grass. There had been a time they'd shared everything, talked about everything, been everything to one another. *Been friends.*

And now she'd ruined it. But she had to think about it with no regrets. She was a mother now, her priority had been her daughter ever since she'd given birth to her. Losing out on a chance to be with Ben was a result of what she'd kept from him, and now Lexie had to be her number one. She might have thought Ben would never come home, not after all this time, but the past was the past. Lexie was her future, because she was fairly certain Ben would never forgive her enough for them to go back to where they'd been, to even be friends again, let alone the lovers they'd been only a week ago.

She heard the gentle clip-clop of hooves on the hard packed earth and raised her eyes again. Rebecca had become so engrossed in her thoughts she'd dropped her head and been gazing at her own toes. Willy was coming her way, and that meant she knew where Ben was heading. He was off toward the river, the place they'd always raced to on his crazy polo ponies.

Ben had his head dipped low, talking to Lexie, her lit-

tle girl smiling with one of her hands on the reins, Ben's
large ones covering hers. For a guy who hadn't known
what the hell to do with the little girl a short time ago,
he looked pretty at ease now.

She was on the bottom step of the porch now and Lexie
saw her. She took one hand off the pommel and waved
fiercely to her, a grin from one ear right to the other.

"Hey, honey," she called.

Her heart was screaming out, she wanted nothing more
to pull her down and protect her, but she knew Lexie
was in good hands. Ben was one of the best horsemen
she knew, and if her girl was safe on any horse, it was on
a horse with Ben. *Lexie's dad*, she thought. It just didn't
sound right. Even though she'd known all this time, it
had seemed more like a dream. A fantasy. But Daddy
was most certainly back in their lives.

As she waved Lexie on, with her so gleefully smiling and waving back, Rebecca sucked down her pride
and glanced at Ben. The look she received in return sent
prickles spiking over her entire body. They rode by, but
Ben's eyes never left hers—a piercing gaze that conveyed everything. *His hurt, his disappointment, his dis-
trust.* But there was something else; the anger she'd seen
in his gaze earlier seemed to have softened somehow, a
look that made her hope…she sucked in a big lungful of
air. She wasn't even going to think it, because she'd only
end up heartbroken all over again.

All that mattered was that Lexie was smiling, and that
from this day on, she'd have a dad who loved her. Lexie
had always had a mom who'd do anything for her and
grandparents who thought the world of her, but nothing
would beat adding a dad to the mix. *Nothing.*

* * *

They still weren't back. It had been two hours since they'd left, and still they hadn't returned. Lexie would be starving hungry, grumpy as hell probably, and Ben should have known better than to take so long. Rebecca knew only too well that something could have happened...a snake bite, a fall, *anything*!

"That's not doing you any favors."

Gus's no-nonsense voice snapped her out of it. She looked up from her seat on the edge of the porch. Eyes that had been trained on the direction they'd left in finally taking a break.

"That worrying. It's no good," Gus said.

"They've just been a long—"

"They're fine." He gave her a sharp look and sat down beside her.

Rebecca started to cry and Gus didn't even attempt to comfort her. She sat there with tears dripping steadily down her cheeks and he didn't say a word until she'd sucked all her sadness back and cleared her throat.

"What you did was wrong, girl," he said, his voice even deeper than she'd remembered it all these years.

She nodded. She'd had a feeling Ben would have confided in him, but knowing she'd let Gus down hurt, too. Seeing him again now, she knew he deserved to be a grandfather. He had been so great to her, and Lexie would have enjoyed spending time with him. It was all such a mess, and the worst part was that it was all her doing. She'd tried so desperately to do the right thing, and all she'd done was make everything a hundred times worse than it had to be.

"You were young, Ben was leaving," he said, before

making a deep grunting noise in his throat. "Bad choices, but I can understand. They weren't choices you'd have made if he'd been home or you'd been able to go with him. Not to mention the two of you needed your heads banged together for not seeing that you were supposed to be more than friends."

Rebecca looked up, hardly able to believe what he was saying.

"You can?"

"Yes, Rebecca. I can." He turned to face her. "But I'm not the one you have to convince."

As if on cue, the trio appeared. Willy plodding along, Ben sitting straight, and her girl, *their girl*, slumped back. Fast asleep.

She looked over at Gus but he was gone, the light tap of the door falling shut signaling that he'd headed back inside again. Part of her wanted to flee before facing another discussion with Ben, but another part of her knew she had to face up to her decision and meet the consequences. Once the weekend was over, she was going to have to admit her lie to her family, and some of her friends, so things weren't exactly going to get any easier.

There was an awfully strained feeling between them, despite them both trying their best for Lexie's sake. Rebecca watched Lexie as her eyes drooped slightly, despite continuing to munch on her sandwich. The kid was starving, but once her blood sugar levels were restored, she'd be bouncing off the walls again.

"You want a nap?" Rebecca asked, as Lexie stuffed the last piece into her mouth.

"Uh-uh," she managed, her cheeks bulging like a little chipmunk settling in for winter. "Ben told me I could meet the foals."

She looked his way and Ben just shrugged. Rebecca knew better than to say no without softening her response, especially when Lexie was having so much fun, so she tried her best to talk around it.

"Maybe later sweetheart."

"Why?"

"Because the foals need a midafternoon nap, too. They're only babies, remember."

That seemed to satisfy her, and she managed to get her upstairs and settled in for a sleep, tucking her up in bed with a blanket pulled up to her chin. She stroked her head and stared down at her, watching as she drifted off to sleep, before heading back to face Ben. He was thumbing through the paper, but she could tell he wasn't really interested. He was turning the pages too fast to actually be reading them.

"We'll be heading off later this afternoon."

Her words seemed to cut through the invisible barrier he'd erected between them.

"When?" he asked, looking up.

"Doesn't matter when, so long as we're home before dark. I have to work tomorrow."

Ben nodded and went back to flicking through the paper. It was so unlike him to be rude, to be so distant. She had no idea what to do. Rebecca felt more alone now somehow than ever before. Worse than being without a loving man by her side giving birth, worse than thinking Lexie would resent her for not giving her a two-parent family, just the pits. It was like watching from above, not actually being part of the scene unfolding before her.

Because in all the years she'd known Ben, all the times they'd been through, she'd never known him to be so resentful, so angry, so brooding.

"Lexie wanted to know when she could come here again. When she'd be able to stay for longer," Ben said, the fact that he was talking to her taking her by surprise.

"What did you say?" she asked.

"I said sometime soon." He met her gaze. "But what I should have said was all the time."

"You can't keep blaming me," she said, refusing to be the bad guy forever. "You know now, so the only thing left to do is figure out how we're going to make this work. I was wrong, I was stupid, but I can't take it back."

"The only reason I know, *Rebecca*, is because you were forced to tell me." Ben ground out his words.

He stood up and went to walk outside, his fists balled at his sides as he moved farther away from her.

"I loved you, Ben," she said to his back. "I loved you then and I love you now, and that's exactly why I didn't tell you. You want the truth? Well that's it. But the day you came back there was no doubt in my mind that I had to tell you, it was just a matter of when. *And how.*"

When he kept on walking, not stopping to look back, not acknowledging her words, not saying anything, she realized it was over. If he was going to forgive her, he would have done it by now.

Rebecca ran up the stairs to the bedroom. Lexie had her arms flung out, in deep sleep, but she couldn't wait for her to wake. Instead, she threw their things into the two bags she had, not stopping to fold, just getting everything of theirs packed and ready to go. It only took her one trip down to fill the car, then she was back upstairs, pulling Lexie into her arms.

She murmured, eyes half-open, and Rebecca smiled bravely down at her. It took her only a moment to put her in the car, fixed into her seat, and then she was behind the wheel. It was time for her to go home and give Ben some space.

CHAPTER THIRTEEN

REBECCA WATCHED LEXIE as she zoomed around with her cousins. Her brother, Ryan, and his wife, Lucy, had twin boys and they ran her girl ragged. They had a blast together all the time, and it wasn't as if she was planning on giving Lexie any siblings, so it was the perfect balance. She couldn't imagine letting anyone else close to them, let alone marrying a man and having more children. And now that she'd ruined everything with Ben... She shook her head, trying to push him from her mind. Being with him the other night had made her hope, *yearn*, for more, but she'd always known what the reality was going to be.

The atmosphere was relaxed and happy, as it always was when her family got together, and that's what she had to focus on. Now that her parents had retired and left her to the day-to-day running of the restaurant, they either enjoyed long days looking after their grandkids, putting on family lunches, or traveling around Australia. She wouldn't give up their Sundays together for anything—family meant everything to her, and if she hadn't had them she had no idea how she'd have pulled through the last few years.

And then she was back to Ben again. She took a deep breath, watching the kids as they ran around the backyard. Every second she had to herself, every moment of not doing something, was spent thinking about him. About the way she'd left, about the look on his face when he'd been teaching Lexie to ride—*everything*. He'd been so awkward with her at first, but it hadn't taken him long to look more at ease.

Her dad called out from the barbecue and she gathered herself up, cringing when she realized her bottom was wet from the grass.

"Meat's ready!" her father hollered, in case they hadn't heard him the first time.

Rebecca's mother appeared at the open door to the house, carrying a big salad bowl. She smiled at her daughter as she passed and Bec felt nervous all over again. Today was the day she was going to tell them. The secret was out and it was time she told her family. The only reason she had hidden Lexie's paternity anyway was to shield Ben, but the lies were over now and she wanted to start fresh. They were her family and they'd be shocked, but they'd forgive her. *Unlike Ben.* Her mother would probably be more upset about the fact she'd kept it from him than from them.

The twins and Lexie came hurtling from their playhouse, and Rebecca scooped up a plate and took a sausage from the grill. Her father swatted at her but she managed to steal it anyway.

"You going to dish out for your two?" she asked her sister-in-law.

Lucy nodded and hauled up from her seat. Rebecca's brother cast her a watchful stare from his spot near the table, and Rebecca followed his gaze, seeing that it was his wife he was keeping a close eye on. Lucy was heavily pregnant and from the look of it he was in full alpha protective mode. It was a look she'd never had cast in her direction before, and she wished she had.

She pushed the thoughts away, ones she'd long since forgotten about that were somehow rising to the surface again, and took a slice of bread, squirting tomato sauce over it before wrapping it around the sausage. Lexie stood at her side, waiting like a drooling Labrador for her lunch.

"Why don't you take this back to the playhouse?" she suggested.

Lexie nodded and reached for the plate, grinning up at her.

"What about Leo and Sammy?" Lexie asked.

Rebecca looked at her cousins and smiled. The boys were slightly older than Lexie, loved her to pieces and always included her in their games.

"Their mommy will get theirs," Rebecca said, licking some sauce from her finger that must have slipped from the bottle when she'd squeezed it "No running with food in your mouth!"

She skipped away anyway, Rebecca's words lost to the excitement of racing away from the adults.

Rebecca took her place at the table that covered the deck and fiddled with the edge of her napkin. This was going to be hard. Around her, the others were tucking in. Lucy was heaping her plate high with food, her mother was fussing over the salad and her dad was dishing steak on to everyone's plates, chargrilled just like always. Only her brother was actually looking at her. Ryan sat across the table, his eyes trained on her, eyebrows raised as he asked her a question without even saying anything.

"Did you have fun at the polo? Or was it all work and no play?" asked Lucy.

Bec smiled, digging her fingernails into her palm. It was now or never.

"It was busy, but good." She was conscious of all the faces now looking her way, everyone listening to her. "We served a lot of food and the crowd seemed to love it, and then I had a catch-up with, ah, Ben."

"Sorry we couldn't help out," Lucy continued, still serving herself food. "Next time you can count on me." She patted her stomach and made them all laugh. "Next year I'll be begging for a day at the polo! I'll just have to leave your brother behind with the kids."

"Must have been nice catching up with Ben again." Her mom made that clucking sound she did whenever Ben's name was mentioned, and Rebecca stifled a groan. They'd loved him like a son, which was why telling them was going to be even harder.

"Bec, are you okay? You seem kind of…" Ryan was staring at her, the question still on his lips. When she glanced at his plate and saw he hadn't touched his food, she knew he wasn't going to let it go. He knew something was up.

She took a deep breath and ran her tongue lightly over her lips. Her mouth was so dry it was like it was full of cotton candy. But here she was, surrounded by the people who loved her most, and she needed desperately to get this off her chest.

Rebecca looked over to make sure Lexie wasn't near, but she could hear their excited shrieks from the back fence. She turned back to see everyone waiting, watching her. It wasn't as if she was often the center of attention and she hated it.

"I, ah, well…" She hesitated.

Her mother placed her fork back on the table. Every

sound, every look, was sending Rebecca's pulse rate higher. She closed her eyes for a moment and drew on all the courage she had.

"As you all know, I've been spending some time with Ben. He's back in Australia for good."

"Oh, that's wonderful news." Her mother beamed at her. "It'll be so nice for you two to reconnect some more."

At least Rebecca could count on her brother for picking up on her feelings—he was giving her a weird look again.

"Anyway, what I'm trying to say is that while I was there, I had to tell Ben something that I've kept from him and from all of you."

That stopped her mother from saying anything else. Rebecca blinked away tears, refusing to break down.

"Ben is Lexie's father." She said it so fast she wondered if they'd heard. But a glance around each face saw there was no mistaking it. They'd heard all right. Only no one was saying anything.

"*What?*" Ryan's face had turned a deep red and he thumped his fist down hard on the table, the first to react.

The clatter of cutlery made Rebecca jump. Her brother hadn't taken the news of her having a baby on her own well back then, so hearing that it was Ben's would have come as a shock. Probably a bigger shock to him than to her parents.

"Before you all jump to conclusions," she said, looking firmly at Ryan, "I want you to know that Ben didn't know. I only just told him, so there's no need to make him out to be the bad guy. If anyone is to blame, it's me."

Her mother looked as if she might cry, her father was back to fussing with the meat, and Ryan was still glaring at her.

"You're telling me that Ben McFarlane left you when you were pregnant?"

Rebecca looked sideways, not wanting to deal with her brother all hot under the collar. Lucy had her lips pursed, and she at least hoped her sister-in-law would be able to keep her brother calm.

"Ben had no idea I was pregnant when he left," she told him. "Had he known, he would have stayed. I can promise you that."

"So when are you getting married?" Ryan asked.

That made her laugh, although the noise died in her mouth when she saw the serious look on her brother's face.

"Ryan, I'm not marrying him!" she insisted. "We haven't even told Lexie yet. It's kind of difficult." She shook her head. "And that's why I didn't tell him in the first place, because he *would* have married me, out of a sense of duty, and the last thing I wanted was Ben giving up his dreams for me and resenting me for having to be tied to us." Not to mention the fact that she'd never really believed she deserved him, that she was worthy of him when she couldn't even face her own fears of getting back on a horse, of trying harder to make the team she'd dreamed about for years.

"I guess she does look like Ben, when you think about it," her mother said, as if she was having a conversation with herself.

"I can't believe you lied to us all this time. All that garbage you spun about…"

Rebecca shook her head and stood up from the table, interrupting her brother.

"You know what? I shouldn't have lied, but I don't owe any of you an apology. The only person I need to say sorry to is Ben, and God only knows I've said that to him a hundred times over these past few days. But Lexie is my daughter, and who her father is, was my business. *Is* my business."

She stormed past the table and fled into the house, rushed into the bathroom and burst into tears. She had never spoken to her family like that, *never*, and she hated that she just had. The truth was, she *was* sorry. Sorry to everyone she'd hurt for not telling them the truth. But was she so bad to have wanted to protect her own daughter? To protect Ben and her own heart, too? Was she that terrible to want to let Ben go and live out his dreams? Because once upon a time they'd been her dreams, too.

A light knock on the door made her haul in a big sob and dab at her eyes.

"Honey, let me in. *Please.*" Her mother's soft voice made the urge to cry even greater.

She swung open the door and fell into her mother's arms, holding on tight and sobbing, her body shaking as she cried and cried. Rebecca felt like a child again, enveloped in her mother's comforting embrace.

"It's okay, honey. No one's angry with you. It's okay."

She knew Ryan wouldn't take long to forgive her, but her mother was wrong. There was someone angry with her, and the way her heart was slowly shattering, piece by piece, told her she'd blown it. Anything that might have been between her and Ben was well and truly over. She'd hurt him so badly and she just wanted to make it right. She wanted *him*. Not just as a friend, but as her something more, as the loving father of her child and as her lover.

Her mother held her tight in her arms, rocked her back and forward like Rebecca did to her own daughter to comfort her. It was not something she'd ever thought her mom would have to do to her again.

"It's going to be okay," her mother soothed.

"I love him," Rebecca choked. "I love him so bad."

"I know, sweetie," she said, and sighed. "I know. You loved him then, you always did."

"But I love him now, too. I never stopped."

Rebecca squeezed her eyes shut and willed Ben's face, his touch, his scent, to disappear from her memories. She'd never stopped loving him, and now, when she had almost had him back, she'd lost him forever. And it was all her fault.

The sun was beating down hard on Ben's bare arms, but he wasn't going to give up. He was sweltering from the heat, sweat pouring from his skin, and he was determined to keep going.

"Ben!"

He heard Gus call out to him, but he refused to listen. He only needed a few more minutes, another half hour maybe, and he'd have cracked the filly. She was still dancing around him, snorting in that arrogant little way of hers, teasing him before skipping away. But if there was one thing he was, it was determined.

"Ben!"

The voice was closer this time. He still ignored it, until a firm hand fell on his shoulder.

"Enough."

The word took a moment to filter through his senses, but the continued pressure on his shoulder made him stop.

"I said, enough,' the slow, steady voice was unrelenting.

Ben turned slowly and looked at his grandfather.

"I want you to get out of here, and don't work with another horse until you've cleared your head."

He bit back a retort, and he was pleased he had. Gus didn't need to be on the sharp end of his tongue, just because he felt lousy. And besides, his grandfather was right. He should never have come out here expecting to work with the young filly in this frame of mind. He knew better, and Gus shouldn't have had to remind him.

Ben gave the filly a look he hoped conveyed his remorse, and exited through the wooden rails. Gus went the long way, walking through the gate. It wasn't that he'd been too hard on her, but he wasn't being patient enough, soft enough to a horse that needed gentle coaxing.

"What do you want, son?"

Ben closed his eyes for a second before turning to watch his grandfather. What he needed was a way to push all the thoughts running through his head away, to just inhale the fresh air out on the farm and give himself a break.

"I said, what do you want?" his grandfather repeated.

Clearly the old man wasn't in one of his chilled out moods. He was asking a question and he expected an answer.

"I don't know."

"Yes, you do," Gus replied. "You know exactly what you want, son. You just need to admit it."

He watched Ben, the two of them looking at one another for a long moment, before walking off with the assistance of his cane. Gus called over his shoulder.

"I'm going to get us a beer. Think about your answer."

Ben sat on the veranda and held the beer bottle against his forehead. The wet, cool feel was helping to reduce his body temperature, but it wasn't helping his thoughts any. He could sense his grandfather's eyes on him, and he knew he had to say something. If he couldn't tell Gus, who could he tell?

"I want Lexie to know I'm her father. I want my daughter." He sucked back a breath, then blew it out slowly. "I want to know how to act around her, just figure out how to be her dad."

Gus nodded. He took a slow swig of his beer, his eyes not leaving Ben's.

"What else do you want?"

Ben shrugged, but his aloofness wasn't fooling Gus. They sat in silence, the only noise the whinny of horses in the distance, and the odd chirp of a bird in the big trees surrounding the house.

"I want Rebecca, okay? I bloody darn well want Rebecca." Ben pushed up to his feet and stormed the length of the veranda, before rounding on his grandfather. "Is that what you wanted to hear?"

Gus just smiled at him.

"You're an idiot, you know that?" Ben glowered at Gus's words. "Get in that car and don't come back until you've told her."

Ben put his beer down and walked toward his grand-dad. He suddenly had this feeling that he wouldn't know what to do without Gus around, that he couldn't bear the thought of life without him. His age had caught up to him fast, and it scared the hell out of Ben.

"Come here you old pain in the neck."

Gus stood and they embraced. The kind of firm, strong hug that men shared when it really meant something. The kind of hug Ben had always been able to count on, when he was a little boy to right now as a fully grown man. The type of support every human being needed in life.

"Call *me* a pain in the neck?" Gus chuckled. "You've been like a bear with a thorn, boy."

Ben grinned.

"You know that little pony we talked about?"

"I'm on it," said Gus.

"Great. I'm gonna head into town and see if I can't get them both back here."

CHAPTER FOURTEEN

THE RESTAURANT WAS BUZZING, which made it easier for Ben to slip in unnoticed. He'd gone straight to Rebecca's house, but then figured she'd be working.

It had always been busy, but it felt different now. He wondered if it was Rebecca's touch, making it that much more special, more intimate, than it had been previously. It had always been one of inner-city Melbourne's busiest Italian restaurants, but the subtle changes made it even more appealing.

Ben kept his head down and sat at a vacant table. He was a bundle of nerves and he hated it. He toyed with the menu but his eyes just skimmed over the words. He didn't care what he ate. For the first time in as long as he could remember he wasn't even interested in food. All he cared about was the woman he'd come here to see.

"Would you like to hear the specials?"

He looked up into pretty blue eyes. *Not Rebecca*. He didn't want to offend the young woman, so he politely said no and just ordered the spaghetti Bolognese. If Rebecca wasn't the one to bring his lunch over, he'd just eat and drink coffee until the rush had died down.

Ben watched the hum of people, coming and going, listening to laughter and conversation, but all he wanted was to see Rebecca. His eyes danced over each table, then out to the kitchen, scanning for her. *And then he saw her.*

Rebecca emerged, holding two steaming plates of food, held high out to each side. Her golden blond hair was pulled back into a loose ponytail, and it swished behind her as she moved. Her mouth was tipped up at each corner into a smile, and she looked happy. He hoped she'd still have that sweet look on her face when she saw him.

He let his eyes follow her as she hurried to a table and placed the two plates down, before saying a few words and heading back to the kitchen. Ben exercised all his willpower to stay seated, when all he wanted to do was take off after her.

His gaze stayed trained on the kitchen, and this time he was rewarded more quickly when she appeared again almost straight away, this time holding only one plate. Ben sat back, trying to look relaxed. She was heading his way. Ten steps, eight, six… She saw him.

Rebecca locked eyes with him, her mouth turning heart shaped with surprise. She looked over one shoulder, and then at the plate, as if wanting it to be a mistake. She hesitated. Ben rose to his feet.

"I think that's my spaghetti."

She still looked stunned, so he walked the few steps to meet her and took the plate for himself.

"Can you sit a minute?" he asked.

She shook her head, looking as though she was about to take off in the other direction.

"Please."

"I can't," she stammered. "We're so busy and I need to get more orders to tables."

He watched her, eyes bonded on hers, and then nodded. "Okay. I'll wait."

Rebecca took a few steps backward before rushing off in the direction of the kitchen. Ben sat down and tried to approach his meal with interest, but his stomach was growling with a different type of hunger. Now that he'd seen her again, he wanted her. Badly. And this time he wasn't going to let anything get in their way. She'd apologized to him enough and it was time to put the past in the past and claim his family. He'd wasted enough time without wasting even more behaving like an idiot.

He'd left her once, walked away when he knew in his heart that he shouldn't have gone without telling her how he truly felt, but now he was back. For good. And there was nothing, *nothing*, going to stand in his way.

There were only a handful of patrons left. Ben pushed his coffee cup away. It was his third and he had enough caffeine in his system to keep him alert for days.

He'd watched Rebecca walk back and forth from the kitchen, smiling her way around each table, and now he was waiting for her to reappear. She'd disappeared out back a few minutes ago and not reemerged. Part of him was worried that she'd done a runner out the fire exit, but he believed in her more than that. Hoped he could trust that she wouldn't just leave him.

But even if she did bolt, he'd track her down and make her hear him out. If she was worried about listening to him fume at her again, she was wrong—he was a big enough man to admit he hadn't dealt with finding out well, but he was going to make up for it now. He was going to be a great dad even if it terrified him; and if she let him, he was going to make up for lost time with her, too.

He smiled as Rebecca finally reappeared and walked toward him—she hadn't bailed after all. She was fiddling with her apron, playing with the edge, and when she got closer she held her hands behind her back and untied it. She was wearing dark denim jeans, ballet flats and a plain black T-shirt, and she looked great.

"Hey," she said.

Ben hadn't seen Bec blush in a long time, but her cheeks were as pink and flushed as he'd ever seen them.

"Hey," he said back.

He stood and pulled out a chair. She sat down, her hands still busy on the cotton of her apron, obviously trying to distract herself from the fact that he was there.

"I had to see you, Bec," he started, pleased when she finally looked up. "When you left like that the other day, I didn't know what to think."

She at least gave him a reaction then.

"What did you expect, Ben?" She kept her voice low but she was clearly angry. "You made it pretty clear you didn't want me around."

"Bec..."

This wasn't going well. He'd come in here knowing exactly what he wanted to say, had practiced the entire conversation while he was waiting for her, and now he could hardly get his words out.

"No, Ben, let me," she said. "I'm not going to say sorry again because you've made it pretty clear there's no chance of me being forgiven. So why are you here?"

He stayed quiet. She was wrong, but he could tell now wasn't the time to tell her otherwise. She had something to say and he was going to sit tight and let her say it.

"Lexie's your daughter, and you have every right to be part of her life. We can work out some sort of an arrangement, something that works for both of us. My family knows now, so it's all out in the open."

Ben nodded. "Where is she now?"

"At my parent's place. She had a little cold, so I let her hang out there all day instead of going to preschool."

"She's okay, though?"

Rebecca nodded and stood up. "Sorry if you came all the way in just to see her, but I've really got to help tidy up. I'm off tonight and I want everything ready for dinner service before I leave."

Ben stood, too. There was so much he wanted to say but clearly now was the wrong time. Wrong place. At least he'd been able to observe these past few hours. If he'd been unsure to start with, he was positive now.

He just needed to figure out how to show her how he felt, so she believed him when he told her that he loved her. It wasn't just because they had a daughter together, or because he wanted to be part of Lexie's life. He wanted Rebecca, whether they had a child or not. And by the end of the day there was no way she wouldn't know exactly what he wanted. *Her*.

Ben pulled his car up outside the Stewarts' place. He hadn't come here that much as a kid, he and Rebecca tended to spend all their time at the stables when they hung out, but he still knew it well.

There was a car he didn't recognize out front, but he could hardly wait until the guest had gone. He didn't have long before Rebecca arrived back, and he needed to talk to her parents before she came home. And he wanted to spend some time with his girl.

He crossed the road and took a deep breath. It was odd knowing that Lexie had no idea he was her father, but he was still desperate to see her. His mind had done nothing other than flick between Rebecca and Lexie for the past few days, and even thought it sounded stupid even in his own head, he'd missed her.

Ben pushed the doorbell and waited. It was only a few minutes before a heavily pregnant woman flung open the door.

"Hi," she said.

"Ah, hi," he said back. "This still the Stewarts' place?"

A scream and a thunder of feet took him by surprise. The woman laughed as three kids, all in various states of undress, ran down the hall toward them.

"Sorry," she said.

"Ben!"

He recognized Lexie straightaway when she slid on the timber floorboards and screeched to a halt. At least he knew he had the right place.

"Hey, Lexie."

Lexie shot straight forward and grabbed his leg, her wet hair colliding with his chest when he bent down.

"What have you been doing?"

"Water fights," she said, shrugging. "I'm supposed to be sick, but I'm fine."

"You're Ben?"

The woman who'd answered the door had a warm expression on her face, smiling as she stared down at him.

"Sorry, Ben McFarlane," he said, standing and holding out his free hand. "And you are?"

"Lucy," she said, letting go and resting her hand on top of her belly. "Ryan's wife."

Ben nodded. "Can I come in?"

Rebecca turned the radio up loud and sung along. Badly. Seeing Ben today had been worse than when he'd first come back. She still felt such a fool for telling him she loved him, couldn't stop playing that day over and over in her mind. She'd managed to keep her feelings for him hidden for years, but now she seemed incapable of not making a mess of everything.

She pulled up outside her parents' place and noticed the black Holden next to the curb. The car looked a little too familiar. It only took a second before her heart hit the footpath. What was he doing here? Had he come for Lexie?

Rebecca rushed up the drive and pushed open the front door. He might only want their daughter, not her, but he couldn't just barge in like this and expect to take her!

"Mom!" she called. "Lexie!"

There was no one in the house. She rushed through the lounge and into the kitchen, worried something had happened. Where were they?

And then she saw the open doors leading out to the backyard and she was greeted with her worst nightmare. Ben was sitting beside her mother, both with chairs they had pulled out onto the grass. Lucy was fanning herself beneath a big tree, and her father was standing beside the water tap. Lexie was squealing with delight as she ran and then slid down some slippery, green, plastic water thing, and the twins were running back and forward with her. One would run and belly flop onto the plastic, then slide to the end, before the next child would start.

Rebecca looked at Ben. He'd obviously just said something funny, because he had her mother with her head thrown back in laughter. She felt physically sick. It was like some sort of weird setup.

"Mommy!"

Lexie was the first to notice her standing there. She

gave her a wave and then shooed her away as she shook out water from her hair.

Ben jumped up and headed her way. Rebecca felt the urge to run, but forced her feet to stay rooted to the spot. He obviously hadn't come here to steal Lexie away, so what on earth was he doing?

"What are you doing here?" she asked, not wasting any time.

He gave her a big smile and shrugged.

"Not quite the welcome I was hoping for." He reached for her arm but she angled herself so he didn't quite connect.

"Look, I get that you want to make up for lost time, but this is kind of hard for me," she told him.

"Rebecca..."

"No, Ben, don't bother. I shouldn't have lied. I know it's Lexie you want, not me, and I should have just kept my mouth shut."

"Rebecca."

She looked up and into his chocolate-colored eyes; eyes she'd dreamed about for months after he'd left, before she was able to just gaze into her daughter's.

"I need you to come with me. I've organized for your dad to run the restaurant tomorrow. I need you and Lexie to join me."

That knocked the wind out of her as if she'd been sucker punched.

"You have no right to come here and change my life around," she whispered, conscious that all eyes were on them. "I can't believe you think you can just rearrange me and tell me what to do."

"You know what, Bec?"

"What?" she fired back.

"Just shut up and do what I say for once. Okay?" He laughed. "And has anyone ever told you that you look damn gorgeous when you're all mad?"

She looked past him to see her mother grinning. She'd probably never heard anyone boss her daughter around like that before. Rebecca glared at her and turned her back. Just when she needed someone on her team her own family was swapping sides. She gave Ben what she hoped was an unimpressed stare, hands on her hips, but she had to admit it was nice seeing him joke around, laugh like that. It reminded her of the Ben of old.

"Fine," she snapped, although her anger was quickly dissipating.

Ben grinned and turned back to the kids.

"Lexie, last round, sweetheart. I've got a surprise for you," Ben called out, as if he was suddenly at ease with spending time with her, hanging out with the child he'd looked as good as terrified of when she'd first told him.

Rebecca shook her head and received only a shrug of the shoulders from her mother. Conveniently her dad was still busying himself with the children's game. Lucy just gave her a thumbs-up and Bec glowered back at her. It was as if everybody but her knew what was going on and she didn't like it at all. She was always the one in control, planning to the last detail, organizing everybody else. Ben had no right to barge in here, into her family's home, and tell her what to do!

She looked back at her mother and her sister-in-law, then to Ben. They were all grinning like dummies.

This was definitely an ambush. She knew when she'd been outnumbered, and right now she was guessing those numbers were at least one hundred to one.

CHAPTER FIFTEEN

REBECCA DIDN'T LIKE SURPRISES, and she wasn't particularly pleased that Ben had spent time with her parents without discussing it with her first.

The car slowed and Rebecca refocused. She could hardly believe they were at McFarlane's all ready.

"Are we here?"

Lexie's sleepy voice broke the silence.

"Yup, we're here," Ben told her.

Was she the only one not happy? Ben had grinned the entire trip here, Lexie had chirped excitedly before falling asleep and was clearly back to her perky self again already, and she felt nothing but miserable. A wave of dread kept looping through her stomach, telling her something was wrong, but there was little she could do. Ben had made it clear he expected her to comply, and she was sick of arguing with him. Of feeling like everything was her fault. She simply couldn't be bothered fighting, saying no, especially with Lexie around. And the way she felt around him even though she knew nothing could happen? *Ugh*. Being in such close proximity to him wasn't doing her any favors.

When the car stopped she got out and helped Lexie, but her daughter made a beeline straight for Ben, trotting along beside him like a loyal puppy dog. So much for her clingy girl, she thought. Someone better came along and she was gone in a flash.

Rebecca wanted to feel happy that Lexie was going to have a dad in her life, she knew it was petty to think otherwise, but she couldn't help it. Ben was so clearly besotted with his child, and so appalled by her, she felt torn. It had been wrong not to tell him, she could see that now, but what more could she do than say sorry? If there was anything that could make things right between them, she'd do it.

"You coming, Bec?"

Ben calling out spurred her into action and she hurried after them.

"Come on, Mommy!" Lexie called.

She had soon caught up with them, catching a glimpse of Gus waving out, then disappearing into the stable. Something was definitely up. She had that feeling like everything was just too quiet, like some sort of set up.

"Are you ready for a surprise?"

Lexie nodded fiercely. If she'd nodded any harder her head would have fallen off.

Ben looked around to Rebecca. He gave her a look and pointed at Lexie. They stared at one another a long while, before she nodded. There was nothing else she could do, the message was conveyed so clearly in his eyes, his desperation clear for anyone to see.

She got it. He was going to tell Lexie that he was her dad. It upset her that they hadn't talked about it first, but she was Ben's daughter, and she guessed it was up to him to decide how and when he wanted her to find out. Ben walked toward her and she felt guilty for wanting to keep it from their little girl.

"You okay with me telling her?" Ben asked in a low tone, his mouth achingly close to her ear when he moved over, his hand closing over her forearm.

"Yes." What else could she say?

Ben beamed at her and whipped Lexie off her feet and up into his arms, as if he'd done it a million times before. He'd obviously decided he wanted to make a huge effort with her, and it showed.

"Lexie, today's a very special day. Do you know why?"

"'Coz I didn't have to go to preschool?"

Lexie squinted up at Ben, the sun in her eyes. Ben laughed and swung her, before hoisting her up onto his shoulders. Rebecca kept her distance. Her entire body was numb, her eyes wet, hands clammy. All she could do was watch, and feel her heart crumble into piece after piece. To an outsider, this would have looked happy, idyllic even. But the reality was Lexie had gained a father and she'd lost a friend. There was no chance for her and Ben to be anything other than civil parents, with no chance of a reconciliation. His feelings toward her had made that clear.

"Today's a special day because today you get to meet your dad." Rebecca listened to Ben's gruff, deep words as Lexie screwed her face up.

"Where is he?" Lexie asked.

Ben smiled. Rebecca didn't think she'd ever seen him look so happy. Not when they used to gallop down the beach, racing side by side on horseback; not when they used to sneak out and sit on the roof, talking for hours well into the night; *not ever.* She had never since she'd known him ever seen him look like that.

"I'm your dad, Lexie," Ben said simply. "It's me."

Lexie looked confused and Rebecca worried she didn't understand.

"How can you be my dad? You're Ben," Lexie asked.

"I know it's hard to understand, kiddo, but I promise you that I'm your dad, and I'm always going to be. I'm your father, sweetheart."

Lexie wriggled and he pulled her down from where she was perched on his shoulders, putting her on his hip so she could look at both of them. Rebecca had tears in her eyes but she tried so hard to stop them from falling.

"Mommy, do you know that Ben is my dad?"

That made them both laugh. Rebecca just smiled, trying to look happy, watching as little Lexie sat back in Ben's arms to look up at him some more. Children were so innocent, she thought. Her darling wee girl was so kind, so sweet and loving, and looking at her in her father's arms did make her happy. She only wished that same man wanted them both in his arms, not just his daughter. That they could be the family she had secretly dreamed of all these years. It broke her heart to think that Ben would meet someone, someday, and that Lexie would be with her daddy and another woman.

"There's one more surprise."

Rebecca looked up. What else was going on?

Lexie was wriggling so much that Ben had to put her down. Just as he did so, Gus came slowly around the corner, leading the cutest, tubbiest little pony Rebecca had ever seen.

Lexie was dead still now. She was holding on to Ben but she wasn't moving.

"This, Lexie, is a present from your dad."

Rebecca watched as Lexie looked from the pony to Ben.

"Since you love horses so much, I thought you deserved your own pony. Especially if you're going to be spending time here."

Lexie zoomed forward. Thankfully the pint-size pony wasn't worried, and just stood as Lexie inspected every inch of him, touching, patting, talking to him all the while.

Ben left her to it, under Gus's watchful eye, and turned to Rebecca. His grandfather was grinning ear to ear.

"We need to talk," Ben said in a low voice. "Keen for a ride?"

Rebecca nodded, still numb.

"Come on, then."

She followed after him, hardly able to process what was going on. She had no idea what to expect, only for the first time all afternoon, she was starting to believe it might be something good. Something so good she didn't even want to admit it.

They rode in silence for a while. Rebecca had no idea where they were going, why she was here, or what Ben wanted to talk about. If he just wanted to talk custody arrangements? She swallowed hard. Surely he wouldn't be making such an effort if it wasn't something more… Rebecca shook her head, as if it would somehow make the thoughts disappear. What she needed to do was just stop thinking.

Ben stopped then. She halted behind him and waited for his lead.

"Let's get off here," he said before dismounting.

She was pleased at least that she had her old riding mojo back. Her brain might have been working overtime, but her body had been loving the easy motion of the horse's walk.

Rebecca followed his lead, wishing Ben had been guiding her down, like he'd helped her mount that first time she'd ridden with him again after he'd arrived home. She craved his hands on her body, palms firm at her hips, the steadiness of his hold on her. They were dangerous wishes, she knew that, but she couldn't help it and it was worse knowing it was never going to happen again. Besides, she didn't need his assistance now. She wasn't the same timid rider she'd been that first day back on the farm.

Ben took the reins from her and tied the horses to a low fallen tree trunk in the shade. The day was hot, but the sun was sitting lower now, a late afternoon breeze keeping the temperature bearable.

He sat down on the same big trunk and beckoned her over. Rebecca complied, keeping her distance from him. She still didn't know why they were here, what they were doing, and the last thing she needed was to be within touching distance to him.

"I hope you didn't mind me telling her back there?"

She shook her head. "She'll have a lot of questions later, once she's had time to process, but that's okay."

"So you're all right with it?"

"She's your daughter, Ben. You had every right to tell her."

"Not too extravagant with the pony?"

Ben was smiling and she smiled back. He was obviously very proud of the cute pony he'd bought, and he deserved to enjoy the moment.

"It was the best present a kid could wish for. It was very kind of you."

They sat a few more minutes. Rebecca was feeling incredibly uncomfortable. This might not be hard for him, but she'd thought about him every day since he'd left. Thought about him double as much since she'd stormed out the other day. Wishing things were different; wishing she'd just told him before ending up confessing the way she had. She just wished she could go back in time and change everything, but she couldn't and she just had to suck it up and get on with her life.

"You don't want to go for full custody or anything, do you?" The thought made her feel worse than sick. "I love her so much, Ben, and I just couldn't deal with..." She bit down hard on her lip, shaking her head. "I just want to protect her."

Ben didn't answer, but he did shuffle closer to her along the rough wood of the tree trunk.

"I didn't bring you out here to talk about Lexie. And I sure as hell don't want to take her away from you "

She looked up. "You didn't? *Wait, you don't?*"

Ben shook his head, his eyes looking straight ahead toward endless parched yellow grass.

"I wanted to tell you that I understand. I know why you did what you did, and I need you to know that I forgive you."

She went to answer but snapped her mouth back closed. *He forgave her?*

"I've had time to think these past few days, and it made me realize that I was a jerk. I was hurt, but I still should have listened to you, heard you out." He shrugged. "We were best friends, Bec. You were the one person in the world who always knew me as well as I knew myself, and I guess it was hard hearing what you had to say the other day, the fact that you knew how scared I was of ever being a parent, of what I'd been through. You were right, I just didn't want to admit to it."

"You had every right to treat me like that, Ben," she answered. "I never should have kept it from you. It was wrong, I know that."

Ben took her hand, and she fought not to pull it away. She didn't want his touch, his pity. Didn't want him to feel sorry for her. She just wanted to figure out how they were going to make this parenting thing work then get on with it. Hoping for something more was stupid, dangerous.

Ben held her hand tighter so she couldn't pull it away. "Did you mean it when you said you still loved me?"

Rebecca's heart collapsed, then kick-started again. She didn't trust her voice, didn't know if she could even force a word out.

"Did you?" Ben asked again.

"Yes," she stammered. There was no point in lying—she'd told him how she felt the other day and it wasn't as if anything had changed.

"Bec," he said, standing and pacing a few steps before coming back to stand in front of her, casting a shadow over her as he blocked out the dappled sun coming through the leaves.

"I'm sorry, Ben," she said, wanting nothing more than to fall to the ground and cry, to shatter into pieces and not have to re-form until he'd gone. "I wish I didn't but I do. I wish I could just want to be friends with you, but it'd be a lie."

"You've said sorry enough," he whispered, dropping to his knees. "I forgive you, Rebecca. *I forgive you.*"

She looked up, warmth slowly trickling back into her veins as she met his gaze.

Ben dropped to his knees and grasped her hands between his. She didn't know where to look. *What was he doing?*

"Bec, will you marry me?"

CHAPTER SIXTEEN

REBECCA SUCKED IN a sharp lungful of air. Marry him? *Was he kidding?*

"Ben, you can't be serious!"

His eyes didn't leave hers, his hands steady as he clasped hers, fingers linked together.

"I'm serious, Bec." He smiled, then repeated his question. "Will you marry me?"

She snatched her hands away from him, hating how desperately she wanted him, how badly she just wanted to throw herself into his arms.

"No," she whispered.

Ben stared at her, long and hard.

"What do you mean, *no*?"

She blinked back a gasp of unshed tears and jumped up, made her way to her horse. Willy stood patiently, but when she made a grab for his reins a heavy, firm grip stopped her. Ben's fingers dug into her arm, not letting her move another inch.

"Let me go." She tried to sound forceful but it came out as little more than a whisper.

"*No*." Ben kept hold, his grip firm on her arm as he reached for her other wrist. His gaze made his intentions clear: there was no chance of him letting her go.

"You're not going anywhere."

"Let go of me, Ben." She fought hard, struggling to release herself. "Ben, you're hurting me!"

He let go of her wrist, his other hand softening over her arm.

"Why?" he asked.

Rebecca slumped against the horse, her resolve long gone. She turned sad eyes in Ben's direction.

"Same reason I didn't tell you about Lexie in the first place," she said sadly.

Ben looked confused, folding his arms across his chest as he stared at her.

"I didn't want you to propose back then just because you thought it was the right thing to do, and I don't want you to have to do it now. You don't owe me anything, Ben. You don't need to marry me out of some sense of, I don't know, duty."

"*Duty*? Is that honestly what you think?"

"Oh, I don't know," she said, trying hard not to cry. "Pity, then, whatever you want to call it. But you don't need to propose to me because you feel you have to."

Ben stepped toward her and placed a hand softly on each arm. She closed her eyes and tried to ignore the fact that he was touching her, of how good it felt to have his skin over hers. The man of her dreams had just asked her to marry him, was touching her, holding her, but it wasn't real, she knew that. She'd always known that he would step up if he knew, and here he was trying to make an honest woman of her.

"Rebecca, look at me."

When she didn't reply, he hooked one finger under her chin, forcing her to look at him. She swallowed, finally returning his gaze.

Ben didn't give her any warning. He crushed his lips hard against hers, taking her mouth with force. Rebecca tried to pull away, halfheartedly, before giving in and kissing him back. His hands were all over her, up and down her back, touching her hair, cupping her face. They stayed like that for what felt like hours, lost to one another's touch, lips locked, hands exploring, skin alight.

It was Ben who pulled back. He still had his hands around her waist, encircling her, keeping her locked in his cocoon.

"Did that feel like a man who pities you?" he asked. "Who thinks he has to marry you just because it's the right thing to do?"

She caught her lower lip beneath her teeth, still not wanting to hope that maybe she'd been wrong all this time.

"No," she managed to whisper in reply.

"I love you, Rebecca. I always have." He leaned in and pressed a soft, barely there kiss to her lips, his mouth hovering over hers. "And I always will. I should have told you years ago."

She let her eyes flutter shut for a moment, fighting the feeling that it was a dream. When she opened them again he was still there, his warm brown gaze locked on hers.

"I have always loved you, Rebecca. You have to believe me when I say I want you to marry me because I *still* love you, not because it's the right thing to do."

She nodded. It was all she could do. Her own voice had been taken captive in her throat.

"I want you to be my wife. I want to be Lexie's dad. And I want us all to be together." He sighed. "No pity.

No sense of duty. Just because I damn well love you, Bec."

She looked up at him. His gaze was unwavering, hands strong on her hips as he held her gently in place.

"So, will you have me?" he asked.

"Yes," she murmured, the word drawing them closer together, her arms looping around his neck, letting herself believe that he actually did want her just for her. "Yes, Ben. Yes a million times over."

Ben pulled her in tight against him then, his lips falling to hers once more. She sighed into his mouth as he kissed her, before he trailed butterfly-soft kisses down her throat.

Rebecca moaned, her legs close to buckling beneath her. Ben didn't stop. He scooped her into his arms, his mouth back on hers. She shuddered as his tongue teased her lips, groaned as he dropped slowly to the ground and put her carefully on the grass.

He tugged his T-shirt off in between long, languid kisses, and Rebecca ran her hands over his strong back, felt his hard muscles coil and tense beneath her touch.

"I've been waiting to do this again for so long," he muttered against her lips.

Rebecca moaned beneath his touch. *So had she.*

"You are so beautiful," said Ben, holding her close.

She looked away, shy at being the object of his words but not wanting him to stop touching her, kissing her.

Rebecca closed her eyes and let Ben caress her. She had dreamed of this for so long, never thinking that one day she would be back in his arms. Back with the man she loved. She had gone all this time alone, with no other human being to keep her warm at night, to be her mate in life, to love, and now she had Ben, and she was never, ever going to let him go. Not if she could help it.

Ben traced a fingertip over Rebecca's skin, starting at her wrist then all the way up to her neck, and to her lips. Rebecca giggled and he dropped another kiss to her mouth.

"You are going to marry me, aren't you?"

She smiled at him, her mouth stretched wide, her face mirroring how he felt.

"Yes, I'm going to marry you, Ben McFarlane. A hundred times *yes*."

"Good."

"Good?" she repeated. "Is that all you think of me? *Good*."

He pinned her back on the grass, his mouth inches from her face, trying to be serious when all he wanted to do was laugh.

"Do you need me to show you again what I really think of you?" he growled.

Rebecca burst out laughing as he held her down.

"Okay, okay," she said, giggling.

Ben let her go and lay back down beside her, their bodies side by side. He kept hold of her hand, fingers interlinked.

"What do you think Lexie will make of us being together? Of me marrying her mom?"

"She already loves you, Ben," she said, squeezing his fingers. "I think she fell in love with you from the moment she met you, like she knew there was some sort of connection there."

Ben propped up on one elbow again, looking down at her. Her golden hair was fanned out around her over the grass and he stared down into eyes that had haunted him for years.

"You know what?" she asked.

"What?" He smiled as she stroked his arm, her touch featherlight.

"I think Lexie would have been happy with you in our lives even if you weren't her biological dad."

Ben opened his eyes. For all his worrying about being a father, of not wanting to screw up like his own mom had, he suddenly wasn't scared of being in Lexie's life. Maybe Bec had been right in letting him go at the time, even though it hurt like hell to admit it. He wanted to be Lexie's father—it was a belly-deep feeling that would be impossible to fight, but if he'd been faced with this before he'd been away, maybe it would have been harder to accept, to man up to. Maybe he wouldn't have realized how badly he wanted Bec as his partner instead of his friend, to be back on home soil, to make a life for himself on the land he'd grown up on.

"She's a great kid, you know?" His voice was hoarse with emotion.

Rebecca nodded her agreement. "Yeah, and you're going to be just as good a dad."

He hoped so. Man, did he hope so. "If I can be half as good a dad as Gus has been a granddad to me, then I guess I'll be fine." He blew out a breath. "I was so scared of her that first day, I didn't know what to do or how to even talk around her, but once I thought about how Gus was with me, it started to come more naturally."

She leaned up and kissed his jaw. Rebecca crawled up into his arms and he tugged her tight, holding her close.

"I was so scared of being close to anyone, and in the process I somehow forgot that I was already close to you.

I pushed you away when I should have kept you at my side. Made you a part of my life."

She sighed, head to his chest. "Does any of that matter now?"

"No," he whispered, kissing the top of her head. "Because I'm going to spend every day from this day forward making it up to you."

CHAPTER SEVENTEEN

REBECCA EYED THE beautiful black filly and bit down a lump of fear threatening to constrict her throat. She had been psyching herself up for this moment for days, but it didn't make it any easier.

She knew Ben was watching her but she didn't turn. He had offered countless times to help her, but this was something she had to do alone. There was no point becoming the first Mrs. McFarlane to take residence here since Ben's grandmother, without proving she could conquer her fear. Ben had been man enough to forgive her, to make her realize that she deserved his love, and that he was acting from his own feelings and not from duty. And now she owed it to herself to step up, take ownership of her past and believe in her own abilities. As a rider, as a woman and as an equal to him on the farm.

"Hey, Missy," she soothed, leaving her fear on the other side of the corral. "How's my girl today, huh?"

As if understanding her, the horse nickered and reached out her nose to run it over Rebecca's forearm, tickling her bare skin.

Rebecca brushed Missy's back, her hands moving along the indent of her shoulder, then down around her belly. Next she softly rubbed her face, before moving to place the saddle on her back. The horse didn't move, and Rebecca gradually tightened the girth. When she moved to tease the bit into her mouth there was no hesitation, and she slipped the bridle over her head.

She glanced over her shoulder at her support crew and smiled. It was nice to see Gus and Ben standing there, but some of the polo guys who'd arrived were a little intimidating.

Rebecca talked in her low singsong voice to Missy and led her out to the center of the corral. A few strokes of the neck and tug of each stirrup later, and she was settling into the saddle.

Missy jumped and quivered, but Rebecca stayed calmed. She kept talking, a running commentary of nonsense that made the horse relax and listen, ears flicking back and forth. Rebecca squeezed her legs and they moved forward at a slow walk. That was all she wanted from today, didn't want to push things too far.

It wasn't the most relaxing of rides, but Rebecca was proud of herself. A few weeks ago, she'd been scared of going near a horse again. Now? She couldn't deny having a belly full of nerves, but she was finding her way back to her past in the best possible way. She was a mom, she ran a restaurant, and now she was going to be Ben's wife, a wife who'd be confident back in the saddle with him, training for polo matches and having fun. She finally felt like *her* again.

Missy jumped beneath her but she just kept on talking, keeping a firm contact with the reins. Rebecca circled her and then pulled to a halt, before swinging her feet out from the stirrups. She praised the horse.

Nothing had turned out the way she'd expected, but she couldn't be happier. She looked across and met Ben's strong, unwavering gaze. When he grinned she blew him a kiss. She was finally with the man she loved, and nothing, *nothing*, could take that away from her.

Ben gave his grandfather a nudge, not even trying to wipe the beamer of a smile from his face. He'd always known she had it in her. There was something exciting about seeing his girl, his wife-to-be, sitting proud on a horse. Gus had known she could do it, he'd hoped she could do it, and eventually Rebecca had believed enough in herself to trust her instincts and give it a go again.

Nobody could have blamed her for being scared, for not wanting to try again, but she had, and he was pleased. He loved Bec, he loved his daughter, and he loved horses. Just thinking about training with her again, playing polo side by side with her, made him grin.

Ben jumped to his feet and moved toward his fiancée. It gave him a buzz just thinking about marrying her.

"Son?"

He turned and looked at his grandfather. Gus looked as proud of his granddaughter-in-law-to-be as he was himself.

"I think it's time Rebecca had a horse of her own again."

Ben gave him a nod and they both walked toward her. She was making a fuss over the adoring horse she had just made look like a quiet donkey, when in fact she was the only one to connect with her at all.

A patter of hooves and a squeal of delight made them all turn. Ben laughed as he watched his daughter come running, as fast as her little legs would carry her, her placid pony in tow. Lexie was holding the end of the lead rope and the pony trotted beside her.

"I thought I told you to wait for us?" Ben said, trying to sound angry and failing. He'd been the same as a kid and he wasn't going to deny Lexie the fun of playing with her pony. That's why he had spent so much getting a kind old horse to teach Lexie the ropes, so he didn't have to worry every time his daughter was out in the field. They were a cute pair, and the pony had been well worth the money.

"You said not to *ride* him on my own," called a breathless Lexie. "See, Mommy? I'm just playing with him, not riding him."

Ben looked at Rebecca and saw her try to hide a smile behind her hand. She had them there; they *had* only said no riding.

"What do you say, *Mommy*?" asked Ben.

Rebecca put one hand on her hip, then burst into laughter as Lexie and the podgy pony ran past.

"Just stay close," Ben called after their adventurous daughter. "And remember she's a horse, not a dog. You need to be careful."

Ben leaned on the rails and watched as Gus approached Rebecca and Missy. He committed to memory the way his grandfather's weathered hand moved in slow circles over the horse's muzzle, then up her neck. The filly certainly responded to Rebecca, but she was partial to Gus, too.

"You did good out there," he heard his granddad say.

Rebecca looked up from grooming. "Thanks."

She gave the filly a final swoop with the brush then untied her lead rope, ready to walk her back out.

"She'd make a great polo pony if we had anyone decent to ride her, you know," said Gus.

"I know," agreed Rebecca.

Gus pushed his hat up higher to look her in the eye as Ben watched on.

"You never should have lost your horse in that accident, Rebecca." He waited till she looked up before continuing. "You're a great rider and you always will be, which is why I want you to have her."

"No! Gus, she's worth too much and I don't even know if I'd make it through a whole chukker now…"

"I've made my mind up. Don't deny an old man a gift."

"Ben, did you hear that?" Rebecca called out. "Tell him I can't take her."

Ben just grinned and shrugged. "Sorry, but I'm not taking your side on this one."

"Rebecca, she's yours. Make me proud. Just promise me that you'll have fun, and look after that grandson of mine when I'm gone. Okay?"

Ben wiped away a tear as he watched Rebecca walk the horse out into the yard and give Gus an impromptu kiss on the cheek, her arm slung around his shoulders.

"You're the best granddad in the world, you know that?"

"No, love, you're the best granddaughter, and I've waited a long time to have you. So if I want to spoil you, then so be it."

Ben jogged the distance to catch up with them, arms looping around Rebecca's waist once she'd let the horse go.

"We *are* going to have fun, you know that, right?" He kissed her neck, holding her tight. "I love you."

She turned in his arms, eyes shining with tears. "I love you, too."

EPILOGUE

BEN SMILED OVER at Rebecca's parents before giving his grandfather a nudge. Gus was standing next to him, dapper in a dark suit and soft pink tie, matching his grandson. He hadn't expected Gus to be on his feet for the ceremony, but the old man was tough as nails and had managed to surprise them all.

A noise from behind stole his attention and Ben laughed when he saw the commotion. Rebecca's brother was trying to coax Lexie down from her pony and wasn't having much luck. From the day he'd given his daughter the friendly little gray gelding, Lexie had hardly given the poor horse a second to relax. It had been love at first sight; his daughter had fallen for the pony as fast as Ben had fallen for his little girl.

There was a whisper through the crowd as the string quartet started to play, and the soft lull of music made Ben stare at the house, at the door where Rebecca was going to enter from. He held his breath and closed his eyes for a second. When he opened them she was walking toward him. Not on her father's arm, not flanked by a gaggle of bridesmaids, just Rebecca walking toward him, a smile on her face that mirrored his own.

For the first time in his life Ben almost cried in public, but he checked his emotion, swallowed hard and just focused on Bec. Her eyes were shining as she held out her hands to him once she reached him, and he clasped them as tightly as he could before pulling her in for a kiss, just a gentle touch of his mouth to hers to tell her how much he loved her.

Rebecca pressed into him and sighed into his mouth.

"We're meant to wait until after we're married," she whispered, throwing her head back to laugh as he kept her encircled in his arms.

Not the guests behind them, the celebrant clearing her throat, even Lexie standing with her pony and a huge smile, could distract Ben. He had the woman he loved in his arms, and he didn't ever want to let go.

Rebecca squeezed her husband's hand and shook her head as she watched Lexie. She'd refused to come in for the party, preferring instead to race around with her pony, and neither she nor Ben had any intention of forcing her to come in. She was sitting under the shade of the big blue gum tree, sharing food from her paper plate with her four-legged best friend, and there was nothing she'd rather see her little girl doing.

"I love you, baby," Ben murmured in her ear.

Rebecca turned to smile at him and press a kiss to his lips.

The small group of guests were all looking up as metal sounded out on glass. There were no planned speeches but…Rebecca smiled. Gus was standing with his wineglass in hand, clearing his throat. If anyone was going to speak, she was pleased it was him.

"I don't want to talk all night or anything like that, but someone needs to say a few words about our lovebirds over there," said Gus.

There was a murmur of laughter until his still-strong, deep voice rang out again.

"You probably all know that I haven't got much longer, but what you might not know is just how much I love these two."

He gestured at Rebecca and Ben and she dabbed at the corners of her eyes with her napkin, trying hard not to let any tears spill. To even think about Gus not being around was heartbreaking, especially when she'd gone so many years without seeing him.

"I always knew these two would find a way to be together. As kids, they were inseparable, as young adults, it was obvious to anyone but them that they were in love, and as full-grown adults they were even more stubborn! All I ever heard was nonsense about how they were just friends."

Ben squeezed Rebecca's hand and she laughed. There was no denying how stupid they'd been.

"What I want to say, though, is that these two deserve to be happy, and I know they'll be together for as long as they're living. Which is why I want to present them with the deed to McFarlane Stables."

Rebecca gasped and Ben dropped his glass with a thump to the table. *He what?*

"Before you two protest," continued Gus, waving them away, "I want you to know that I've thought long and hard about this, and the paperwork's already done." He paused, his eyes meeting first hers then Ben's, his smile wide. "So please join with me in raising your glasses in toast to the new Mr. and Mrs. McFarlane, custodians of McFarlane Stables."

Rebecca leaned into Ben and he dropped a kiss to her head. If life couldn't get any more perfect, it just had.

* * * * *

"I'd be lying if I said I wasn't interested in you."

"And I'd be lying if I said I *was* interested in you." Peyton brushed at her skirt as if kissing him had left her dusty, or as if she just wanted to whisk away the memory of his touch. "I'm here so you have a chance to get to know your daughter. Nothing more. And I mean that, Luke. *Nothing more.*"

"Then why did you kiss me back?"

"I..." She opened her mouth, closed it. "I didn't mean to. I got caught up in the moment and—"

"Overcome by the heat? Swept away by the romantic atmosphere of a children's zoo?" He shifted closer. Still, she kept her distance, stood strong and cool, dispassionate. If he hadn't been there himself, he wouldn't believe that ten seconds ago this same woman had been leaning into him, letting out soft mews of desire. "Don't pretend you didn't enjoy that. Don't pretend it was nothing."

***

The Barlow Brothers:
Nothing tames a Southern man faster...
than true love!

THE INSTANT
FAMILY MAN

BY
SHIRLEY JUMP

Published in Great Britain 2015
by Mills & Boon, an imprint of Harlequin (UK) Limited,
Eton House, 18-24 Paradise Road, Richmond, Surrey, TW9 1SR

© 2015 Shirley Kawa-Jump, LLC

ISBN: 978-0-263-25140-1

23-0615

To my husband, Jeff, because he is amazing—
as a dad, as a husband and as a man.
He's the family man I always dreamed of
meeting and am blessed to have married.

Chapter One

When Peyton Reynolds was a little girl, tearing through her grandmother's house on her way to whatever excitement waited outside the front door, her grandma Lucy would reach out, corral her granddaughter in a fresh-baked-bread-scented hug and say, "Goodness gracious, child, you gotta slow down. Life is just gonna pass you by if you don't learn to take a breath or two."

Peyton never had learned to slow down. She'd taken every day of her life ten steps at a time, running from high school to college, graduating in two and a half years instead of four, and putting in more hours at Winston Interior Design than any other designer—earning her four promotions in three years. Then, a month before her twenty-third birthday, her world turned upside down when her older sister Susannah died in a car accident, suddenly leaving forty pounds of cuteness and need in Peyton's full-time care.

In that instant, Peyton had put the brakes on her rising career while she figured out how to be a surrogate mom to her niece, Madelyne, and still stay on the fast track in the design industry. She'd been so very close to a promotion to associate, just a step below her goal of partner, but in the past four weeks, everything she had worked for started to fall apart. And it wasn't just her career self-destructing that had Peyton worried...

It was the quiet. The words unspoken, the tears unshed.

Maddy hadn't grieved, hadn't asked about her mother, hadn't wanted to talk about it. She'd gone on playing with her toys and eating her meals and brushing her teeth, but her mood was more somber, her heart more distant. Her laughter dulled, almost silenced.

That sad quiet was what finally spurred Peyton to go back home from Maryland, arriving yesterday in Stone Gap, North Carolina, one of those small Southern towns where it seemed the world stopped spinning. Where the trees and green landscape seemed to offer peace, and quiet, and healing. And where the last man on earth she wanted to see lived. A man who had no idea she was about to upend his world in a very big way.

For a very good reason. Peyton could only pray that he would see it that way, too.

"Auntie P?"

The soft voice of Madelyne, four years old next week and as beautiful as a ray of sunshine, rose from the space on the carpet between the two double beds in their hotel room. Peyton's only niece, and the only real family she had left. There were times in the days since her sister had died that Peyton wondered how she could move forward, take a breath, without letting the grief drown her. Then she'd look at Maddy, at her bouncy blond curls and her lopsided, toothy smile, and a blanket of warmth would surround Peyton's heart. For Maddy, Peyton would do absolutely anything.

Peyton came around the beds, then bent down and offered her niece a warm smile. "What do you need, kiddo?"

"Can you play dolls with me? I gots a house set up and everything." Maddy waved toward an empty suitcase tipped on its side, flanked by a quartet of blond-haired, blue-eyed Barbie dolls in various stages of mismatched glamour. The moment Maddy had arrived back in Stone Gap, she had made herself at home in the hotel room, taking over every square inch of space with toys and clothes, a bright explosion among the tired and boring cream-colored decor.

"Wish I could, but remember I told you I had a meeting this morning? My friend Cassie is coming over to watch you."

"I like Cassie," Maddy said. "She always likes to play dolls."

"She sure does, buttercup!" The loud, happy voice of Cassie Bertram boomed into the room, followed immediately by the woman herself—platinum blonde, dressed in a bright pink sundress and flip-flops sporting giant plastic flowers. Cassie had always been larger than life, and that was part of what Peyton loved about her best friend.

A peacock, Grandma Lucy had dubbed Cassie, for all her sass and snap. Cassie lit up a room when she walked into it and lived her life out loud, in ways that Peyton could only envy. Cassie had traveled all the opposite roads from Peyton—married shortly after high school, settling down in Stone Gap with her husband, and then becoming a mother to five kids while working part-time in the school office. Cassie did the bake sales and cookie walks and all the craziness that came with kids, and more often than not, she sported glitter glue on her arms from the craft project du jour. She'd been Peyton's first call when Peyton had decided to come back home for a couple of weeks, and her biggest support system in the chaotic weeks since Maddy had become Peyton's charge. Cassie had visited Peyton often enough over the years that Maddy knew her well and loved her like another aunt.

"I've got a couple hours before I have to pick up the youngest rug rat at preschool," Cassie said to Peyton. "Is that enough time?"

"More than enough. It won't take me long to tell a certain someone that he should..." She glanced down at her motherless niece, then stepped toward the window and motioned for Cassie to follow, saying "Be a grown-up. And do his part. Or walk away for good."

Cassie grinned. "I wish I could be a fly on the wall to watch this particular conversation unfold."

"It'll be fine. I'll make a logical, reasonable argument, and he'll see the wisdom in my plan."

"Logical and reasonable? With that hunk of testosterone?" Cassie grinned. "Good luck, honey."

Hunk of testosterone. Definitely three words that described Luke Barlow. Or had when Peyton had been a young, infatuated high school freshman, watching the much older Luke turn his charm on Susannah. Her sister's old boyfriend—and also Maddy's irresponsible, never-involved father. According to Susannah, he'd washed his hands of her from the day she told him she was pregnant. She might have let it go, but Peyton sure as hell wasn't going to let the man get away with shirking his fatherly responsibilities, not for one more second. Especially now, when Peyton was nearly at her wit's end. Every decision

Peyton made right now was driven by the urgent need to make Maddy whole again.

"How's the little peanut doing?" Cassie asked softly, as if reading Peyton's mind.

"Same. Won't talk about it. She plays and eats and does what she's told, but there's a…wall there. I can't get past it."

Cassie put a hand on Peyton's shoulder. "It'll get better."

Peyton sighed. That was what she had been telling herself for a month now, and if anything, things were getting worse, not better. "I hope so. And I really hope I'm making the right decision today."

"Auntie P?" Maddy rose, peered over the bed at Peyton. "Are you leavin'?"

"Just for a little bit, sweetie."

Maddy's face flushed, and her right hand curled tight around the hem of her shirt. "Are you comin' right back?"

Peyton swung over to Maddy and lowered herself to her niece's level. "Right back, sweetie. I promise. Cassie will be here the whole time, and she's going to play dolls with you."

Maddy's lower lip quivered. "How long's a little bit?"

Peyton glanced at Cassie. These were the days that made it hard. Explaining to Maddy that just because she walked out the door didn't mean she was going to disappear forever. "Faster than you can watch *Frozen*."

"And we'll sing 'Let it Go' together, munchkin." Cassie grinned at Maddy. "I'll dub you honorary princess for the morning, too."

"Okay," Maddy said, though there wasn't much enthusiasm in her voice. She dropped back onto her Barbie-riddled carpet space and went back to her dolls. Every couple of seconds, her gaze flicked to Peyton, and her shoulders tensed with worry.

Cassie and Peyton crossed to the other side of the bed and lowered their voices again. "You're doing the right thing, Pey. That poor little thing needs family and you need help. And if that foolish man can't be bothered to spend time with that precious gift from heaven…" Cassie cast a smile in Maddy's direction. "I'd be glad to keep an eye on that little doll."

"Thanks, but you have your hands full with that basketball team you gave birth to and everything else you're doing. Besides, it's his responsibility to do the right thing." And the sooner Peyton got there to make sure Luke did that, the better. Peyton grabbed her purse, then darted over to plant a quick kiss on Maddy's cheek. "See you in a little bit, sweetie. Be good for Cassie."

"I will." Maddy's eyes were round and full, but she pressed her lips together and affected a brave front.

"A little bit," Peyton said softly, ruffling Maddy's curls. "I promise."

At the door, Cassie drew Peyton into a tight, quick hug. "Good luck. And go easy on Luke. He's a flirt, for sure, but he's always been a nice guy and maybe he had a good reason for what he did."

"The only good reason is being stuck in a cave for the past four years. Something I can arrange, if need be." Peyton grinned.

"I hope you're only half kidding," Cassie called after her. Peyton just grinned again and slipped out the door.

But when she climbed into her car and started the engine, the frustration and worry she'd been feeling for weeks flared anew. Luke Barlow was the town's most eligible bachelor for as long as anyone could remember— one of those charming, handsome, could-do-no-wrong playboys—but who had never had anything to do with his daughter. A daughter who had lost her mother, and desperately needed a caring father.

Peyton remembered those tearful conversations with Susannah, who said she told Luke about the baby the minute she'd taken the home pregnancy test. When he'd told her she was on her own, nineteen-year-old Susannah had left town, leaving behind her chaotic childhood home—the Reynolds parental storm mitigated too rarely by visits to grandma's when they were little—determined to raise her baby alone. Peyton had followed soon after, switching colleges to be near her sister, and working part-time all through school, helping Susannah financially, emotionally—in all the ways Luke should have and never did.

How could anyone not want to be a part of Maddy's life? From the second she had held her niece in her arms, Peyton had fallen in love. She'd spent every spare minute with Susannah and Maddy, even moving Susannah into her condo in Baltimore so she could be sure they had a solid roof over their heads and a full refrigerator. It had been odd at first, coming home to the responsibilities of a full house when she was barely a grown-up herself, but Peyton had found she liked having a pseudo-family. And though her relationship with her sister had been rocky at best—the two of them butting heads daily on Susannah's refusal to give up her partying habits—the blooming bond with Maddy had been the highlight of Peyton's days.

How long's a little bit?

The heartbreaking words from her niece, so unsure and lost in the wake of her mother's death, told Peyton that Maddy needed a father, now more than ever, and the days of Luke Barlow running around town, as footloose as a loose kite in the wind, were over.

Peyton double-checked the address, then drove the few miles across town to Luke's house, located only a few blocks away from where the Barlow boys had grown up. She parked her car, strode up the walk, then pressed the doorbell, reminding herself to try to be calm, logical. To keep emotion out of it.

Uh, yeah, considering the riot in her gut right now, she had a better chance of being hit by a snowstorm.

The bell chimed, a dog barked, and then...nothing. Peyton waited in the hot North Carolina air, while the cicadas buzzed in the deep woods to the east side of the house.

Luke lived in a modest bungalow, which surprised her. A house smacked of dependability. A mortgage or a lease. Permanence. She would have never thought he would buy a house, much less live in one.

An old wooden swing much like the one Grandma Lucy had hung for Peyton when she was a little girl drifted in the breeze on ropes hanging from an oak tree just down the hill sloping away from the driveway. The painted white mailbox hoisted a bright red mail-to-take flag, while an audience of pansies waved in the shade underneath. The whole property seemed to beckon her back in time, to the days when life had been unfettered, uncomplicated.

She rang the bell again. Waited some more. The dog kept barking, but there was no movement from inside. A restored Mustang convertible sat in the driveway, like some throwback to the '80s. Peyton shifted her weight, then pressed the bell one more time. If there was any justice in the world, Luke would have gotten bald and fat in the years since she'd last seen him.

The dog barked again, then shushed. A clatter of footsteps, and a moment later, the door was opened.

Luke Barlow stood on the other side, looking sleep-rumpled and scruffy with a five o'clock shadow dusting his chin. Her gut tensed, her breath caught. Definitely not bald or fat. At all. If anything, he looked better than he did when he was in high school, damn him.

"What can I do for you?" he said.

There wasn't a hint of recognition in his eyes. She told herself she wasn't disappointed. After all, she'd grown up a lot in the past five years, ditched the nerdy glasses and khaki pants for contacts and skirts. She'd let her hair grow long, made workouts a daily item on her to-do list and developed more curves than she'd had at graduation. When she was younger, she'd been the annoying little sister, while outgoing, flamboyant Susannah had always taken center stage. Now, though, she was an adult. A woman.

Hopefully, a woman to be reckoned with.

"I take it you don't remember me," she said. "I'm Peyton. Susannah Reynolds's younger sister."

Now recognition dawned in his eyes. His gaze swept over her, lit surprise in his features as he took in her dress, low heels, long hair. "Peyton? Peyton *Reynolds*? Holy hell, I haven't seen you in years. What are you doing here?"

Luke's deep Southern voice slid through her like honey drizzled over toast. Once upon a time, she'd had a crush on him. But that was a long time in the past, and a lot had happened in the years since. Except his damned voice still made parts of her warm.

She drew herself up. Calm, cool, collected, that was her. Maybe if she thought it enough, the words would be true. "I came by to…see you."

She'd meant to say *talk to you*, but her eyes lit on

Luke's tall, trim frame, and the word stuttered into *see*.
He was wearing a bathing suit, the dark blue trunks hanging low on his hips, exposing a defined, tan chest, with a
scattering of dark hair running a tempting line down the
center of his belly. Her gaze followed that line, then she
caught herself and jerked her attention back to his face.
Damn. What was wrong with her? She was no longer a
silly schoolgirl with an unrequited teenage crush on the
older captain of the football team.

He quirked a lopsided grin. Busted. "See me?"

"*Talk* to you."

The dog took advantage of the open door and scampered onto the porch. Luke waved a hand at the dog.
"Charlie, sit."

The terrier glanced up at Luke, as if to say, *Do I really have to?* When Luke didn't relent, the dog let out a
sigh and plopped onto the porch. His tail swished against
the wooden floor, hopeful, anxious. It took a second, but
then Peyton remembered.

"Is that…" Peyton asked, as she leaned forward, peering at the lopsided brown ears, the big chocolate eyes,
"…the same dog?"

A slow smile spread across Luke's face. "You remember that?"

Oh, she remembered a lot of things about Luke. Some
memories that made her heart trip, some that tripped
her common-sense alarms. "I thought you said you were
going to bring him to a shelter."

Luke shared his smile with the dog, then shrugged.
"What can I say? I'm a softy."

Peyton's doubts about bringing Luke into Maddy's
life eased a fraction. But only a fraction. Just because
the man had kept the dog they'd rescued years ago didn't
make him a suitable parent. And if he wasn't going to be

a good father figure, she was damned well going to make sure he either signed over custody or at least paid child support. He owed Maddy that much, at a minimum. Susannah might have been easy on Luke, but her younger sister had no intentions of doing the same. She needed to keep all that in mind and not get distracted by feelings half a decade old.

Luke gestured toward the wicker love seat and chair on the veranda. A ceiling fan swirled a lazy breeze over the white furniture and pale gray plank floor. Peyton's gaze kept drifting to Luke's bare chest. Damn, he looked good. Too good. He was distracting. Would it be rude to ask him to put on a shirt, so she could think with the rational side of her brain?

"So what brings you by?" Luke asked, settling into the love seat and draping one arm over the back.

She had thought this through on the long drive from Baltimore to Stone Gap. As much as she wanted to leap to the reason she was here, she needed to finesse the situation first. Feel Luke out. See if he had changed. Then she would decide which tactic to take. It was the way she approached her work—get a feel for the space, the dimensions, the history, the very air and let that influence the tone of her design. She perched on the opposite end of the small wicker couch. "Just wanted to catch up with some old friends while I was visiting town. I saw Cassie Bertram this morning and heard you were living on this side of town. I was in the area and thought I'd stop by. So, how have you been?"

If he thought her reasoning for coming to see him was strange, he didn't show it. "Good. Can't complain."

Awkward silence. She flicked her gaze away from his chest—what did he have on there, magnets?—and at the clapboard siding. "Nice little house you have here."

"Thanks. It's a rental, but I like it a lot. Kinda growing on me. And it has a pool. Pretty much all I need is that and a fridge." He grinned.

"To make it party central?"

He scoffed. "If I was eighteen, yeah, maybe. I'm still a pretty simple guy, Peyton. Though my mother keeps haunting garage sales and tries to talk me into crazy things like spice organizers, whatever the hell those are. Jack's built me a table and chairs, so I guess you could say I'm settled in here."

Okay, so maybe he wasn't the party-hard guy she remembered. Maybe he had matured a little. "Jack's building furniture?"

"Building whatever he can with a hammer and nails. He likes working with his hands. I convinced him to get serious about that a few months ago, after he got home from Afghanistan and was kind of at loose ends, trying to figure out what to do next. Now he's got business cards and orders and everything."

"And Mac? How is he?" She hadn't seen the oldest Barlow brother since graduation. He'd been the studious one, excelling in school, graduating at the top of the class.

Luke chuckled. "Still the rebel without a cause. Working a zillion hours a week at building the Maxwell Barlow empire, I'm sure."

She wasn't surprised. Jack had always been the adventurous one, strong and loyal, a good choice for the military. She had no doubt he'd be as excellent at furniture, putting the same care and detail into that job, as he had everything else in his life. Mac was the overachiever, constantly trying to do more, better and faster than anyone else. Luke had always sat square in the middle, great at sports and popularity, but so-so with academics. She didn't remember him being particularly ambitious, but then again, none of the girls who had wilted at the sight of Luke cared if he only had a part-time job. Now, however, a regular paycheck was a necessity for supporting a child. "And, uh, where are you working now?"

He leaned back against the love seat. "Why does this feel like a quiz?"

"I'm just…curious." She smiled. "Haven't seen you in a long time and I was just catching up."

"Yeah, catching up. That's what we're doing." Reservations still lingered in his gaze, and she got the feeling he was assessing her as much as she was assessing him. "I've been working with my dad in his garage. Jack and I were helping him out back when he had his knee surgery, but now that Jack is getting busy with his new business and my dad is thinking about retiring, I've been there more often." Luke ran a hand through his hair, and his eyes took on a faraway look for a moment. "The future of Gator's Garage is still up in the air, though."

"You aren't going to take it over?"

"That's a lot of responsibility. A lot of hours. And a long-term commitment." He grinned again. "Those three things aren't usually on my personal résumé."

"I remember." She tried to act as if it was a joke, but inside her chest, disappointment was sinking her dream of Luke being the parent that Maddy needed. Only now did Peyton realize how much she'd been hoping Luke would have grown up in the years since she'd last seen him, and that he would want to be an involved parent. Not that Peyton couldn't raise Maddy on her own, but it would be good for Maddy to have a male role model, and even better, a biological parent who could be a big part of her life.

"So how about you?" Luke said. "You look…amazing."

She blushed, and cursed herself for it. "Thanks."

"You said you're visiting Stone Gap. Where is home now?"

And the tables were turned. Because he was trying to beat her at her own game or because he was truly interested? "Baltimore. I'm an interior designer and I work with a relatively large firm there."

He considered that and nodded. "Makes sense. You were always the kind of kid who wanted to make things more beautiful, leaving flowers in my manly tree forts and painting your bike's spokes pink and purple. What am I saying? Kid? You're a beautiful woman now."

Two compliments in the space of a minute. The blush crept into her cheeks again, but she reminded herself that this was Luke, the man who could charm the leaves off the trees in the middle of summer.

"Well, thank you. Again."

A car went past, its noisy muffler putting a pause in their conversation. "How's your sister?" Luke asked.

She blinked. The air took on a chill, the sky seemed to darken. "You don't know?"

"Know...what?"

Peyton drew in a breath, then pushed out the words. "Susannah was..." Her voice wavered, her breath skipped. *Damn, why was this still so hard to say?* "She was...killed in a car accident a month ago."

Luke sat back against the seat, his face paling. "Really? That's terrible. I hadn't... I hadn't heard. She was so young. Way too young." He cursed, then leaned forward, his blue eyes intent on hers. "Oh, God, Peyton, I'm so sorry. Are you...okay?"

He touched her hand, a gesture of comfort, connection. The tight lock Peyton always held on her emotions loosened, and tears rushed to her eyes. She'd never expected him to ask her how *she* was. For a second, she wanted to tell the truth. *I'm falling apart. My life is a mess. Everything I thought I had under control is careening off a cliff and for the first time in my life, I don't know what to do.* "I'm…I'm fine."

"I'm so sorry," he said again, his hand curling over hers, solid, there.

She started to speak, then realized he'd left off the most important part. No questions about his daughter? About how Maddy was coping with the loss of her mother? Did the man feel no remorse that he had left Susannah to fend for herself for so long?

She tugged her hand out of his, reached into her purse and withdrew her phone. Peyton turned the phone to face Luke. Maddy's picture, a recent one from a happy day at the park shortly before Susannah died, filled the screen. "Aren't you even going to ask how *she's* doing?"

"Pretty girl," Luke said. Charlie the dog padded over and lay down at Luke's feet. "Is she yours?"

"No, she's not mine. You know that. I can't believe you don't even recognize her."

"I don't know that kid at all, sorry." Luke shrugged. "What is she, three? Four? Good age. They're still cute then, but don't have diapers. I think. I don't know much about kids, though."

"Because you have done your level best to avoid your own." She stopped herself from adding, *you selfish, self-centered jerk.* Good thing she hadn't fallen for that whole concerned-about-you act, with the nice little touch of his hand on hers.

"My own? My own what?" Luke met Peyton's gaze, wariness creeping into his expression. "What the hell are you talking about?"

"This is Madelyne. *Your daughter.* Remember?"

The words hung between them in the heavy, humid

air, lead weights on the end of a fishing line. Luke's mouth opened, closed. The cicadas kept up their steady hum in the heat.

"Mine? But how... What..." He shook his head, cast another long glance at the photo of Madelyne. "Is this some kind of joke? I don't have a kid."

"Don't play dumb with me, Luke. I know my sister told you about the baby and you wanted nothing to do with her. Left her to raise Maddy on her own. Well, now Maddy has lost her mother and I think it's about damned time her father was responsible and helped take care of her or at least supported her financially. She's gone through enough for one little girl."

There, she'd said it. And without all the cursing that usually accompanied that lecture in her head.

Luke tapped the phone's screen. "I don't know anything about this kid, Peyton. I don't know what your sister told you, but Susannah *never* told me she was pregnant."

A doubt tickled the back of her mind. "She said she did, Luke. She told me a hundred times how you broke up with her the instant she said she was pregnant. Either way, how can you not see the truth when it's right here? Don't you see your eyes and your smile in that face?"

He took her phone and held it closer. He studied Maddy's picture for a long, long time, then hesitated before handing the phone back, almost reluctantly. "Maybe. She does look like me, a lot like me. You gotta believe me, though, Peyton. I had no idea Susannah had a baby. That's the God's honest truth."

Was it possible? Would Susannah lie? Her sister had never been the most conventional of women or mothers, but lying about something as big as this? Peyton couldn't see why Susannah would do such a thing, even though the doubt still haunted her thoughts. Susannah, the irresponsible. Susannah, the flighty. Susannah, who had told lies to the grocery clerk and the bill collectors and the boss of the week. Would she really have lied to her younger sister—about *Maddy*?

"Well, now you know. And if you want proof, I am more than happy to pick up one of those mail-in DNA tests. We'll have results in less than two weeks."

"You have all the bases covered," he said.

"I have to. Someone has to be responsible here, and right now, that's me." Peyton started to get to her feet, suddenly anxious to be out of there, to go back to Maddy and hug her niece. "Once the DNA test proves you are Maddy's father, I expect you to support her financially, if nothing else."

He reached out, captured her hand. The touch cemented her in place, unnerved her and had her glancing at his chest again. God, what was wrong with her? Why did she keep getting so off track?

"What, that's it? You come here, tell me I have a kid, tell me I need to do my part, then run off?"

She didn't want to tell him she was rattled by the idea that Susannah could have lied. That her years of righteous indignation might have been wrong. That she wanted to get out of here, so she could breathe, digest it, get her mind back on track. "I'm not running off. I'm just going back to my hotel. I'm in town for a couple of weeks, should you want to discuss this further." Two weeks, that's all she had, to help Maddy feel grounded again, and then Peyton could go back to work and start building a solid foundation for the next phase of their lives.

"Should I want to discuss this further? Hell, yes, I want to discuss this further! Is the kid with you?"

"The *kid* is named Madelyne. And yes, she's at the hotel, with Cassie. But don't worry about it. I have it all under control." She nodded toward the house, the bachelor pad with a fridge and a pool. "I'm sorry for interrupting whatever...fun you have going on. I only came here to tell you about her, because she needs..."

She couldn't finish the sentence. Right now, Peyton wasn't sure what Maddy needed. The child psychologist Peyton had taken Maddy to had said the little girl needed time, space, love. Three things Peyton thought she'd been giving Maddy in heaps, but it hadn't worked. Nothing had brought Maddy out of her quiet little shell.

"She needs her family, and right now, that's just me," Peyton said, her voice catching again, damn it. "You're her family, too, whether you accept it or not, and I'm asking you to either be a part of her life and get to know her, or..."

"Or what?" Luke said.

Peyton drew herself up, all business again, pushing that moment of vulnerability away. She tugged the papers out of her purse and flashed them at him. Peyton Reynolds, nothing if not prepared. "Sign over custody once and for all. The one thing Maddy doesn't need any more of is uncertainty. I need to make some decisions for her future, and I need to know if those decisions include you or not."

"Whoa, whoa, whoa. Peyton, you are springing a lot on me in a very short period of time." Luke ran a hand through his hair. It gave him that mussed, straight-from-bed look, and something in Peyton's gut flipped. "I...I'm still processing the fact that I have a kid."

"Like I said, you don't need to accept this responsibility if you don't want to. So here, just sign." She drew out a pen from her bag and turned it in his direction. All she wanted was to be done here, done talking to Luke Barlow and all the questions he had dropped into her world.

He shook his head. "Hang on a second. I'm not sign-ing anything yet. You show up on my doorstep, tell me I have a kid. And now you're giving me a hard time for not being ready for this news? Susannah kept this from me for four years, and here you are, accusing me of being a terrible father without knowing the whole story. Maybe things would have been different if she'd told me, but she didn't, and now this is hitting me. Give me five minutes at least to digest it all before you stomp out of here in a self-righteous fit."

"I am not—" An angry retort sprang to her lips, but she cut it off. He was right. She had just dumped a lot on his plate. Whether he'd been a jerk four years ago or not wasn't the issue anymore. If Luke wanted to be part of Maddy's life now, she had to give him a chance. Maddy deserved that.

Peyton took in a deep breath, let it out. "I'm sorry. You're right. I'm just at my breaking point here trying to be a parent to Maddy, and I need…help."

Damn, it grated on Peyton's nerves to say that. She was the kind of woman who could do any task, by herself.

Any task but heal a wounded child who had lost her center.

"Whatever you need. Just say the word."

She hadn't expected his easy, quick response. She shouldn't be surprised. The Luke she'd known—the Luke she had once fallen for—had been as fast to forgive as he was to lend a hand to a friend. He might not be big on commitment or permanence or anything approaching a long-term relationship, but he was one of those guys you could call in a pinch. The guy who would jump-start your car at two in the morning or help you move a couch in the middle of summer. She was hoping that guy was still there, beneath the chest her gaze kept drifting toward, and that he would be there for her for the next few weeks. "Maddy hasn't handled the loss of her mother very well. I guess you'd say not at all."

"What do you mean?"

"She won't talk about it. Won't cry about it. Just acts as if it never happened, except for being really clingy to me, as if she's afraid I'm going to disappear any second. I've been trying to juggle my job in Baltimore and be her surrogate mom and help her through this and..." *Failure* wasn't a word in Peyton's vocabulary. She had never failed at anything in her life and refused to fail now. "And I think she and I need a recharge. A vacation. So I came here, where I can have two weeks to just be with her and take her places and see her smile again. And I thought it would be good for her if she got to know her father."

"If you wanted me to be a parent, then someone should have told me about her four years ago." He got to his feet. Charlie snapped to attention, pressing his body against Luke's, the dog's tail moving in a slow wag, as if he was worried about his master. "I take it she doesn't know who I am? Or that I even exist?"

"No. Over the years, Susannah chose not to talk about you to Maddy. I haven't, either, because...well, I assumed you didn't want to be an active part of her life."

"You assumed wrong. So if I see her, what am I supposed to be?" He scowled. "Temporary Uncle Luke or something?"

Peyton could see the Mustang in his driveway, imagine the parties he probably had in his pool. Her niece had suffered enough heartbreak for one lifetime, and the last thing Peyton wanted was for Maddy's father to disappoint her. If he hadn't grown up, if he wasn't ready to be a responsible part of her life, then it was better not to set

Maddy up for disappointment. "I think it might be best if I tell her that you're an old friend of mine."

He snorted. "Hedging your bets in case I'm not a good influence?"

"Giving you an out, if you want it. My offer still stands. If at the end of two weeks you don't have any wish to be a part of Maddy's life, you can sign over custody and I'll raise her myself. I just wanted to give you an opportunity to step up." Peyton met his gaze head-on, not on the ridges of his chest, or the way his bathing suit hugged his hips. "Maddy needs someone she can count on, now more than ever. And that means if you're still dating everything with breasts and a smile, still driving a car meant for a sixteen-year-old and still working a job no more permanent than snow in North Carolina, then maybe you aren't the best choice to be in her life."

He took a step closer to her, so close she could feel the heat from his body. She could reach out and touch him, feel those hard muscles beneath her palm, trail a finger along that dark V that led to the parts of him the bathing suit kept hidden. Why hadn't that crush died long ago? Why did she still find the man attractive?

"If I'm so terrible, why do you want me around her?"

Her breath hitched a little and she cursed inwardly. "I never said you were terrible."

His smile tipped up on one side, and his eyes held that charm she remembered. "You're not the only one who's changed a lot since high school, Peyton."

"I'm counting on that, Luke. Your daughter is, too." She paused and squared her shoulders. Calm, cool, collected again, though with every second the heat simmering in his blue eyes made it exceptionally hard to maintain anything approaching cool and calm. "So, will you be there for Maddy? At least, for the next two weeks? Will you try?"

His gaze lifted over her head, to the swing a few dozen yards away. He didn't say anything for so long, she wondered if he was going to answer.

"Just little bits of time," Peyton said. "An hour here or there, maybe more if you're up to it. Nothing big. I don't..."

"Trust me with her."

"Well, no. She doesn't know you and I haven't seen you in almost five years."

"You know me. I'm not perfect, but I'm a decent man at my core, Peyton." His gaze locked on hers, and Peyton's heart stuttered again. "Trust me."

That was the hardest part. Trusting anyone with Maddy. Susannah had always been busy and scattered, flitting in and out of Maddy's life like a butterfly. Peyton was the one who had enrolled her in preschool, cut the crust off her sandwiches, enforced a bedtime, set all the doctor and dentist appointments. To let someone else control even five minutes of Maddy's life took a Herculean amount of trust.

Charlie crossed over to Peyton, nosing at her hand until she lifted it to scratch his ears. It almost seemed as if the dog remembered her, remembered that day they had found him. More than five years ago, she had been walking home from her part-time job with Luke—Susannah had ditched her promise to drive Peyton home and headed off with her girlfriends. Luke had offered to walk Peyton home. Along the way, they'd found this mutt, shivering and shaking and curled into a ball under a tree. No collar, no tags, nothing but skin and bones and big eyes. Luke had scooped the dog into his arms and carried him a mile back to his house and straight into the kitchen, ignoring his mother's protests.

Luke had fed the dog the steaks defrosting on the counter, then given him a bath in the second-floor tub. *We should call him Charlie, because he had an angel looking out for him,* Luke had said. Then he'd looked in Peyton's eyes, in that way he had of making her feel as if nothing else existed in the world but this man, this moment.

An angel? she had asked.

If you hadn't seen him, Charlie might not have lasted another day. He's lucky to have you in his life.

In that schoolgirl-crush way, she'd thought he was talking about more than just the dog. She'd been head over heels for Luke, her heart breaking a little every time she saw him with her sister. But the Luke she remembered, the same one who had let down her sister when she'd gotten pregnant, had no more permanence than wet tape. She didn't think that side of Luke had changed one bit—

But then there was the dog.

A dog required commitment. A home. A dependable adult.

Maybe Luke could handle Maddy. It was only two weeks, after all. A blip in time.

A test...

Was she really basing her decisions for Maddy on a *dog*, for Pete's sake?

But what choice did she have? Maddy needed time, love and connection, and there was no better person to do that than the man who shared her DNA. Peyton had done her best, but even she had to admit her best might not be enough. Maybe spending time with Luke, with the man who had once loved her mother, would allow Maddy to heal.

And at the end of the two weeks, if Luke still wanted to be part of Maddy's life, Peyton could make arrangements. Call up a lawyer, draw up a plan.

"I'll do it," Luke said, "but on one condition."

Her gaze narrowed. "What?"

"I'm not going to be Uncle Luke or Friend Luke or anything else. I'm Dad. So you better figure out a way to tell my kid she has a father, and also that I'm not going anywhere two weeks from now. Or ever."

Chapter Two

Two hours later, Luke sat in a lounge chair in the shade of the lanai roof at the back of his rental house, nursing a beer that should have taken the edge off his hangover, but instead churned in his stomach. Across from him there were splashes and laughter and bawdy jokes, but he stayed where he was, feeling older than dirt.

A kid. *He* had a *kid.*

He let the thought settle over him, but it didn't become any more real or concrete. He'd seen the photo of Madelyne, seen his eyes in her wide blue ones, but still couldn't compute him + Susannah = Kid.

Being a parent meant being responsible. Growing up. Stepping off the hamster wheel of parties and hangovers. Considering he had a party going on right in front of him while he was still battling the hangover from yesterday, Luke Barlow clearly wasn't stepping off that hamster wheel anytime soon.

Except a part of him had been growing weary of the life he'd been leading, had been for some time. The problem was whether he was ready to change. Or if he was even capable of change.

Change like agreeing to spend time with a four-year-old? It didn't sound hard—what did a four-year-old do anyway?—but it sounded like something better suited for a relative or a good friend or someone other than Luke. Someone with experience. Someone who knew what to do when a kid cried or fell down.

Except he was Maddy's *father*. A father should know what to do. A father should have no problem spending time with his daughter.

A father who hadn't known he was a father until Peyton showed up on his doorstep. From the minute she started speaking, the world had dropped away. Part of it was the bomb she'd exploded in his life, part of it was Peyton herself.

Hell, he hadn't even recognized her at first. Gone was the geeky girl who had tagged along with him and Susannah. The girl who more often than not carried a book in her backpack and buried her nose in the pages every spare second. That girl had turned into a beautiful woman, the kind who stopped traffic, made a man forget every coherent thought in his head.

And lingered in his mind long after she had pulled out of his driveway.

Peyton had always had this way about her, an air his mother had called it, that wrapped people in a spell. Okay, maybe not people. Maybe just him. Because today he'd agreed to the one thing a man like him should never do—

To be a responsible role model and parent. Ha. Luke had his position in the family—sandwiched between his military hero younger brother and his overachieving CEO elder brother—serving as the family screwup. Yeah, he'd been good at sports, but he'd never been good enough to become a star player, the way Jack had been a leader in the military or the big-bucks moneymaker Mac was. Maybe it was because Luke hadn't found his niche, his place in the world. Or maybe it was because he was no good at doing responsible or role model or anything even close.

He'd tried, once. Tried to be the kind of guy someone else could rely on.

And he'd screwed it up. Royally. No one talked about the fallout from that day, the accident that had left Jeremiah in a wheelchair. Nowadays, Jeremiah rarely left his house, rarely returned Luke's texts, rarely did anything other than play video games in the dark and wait for his life to unwind.

Damn.

Luke twirled the beer in his hands, but didn't drink. The weight on his shoulders hung too heavy for him to do anything other than sit there and wonder if Peyton had made a huge mistake in bringing a kid into his life.

Not a kid. His own child. His *daughter*.

Ben Carver plopped down into the seat beside Luke, clutching a nearly empty beer, his hair wet from the pool. Ben grinned, and the gesture lightened the heavy air around Luke. Friends for almost all their lives, Luke and Ben had been named Most Likely to Cut Class in high school, gone on more adventures in twenty-six years than most people went on in eighty and served as each other's wingman almost every night of the week. They were bachelors—and damned good at it, if you asked anyone in Stone Gap. If there were ever two men in this town least likely to grow up, it would have been Luke and Ben.

Except now Luke had a child, and that changed things. A lot.

"You going to sit there all day or join the party?" Ben said. "There are some hot girls waiting for you to join them in the pool. Actually, they're waiting for me, but they said you could tag along. Pity dates."

"Yeah." Luke tipped his beer in the direction of Tiffany and Marcia and...Beth? Barbara? He couldn't remember. There were three other women in the pool, and two other guys Luke had known since high school. A typical Sunday afternoon at Luke's house, a small rental he'd had for about a year now. He should have been enjoying himself. Should have been in that pool, living it up with Beth/Barbara/whatever her name was. But his mind kept straying back to Peyton, back to the earnest intent in her eyes, to the obvious protectiveness she felt for Madelyne and, most of all, to the way Peyton had dropped a detour into his life. "Nah. Got a lot on my mind."

"Dude, it's Sunday. Party day. Not the time to think about anything other than Coors or Yuengling."

Luke propped his elbows on his knees, let the beer bottle dangle from his fingers. "You ever think we're too old for this? That maybe it's about time we grew up?"

"What is wrong with you? Hell no, we're not too old for this. When your AARP card comes in the mail, then *maybe* it might be time to grow up."

Luke smiled, but the gesture felt flat. "Jeremiah might disagree."

"Jesus, Luke. What the hell is wrong with you? Why'd you go and bring that crap up?"

Luke saw his own reflection in the mirror of Ben's sunglasses. The image seemed distorted, small, as if there was a lot more Luke could do to be a bigger presence. "Just thinking through my life choices, that's all."

"Well, that isn't going to get you anywhere but depressed. And that doesn't work on party day." Ben clinked his bottle against Luke's. "So come on, have another beer and let's go join our hot friends."

Luke glanced over at the others. "You go. I'm going into town. Pick up some snacks and beer."

"We have plenty—"

But Luke was already out of his seat and heading into the house. He left the full beer on the countertop, threw on a T-shirt, then climbed into his Jeep and headed toward downtown Stone Gap. He didn't need to go to the store. Didn't need to do a damned thing today except mow the lawn, but for some reason, he couldn't stay in that lounge chair for one more second.

All he could think about was his daughter. With her blond ringlets and blue eyes and a wide, toothy smile.

She still didn't feel any more real. He needed to know, to see, to really believe. Luke drove for twenty minutes, passing through downtown Stone Gap, turning right at Gator's Garage, closed on Sunday, as it had been for the past forty years, then another left and a right before he realized where he had ended up.

The Stone Gap Hotel sat atop a tiny hill a few blocks outside town. The white wood clapboard building wasn't doing much to live up to its name, considering it held about twenty rooms and room service was provided by Tony's Pizza across the street, but it was the only thing Stone Gap had for out-of-towners, and this, Luke figured, was where Peyton would be staying. Peyton's mother, long divorced, had died a few years back, and that meant Peyton had no real family left in town, so the hotel was the most logical choice.

Luke tried to imagine that—a loss of the family that had surrounded him since birth. Two brothers, a mother, father, numerous aunts and uncles and cousins, a whole army of family at every holiday and gathering. Peyton had always been part of the little Reynolds crew of three, and now two of those three were gone.

Except for Madelyne, her niece. Susannah's daughter. *His* daughter. A connection between two families, one big and boisterous, one so tiny it almost didn't exist.

He parked, got out of the car and headed up to the front desk. The blonde behind the desk smiled when he entered the air-conditioned office. Karen Fleming had been a year behind Luke in high school and had dated half the football team—but not Luke. Something Karen tried to rectify every time she saw him.

"Why, if it isn't Luke Barlow here to brighten my day." She flashed him a broad smile and leaned over the counter, a move which brought the tops of her breasts into view. Any other day, Luke might have flirted back, but not today.

"Is Peyton staying here?" he asked.

Karen pouted. "And I thought you were here to see me."

"Peyton?" Luke prompted again.

Karen sighed. "Room ten. Down the hall and on the right. What's she doing back in town anyway?"

Luke was already heading away from the front desk. The maroon-and-gold-carpeted hall muffled his footsteps as he passed the other faux oak doors and stopped before room ten, his stomach doing backflips.

Sorry, Peyton, I'm not father material.

He shifted his weight. Tried another tack in his head.

Sorry, Peyton, but I can't do this. I'm...busy.

Oh, yeah, that sounded even better. Just a simple *Sorry, Peyton, I can't* was all he should say. Except that sounded empty, too. None of the three options captured what he really wanted to say—

No way, no how, do I want to be responsible for a kid that I didn't know I had; a kid I have no idea how to connect with; a kid who is a mystery to me.

A kid who has no other living parent but me.

Well, hell. That was the truth, right there. Madelyne had no one but him, and her aunt. If he didn't step up, then, for all intents and purposes, as Peyton had said, this child would be an orphan.

How could he possibly say no?

He raised his hand, but the door opened before he could knock, and the four-year-old from the photo came barreling out and straight into him. He let out an *oomph*.

"Sowwy," she said, backing up and sending Peyton an uncertain glance.

And in that moment, there was no doubt. He could see his eyes, Susannah's high cheekbones, in Madelyne's face. She could have been a carbon copy of their baby pictures.

This was his daughter. The thought settled into him, not as foreign now.

"Madelyne, don't run—" Peyton stopped in the doorway. Her eyes widened. "Luke. What are you doing here?"

"I…uh…" His brain cells misfired when he took in what Peyton was wearing. Earlier today, it had been a soft peach dress that swirled around her legs, with low heels, and her straight blond hair down around her shoulders. But in the interim, she had changed into a dark green two-piece bathing suit and one of those knitted cover-up things that seemed designed to entice a man with flashes of skin and swimsuit. Her hair was swept up into a clip, with a few tendrils tickling against her long, elegant neck. Holy hell, Peyton Reynolds had grown up. And done it well.

He cleared his throat, refocused his mind on why he had come here. "I wanted to talk to you."

She put a protective hand on her niece. Madelyne stepped back, ducking her head and pressing her body against Peyton's leg. Madelyne turned big blue eyes—the same eyes Luke saw in the mirror every morning—up toward the stranger at the door.

Her eyes widened and she shrank farther behind Peyton. Damn. The kid was scared of him. She didn't know him.

And whose fault is that? a little voice whispered in his head.

That was the moment that cemented it for Luke. He might suck at being a father, might have just found out he even *was* a father, but no way was he going to let another four years go by with his kid thinking he was a scary stranger.

Peyton gave Madelyne a reassuring squeeze. "This is not a good time, Luke. We were just heading for the pool."

Not that he'd expected some instant bond just because he and the kid shared some DNA. But her wide-eyed trepidation made him feel like an interloper.

If he had a snowball's chance in hell of changing the look in Madelyne's eyes, then he better start now. "How about I join you?"

Surprise colored Peyton's features. "Don't you have other things on your agenda today?"

The way she said *other things* almost sounded as if she was jealous. Which was impossible, considering he and Peyton had never been involved, never been anything more than friends.

"Not anymore," Luke said, though he was pretty sure the party would go on, with or without him. Seeing Peyton now, in that teeny-tiny bikini partially hidden by the knit dress, made whatever was happening back at Luke's house seem very, very far away. To his recollection he had never seen her wearing a bikini before. And it made him realize that Peyton Reynolds had some very nice curves.

Peyton gave him a dubious glance. "Okay. Let me grab another towel." Maddy followed her, as close as an extra leg.

"Auntie P, who's that man?"

Peyton, her hand halfway to the towel, turned and looked at Luke. Her eyes were wide and scared, like Madelyne's had been a second ago. The look said *Don't upset this little girl's world. She's been through enough.*

He wanted to tell his daughter the truth, but some instinct deep in his gut said springing the fatherhood connection on a preschooler wasn't the best choice. What was it that Peyton had said? Maddy had had enough uncertainty for now.

It would upset her world, and that was the last thing he wanted to do. He might not be good at being a father, might not have the slightest clue where to start with a child he didn't even know, but he knew this much—dropping that shocking news into the life of a kid who'd just suffered a major loss would be a stupid move on his part.

She needed get to know him first, and he needed to get comfortable with the idea of being a dad. He thought of his own father, of the impromptu wrestling matches in the living room; the way Bobby Barlow had cheered for each of his boys at every sporting event, all the times he'd taken them fishing or showed them how to fix a broken gate. *That* was being a dad. Walking into a room and announcing fatherhood was not. Right now, the truth was, he wasn't a dad at all; he was just the sperm donor.

And as scary as it seemed, a part of him wanted to change that.

"I'm a friend of your mom's and your aunt's," Luke said, taking a step into the room. Relief flooded Peyton's features. "Just a friend."

He bent down and put out a hand. "I'm Luke."

Madelyne slid her tiny hand into Luke's, her fingers as delicate as twigs. But she had a firm grip and her gaze was direct and assessing. It was weird, Luke thought, holding the hand of this tiny person who was half him.

"I'm Madelyne," she said. "I'm almost four."

"Nice to meet you, Madelyne." He shook hands with her, then gave her a grin that he hoped spelled trustworthy and friendly. "Is it okay if I go swimming with you?"

Madelyne bit her lip. Behind her, Peyton did the same, probably completely unaware she was mimicking her niece. There was a hushed anticipation in the air, a sense of worry and fear, and Luke got the feeling that this moment would set the tone for what was to come.

"I dunno." She cocked her head, sending a few of those curls springing off her shoulder. "Do you like doggies?"

The non sequitur caught him off guard. "Uh, yeah, sure. I love doggies. Even have one of my own. His name is Charlie."

That made her brighten a little. "Can he come swimmin' wif us?"

"I didn't bring him today, but if you come over to my house, you can see him. Would you like to come over sometime? With your aunt, of course." He felt as nervous as a teenager waiting on Madelyne's answer. Here he was, asking his own daughter, whose bright pink cheeks made her look like a porcelain doll, if she wanted to come over.

If Madelyne said no, or shied away again, Luke would take it as a sign. Back away and leave her in the undoubtedly highly capable hands of Peyton.

Madelyne toed at the carpet, then met his gaze with her own. Her eyes were dark pools, unreadable and still. "You promise? I can play with the doggy? I love doggies. They're so furry and soft and they give kisses and eat cookies and play lots."

"I promise you can play with Charlie. Cross my heart." Luke made the gesture across his chest, and for a second, he was four again himself, swearing allegiance to some pact he'd made with his brothers. *Cross my heart and hope to die,* they'd said back then, in that cavalier way of kids who thought the world lasted forever and mothers never died too young. "Sound good?"

A tentative smile filled Madelyne's face, and to Luke, that smile felt a lot like winning the lottery. "Okay."

A second later, the three of them were heading down the hall. *Like a family,* he thought, though they were far from any such thing. He was still the stranger, uninvited at that, tagging along on the visit to the pool.

"Well, you clearly passed her test," Peyton said.

"I think the kid grades on a bell curve."

Peyton laughed. "Maddy's pretty easy to please, most days. Plus, she figures anyone who loves dogs is okay. That's her big criteria for everyone she meets."

"I'm lucky she sets the bar low." He tossed Peyton a grin. She returned it, and the dark, threadbare hall seemed brighter for a moment.

"Charlie to the rescue again," she said. "That dog is quite the miracle worker, and he doesn't even know it."

"That he is." Luke's gaze went down the corridor, but his mind reached into the past. To the days after he'd found Charlie, the dark days that haunted Luke still, when he would sneak Charlie into his room at night and whisper his regrets into the mutt's caramel-colored fur. The dog would lean against him and listen, patient and true.

"Honestly, I think that dog saved me rather than the other way around." The admission slipped from Luke's lips before he could stop it.

"What do you—" Peyton's question was cut off when Madelyne dashed ahead, reeling back when Peyton called out to her to take it easy, to walk instead of run. Dash, slow, dash, slow. It was like watching a yo-yo.

Luke turned to Peyton. "She always this hyper?"

Peyton laughed. "Hyper? Honey, this isn't hyper. This is normal."

Something inside him tripped at the word *honey*. He knew it was an offhand comment, a word Peyton probably hadn't even realized she'd said. He shook it off. He was here to figure out how he was going to be a father to a kid he never knew he had, not get wrapped up in the way Peyton looked or the words she used.

Madelyne started skipping from diamond to diamond on the patterned rug while she sang a rhyming song about a whale and a lemon. She was wearing a pink-and-white polka-dot one-piece swimsuit with a ruffled skirt, matching sandals, and even had pink ribbons tied in bows around the twin braids in her hair. She seemed awfully dressed up just to get in the pool. Reason number five hundred and seventy-two why Luke wasn't going to be very good at this fatherhood thing. He couldn't braid hair or tie ribbons or color-coordinate shoes and bathing suits.

But the more he looked, the more he could see himself in her eyes, her mannerisms. He saw Susannah in Maddy's impish smile, in the way she danced down the hall. No doubt—this was his daughter.

"I gotta warn you, I have zero experience with kids," Luke said. "I could screw this up without thinking twice."

Peyton shot him a smile. "You'll be fine. Spending time with a four-year-old can be challenging, but it's also not as hard as you think. I'll be right there the whole time, ready to give you plenty of instructions and worried-auntie input."

He watched the girl stop and twirl in the hall, spinning and spinning and spinning while she went on and on about the whale and the lemon, and their new friend, a lime. Those braids spun out from Madelyne's head, loosening a ribbon. Without missing a beat, Peyton stepped forward, retied the bow and sent Madelyne on her way.

Maddy pushed on the door handle, flooding the hall with sunlight. "Wait, wait," Peyton said, running up to Madelyne and putting a cautionary hand on the little girl's shoulder. "Remember, you can't just run out there. You need to take Auntie P's hand."

"But I'm a big girl," Madelyne said. "I can walk."

"Uh-huh. I'm sure you can. But it's slippery around the pool."

Luke watched Madelyne slide her hand into Peyton's and realized he would have never thought to hold the kid's hand when they were near the pool. Heck, he probably wouldn't even have stopped her from running in the halls. All clear signs that he would be a terrible babysitter. An even worse father. Was that even something he could learn? Was there a Dummies book he could read overnight? Or was he better off just staying clear of this whirling, busy girl?

What if something happened to her? What if she ran into the street or tried to climb on the countertop? What if he wasn't as attentive as he should be? Things could happen when he looked away, he knew that too well. The conviction that he could handle this—handle his own child—began to slip. "Peyton, we should talk."

"Can it wait a minute? I've been promising Maddy that she could go swimming all day and we only have an hour until I need to feed her lunch."

"Uh, okay."

Peyton led Madelyne outside, then pulled some kind of blown-up triangular things out of the bag on her arm and slipped them onto Madelyne's forearms. Madelyne flopped her arms and giggled. "I's ready now."

"Okay, give me a second." Peyton reached down and tugged the hem of the white knit dress, sliding it off her body and tucking it into the bag.

Luke swallowed hard. Holy hell, Peyton looked good. Amazing, in fact. She filled out the dark green fabric of the bikini in a perfect hourglass. He had to force himself not to let his jaw drop, or to say any of the numerous stupid things a man could say when standing beside a beautiful woman in a bikini.

Peyton took Madelyne's hand and led her toward the pool. The little girl lingered on the top step, her eyes wide and worried again. Peyton kept going, the bottom half of her body disappearing into the shallow end.

Luke pulled off his t-shirt and tossed it, along with his car keys and wallet, onto an empty chair, then slipped into the pool beside Peyton. "Water's a bit cold."

Peyton grinned. "Are you saying the big, strapping football captain is feeling a little wimpy?"

"Not at all." Though he was feeling a little pleased that she'd called him big and strapping. Jeez. He really needed to start thinking with the parts of his brain that existed above his waist.

"Come on, Maddy girl. Your turn." Peyton put out her arms.

Madelyne stood on the first step, water swirling around her ankles. "I just stay here, Auntie P."

"Come on, you can swim with me. I'll hold on to you. You'll be safe and snug as a bug in a rug."

Madelyne shook her head and toed at the water. "I just stay here."

"You can do it, sweetie pie. I know you can."

Madelyne dropped onto the edge of the pool and swished her feet back and forth, creating little ripples. Her mood had shifted into reserved and distant, her shoulders tensed. "I just stay here," she repeated.

Peyton sighed. "Are you sure? Because Luke and I are having fun in the water." Peyton sat back, sweeping her hands back and forth. She arched a brow in Luke's direction. "Aren't we?"

"Oh, yeah, uh, sure." He did the same as Peyton, but felt like an idiot pretending to have fun in the shallow end. He forced a grin to his face even though the water was about ten degrees too cold. "Lots of fun."

"Swimming is awesome, Maddy. And the water is warm." She glanced at Luke.

"Yeah, warm."

"A little enthusiasm, Mr. De Niro," Peyton whispered to him.

He widened his grin. "It's super warm!"

Peyton shook her head and bit back a laugh. "You are hopeless. Don't quit your day job."

Madelyne just kicked her feet back and forth, watching the adults make fools of themselves. "I just stay here. I swim next time, Auntie P."

Sadness flickered across Peyton's face, then she smiled. "Okay, sweetie. That's fine."

"She doesn't swim?" Luke asked.

Peyton shook her head, then lowered her voice. "She's

scared of the water. I don't know where she got that from because Susannah and I loved the water."

He remembered. A lot of his best memories centered around those times at the lake with Susannah and Peyton. Those were the best summers he could remember, before his life had taken a left turn he hadn't seen coming. "That summer of senior year, I swear the three of us spent every single day at the lake. Me and Susannah and…" He flicked some water at Peyton. "Tagalong."

Her cheeks colored at the old nickname. "It was just because there wasn't anyone my age at the lake that summer."

"Jack and Mac were there."

"Your brothers?" Peyton snorted. "They were always busy. Jack, off hanging with his own friends and Meri's family. As for Mac, he never wanted anything to do with any of us. I swear, Mac was born an adult."

Luke laughed. "Very true."

Then he sobered, because he thought of how long Mac had been gone, how his older brother's absence had created a vacuum in the family. When they were kids, Jack, Luke and Mac had been the three musketeers, as their mother dubbed them, in trouble more often than not. But as they got older, Mac became the serious one, the determined one. He'd worry over his grades, obsess over every word in an essay, work harder and more than anyone else to keep the T's crossed and the I's dotted. He'd been the one who butted heads with their parents the most, the one who thumbed his nose at curfews and rules. The black sheep with the straight As, which made it awful hard to justify grounding him. The minute he was old enough to leave, Mac headed out of Stone Gap, his returns on par with sightings of Halley's Comet.

Luke glanced over at Madelyne, sitting on the step,

prancing a Barbie doll around the edge of the pool. She was his daughter, though he didn't feel a single thread of emotional connection to what was, essentially, a child stranger. He could see their link in her features, in the way she cocked her head to study him, in the offbeat way she assessed people's worth. In those ways, they were alike. And maybe he was hoping for too much, expecting some instant bond.

Madelyne, he realized, had a hole in her life now, too. One that was never going to be filled by a quick visit at Christmas, a few checks here and there. What was it the statisticians said? Kids raised with a strong male and female role model did better. They were happier, more grounded. Madelyne clearly already had a strong role model in Peyton, but Luke—

Well, no one was holding him up as an example of what to be when you grew up.

"So, what does this spending-time-with-Madelyne thing entail?" Luke asked. *"Exactly."*

Peyton grinned. "Don't look so panicked."

He waved a hand. "Does this face say panicked?"

She took a step closer to him, swirling water around their hips. She feigned deep scrutiny, peering into his eyes. Her perfume, something light and airy, wafted in the space between them. "Terrified."

"Me? I'm only terrified of anacondas and great white sharks. Not kids."

That made Peyton laugh. He'd never noticed her laugh before, but decided he liked the sound of it. "Wait till she's having a complete meltdown because she wants to eat cake for dinner or stay up past her bedtime or buy that six-foot teddy bear at the mall. Then we'll see how the big, brave bachelor reacts."

"I'll be fine," he said, speaking with a confidence he

didn't feel. Hell, he could barely take care of himself. And the thought of being responsible for another person—

Damn.

"I'll be fine," he repeated, more for himself than Peyton.

The tease dropped from Peyton's features. Her voice sobered. "You better be, Luke. A kid isn't a watch you can return to the store because it doesn't match your suit."

"If you haven't noticed, I don't wear a watch or own a suit." He tossed her a grin, slipping into the familiar role of class flirt. "And I'm still a big kid myself."

"*That* particular fact I noticed."

For some strange reason, the fact that Peyton had noticed anything at all about him made Luke smile. Years ago, he'd barely known she existed, except as a thorn in his side when he'd been trying to be alone with Susannah. But now, standing in the water with this older, sexier, more intriguing Peyton—

"Auntie P? Can I play with my other dolls now?"

"Sure, sure." Peyton strode out of the pool, reaching for Madelyne as the little girl was heading for the table where Peyton had placed their things. "Wait, let me get the bag for you."

Luke's gaze followed the cascade of water running down Peyton's back, over her buttocks, down her shapely legs. There were a few things that improved with age. Cheddar cheese. Red wine. And Peyton Reynolds.

He reminded himself he wasn't here for Peyton or for anything other than his daughter. He was trying to be responsible, for once in his life, and being responsible didn't include lusting after his kid's aunt.

He was a father now, whether he was ready or not,

and that meant being a whole other person than the one he had been for the past twenty-six years. He could only pray he didn't screw it up.

Chapter Three

Peyton woke up on Monday morning with her stomach in knots. She lay in the hotel bed, staring up at the white popcorn ceiling for a good ten minutes before she heard Madelyne stirring beside her. Ever since Susannah's death, Maddy had slept curled up against Peyton, one hand on Peyton's arm, as if she was afraid she, too, would disappear.

Peyton placed a gentle kiss on Maddy's temple, then lay against the pillows and did what she always did before putting that first foot on the floor—she ran through a quick mental to-do list, setting goals and ticking off tasks. The activity almost always energized her for the day ahead, infused her with that can-do spirit that had fueled her rise in one of the biggest interior design firms in Baltimore.

Today, though, lying there with a sleeping Maddy tucked beside her, the image of innocence, that to-do list was short and empty, sending a rising tide of panic through Peyton's stomach.

Two days ago, Peyton had been sitting in her boss's office, listening to him tell her that she had screwed up on a big job—missed an important deadline—and that she needed to get her act together if she hoped to stay at Winston Interior Design. "Take two weeks off," he'd said, "get some reliable child care in place, a maid to do the laundry and a priority list that puts your job back at the top, and then come back."

In other words, quit running out of the office because Maddy had a meltdown at preschool. Stop coming in late because Maddy hadn't wanted to eat breakfast or get dressed. Quit leaving early because Maddy had been crying on the phone when Peyton called to check on her.

Not to mention how the added responsibilities and worries had taken a toll on Peyton's sleeping and eating habits. She was a walking zombie at best most days. As much as she needed the sleep, the break, the mere thought of a day that stretched long and empty scared her. They had the trip to the zoo, then lunch, then a trip to the playground, dinner, bath, followed by the endless hours after Maddy fell asleep and Peyton lay in bed, thinking. Thinking far too much.

From the day the police had come to the door with their long faces and somber tones, Peyton had worried ten times more about Maddy than she ever had before. How would Peyton make this work? Would she be a good mother? A strong role model? Had she made the right choice coming here? Or would these days in Stone Gap make Maddy withdraw even more?

Peyton stared at the ceiling, her heart heavy, her chest tight. *Suzie, why did you leave her with me? I'm not a mom. I don't always know the right thing to do.*

Susannah had been a distracted mother at best, one who seemed perpetually in need of money or help, but she had loved her daughter fiercely, and Peyton always believed that when it came down to the wire, her sister would put Maddy above everything else. In the end, Susannah hadn't had the chance.

Now Luke had a chance to step up and be a parent, but Peyton worried he would let her down—and worse, let Maddy down. If there was one thing Maddy desperately needed, it was structure, stability. Luke had never been the kind of guy who built fences and planted vegetable gardens and ate dinner at six.

She needed to remember that when she met Luke at the zoo in a little while, and not delude herself into thinking that just because the man was handsome, and seeing him caused a little flutter in Peyton's gut, that the three of them were forming some kind of happy little family. She was doing all this for her niece—not to resurrect some silly teenage crush.

All Peyton wanted was to help Maddy become a happy little girl again. Stone Gap was the best place Peyton knew of for Maddy. Here, where the town sprawled among the lush green landscape, there were memories in the streets and the houses. Memories of Susannah, of Peyton, and a foundation for Maddy, who had stood on shifting sand for far too long.

Staying in bed wasn't going to get her any closer to that goal, so Peyton got up, got ready, then woke Madelyne. "After breakfast, we're going to the zoo with my friend Luke," Peyton said, as she tugged Madelyne's nightgown over her head and helped her slip into shorts and a T-shirt.

"Are you gonna be there, Auntie P?"

Peyton nodded. "I sure am."

"The whole time?"

"Every single second." Peyton paused in helping Maddy dress to hold her arms and grab her attention. "I promise."

Relief washed over Maddy's features. "Is there gonna be monkeys at the zoo?"

"Monkeys and lions and giraffes," Peyton said, lifting one of Maddy's legs to slip on a sock, then repeated with the other foot. "And one very pesky monkey in particular." She tapped a finger on Maddy's nose, and the little girl almost—*almost*—giggled.

"I's not a monkey, Auntie P. I's a big girl."

Peyton pretended it didn't bother her that the jokes that used to make Maddy smile had lost their touch, that Maddy's sparkle had gone as flat as a pancake. *Time,* the psychologist had said. *Time will help.* How much time was the question that bothered Peyton in those dark moments late at night when she was struggling to be sure she was doing the right thing. "Go get your shoes on, monkey, and we'll go to breakfast. We have to be at the zoo at nine-thirty."

Maddy, of course, couldn't tell time yet and had no idea if it was nine-thirty or five-thirty. But Peyton liked having the schedule, liked saying it out loud, as if putting the numbers in the air would cement the plan in place. When things ran on time and as planned, it gave Peyton room to breathe.

So at eight-twenty, they left the cozy room at the Stone Gap Hotel, took Peyton's car to downtown Stone Gap and walked into The Good Eatin' Café, pretty much the only breakfast choice in town. The second the door opened, Peyton regretted her choice. Stone Gap was a small town with long memories and gossipy residents. All she needed was someone recounting Susannah's wild past in front of Maddy.

"Oh, you cute little button!" Vivian Hoffman, the owner of the diner, came bustling around the counter, a petite gray-haired woman who had worked at The Good Eatin' Café for so long, Peyton figured she had to be close to a hundred, though she moved at the speed of people half her age. Vivian bent down in front of Maddy. "What's your name, sweetheart?"

"Madelyne." She drew herself up. "Madelyne Reynolds."

"Oh, what a cutie. And as serious as a judge in church." Vivian put out her hand and gave Maddy's a little shake. "Pleased to make your acquaintance, Miss Madelyne. I'm Miss Viv, and if you need anything at all, you just let Miss Viv know and I'll get it from the kitchen."

"Can I have pancakes that look like cookies?"

"She means chocolate chip pancakes," Peyton explained.

"Oh my, of course you can, sweetheart." Miss Viv's smile crinkled her eyes. "Why, we make the best cookie-looking pancakes in all of North Carolina. How about some chocolate milk to go with that, too? With one of those crazy bendy straws?"

Maddy started to say yes, but Peyton put a hand on her shoulder. "Apple juice will be fine, Miss Viv. Thank you."

Vivian looked at Peyton now, really looked at her. "You're the younger Reynolds girl, aren't you? Peyton?"

"Yes, ma'am," she said, as if she was still a child and trying on her best manners in front of Grandma Lucy.

"And this adorable angel is your little girl?"

"No, she's my niece."

"Niece? That means Susannah…" Her voice trailed off and she dropped her gaze to Maddy's blond curls. "Well, I'll be. And I thought I knew 'bout everything that happened in this town." Miss Viv brightened and put an arm around Peyton, drawing her deeper into the diner and steering her toward a booth that overlooked a shady corner of the park next door. "Best table in the house, though that busybody Mort Williams will say otherwise."

From the far corner of the laminate bar that fronted the kitchen, Mort, a gray-haired man with a hunched back who owned the Page In Time Bookstore a block away, raised his cup of coffee in Miss Viv's direction. He had a book in his hands now, a leather-bound volume. Probably a classic he'd read a hundred times before, if Peyton remembered correctly. "Howdy, Peyton," he said, raising his book in her direction. "Stop on by the bookstore while you're in town."

"I sure will," Peyton said. "I think I spent more time there than at home when I was young." The bookstore had been her escape, a quiet place with cozy chairs, where she could read and get away from the roller coaster that had been her childhood. An alcoholic mother, a never-present father and two girls who had few, if any, rules or expectations meant Peyton could count on nothing but the happy endings she found in the books she read.

"Looking forward to seeing you." Mort smiled. "And though that booth Miss Viv gave you is good, if you ask me, the best seat in the house is this one. Lets me watch all the comings and goings."

Miss Viv leaned in toward Peyton. "He likes to think himself the town gossip. I told him Anna May Robicheaux has had that job for going on ninety-one years and given her constitution, she's not giving up her title anytime soon. Would that she did, because Mort here is near as old as Methuselah himself."

"It's your coffee keeping me young, Miss Viv," Mort said, hoisting said mug again for a refill. "That and your sweet smile."

"That man is far too old to flirt. Goodness. Now, you two sit right here," Miss Viv said, reaching over to pluck two menus from a vacant table and lay them before Peyton and Maddy. "Tell me what you want, Peyton, and I'll get it started right quick."

"Uh…just coffee, please."

Vivian waved that off. "You can't start your day with just coffee! You'd, like, about die from starvation before ten. 'Sides, I can't let anyone leave the Good Eatin' Café saying Miss Viv didn't fill their bellies from the bottom up." She stepped back, put a finger on her chin and studied Peyton. "Let's see if I can remember your favorite order."

"Oh, Miss Viv," Peyton began, "it's been at least ten years since I've eaten here with my grandma and—"

"Two eggs, sunny-side up, not too hard, not too soft. With a side of pancakes, and extra syrup."

Miss Viv had nailed her order, as easily as if the last time Peyton had been here had been last week, instead of over a decade. "That's…that's exactly it."

The older woman patted Peyton's hand. "I never forget a customer, especially one as pretty and nice as you." Then she bustled away toward the kitchen, sending over one of her waitresses to give Peyton a hot cup of coffee.

Maddy settled in the booth, dwarfed by the red leather back. "Auntie P, how's come that lady knows you?"

"I used to come here when I was a little girl with my grandma. I sat at that stool right there." She pointed toward the one in the middle of the bar, wondering if it still squeaked when you turned right. "And we'd have our Sunday-morning breakfast here."

Maddy considered that for a while, taking in the seat, the covered platter of sugar-dusted doughnuts beside the glass cookie jar raising money for a local boy whose beaming face filled a photo on the front, then lifted her gaze to Peyton's. "Do I have a grandma like that, Auntie P? Can she bring me here on Sundays, too?"

Peyton started to say no. Peyton's grandmother Lucy, the one who Peyton could run to for cuts and bruises and happy moments, had died when Peyton was eleven. And Peyton's own mother...

She'd never been the motherly type, much less the grandmother type, even after Maddy had been born. Three years ago, Peyton's mother had died of cirrhosis. The girls had never known their father, so if there were paternal grandparents, Peyton had never met them.

But there was another woman, another grandma, who would take one look at Maddy and spoil her rotten for all the days of her life. The kind of grandma who would take her for chocolate chip pancakes every Sunday and go to all her school plays and exclaim over every hand-made lumpy clay ashtray.

Peyton knew that, because she knew that woman well. Luke's mother, Della, the one woman in Stone Gap who Peyton had wished was her mother from the minute she met her.

Maddy was still watching her, waiting for an answer. If Peyton told her the truth, Maddy would want to meet Della. If Peyton lied, it would be one more blow to a little girl who'd already had too many.

"Yes, Maddy, you have a grandma like that."

A smile, a genuine, joyful smile as bright as a June day, bloomed on Maddy's face. "Does she know I like pancakes that look like cookies? Does she know I'm al-most four? Does she know I can count to a hun-red all by myself?"

Damn. How to answer these questions without telling Maddy everything? "She doesn't yet, but she will, when you meet her."

"When am I gonna meet her? Is she coming to my house? Is she gonna make me cupcakes like Kayleigh's grandma? Cuz she makes cupcakes all the time and puts sprinkles on them and they're really yummy."

"I don't know when you'll meet her," Peyton said. The waitress came by and laid plates of food before them. Peyton thanked her, then nudged Maddy's plate closer to her niece, hoping to shift the conversation away from a comparison of Maddy's friend Kayleigh's grandma and her own. "Why don't you eat your breakfast, so we can go to the zoo?"

"I don't wanna go to the zoo. I wanna see my new grandma."

"We can't right now, sweetie. But...soon."

"When?"

"I..." Peyton sighed. "I don't know. Just eat, please."

Despite much cajoling on Peyton's part, Maddy only picked at her chocolate chip pancakes and took two sips of her juice. She kept her eyes down, her hair swinging like a curtain over them. The bright mood evaporated.

Why had Peyton brought her to Stone Gap? Why had she brought Luke into Maddy's life? All it had done so far was complicate things and open up questions that Peyton wished she didn't have to answer. She never should have mentioned Della or told Maddy that she had another grandparent. Two, in fact, who would probably love nothing more than to spoil Maddy with love and kisses.

This little girl deserved that—deserved those moments when the world was full of sunshine, those brief snippets that Peyton herself had enjoyed on the rare weekends when she had stayed at Grandma Lucy's—but bringing Della and Bobby into Maddy's life meant exposing Luke as Maddy's father. Creating a permanent bond with the man and his family.

Was that what Peyton wanted? What was best all around?

Peyton slid her plate to the side, the food mostly untouched. Maddy did the same, with even less of her food consumed. "Come on, sweetie, eat some more. Aren't you hungry?"

Maddy shook her head. "I don't wanna. I wanna go home."

"We're going to the zoo today. We can go back to the hotel later."

Maddy looked as though she wanted to argue, but instead she just nodded. The acquiescing, resolute and sad Maddy that so worried Peyton had returned.

"Well, we need to go if we want to get to the zoo on time." Peyton dropped a few bills on the table for the tip, then waved a thank-you at Miss Viv as they left. Maddy dutifully fell into place beside Peyton, taking Peyton's hand as they went back to the car, but the spark was gone from her niece's face.

Even when they pulled up to the zoo, located a few miles from Stone Gap in a nearby city, Maddy didn't seem any more excited to go. Peyton parked, exchanged her purse for an easier-to-carry backpack, then unbuckled Maddy. She looked around the still-empty parking lot—the zoo opened at nine-thirty and had yet to fill with patrons—but didn't see Luke or his Mustang.

Typical. He was probably late or had forgotten all about it. Why had she thought she could count on him?

"Come on, sweetie. Let's go get our tickets." Peyton led Maddy across the lot to the bright ticket booths, each shaped like a different animal head.

And then, standing beside the giant polar bear booth,

dark shades blocking his incredible blue eyes, was Luke. He was leaning one shoulder against the booth, as casual as a summer breeze. He smiled when he saw her and something warm unfurled in Peyton's belly.

He pushed off from the wooden building and met her halfway. "Bet you didn't think I'd show."

"The thought crossed my mind."

"I'm more responsible than you think, Peyton." He held up three colorful slips of paper. "And I already have tickets."

Peyton's brows arched. "You do? Wow. Thanks." That surprised her, even more than him being on time. "Where's your sports car?"

"My sports car..." It took him a second, then he nodded. "Oh, the Mustang. That's Ben's. My car's a plain old Taurus. It was at Gator's the day you came by, waiting on some parts for the brakes."

"Oh."

"Didn't expect me to be driving a car as boring and dependable as a picket fence, did you?" He didn't wait for Peyton's answer. Instead, he turned and handed Maddy one of the tickets. "Here, kiddo. Here's yours."

"Oh, I don't think she's old enough—"

But Maddy was already running ahead, dashing toward the ticket taker at the entrance to the zoo. The woman smiled down at Maddy, tore the paper in half and handed one half back to Maddy, who clutched it in a wadded ball in her palm. "Be sure to keep your half of the ticket," the woman said. "You need it to take the train around the zoo."

"Okay. T'ank you," Maddy said, as solemn as a preacher.

Peyton followed behind, with Luke right beside her. She moved fast enough to be sure Maddy never got more than a couple of feet away, scanning the ground as she walked. Partly to watch for the ticket when it dropped, and partly to keep her gaze from straying to Luke. Damn the man for looking good in something as simple as a button-down shirt and khaki shorts.

Thirty seconds later, Peyton bent down and picked up a familiar crumpled paper. "This is why I don't let her hold her own ticket," Peyton said to Luke. "She's too little for that responsibility."

"People don't learn responsibility unless you give it to them," Luke said.

"And you, Mr. Unmarried, are the model for responsibility?"

"How do you know I'm not married?"

"I…well, I…I assumed because, well, there's no ring and…" She cursed the heat in her cheeks. Why did the man make her stammer?

He grinned. "You checked my hand to see if I was married?"

"Only because I didn't want to intrude upon your life if you were with someone else. This," she said, gesturing toward Maddy, who had dashed over to the fence outside the mountain lion enclosure and was peering into the shaded space, looking for the sleeping cat, "is a lot to take in, and even more so if you had a wife and kids already."

"Auntie P, where's the big kitty?"

Peyton bent down and pointed to a long tawny body curled in a ball under the shade of a thick oak tree. "He's right there. Taking a nap."

"But it's not nap time," Maddy said. "I wanna see him."

"You want to see some lazy nappers, check out these sloths." Luke pointed to a trio of sleeping animals in the next enclosure, flopped among the branches of a man-made tree. Bugs fluttered around them, but the sloths paid them no mind.

Maddy scampered over to the next cage, and the one after that, her mood a little lighter with each sleepy animal who had apparently decided 10:00 a.m. was early enough to call it a day. "They're so silly." She waved at the sunbathing otters, who barely even raised an eyelid in response.

Luke slipped into the space beside Peyton. The zoo was beginning to fill with children and adults, raising the noise level around them. "So it doesn't matter to *you* personally if I'm married? Only for…this."

Instead of answering him, Peyton turned to follow Maddy to the antelope exhibit. Miniature antelopes were mixed in with fully grown ones. Peyton waited, sure that Maddy would make a comment about mommy antelopes and baby ones—something she always noticed before— but Maddy just gave the animals a cursory glance before moving on to a towering birdcage. Peyton bit back a sigh. "This is all that matters right now, of course."

Luke chuckled. "Of course."

She shot him a glare. "I am not interested in you on a personal level, Luke. At all."

Uh-huh. Which is exactly why her gaze kept straying to his broad shoulders. His muscular calves, his long fingers. His lips. His eyes.

"Good. I'm glad. Takes the mess of attraction out of the equation."

"You think being attracted to each other would be messy?"

He leaned in close, his breath warm against her throat. His pulse ticked in his neck, and the dark scent of his cologne whispered between them. The air filled with Luke…just Luke.

"Doesn't sex always mess up everything?"

"Sex?" she whispered the word, so low and sharp, it almost sounded like a curse. "Who said anything about that?"

"Isn't it always part of the conversation between a man and a woman?"

"You think a man and a woman can't be just friends?"

"Sure they can. If the man is a eunuch."

Maddy turned around. "Auntie P, what's a you-knock?"

Peyton sent Luke a glare, but he just grinned back. "One of those things you will learn about when you are older. Oh, look, did you see the sign for the zebras? Want to go see them, Maddy? You love zebras."

Maddy just nodded and smiled, none of the usual excitement in her face. She was being good—she almost always behaved—but the whirling cloud of joy and discovery that normally surrounded her had morphed into something dark and gray, listless. Like a sail that had lost its wind.

Peyton bent down and took both of Maddy's hands in her own. "Sweetie, are you feeling sad today?"

Maddy shook her head but her eyes welled and her lips pressed into a tight line.

"I bet you wish your mommy was here," Peyton said softly. The words choked Peyton up, but she kept her composure. If she cried, if she showed that weakness, then she was afraid that it would make this harder on Maddy. "I do, too. She loved the zoo, didn't she?"

Maddy looked as if she wanted to say something, wanted to open up, but then she glanced away, and the moment passed. "Can we go see the zebras?" The space behind Maddy's eyes filled with that wall that Peyton knew too well. Stones built out of the holes in Maddy's life, the yawning cavern that stretched ahead for a girl who had lost her mother.

Peyton wanted to draw Maddy close, hold her tight and promise her everything would be all right, that nothing bad would ever touch her life again. But the words would be a lie, and they both knew it. So instead, Peyton nodded, forced a bright, happy smile on her face and said, "Zebras it is. Let's go."

The other kids ran ahead of their parents, running zigzags past the lines of strollers and rented plastic red wagons for the little ones. The volume of excitement rose and fell in waves around them, while the animals watched with bored expressions. Maddy stayed close, falling into place between Peyton and Luke, her little light-up shoes making a spark from time to time. But her mood was still somber, her gaze cast on the winding paved path.

"Cool shoes," Luke said. "When I was a kid, we didn't have shoes that lit up. Just boring old regular shoes."

"These're my favorites," Maddy said. "Auntie P bought 'em for me."

"Well, if I had shoes that lit up, I'd be making them do it all the time. What happens when you do this?" Luke stomped on the ground.

Maddy did the same. A shower of lights burst from the LEDs running along the sole. She did it again, and let out a little laugh when the LEDs responded with a strobe of red lights. "They lights up a lot."

"That is cool," Luke said, giving her an admiring smile. "Let's stomp to the zebras." He stepped forward, stomp, stomp, stomp.

"Like elephants?"

"Yup. Though it helps if you do this, too." Luke leaned forward, pressed his arm to his cheek and swung it like a trunk, then stomped again.

Maddy giggled, actually giggled, and followed along behind Luke, stomping and swinging her arm. The other adults in the zoo looked on with amusement, and maybe a little envy, because Luke had that rare ability to let go and be as much of a kid as the child with him.

At least that was the emotion running through Peyton. Envy at his easy way, envy at his intuitive grasp of making a kid happy and, most of all, envy at the way Maddy was laughing. Peyton would have paid any amount of money to hear that laugh in the past few weeks, and here, in the space of five minutes, Luke had broken down that wall.

"Come on, Auntie P! Be a elephant!" Maddy swung her arm and stomped ahead.

"Yeah, come on, Auntie P." Luke grinned at her and did the same.

"Oh, I can't." Peyton shook her head and walked like a normal adult. "You guys go on ahead."

"Come on, you have to do it. We're at the zoo. What better place to act like an elephant?"

She shook her head again, her cheeks heating. "I'd feel silly."

"Oh, that'll pass." Luke took her hand and swung her arm forward. "You heard Madelyne. She wants her Auntie P to join in on the fun."

"Luke, really, this is silly. You guys just go."

Luke met her eyes, while Maddy waited to the side, watching the adults. "Didn't you ever act silly as a kid?"

She glanced over at her niece. The swarm of kids entering the zoo parted like a wave around the three people stopped on the path. "I was never really a silly kid."

Luke reached up and cupped her jaw, a momentary touch, but coupled with the searing connection in his eyes, the light caress of his fingertips along her skin sent shock waves through her veins. "Every kid should have time to be silly. It's part of growing up."

"Some kids have to grow up too fast." She cut her gaze away. "That's part of growing up, too."

"Nobody should have to grow up too fast." Luke's hand touched her cheek again, his thumb tracing a half-moon along her cheek. "Take some time to be silly, Peyton. Better late than never."

"Okay," she said, if only to get him to release her. She stepped back, bent her head a little and brought her arm alongside her nose. "There."

"Oh, no, you have to stomp and swing. Like us. Let's show her, kid." Luke and Maddy repeated their elephant walk, going ahead of Peyton two by two.

Like a father and daughter.

Dare she hope that maybe he would be a real part of Maddy's life? That he would help fill those gaping wounds in Maddy's life?

Peyton came up behind them, laughing too hard to act like an elephant. The three of them stopped in front of the zebras, a wide-open plain dotted with the striped animals, a trio of elephants, a pair of giraffes and a lone ostrich. Maddy delighted over the animals, spending nearly an hour running along the fence, peering past the posts and asking questions about each and every animal. She was as busy as a bee on the first day of spring, flitting here and there, her little shoes making sparks along the paved path.

And most of all, Maddy was happy. Having fun. Because Luke had gotten her to stomp her feet and trumpet her arm, and forget the shadows that troubled her. It was the best moment Peyton could have hoped for, and exactly the kind of moment she had come to Stone Gap for.

Would Luke really stay in Maddy's life after the two

weeks were up? Would he be there to make her laugh, encourage her to act silly?

Maddy ran over to Peyton. She was out of breath and tiny beads of sweat dotted her forehead. "I's tired, Auntie P."

Peyton bent down and lifted Maddy's long curls off her neck, giving her a moment of cool air. "I'm not surprised. You were busy talking to all the animals." Peyton waved toward a bench located in a shady copse of trees between the main path of the zoo and the splash pad to the rear. "Let's take a load off for a few minutes, then go get lunch."

Maddy clambered onto the bench, settling her body against Peyton's left side. A minute later, she was asleep, falling into a fast, deep nap, something Maddy had done since she'd been born. Peyton had never known anyone who could fall asleep so quickly and so deeply, then be back up again a few minutes later, ready to tackle the rest of the day. If there was one thing Peyton had been grateful for when she'd brought the newborn Maddy and Susannah into her home, it was Maddy's ability to sleep.

Luke sat on Peyton's right side, leaning forward and peering around at Maddy. "She's out that fast?"

"Yup. She's always been like that. Even when she was a baby. I'd put her in her crib, and five minutes later, she'd be asleep."

"You put her to bed every night? What about Susannah?"

"She was…busy." Out on dates. Out at bars. Just plain out. Peyton didn't add that. It wasn't right to speak ill of the dead, and never right to speak ill of the sister who had brought the precious Madelyne into the world.

"That kid is the definition of busy. I've never known anyone with so much energy."

Peyton laughed. "Look in the mirror. You were like a tornado when you were young. Going here, there, running this, running that."

"Me? Nah, I was the lazy one."

Lazy was never a word she would have associated with Luke. Irresponsible, yes, a charmer, yes, a serial dater, for sure. But lazy...no, never him. "You were captain of the football team—"

"Because no one else wanted the job."

"Class president—"

"Again, no one else wanted the job."

"You worked part-time at your dad's garage and—" She put up a finger to stop him when he started to protest. "You were at every party that anyone threw in Stone Gap."

"Which was my main job." He grinned. "That doesn't make me anything other than a party animal."

"Maybe so, Luke, but you also had a lot of good qualities."

Surprise lit his face and curved across his lips. "You think I have a lot of good qualities?"

"You made Maddy laugh and smile today. That's the only quality I care about."

He reached up and cupped her jaw, just as he had earlier, only this touch was more tender, softer. "And what about you? Did you laugh and smile, too?"

She swore she could feel her heart beat in the places where he touched her. "Maybe."

His thumb traced across her bottom lip. Heat chased through Peyton's veins. "Ah, Peyton, you are a stubborn woman." But the words held no malice.

"I prefer to think of myself as strong, not stubborn. Somebody has to be in charge and make sure everything happens on time and the way it's supposed to. Someone has to be the one who keeps it together so that no one else falls apart." She tore her gaze away from his hypnotic blue eyes and glanced at her watch. Calm, cool, collected. Not at all affected by Luke's touch, or his cologne, or his warmth. Or every inch of him. "Speaking of which, it's time for lunch. I should wake Maddy and—"

"Let her sleep another five minutes. The world won't end if you do."

Her eyes connected with his again. "Oh, it might. It very well might."

His gaze dropped to her lips, then back to her eyes. Hunger colored the blue dark, and heat rose in the space between them. A heartbeat passed between them. Another. The shaded bench seemed a million miles away from the busy zoo, lost in the quiet of the shrubs and trees that had carved out their own private niche. "I'm going to kiss you, Peyton."

Anticipation warmed her, made her want in ways she hadn't wanted in a long, long time. "I…I… We shouldn't."

"You're probably right. But when have I ever done what I was told?" He grinned, then leaned in and caught her mouth with his own.

Chapter Four

The kiss was a mistake. An accident.

Or at least that's what Luke told himself for the first five seconds, when his lips met hers and she sat there, ramrod still, for a blip of time. Then something softened between them, a wall crumbling, and she leaned first into the touch of his hand against her face, then into him. And in that moment, Luke wondered if any of this was an accident, or if a part of him had intended to kiss Peyton ever since that first day when she'd shown up on his porch.

Her lips were hot beneath his, and her perfume, something with a dark floral scent, lured him closer, made him think of hot summer nights with a breeze drifting into open windows, the two of them in a bed, tangling in the sheets, their bodies slick with sweat, the rush to be in her, with her, overpowering every other thought. He tangled one hand in her long blond hair, the other going around her waist, drawing her closer, breast to chest, thigh to thigh, an electric current charging every place they touched.

Then a kid let out a shriek from the splash pad. The piercing sound broke the spell between Peyton and Luke, and she jerked away from him. "That…that shouldn't have happened."

"Maybe," he said. "But it did."

She pushed her hair away from her face. The movement seemed to drop a mask of calm over her features. The flush in her cheeks dissipated, and her breathing evened out. In an instant, it was as if the kiss had never happened. "I'm not here for…that."

"Me neither. But I'd be lying if I said I wasn't interested in you."

"And I'd be lying if I said I was interested in you." She brushed at her skirt as if kissing him had left her dusty, or as if she just wanted to whisk away the memory of his touch. "I'm here so you have a chance to get to know your daughter. Nothing more. And I mean that, Luke. *Nothing more.*"

"Then why did you kiss me back?"

"I…" She opened her mouth, closed it. "I didn't mean to. I got caught up in the moment and—"

"Overcome by the heat? Swept away by the romantic atmosphere of a children's zoo?" He shifted closer. Still, she kept her distance, stood strong and cool, dispassionate. If he hadn't been there himself, he wouldn't believe that ten seconds ago this same woman had been leaning into him, letting out soft mews of desire. "Don't pretend you didn't enjoy that. Don't pretend it was nothing."

"It wasn't anything, Luke, and the second you accept that is the second we can move forward." She bent over, roused Madelyne and helped the little girl into a sitting position. "Come on, sweetie. Time to wake up.

Let's go get some lunch, and then see the rest of the animals. Okay?"

The air between him and Peyton had chilled. She was as cordial to him as she would be to her dry cleaner. He told himself he didn't care, but damn it, he did.

She intrigued him, this grown-up, confident, capable Peyton Reynolds. He saw all the order and schedules in her life and wondered what it would be like to get her to let go, to see her with her hair down—literally. Even now, with her hair loose around her shoulders, everything about her seemed restrained, as if her entire body was held in place by extra-strength hairspray. For a moment there, a brief, sweet, hot moment, that control had been relaxed. The taste of that other Peyton—the Peyton she could be—lingered in his mouth, pooled desire in his gut.

But she was right on one thing—neither one of them was here today at the zoo for what had happened on that bench. They were here for Madelyne, so he could get to know his daughter, and so that Peyton could bring some joy into the life of a kid who seemed to carry a cloud over her head. And rightly so.

He thought of the childhood he'd had—all the creeks he'd explored, trees he'd climbed, adventures he'd embarked upon. He'd had a good childhood, the kind that would have made Norman Rockwell fill a gallery. Every kid deserved that.

Especially his own.

Peyton held Maddy's hand, heading for the food court on the right side of the path. Madelyne kept looking over her shoulder, though, watching the kids on the splash pad with a longing that was nearly palpable. Luke caught up to Peyton and put a hand on her shoulder. "Hey, before we eat, why don't we take her over there?" He nodded toward the splash pad.

Madelyne stopped walking and looked up at Peyton, silent.

"It's lunchtime," Peyton said.

"And the world won't fall off its axis if we stop for a little fun."

"A schedule is important—"

"But not written in stone." He took a step closer. "Come on, Peyton, live a little. Let the munchkin live a little. She's been eyeing that splash pad like it's Santa's summer home."

He could see the hesitation in her eyes, the war between what she was tempted to do and what she had planned to do. Madelyne stood at Peyton's side, her body quivering a little with anticipation. Then a shadow dropped over Peyton's features and she shook her head. "We've already gotten off track enough for one day. It's time for lunch."

Madelyne sent one last longing glance over her shoulder, then ducked into the faux tiki hut restaurant with Peyton. Luke followed behind, quelling the urge to argue with Peyton. She was, after all, the kid's de facto mother and had way more experience at this parenting thing than he did. Maybe she was right, and maybe a schedule mattered more than a few minutes splashing in the sun.

And getting off track. In more ways than one.

Peyton tucked the blankets around Maddy, then smoothed the hair on her forehead. The day was winding to a close, after the morning at the zoo with Luke, a trip to a playground after they'd left the zoo, then a spaghetti dinner at the diner. Before Luke left, Peyton had given him the DNA test swab she'd picked up at the drugstore after leaving his house. She'd taken a swab from Maddy, too, telling her niece it was a game of sorts. Then she'd sealed up the already stamped envelope and slipped it into a mailbox. Even though Maddy looked every bit Luke's daughter, the best course was the prudent one, and that meant sending in the test and covering all the bases. Luke had gone to work after they'd finished at the zoo, and Peyton told herself she was glad. Still, a hole had lingered after he was gone, as if the circle was incomplete without him. Crazy thoughts. Peyton was just fine on her own with Maddy, just fine. "Did you have fun today, monkey?"

Maddy nodded, her eyes half closing. "I liked the zebras. And the elephants. And the hippos. They were really big."

"They were." Peyton smiled. "How about we go to the children's museum tomorrow?"

"Is Luke gonna go? He's really fun, Auntie P. He likes to be an elephant, like me. And he makes funny faces when he eats his chicken nuggets."

And he makes my heart sing when he kisses me. Peyton brushed off that thought. Kissing Luke was not on her agenda, not now, not ever. He was a mistake she didn't need to make in order to learn her lesson. Hadn't Susannah told Peyton over and over again that Luke was no good, that he was a man who wanted a conquest, not a relationship?

Yeah, being around Luke was a bad idea, all around. Somehow she'd find a way to let him spend time with Maddy—and keep Peyton far from stupid decisions. Like kissing him again.

"I thought maybe just you and me should go. Girl time. Then we can go back to the playground, and you can play on the jungle gym while I get a little work done." Peyton gave her a grin. "How's that sound?"

"Okay." But Maddy's voice was heavy, and her gaze shifted away.

"You really like Luke?"

"Uh-huh. He's silly." Maddy clutched her teddy bear, a worn cream-colored stuffed animal she'd dubbed Bo a long time ago. At the end of the day, after she was done with all the Barbies and baby dolls, it was Bo she reached for, Bo she tucked under her arm and nestled beneath her chin.

The silly bear had been with Maddy for as long as Peyton could remember. It was the first thing Peyton had bought when she found out her sister was pregnant, the first gift she brought to the hospital when she visited a newborn Maddy and the first thing she had packed when they'd made the trip to Stone Gap. Maddy plucked at the fur on top of Bo's head, giving him a short, spiky Mohawk, something she did when she was nervous or scared.

"Do you like Luke, Auntie P?" Maddy asked.

"Of course I do. I've known him a long time."

"Is he your friend? Cuz he's my friend."

"Yes, I'd call him a friend." Nothing more than that, of course. Anything more would be silly.

Except friends didn't kiss the way they had kissed. And friends didn't have the kind of late-night thoughts about each other that she had been having about Luke. "Definitely friend," Peyton clarified, mostly for herself.

"Then how come he can't go wif us?"

How come he couldn't go? The question lingered in Peyton's mind as she finished tucking Maddy in and settling her down for the night. Peyton sat beside her niece, as she had every night for the past month, with Maddy's hand clasping her aunt's, seeking security, comfort. A few minutes later, Maddy nodded off, curled in a tight ball with Bo pressed to her chest.

There was a soft knock at the door. Peyton hurried to answer it, before the sound woke Maddy. Peyton peeked through the peephole, one hand on the doorknob. She'd expected to see housekeeping or a traveler at the wrong door.

What she saw instead was a pair of tempting blue eyes and a lopsided smile that caused a hitch in her breath. She drew in a fortifying breath, then pulled open the door, ridiculously regretful that she'd changed into sweats and washed off her makeup. "Luke, what are you doing here?" Peyton whispered.

"I wanted to see you and Maddy."

"It's eight-thirty. She's already asleep."

"That early?"

"She's four, Luke, not fourteen." She chuckled. "I bet even you went to bed that early when you were little. Unless there were parties in your nursery, of course."

He took a step closer and cocked his head. "Why do you insist on thinking the worst of me?"

"I don't think the worst of you." Okay, so maybe she had. But only because he had a past that spelled out what the future could hold. What was that old adage? History is the best predictor of the future? He'd broken countless hearts and been as fickle as a summer wind.

Amusement lit his blue eyes. "Then what *do* you think of me?"

She gripped the door handle tighter. She didn't want to answer that question, because the only answer she had was *it's complicated*, as if standing here in the doorway with Luke Barlow was some kind of Facebook status. "Listen, Maddy's sleeping and I was about to turn in…"

"At eight-thirty? Even you stay up later than that, don't you?" His grin softened the tease in his words. "Come on, let's sit and talk for a little while. We can sit out on the balcony and look for Orion."

Just like that, Peyton was fourteen again and sitting on the bank of the lake with a seventeen-year-old Luke late at night. Susannah had drunk too much and fallen asleep on a blanket beside them. Peyton had heard her mother calling for her, but she'd ignored her curfew, because all she'd wanted—all she'd ever wanted since the day she'd met him—was five more minutes with Luke. He'd sat beside her and pointed out the stars, weaving hypnotic tales of ancient Greek gods and goddesses with each constellation he'd named. Of all her summer memories, that one stayed high and bright in her mind, like the North Star.

"I have a couple of mini wine bottles in the room fridge," she found herself saying, words overriding common sense and her weak resolve. "If you want something to drink."

"Are they pink and fruity?"

She laughed. "Definitely."

"That's my favorite kind." He stepped through the open door and into her room.

Peyton stepped aside, turning to lead Luke to the balcony, but he had stopped, just a few feet inside the small space. His gaze shifted to the bed, to Maddy still tucked against her bear, her hair splayed in a wild curly halo around her head. She'd kicked her feet free of the blanket, and her sparkly pink toenails caught the soft light from the bedside lamp. "She looks like...an angel."

Peyton heard the soft wonder in Luke's voice, the same wonder that had filled her a million times in the days since Maddy had been born. "She is an angel, though you might need to remind me of that when she's seventeen and sneaking out at night to see some boy."

"She really is mine, isn't she?" It was a rhetorical question, the kind that people asked when they couldn't believe their good fortune. The truth was settling into Luke, Peyton could see, filling in the cracks of shock and doubt. "I mean, I know we're waiting on the test results and everything, but I feel it, here." He pressed a hand to his chest. "She's mine. And that's pretty amazing."

Peyton stood beside him in the dim light of the hotel room, both of them caught in the spell of one little girl. Maybe Peyton was biased, but she'd always thought Maddy had a way about her, something special, that drew people in and made them fall in love with her winsome smile and big, curious blue eyes.

"I still remember the day she was born. It was like... magic. Susannah, me, the doctor and nurse were in this bland, gray hospital room, had been for hours, while Susannah was in labor. Then, all of a sudden, there was another human being in the room, a perfect, beautiful, crying human, and just like that—" She snapped her fingers. "I fell in love."

"I wish I'd been there," he said softly.

"You should have been." The words held no harsh edges, no recrimination. The past was in the past, Peyton realized, and she couldn't change or undo any of it. Susannah should have told him, and he should have come. He had the right, as Maddy's father, to be there for every first, from the first breath to the first step.

Though, if Luke had been present at Maddy's birth, maybe he would have insisted on moving Susannah and Maddy back to Stone Gap, and Peyton would never have had the years she'd had with her niece.

There was only today. Luke might not be there tomorrow or two weeks down the road, but he was now, wanting to know more about Maddy, wanting to be more involved, and that was a good thing. "Come on, let's go outside, so we don't wake her up."

Peyton grabbed the two bottles of wine and a couple of clean glasses from the minibar, and she and Luke settled into the cheap white plastic chairs that filled the small space on the hotel room's balcony. It was a tiny square, no more than two feet by three feet, but it had a view of the woods and, far in the distance, the lake where she had spent many a summer day. Ironic, Peyton thought, that more than ten years later, she and Luke were again sitting under a night sky with the lake in the distance.

The night was quiet, the distant sounds of traffic a low whisper. Night birds called out to each other from time to time, and a soft breeze rippled over the balcony, bringing with it the sweet scents of clematis and osmanthus.

"Cheers," Peyton said, tapping her glass against Luke's.

"To old friends," he clinked her glass, saying, "and new beginnings."

Old friends. Was that what they were? Was that what she wanted them to be? After that kiss today, she wasn't so sure. It had been the kind of kiss that lingered, hung on the edge of her every thought. It was still there now, unspoken but part of the conversation, of the fabric woven between her and Luke. It could never be erased, never be undone, and at some point, she was going to have to think about what it had meant and how it had shifted everything between them.

Luke propped his feet on the balcony rail and raised his gaze to the twinkling sky. "Do you remember how to find Orion?"

With that one question, she was fourteen again, sitting in the dark shadows along the lake while the water lapped against the shore. A younger, more wiry Luke sat beside her, sharing the small space on her towel. In the dark, she hadn't been the nerdy kid sister with glasses and a book under her arm. In the dark, she could be anyone, and for those couple of hours, she'd pretended she was Luke's girlfriend. He'd leaned back on his elbows and smiled at her, and asked her if she knew how to find Orion. She could have been an astronomy major and she still would have said no, just to have him reach past her into the sky and tell her the story of the eternal hunter.

"Show me again," she said now.

He leaned over as he had years ago, his shoulder close enough to brush hers. In the dark, the spicy notes of his cologne settled into the space between them, luring her closer, urging her to touch him, to press her face against his neck. Her muscles tensed, and she curled her palm around the hard plastic arm of the chair instead of caving to the desire rushing through her veins.

Luke pointed up at the sky. "Look to the west. See those three stars close together?"

She breathed. In, out, catching that spicy scent again, pretending to be looking at the stars and not the five o'clock shadow that roughened his jaw. "Yes."

"Those form Orion's belt. There, those two to the north are his shoulders and the two to the south," Luke lowered his hand, continuing, "are his feet."

She remembered all of this from that night by the lake, but she didn't want to tell him, didn't want to undo the threads that bound the past to this moment. "And who was Orion? I've forgotten."

"The legend says he was the son of the great and mighty god Poseidon. He was able to walk on water, and he was the greatest hunter of the day. But he fell in love with one of the seven sisters in the Pleiades and Zeus, angry at Orion for falling in love, plucked him from the earth and placed him in the sky, where he is perpetually hunting for the love that he lost."

She smiled up at the constellation, a smattering of stars wrapped in mythical legends that had been passed down for centuries. "How do you know so much about one particular constellation?"

"I never told you this story?"

She shook her head.

Luke leaned back in the chair, and the little extra distance sent a shiver of disappointment through Peyton. "My father was in the army when he first married my mom. They were newlyweds when he was stationed overseas, and she was pregnant with Mac, so she stayed stateside. They were miserable without each other, and because they were on opposite sides of the world, they had a hard time making phone calls work. So they decided that they would each go out at night and look for Orion, knowing that the other one would be looking at that same constellation a few hours later. My father said he chose Orion because the woman of his heart was just out of reach, like the Pleiades sister for Orion, and he could hardly wait for the day when he would cross the world and be with her again."

"That is so romantic," Peyton said. "I never knew your dad was like that."

"He's a big old softy, but don't tell him I told you. He says he'd have to turn in his man card if anyone found out he cries at sad movies and stares up at the stars when he's missing the woman he loves."

Peyton looked up at the steady constellations caught in an eternal quest for true love. "How wonderful it must be to be loved like that," she said softly. "Across oceans and time and stars."

"It is kind of wonderful," he said. "Makes my parents

cool, in a way. They're still as much in love today as they were the day they got married." Luke's voice was tinged with affection for his parents—and maybe a little envy.

The same emotions rippled in Peyton. She'd known Della and Bobby for years and always thought they were a wonderful example of what marriage—and family— could be. Luke had no idea how lucky he had been to grow up in a house like that, one with warmth and love, built on a solid, constant foundation. Her own had never been solid, with a mother who battled alcoholism and traded boyfriends as often as she traded her hair color. No weekly Sunday dinners, no Christmas traditions, just a sort of cobbled-together existence. "That kind of life-time love is such a rare thing."

"Very, very rare. Though Jack seems to have found that with Meri. They're getting married in a few weeks."

"Jack and Meri Prescott? They got back together?" She remembered the beauty queen who had dated Luke's younger brother. They'd made a nice couple back in high school, though Peyton had been in a different group of friends and hadn't really known either of them very well.

"Yup. And now they're always mooning over each other, just like my parents." Luke grinned.

"You almost sound envious."

"Me?" He scoffed. "Nah."

"You don't want to find someone to love like that? Someone who would love you back the way Orion loved that woman?"

"There's a reason loves like those are immortalized in the stars, Peyton. They're few and far between." He took a long sip of wine, then set his glass on the concrete floor. "What about you?"

She clasped her hands around her glass, the conden-sation cooling her palms. "What about me?"

"Are you holding out for a man who will hunt the skies for eternity, just for the chance to be with you?"

She let out a chuff. Years ago, she might have dreamed of that kind of thing, but then she'd grown up and realized fairy tales rarely came true. "Come on, that doesn't happen. I mean, your dad and mom, and Jack and Meri, got lucky, but like you said, that's the exception, not the rule. I'm focused on raising Maddy and as for the rest..." She shrugged.

"What happened to the girl who used to read love stories and dream about knights in shining armor?"

"I grew up," Peyton said. "Got a job, a mortgage and, now, a child. I don't have time for fantasies about white horses and sunsets."

"Sounds like we're the same that way."

"Realists unite." She raised her glass and tipped it in his direction.

"Is that what we are?" he asked. "United?"

United. Together. It was a strange thought, coming years after she had dreamed of that very thing. Truth was, they were united, but for something that had nothing to do with romance. "For now. With Madelyne."

"A temporary alliance."

She nodded, maybe a little too vigorously. "*Alliance*. That's the perfect word."

"None of that silly romantic notion stuff." He waved at the sky, as if Orion himself would agree.

He'd echoed her thoughts. That kiss had been an aberration, a mistake they both regretted. No worries about Luke taking this any further, or wanting more from her than she was willing to give. "Exactly."

Which meant she should stop looking up at the sky and picturing herself back beside him, on the banks of the lake, ever hopeful that this time, this moment, he would notice her and realize he had been dating the wrong sister. None of that silly romantic stuff meant focusing solely on Madelyne, and nothing else.

Peyton cleared her throat. "You said you came to talk about Madelyne. What did you want to discuss?"

"I'd like to spend some time with her—"

"We can arrange that. I was thinking maybe all of us could go to the children's museum tom—"

"On my own," Luke cut in. "I want to get to know her and I think that would be easier without a go-between."

"I don't know if that's such a good idea. She's nervous about new people and she's used to me and—"

"And I'm her father, as far as we know, though I'm willing to wait on the blood test results for confirmation, if need be. And if the DNA comes back a match, you know I have the right to see her."

He was right, of course, and if they went to court—not that it would ever get that far—but if they did, Luke would have every legal right to share custody, and maybe even get sole custody. He was, after all, very likely the only remaining biological parent.

Maybe she could use the time that Maddy was at Luke's to do some work from the hotel room. Follow up on the Drexel Avenue job that had been on her desk before she left, check on that order for the silk wall covering. Try to resuscitate her career. She was supposed to be on vacation, but that didn't have to stop her from doing some damage control.

Maybe then she could return to Baltimore with a plan in place. Her career could get back on solid ground, and that would give her more time to devote to Maddy.

Peyton twirled the glass between her palms and stared at Luke. "You're asking me to trust you with Maddy."

"I'm a trustworthy guy, Peyton." He grinned.

"It's just…I don't leave her often with people I don't know really well."

"Why?"

She could lie and tell him that Maddy didn't like new situations or got upset in new places. But that wasn't true. Until Susannah's death, Maddy had been a pretty adaptable kid, easy to please, friendly to everyone she met. Peyton could say it was because she was still worried about Maddy's fragile emotional health—which was true—but that wasn't all of it. "I've made most of the decisions for Maddy since she was born," Peyton said. "And to be honest, it's hard for me to let someone else be in charge, even for a little while."

"Where was Susannah during all this?" Luke asked.

Peyton leaned forward and propped her elbows on her knees. Her gaze traveled across the tops of the trees, now just blotches against the night sky, to the lake that sat in a thick black line in the distance. "Susannah wasn't much for being a mom. She was a great friend, but kids don't need friends. They need parents who set schedules and make them eat vegetables and remember to put on their winter coat when there's frost on the ground."

"And Susannah didn't do that?" Surprise colored his words.

Peyton thought of all the arguments she'd had with her sister, all the times she'd told Susannah that she needed to step up, be responsible, be the mother that Madelyne needed. Peyton would trade every one of those arguments to have her sister back, with her quirky sense of humor and her silly cards. "Susannah wanted to be a good mom, and she loved Maddy more than anything in the world. In the end, that's all that really matters." Peyton shifted her gaze to Luke and let out a long breath. "And that's all that really matters to me—that Maddy is loved."

"That's all that matters to me, too, Peyton." Luke's gaze turned to the night sky again. The stars flickered above them, as if Orion was blinking his approval.

Chapter Five

Luke Barlow had made a lot of mistakes in his life, some he had made amends for, some that still lingered like scars. In the few days since Peyton had arrived with Maddy, he began to have a glimmer of a different life, of a future that frankly scared the hell out of him as much as it excited him. Rather than push off the next steps he needed to take, as he might have done last month or last week, he got up early and showed up on his brother Jack's doorstep just as the sun was beginning to rise and kiss Stone Gap with gold.

Jack was already out in his workshop, the whine of the table saw drawing Luke over to the detached garage that Jack had converted a couple of months ago. Luke knocked on the open door. "You got a minute?"

Jack shut down the machine and laid the newly cut boards against the machine's leg. His younger brother had the same dark hair and brown eyes as Mac and their father, but had retained the leanness and hard edge he'd picked up during his time in Afghanistan. "I must be hallucinating. Because I'm seeing my brother before noon."

"Hey, I've been getting into the garage early for weeks now."

"Yeah, I know. I'm just teasing." Jack grinned, then reached for a bottle of water in a nearby cooler. He handed a second one to Luke. "You thinking about making it a full-time gig? Dad needs that second knee operation and really shouldn't be—"

"I know. I know."

"Wouldn't hurt you to step up, Luke."

He scowled. "I didn't come here for a lecture about my life choices. I came to ask a favor."

"If it involves lying to some girl, call Ben. I'm not your alibi." Jack took a sip of water. "Though I still want to hear all the details."

"It does involve a girl, but it's not what you think." Luke sat down on an overturned five-gallon bucket. The day was starting out hot, but the workshop, built under a wide tree, was still cool inside. "I need you to take my shift at the garage this morning. Nothing big on the schedule, just Ernie Franklin's brake job. I did the front two yesterday afternoon but the rear—"

"What girl?"

"Doesn't matter."

"Peyton Reynolds, by any chance?"

"How do you know she's in town?"

"Luke, Stone Gap is smaller than a mouse's shoebox. Someone sneezes in this town, and half the residents are lining up for their flu shot ten minutes later."

Luke chuckled. "True."

"And I know she always had a thing for you, so I just figured maybe now that she's all grown up, and hot as hell—"

"Hey!" The words had struck a match to Luke's temper. "You're practically a married man. You shouldn't talk like that about Peyton."

"And that," Jack said, tipping his bottle in Luke's direction, "answers my question about whether you are interested in her. So, what do you have cooking with Peyton Reynolds? She's a mother, too, I hear."

"It's not her kid. Well, it is, but…" Luke let out a long breath. He'd come here for a little advice and support, and telling only half the story wasn't going to do much good. "Promise you won't tell Mama, not till I'm ready to tell her myself?"

Jack dropped onto a second bucket and draped his arms over his knees. "Cross my heart, hope to die."

Luke smiled at the echoed promise, the same one he'd made to his daughter. "Peyton is raising Susannah's child. Susannah's and…mine."

Jack's jaw dropped. "Whoa, wait. Did you just say *your* child?"

Luke nodded, then ran through the story. "So today, I get to spend some time alone with her. Just me and Maddy. A garage isn't a safe place for a kid, so I was hoping you'd take my shift."

"Sure, sure. No problem. I can move things around with my schedule." Jack peeled off the paper label on his water bottle, then wadded it into a ball and tossed it into the trash. "You know you have to tell Mama and Dad. They're bound to find out, and woe to you if the information doesn't come straight from your lips."

Luke chuckled. "Yeah, probably not the kind of news that should be delivered through gossip. I will tell them. I'm just…getting used to the idea myself."

"And trying to decide how you want to handle the future?"

"Pretty much." He ran a hand through his hair and let out a long breath. "Peyton's a hell of a mom. She's all organized and scheduled and she thinks about all those little things like tying shoelaces. I'm not exactly Joe Father Figure here, and I don't know..."

"Don't know what?"

"I don't know if I'm the best role model."

"Hell, who is? Nobody's perfect, Luke. Not me, not you and not even Peyton. If there's one thing I've learned from Mama and Dad, it's that you do the best you can and don't sweat the small stuff."

"You sound like Anthony Robbins and Oprah Winfrey's love child."

Jack laughed. "I'm not saying I have all the answers, but I do have a few. After all, I'm the youngest one, so I've learned from the mistakes of those before me."

"Being last doesn't make you the smartest," Luke said, repeating an oft-told joke. "Or the one Mama likes the best."

"She just tells you that you're her favorite so you won't feel left out, being in the middle." Jack grinned.

"And she tells me she had me because she was so disappointed in the first kid." Luke grinned back.

"Well, she tells me you're the spare, after she had Mac. And that makes me—"

"An accident," Luke said, the same jokes from the past two-plus decades causing a burst of laughter between the brothers. Their mother told each of them that they were her favorite, and all three boys tried various ways to get their mother to pick one of them as the numero uno kid. She never had, and probably never would, which only made them try all the harder.

"You still working on that playground downtown?" Luke asked. His brother had started building a playground in the heart of Stone Gap as a way to memorialize his friend—and his fiancée Meri Prescott's cousin—Eli, who had been killed in action in the war.

"Yup. I'm adding in some handicap-accessible sections this week. Trying to make it a playground for all kinds of kids, you know?"

"I'd love to help out. Let me know if you need me this weekend."

"I can always use another pair of hands." Jack got to his feet and set his water bottle on a nearby counter. "Speaking of which, I better get cleaned up if I'm going to be at the garage in a little while."

Luke clapped his brother on the shoulder. "Thanks, Jack."

"No problem. Just do me one favor."

"Anything."

"Don't screw this up," Jack said, his tone serious, his gaze direct. "A child is a gift, Luke, and the last thing you want to do is throw it away. You might not get a second chance."

At eight that morning, Peyton stood in her hotel room, in her third outfit choice of the day. Not that she cared what she wore, of course, or who might see her in this dress or that dress—

Okay, so maybe she did care. She'd changed dresses over and over, put her hair up, let it down and finally settled on a dark green cotton dress she often wore to work.

Maddy tugged at Peyton's hand, bringing her back to what was important. "Auntie P, are you gonna stay with me today?"

"No, honey, I explained this to you earlier. You're going to stay with Mr. Luke for just a little while, and

I'm going to get some work done. I'll be back before you can miss me."

"I don't want you to leave. I want you to stay wif me."

"It'll be fun. Remember, he has a dog and you love dogs."

"Okay," Maddy said, but her voice was small, almost resigned. How Peyton missed the excited Maddy who used to run up and greet her at the end of the day, who found wonder in everything she saw and touched. This sad, empty little girl broke Peyton's heart.

Peyton bent down beside her and took Maddy's hands in both her own. "If you don't want to go, just say the word. We can do whatever you want. Do you want to do something else today?"

Maddy shook her head, her gaze downcast.

"Do you like being here, sweetie?" Peyton asked. "In Stone Gap?"

Maddy shrugged.

"Because if you want to go back to Baltimore, and go back to day care—"

Maddy was already shaking her head. "I wanna stay with you, Auntie P."

"And I want to stay with you, monkey. No matter where we go, we'll be together."

"But not...not when you goes to work and I gotta goes to day care and then I gots to wait a long, long time for you to come back and I get sad and wanna go home."

"Oh, honey, I know." Peyton drew Maddy into her chest and held her niece tight for several long seconds. Her heart filled with love, and she wished she could hit the lottery, or inherit a gazillion dollars, just so she never had to leave Maddy again. "When we go back to Baltimore, I'm going to try my best to work less and be with you more. Okay?"

"How's come we can't live here? With Mr. Luke and his doggy and the zoo and the pancake lady?"

Peyton brushed Maddy's bangs off her forehead. "Because my job is in Baltimore. But we can visit Stone Gap a lot. Would you like that?"

"I don't like Baltimore." Maddy's eyes welled. She gripped the hem of her shirt again. "I like here. I like the pancake lady and I like the zoo and I like the park."

"We have all those things in Baltimore, too."

"And I like Mr. Luke," Maddy added.

That was the only thing that she didn't have in Baltimore. And Peyton didn't have an answer for Maddy about making Luke magically appear in Maryland anytime soon. "Then do you want to go to Mr. Luke's house today for a little bit? I bet it will be fun."

Maddy nodded but didn't release the edge of her shirt. "Okay."

"I'll stay for a little bit, okay, sweetie?" Peyton said. "And if you change your mind after you meet Charlie the dog, you don't have to stay." Peyton bent down to retie a loosened shoestring on Maddy's sneaker. "Remember, Luke isn't used to watching a little girl like you, so try to remember all your manners and to not be a messy monkey."

Maddy smiled. "I's not a monkey. I's a big girl."

Peyton chuckled and tapped Maddy on the nose. "You are indeed."

Maddy dropped onto the bed and sat as still as a stone while Peyton brushed her hair and fashioned it into braids. Peyton kept an eye on the clock, working fast on Maddy's hair. "Does Luke like dolls?" Maddy asked.

Peyton thought of the manly jock she used to know and couldn't keep the wicked grin off her face. "I bet he *loves* dolls."

"Okay. I'll bring Sammie and Lucy and…" With her hair done, Maddy went over to her pile of toys stacked on the chair beside the bed, grabbing one after another and handing them to Peyton to add to the pile inside the bag. "Macy and this one. She doesn't have a name yet." Maddy gnawed on her bottom lip. "Maybe Mr. Luke will wanna name her."

"I'm sure he will." He'd probably hate Peyton for suggesting he play with dolls, but hey, that was part of being a father. She could only hope Maddy asked for a tea party, too. "Okay, it's getting late. We need to eat and get going, kiddo."

She piled Maddy, the bag of toys, a change of clothes and a few snacks into the car, then stopped off for breakfast at Miss Viv's again. This time, Maddy slid into the booth and beamed up at Miss Viv when she ordered her favorite pancakes.

Miss Viv gushed and fussed over Maddy, and dotted the pancakes with whipped cream at the table. Maddy ate up the attention, then finished off her breakfast in record time.

Relief washed over Peyton. Maybe being here in Stone Gap was exactly what Maddy needed. It was the most she'd seen her niece eat in one sitting since Susannah had died, and it gave Peyton a surge of hope. The emotion was chased by reality—would these changes hold when they went back to Baltimore?

At nine on the dot, Peyton pulled up to Luke's house. She rang the bell, and an instant later, the door opened. Peyton's heart skipped a beat, and her belly tightened.

Luke wasn't bare-chested today, and a part of Peyton was disappointed. He had on an old, faded concert T-shirt, with Bruce Springsteen's face on the front, and khaki shorts. His feet were bare, his hair still mussed as if he'd just gotten up. Charlie sat beside Luke, tail swishing on the entry carpet. The whole thing felt too intimate, too close. "Bet you thought I wasn't going to be awake," he said.

"Twice in a row, on time and up early. I daresay you're becoming a true card-carrying adult now."

"Well, I wouldn't go that far."

"Is that your doggy?" Maddy said. "He's cute."

"Yup, this is Charlie. He's awful excited to meet you, Maddy."

Maddy stayed pressed against Peyton's leg, still shy and wary. Peyton laid a protective hand on her niece's shoulder. "If you just wait a bit, Charlie can get to know you, like he's doing now with sniffing. Then you can play with him."

Maddy nodded. "And I can smells him, too." She sniffed, but stayed where she was.

Luke bent down and gave Maddy a wide smile. "And look at you. Is that a little chocolate from Miss Viv's famous pancakes on your chin?"

Maddy nodded. "Uh-huh. She makes yummy ones. And she puts this cool white stuff on 'em and it looks like ice cream, but it's not. But it's yummy. Auntie P said I can only eat a little, cuz it's not good for my tummy."

"Oh, a little of the bad stuff can be very good sometimes." He raised his gaze to Peyton. "Isn't that right, Auntie P?"

Heat curled in her veins. Was he talking about whipped cream or something else? And what if he meant something else? Was she interested? No. Definitely not. Not at all. "Sometimes, yes. Most of the time, no."

His gaze swept over her, and a smile curved up one side of his face. "Look at you. You always dress like that on vacation?"

She adjusted the collar on her dress. "I was going to go to a coffee shop and get some work done. It helps me feel like I'm working if I dress the part."

Appreciation shone in his eyes, in the devilish tilt of his smile. "You're making a good impression on me."

The compliment warmed her. It had been a long time since she'd been complimented this many times in a week. She worked with men, of course, but always did her best to keep everything all business, and no dating. Dating detracted her from her goals, so she had decided to put that part of her life on hold. But ever since that kiss with Luke—that too-short, soul-shattering kiss on the zoo bench—she'd begun to wonder if she was missing something.

Missing his lips on hers, that was for sure. More than she liked to admit. And really enjoying the way he was looking at her. More than she wanted to admit.

"Are you flirting with me, Luke?" She propped a fist on her hip and felt a tiny thrill when his gaze flicked to her curves.

"Me? Never." He grinned.

She hoped he was lying. That kiss had told her one thing, but her common sense told her another. Luke had been Susannah's boyfriend at the end of senior year of high school and a little after, and Susannah was as far removed from Peyton as two aliens raised on different planets. Plus, the Luke she remembered from high school had dated as if it was a sport, rarely staying in one relationship for very long. Peyton needed to remember that before she got too caught up in a couple of innuendos and a compliment.

And besides, Peyton had priorities. Priorities that didn't include a relationship with Luke, even if that kiss lingered at the edge of every thought. "Well, good," she said, to him, to herself, as a reminder that she shouldn't be kissing him at all, "because I have other things on my mind right now besides…" She waved a hand between them, then down at Maddy, who was watching the adult exchange with wide-eyed interest, continuing, "Whatever this is that you're doing."

"This—" Luke gestured between them "—is nothing more than me giving you a compliment. All you have to do is say thank you, Peyton. Not run off into the sunset with me."

Maddy tugged on Peyton's sleeve. "Auntie P? I gotta go potty."

"Oh, sure. Uh, bathroom's inside, to the left." Luke pointed. Charlie popped up his ears, but stayed by his master. "Do you need me to do anything?"

He looked so panicked at the idea that Peyton almost laughed. "No. I got this." She hurried inside with Maddy, mostly as a way to avoid having a discussion with Luke that she didn't want to have.

Run off into the sunset with him? Goodness, no. She wasn't interested in him—even if that flutter in her belly belied her statement—and she was only here so he could do his part with his own flesh and blood. Even if she did succumb to Luke's charms again, she had no intentions of dating him. He was Maddy's father and that alone screamed *best to keep a strong line in the sand.*

She wasn't a silly romantic girl anymore, Peyton reminded herself. Just because the man was still handsome and was being nice to Maddy didn't mean they'd all end up in some house with a white picket fence. This was reality, not a romance novel, and Peyton needed to keep a steady focus on the facts. Luke was Maddy's father, not the boy she'd once had a crush on. This wasn't her chance to tie up loose ends from high school—it was

Maddy's chance to build a relationship with her sole biological parent.

"Auntie P?" Maddy asked, as she rubbed her soapy
hands together under the running water. "Do you like
Mr. Luke?"

"Sure I do." *As a friend. Just a friend.*

"Then how's come you make this face sometimes?"
Maddy screwed up her nose and pressed her lips together.

Oh, the simple questions of children that merited complicated answers. "Are your hands all clean?" Peyton
asked.

"Yup!" Maddy raised her hands, sending water dripping onto the tile floor. Peyton snagged a towel from the
rack and dried Maddy's hands.

"Let's go see Charlie the dog. I bet he's as ready to be
friends now as you are. Okay?"

Maddy nodded, her earlier question forgotten. She
hurried out of the bathroom, and they returned to the
front hall. Luke was waiting for them, his dog sitting
patiently a few feet away.

"Can I play with the doggy now?" Maddy asked Luke.
"Does he like dolls?"

Peyton had never had a dog, so she wasn't sure if the
dog would chew up the toys or allow Maddy to pile them
near him. Peyton wanted to tell Maddy no, to throw up
the flag of caution—all those *what-ifs* that plagued Peyton's every decision with Maddy rising in full force—but
Luke stepped in before she could.

"Charlie loves dolls," Luke said, with a confident
smile. He snapped his fingers and the dog scampered
forward, then settled on the beige rug beside Maddy.
Charlie's tail slapped the carpet. He sniffed the air around
Maddy, and whatever scent he got made his tail wag even

faster. "You can pet him, if you want. Tell him your name first, so you can meet all proper."

"Hi, Charlie. I'm Maddy." She reached out a tentative hand, holding it just a hair's breadth away from Charlie's muzzle. The dog nosed forward and pressed his snout against her hand. She let out a happy squeal, then did it again. An honest-to-goodness joyous sound, something Peyton had wondered if she would ever hear again.

"She loves him," Peyton whispered to Luke.

"I told you, he's the miracle dog." Luke shared a smile with Peyton, then moved over to Maddy. "Charlie's a big baby, you know. He'll be your best friend for life if you scratch behind his ears. Like this." Luke bent down and gave Charlie's ear a rub. "Wanna try?"

Maddy looked up at Luke, uncertainty shimmering in her eyes. "He won't bite me?"

"Charlie is the sweetest dog in all of Stone Gap, maybe in all of North Carolina. He wouldn't bite anyone."

Maddy hesitated a second more, then ran a tentative hand along Charlie's head. The dog, as if sensing he needed to be more relaxed around the little girl, lowered his head to his paws and let out a happy groan. Maddy giggled and, within five seconds, was petting Charlie and chattering about her dolls, as if the mutt might jump in and play at any moment.

It was the most relaxed Peyton had seen Maddy in a long, long time. There was no more worry in Maddy's face, no more indecision about staying here at Luke's. She was happy—honest-to-God happy—and for the first time in a long time, Peyton felt good about leaving Maddy for a little while.

Maybe being at Luke's, with the dog and the swing, would help Maddy loosen up and find some joy again. Peyton got to her feet and straightened her skirt before crossing to Luke. "That was nice, what you did with the dog."

He shrugged. "All kids love dogs. And Charlie loves all kids."

Maybe Luke would be better at this than she thought. The tension in Peyton's body eased a fraction. "Maddy should have everything she needs in this bag," Peyton said, handing over a tote bag to Luke. "A change of clothes, some ibuprofen if she gets a fever. Everything is labeled, and there's a schedule in the bag—"

"Schedule? For the next two hours of her life?"

"Kids do best when they are on a schedule." She tugged it out and showed him the slip of paper. "Do you want me to go over it with you?"

"Uh, I think I can read. I do have that high school diploma, you know."

She made a face at him. "Okay, but if you have questions, call me. Maddy eats lunch at twelve so I will be back in time for that."

"I can feed her here."

"No, I'll pick her up." Peyton wasn't worried about Luke's ability to watch Maddy for a little while, but long-term...

Maybe not such a good idea. Besides, she had promised Maddy she would be back soon, and returning before lunch, so that lunch could be followed by the hotel pool, then dinner, then bath, then bedtime, would put them both back on track, something she seemed to forget whenever Luke was around. Peyton liked the schedule, the tightness of it, the way it wrapped her days in predictability. That was what Maddy needed, and what gave Peyton comfort. "I always make sure Maddy has a good lunch."

"You do?" He hesitated, then asked, "Didn't Susannah do that?"

"Susannah was…busy." Peyton didn't say that her sister often slept until Peyton had to leave for work, and rarely made anything that didn't come loaded with fat and carbohydrates. Rather than battle her sister about doing the right thing, Peyton had gotten in the habit of making lunch for all of them before she left for work each day.

"I have an idea. Why don't you come here, and have lunch with me and Maddy?"

"Do you have something healthy to eat here?"

"Of course. Pizza and beer." He grinned.

"Are you serious? She can't have—"

He put up a hand. "It's a joke, Peyton. Lighten up. We'll be fine. I might not have any experience at this, but I'm not a total idiot."

She arched a brow.

"Trust me," he whispered. "Just trust me."

That was the trouble. She didn't fully trust him. Didn't, in fact, trust anyone but herself when it came to Madelyne. Susannah had accused Peyton of being too much of a worrywart, constantly yelled at her to just relax. *Kids have been growing up for centuries without all that crap you keep reading in those silly books, Peyton,* Susannah would say. *When they're hungry, they eat. When they need to sleep, they sleep. Stop worrying about the freaking nutritional labels and the daily schedule. She's a kid, not a science experiment.*

Peyton took Luke's hand, wanting only to get his attention, but a *zing* went through her when they touched. It made her want to kiss him again, to do a whole lot more than just kiss. She wanted to hold his hand forever, to prolong the moment as long as she could. But she wasn't here for that, or for herself, so she released his hand. "Maddy means more to me than you can ever understand, and for me to leave her here with you takes a monumental amount of trust. Don't. Screw. This. Up."

He glanced over at Maddy, still happily chatting with Charlie and showing him each of her dolls, then back at Peyton. "You can count on me, Peyton."

But past history had proven differently, and as Peyton walked out of Luke's house, she wondered if she was putting her faith in Luke because she was a hopeless romantic—or a hopeless fool.

Chapter Six

The second the door shut behind Peyton, Luke had a moment of panic. Then he reminded himself that Maddy was sitting on his living room floor, surrounded by dolls and the dog. She seemed happy enough right now, which meant maybe this wasn't going to be so hard. After all, it was only for a couple of hours, and they'd gotten along well at the pool and the zoo. He could handle this, no problem. What could possibly go wrong?

Luke had his answer to that five minutes later. He was in the kitchen, pouring a third cup of coffee—contrary to what he'd told Peyton, 9:00 a.m. was pretty damned early for him— when he heard a cry followed by, "Auntie P! I wanna see Auntie P!"

Luke headed into the living room. He saw Charlie tucked in a ball in the corner, his head down, as if saying, *I didn't do it, man,* and Madelyne dwarfed by the big armchair, her arms wrapped around her chest, the toys forgotten on the floor. Crimson bloomed in her cheeks and her blue eyes were puffy. She scrubbed at one eye with the back of her fist, then stared up at him, expectant. "Where's Auntie P?"

"She's working," Luke said. "How about we, uh, read a book?"

Did the kid even read yet? He had no idea. More to the point—did he own a single book appropriate for a child? Probably not.

"I don't wanna." Maddy popped a thumb into her mouth.

Wasn't she too old for that? He was pretty sure she was, but he kept his thoughts to himself. The full extent of his knowledge about kids could fit on the back of a wasp, with room left over. "Uh, want to watch TV?"

The thumb stayed put. She shook her head again. Her eyes glistened with unshed tears. Damn.

"Hey, look, your dolls." He waved toward the pile on the floor, trying to work some enthusiasm into his voice. "You should play with them. Charlie loves the dolls." But the dog had skulked away, as if saying, *This is your gig, dude.*

"I want Auntie P," Madelyne said, then the thumb went back in her mouth. Her free hand twisted into her shirt, gathering the hem into a worried knot.

"We could go outside." *Just say yes, Maddy, and quit looking at me like I ran over your puppy.*

Now the tears brimmed, rivers standing on the edge of big blue banks. "When's Auntie P coming back?"

"Lunchtime."

"When's that?"

"I…I'm not sure. Let me check the schedule." He hurried back into the kitchen, dug through the bag until he found the neatly printed paper. Glanced at the clock, back at the schedule.

One hour and forty-five minutes to go. Luke stood there, feeling helpless and frustrated all at the same time. A few minutes in and he was ready to throw in the towel. Reason number four hundred and thirty-seven why he shouldn't be a father.

"You want lunch?" he asked. Because Maddy was still sitting there, staring at him.

"I dunno. It's not lunchtime, is it?"

"Not really. But the real question is, are you hungry now?"

She nodded.

"Well, how about having second breakfast?"

Madelyne's face scrunched in confusion. "What's that?"

"Second breakfast is the best meal ever," Luke said, bending down to the kid's eye level. Her eyes had stopped looking like tidal pools, and she'd let go of the corner of her shirt, so he figured he was making progress. That made him feel good. Damned good. "It's when you're still hungry from first breakfast, so you eat it all over again."

He vowed to show Maddy all the Lord of the Rings movies as soon as she was old enough. He'd bet good money his daughter would love them as much as he did.

She considered that. "I never had a second breakfast."

"Well, I have them all the time, and I think they're awesome. Wanna come see what I have to eat?"

The short answer, Luke realized a few minutes later, was nothing. That was when he remembered that most days he had second breakfast at Jack's, or his mother's, or at the Stone Gap Sip and Chew, which wasn't near as nice as Miss Viv's restaurant, but was cheap and only a half a mile away.

Madelyne peered around his hip and into the fridge. "You don't have a lotta stuff."

"Nope. I forgot to go grocery shopping." Though Luke's version of grocery shopping was usually bringing home leftovers from his mother's Sunday dinners, and grabbing something at a drive-through midweek.

"Auntie P goes shopping lots. We buy bananas and apples and cereal and toast and chicken nuggets, 'cept not the kind of chicken nuggets I wanna buy. Auntie P says we gotta have the healthy ones. Cuz they don't have... filleruppers."

"Filleruppers?" Luke asked, then thought a second. "Oh, you mean fillers."

That was good. Meant Peyton was watching what went into her niece's belly. Probably why she'd nixed the extra whipped cream on the pancakes, too. Luke never would have thought to read a label or consider the full ingredients list. Good thing at least one adult in Madelyne's life made sure she didn't grow up eating Red Dye #40, or whatever it was that kids weren't supposed to eat.

Clearly, if he was going to be spending time with his daughter, he needed to check a few nutritional tips on Google. And get to the grocery store more than once a month.

Madelyne looked up at him. "Do you have chicken nuggets?"

He glanced again in the fridge, as if food would magically appear. "Nope."

"Peanut butter?"

A quick peek in the cupboard. "Nope. Uh, but I do have a can of beans."

She shook her head. "Beans are icky."

"That's because they're good for you." He took out the can, showed it to her. "See? It says healthy right there."

"I don't want beans. I want what Auntie P makes me."

"What does Auntie P make?" He knew he could call her and ask her, but that would mean admitting defeat less than twenty minutes into the whole *trust me, I can handle this with one hand tied behind my back* promise earlier this morning.

"Good stuff." Madelyne shrugged. "Yummy stuff."

Stuff without filleruppers, he assumed. "Uh, I have beans."

Jeez, he really needed to grow up and get his ass to the grocery store once in a while. A six-pack of beer, a half-empty container of very likely expired milk, one pack of cheese and a can of beans did not constitute a full pantry.

Madelyne started to cry again. Except this time it was worse. Because she did it silently, just standing there, tears sliding down her cheeks in slow, steady rivers, as if he had run over her puppy and stolen her best friend at the same time.

Okay, so he sucked at this. Sucked royally. It was time to call in reinforcements. Reinforcements who would be pleased as punch to know Maddy existed. And truth be told, a part of Luke was damned proud he had a child as perfect as this one, and he wanted to share that with his family. He might not have accomplished much in his life so far, but he had been part of this four-year-old miracle, and that, he knew, was a pretty amazing thing.

"You know what, Maddy?" he said with a sigh. "You're right. It's time to make a call."

"Auntie P?"

"Better. My mom." He grinned, then picked up his phone.

Peyton stared at her cell phone. Checked it for text messages, even though the sound was up, the screen was bright and she would have seen and heard a message or a ring from ten miles away. Her finger hovered over the call button, debating whether to call Luke and check on Madelyne. It had, after all, been over an hour since she'd dropped her niece off.

Trust me, Luke had said.

But she couldn't bring herself to do it. And now, all of a sudden, she had put the most precious person in her life in someone else's hands.

She glanced at her phone again, just as her computer screen lit up with an incoming Skype invitation. The client she was working with, one of the most important and demanding ones at Winston Interior Design. Catherine Madsen bought and redecorated houses as often as some people changed out the photographs on their mantel. She said it kept her young, and kept her from thinking about the loss of her Realtor husband a few years ago. He'd left her with a generous nest egg, and a treasure trove of properties located throughout the historic area of Baltimore.

Tom Winston had said Peyton should take some time off. He hadn't said she couldn't work at all—which meant it was totally fine that she'd sent a follow-up email to Catherine about her latest project and arranged for this Skype conference call today. If Peyton could just get past that screwup where she had forgotten to schedule the installation of both the countertops and the flooring, making the client miss an important open house, just prove herself again, maybe the promotion she'd been working toward wouldn't be such a lost cause.

Peyton had found a table in a quiet corner of Miss Viv's diner. It offered Wi-Fi and unlimited coffee refills, which was perfect for Peyton. She'd been working since she sat down, finishing up the ideas she'd been working on ever since her boss had ordered her to take a two-week break. As much as Peyton knew she should, she just couldn't let that much time go by without working.

"Hi, Catherine," Peyton said, when the computers connected and the screen filled with the live image of her client's elegant features. "How are you today?"

"Overwhelmed and scattered, as usual." Catherine let out a throaty laugh. "I swear, one of these days, I'm going to take on a challenge bigger than I can handle."

"I doubt that. Every house you flip is more amazing than the one before."

"Thanks to you and your creative eye. We make a good team, Peyton."

A smile curved across Peyton's face. "All thanks to you and giving this fresh-out-of-college girl a chance years ago. And another one now."

Catherine waved a hand. "We will move past that. Everyone has a bad day, just not two in a row, hmm?" Catherine shifted in her seat, a reupholstered fauteuil armchair she had rescued from a trash pile two years ago. She'd brought it and a parlor makeover project to Peyton. It had been the first project they'd undertaken together, a test that Peyton had thankfully passed. Until she'd missed several critical deadlines on the Devall Street house. Another designer at Winston had stepped in at the last minute, but Catherine had not been happy about the necessary reschedule of the open house and nearly fired the firm.

Peyton had been on pins and needles ever since she sent the email to Catherine earlier this week, asking for a second chance. "Everything is back on track on my end," Peyton said now, though she knew that was a bit of a stretch, "and I'm eager to work on the next house with you. I took the liberty of checking on the progress of Drexel Ave., and drawing up some ideas for Market Street, in case you still had that one next in line."

Catherine assessed her, peering over her reading glasses and into the computer screen. She might be a difficult, exacting client, but she was also a straight shooter, something that Peyton respected. "Okay. What do you have for me?"

Peyton clicked on her computer and brought up the image of the design board she'd created, then shuffled the samples from her bag into a pile for quick reference. As she did, she gave herself a quick mental pep talk. Yeah, it had been a while since she had done this job, and yes, pretty much everything in her future relied on her making a good impression with this one project, but she could do this. So she gave herself the advice she had been whispering in her head for years, when she was standing outside the nursery window while little underweight Maddy struggled to hold her own those first few days, when she watched Maddy take those first tentative steps, and in those weeks since Susannah's death when Peyton had worried incessantly about the right decisions.

Take a breath, and just…go.

"For Market Street, I know you wanted a modern, upscale feel, while still staying true to the building's Southern roots," Peyton began.

Catherine grinned. "You paid attention. I think we had that conversation a year ago."

"I remember being excited about it, even then. A nice challenge, instead of another cookie-cutter design."

Catherine laughed. "You know me. I am far from cookie-cutter."

Peyton picked up a few samples and held them in front of the webcam as she walked Catherine through the elements on the design board, referencing images of the house. "This house has great bones, and with its old-world roots, I think we can really make it amazing, by combining history with modern touches." As she ran through her plans, her confidence grew—and she could see Catherine responding to her ideas.

Catherine put a hand up. "Let me stop you there."

Peyton's breath caught.

"I love it. All of it. The colors, the design." She waved at the screen. "Go forth and decorate."

"But don't you want to see—"

"I trust you. Despite what happened on Devall Street, I think you're going to do great. I'm thrilled you're staying on top of Drexel Ave. and glad to have you on Market Street. And I'm pleased to hear you have gotten your personal life straightened out."

"Thank you. I appreciate the work. I'll have Tom draw up the contract."

Catherine nodded. "Construction should be done in two weeks, so be ready to run with this a week from Monday."

It took a solid minute after Catherine signed off for Peyton to realize that not only had she made her boss happy, but she'd also been given carte blanche to decorate the house the way she wanted. It was the most control Catherine had ever handed over before—and a chance for Peyton to go back to Tom and show him she was ready for the promotion.

She had a monumental to-do list in front of her, but first, her phone sat there, silent and black. Still no texts or calls from Luke. Her finger hesitated over his number. Five more seconds to make a quick call wouldn't hurt, Peyton decided. The phone on the other end rang four times, then went to voice mail.

Peyton pushed away the little tickle of worry in her

gut. Luke could be busy playing with Maddy, or making Maddy a snack or any of the other hundreds of things that comprised a day with a four-year-old. Shrugging off the nagging sensation, she turned back to her laptop.

"Peyton?"

She glanced up to see Jack Barlow standing beside her. Luke's younger brother, and almost a carbon copy of him. Luke had that twinkle in his eye, though, and that little curve to his grin that made it dimple on one side. Jack had shorter hair, a longish military cut, and a serious cast to his face. She rose and they exchanged a quick, friendly hug. "It's nice to see you, Jack."

"I just stopped over for a quick bite and some coffee before I get back to work. I took Luke's shift at the garage this morning. It's good to see you. I heard you were back in town."

"For a couple weeks, yes."

"Stay an extra week and you can come to my wedding." Jack grinned, a smile as wide as the state of Texas blooming on his face. "Meri Prescott is making an honest man out of me at the end of the month."

"That's wonderful. Congratulations." Meri had been one of those stunningly beautiful women who made everyone around her pale in comparison. She'd been as nice as she'd been pretty, and Peyton was glad to see both Meri and Jack get a happy ending.

But also a little jealous. She'd never had anyone light up when they talked about her, the way that Jack lit up about Meri. The man was definitely in head-over-heels, heart-thumping, rainbows-and-sunsets love. The kind of crazy love that flooded a person's world, made them do insane things like get married a few months after reuniting.

Not Peyton Reynolds. She was far too sensible and

grounded to do something like that. When and if she met her Mr. Right, she'd take it slow, one step at a time. No rushing into the biggest decision of her life. Uh-huh. Just as she'd made a slow, calculated decision to kiss Luke on that bench. Every time she was around the man, he made common sense disappear.

"Luke must be glad to see you again," Jack said.

Luke. Just hearing his name sent a flutter through her, a wave of heat that filled her cheeks. Exactly the opposite of being sensible and grounded and slow. Which was her number one reason for staying far, far away from a romantic entanglement with the man. "It's always nice to connect with an old friend," she said.

Jack scoffed. "Uh-huh. That's what I said about seeing Meri again. And look where we are now. Don't be too sure the same won't happen with you and Luke."

She scoffed. "Luke isn't going to turn into Mr. Settle Down just because I'm in town."

"Stranger things have happened. Luke's a different man these days. I think it's because of you and the changes your return brought to his life." He reached out to squeeze her shoulder. "It's good to have you back, Peyton. Real good." He gave her a grin, then headed off to his car.

Peyton turned back to her work, determined to put Luke far from her mind. But the little tickle of worry about Maddy didn't disappear, and grew to become a full-out fist clawing at her gut when her second, third and fourth calls to Luke's phone all went to voice mail.

Ten minutes later, Peyton could stand it no longer. She gathered up her computer and samples, hopped in her car and drove like hell to the other side of town.

Chapter Seven

Rainbow swirls of paint formed concentric circles that overlapped on the white paper, and sometimes skittered onto the laminate kitchen table. Madelyne was wearing one of Luke's old dress shirts—or rather, the shirt was wearing her, considering that the blue cotton fabric dwarfed her tiny body and bloomed like a cloud around her slender frame. Her nose was red, her cheeks green and her chin blue, but there was a smile on her face the size of Texas, and that made Luke feel...

Good.

Which was weird, because Luke had never felt anything one way or another when a kid smiled. He had never, in fact, really interacted with kids before. Sure, packs of cousins ran around at family get-togethers, but they mostly stayed clear of the adults, barreling past in a giggling, screaming horde. But this kid—his own child—had stolen his heart in less than twenty-four hours, and he suspected he was never going to get it back.

"What'd I tell you?" his mother said, leaning in close and lowering her voice so Maddy wouldn't overhear them. She'd come the minute he'd called today and set to work right away, spoiling Maddy mercilessly with lollipops and a new doll, finding ways to keep her entertained and doing everything a grandmother would do. Luke hadn't told Madelyne who his mother was, of course, because he had to tackle the whole *Maddy, I am your father* conversation before he could do that. He wanted to tell Maddy he was her dad, wanted in some deep, base way to hear her say *Daddy*, but he sensed Maddy was still in a fragile place, and waiting was the best decision.

At first, Della had been mad at him for not telling her, then tickled pink to find out that she had a grandchild. Later, Luke suspected, there'd be a lot of questions to answer, but for now, Della was beaming at Madelyne as if the sun rose on the little girl's face.

"Grandma always knows best," Della whispered to her son.

"I'm just glad Grandma knows all the sh—" he caught himself before he cursed "—stuff I don't know."

He'd been at a complete and total loss for how to soothe Maddy when he'd called Della an hour ago. His mother had been the one to get the little girl's attention with a snack. His mother had been the one to dig around in Luke's fridge to find enough ingredients to fix Madelyne a grilled cheese sandwich, complete with a smiley face and a side of matchstick-thin apple slices, just the way she'd made lunch when Luke was little—something he'd completely forgotten in his panic. His mother had been the one to run over to the dollar store and return with finger paints and giant sheets of paper, creating a diversion that had entertained Madelyne for the past hour.

"Oh, you'll learn." She laid a gentle hand on his shoulder. "Having kids is like an instant learning curve."

"This is just temporary. Peyton's going back to Baltimore in a couple weeks."

His mother arched a brow at that. "You think you can just walk away at the end? That she isn't going to need you for the rest of her life? You're her father, Luke. That's something that lasts a lot longer than summer camp."

He chafed at the thought. He hadn't signed on for a lifetime of parenting—hell, he could barely commit to a car lease for three years, never mind a relationship with someone who was going to expect him to be a perfect role model. He'd help out financially, of course, that went without saying, but as for all this relationship stuff—

"I don't know," he said. "I mean, I had to call in reinforcements before lunch, for God's sake."

"Hey, kids are tough. But you can handle this. She adores you," Della said. "I can see it every time she talks to you. You'll get the hang of it, I promise."

His mother had a good point, but Luke still worried he might not be good at this parenting thing.

Except...

There was something nice about the way a four-year-old brought chaos to his house, nicer than the chaos he usually had with his messy friends. The paint puddling on his table, the toys peppering the living room like shrapnel, the crumbs piled under the kitchen chairs—it all sort of felt like being in the center of the living room floor right after the Christmas presents had all been unwrapped. Messy, but homey.

Della seemed completely unfazed by it all, as always. Of course, she'd raised three rough-and-tumble boys, so a few crumbs and drops of paint weren't a big deal to his capable and easygoing mother.

Luke wrapped his mom in a one-armed hug. "Thanks again."

"Anytime." Then she met his gaze. "Did you call your dad back yet?"

"Tonight. I promise."

Della put a hand on his cheek. "You're a good son."

Luke scoffed. "No, I'm not. But I'm working on it."

"Luke, look what I made!" Madelyne held up the finger paint blur of colors. Rivers of excess paint dripped off the sheet and onto the table. Great globs stained the tile, slid under the feet of the chairs.

He reached for the paper towels, but his mother put a hand on his arm. "The cleanup can wait. When a child shows you something she made, you make a big deal out of it."

His mother was right. How many times had she paused in baking bread or weeding the garden to gush over one of her boys' projects? Whether it was a lumpy clay dish fired in art class or a lopsided birdhouse clumsily hammered together in shop, every creation made by a Barlow boy had earned a place of honor in her curio.

He bent down to Maddy's level. "That is the prettiest picture I've ever seen," he said. "Awesome job, kid."

Madelyne beamed as if he'd just told her the concentric circles of color, blended into a ruddy puke color, was the next Jackson Pollock. "I gonna put it on the fridg-rator. That's where Auntie P puts my pitchers."

He noticed she didn't mention her mother. Every time Madelyne talked about her life, it was with Peyton at the center. Because Susannah had been uninvolved? Or because it hurt too much for the child to mention her late mother?

Madelyne scrambled out of the chair and slapped the messy painting onto the front of his stainless steel refrigerator. It slid down the smooth silver surface and landed with a plop on the floor.

"Uh-oh." Madelyne toed at the mess, creating another circle of paint. She raised big, wide eyes to him. "Sowwy."

"It's okay. My floor was boring." He dropped to his knees beside the kid and plopped his palms in the mess, then swiped left, right. "There. It's not boring anymore."

A pair of long, lean legs moved into his peripheral vision. High heels flexed Peyton's calves into tight round hearts. "Oh. My. God. What did she do?"

"Made art." Luke grinned. Which was exactly what Peyton was. Damn, the woman stopped his heart every time she came into the room.

"Oh, my God," she said again.

Exactly what I was thinking. He forced his gaze away from her legs and stood. "It's no big deal. It's washable."

"Auntie P!" Madelyne ran over to Peyton and plowed into her arms. Peyton scooped her niece to her chest and hugged her tight, heedless of the paint smearing her dress, her hair.

Luke watched the two of them, hugging as if they had been separated for a year instead of a couple of hours, and felt something tug in his chest. Something a lot like jealousy. He grabbed a roll of paper towels and started cleaning up the floor and the fridge while his mom made small talk with Peyton. Because it hurt too much to see the way Maddy loved Peyton.

"You look like you haven't aged a minute," his mother said to Peyton. "Still as beautiful as always, Peyton. And I'm so sorry to hear about your sister. Such a tragic loss."

"Thank you, Mrs. Barlow." Peyton hefted Maddy onto one hip. "Though I'm very surprised to see you here. Today." She cast a worried glance in Luke's direction.

"I just stopped over to give Luke a hand. And make a new friend." She grinned at Maddy.

"I gots lots of new friends, Auntie P. Luke, and Miz Barlow, and Charlie." Maddy wagged her fingers in the dog's direction.

"You've got one amazing little girl there," Della said. "Smart and sassy."

Maddy giggled. "Miz Barlow says bein' sassy is good. Cuz then boys don't wanna mess with you."

Peyton laughed, then tapped a finger on her niece's nose. "An excellent life policy."

"Well, Luke, I've got to get home and make dinner for your father." His mother grabbed her purse, and the stack of finger paintings Maddy had made for her earlier. "So nice to meet you, Miss Madelyne."

"T'ank you, Miz Barlow." Madelyne gave Della a toothy smile. "I liked my sammiches."

"I'm glad. I hope to get to see you again sometime while you're here in Stone Gap." She sent a pointed glance at Peyton. "Perhaps for dinner on Sunday night? So the *whole* family can be together?"

Peyton hesitated, as if she wasn't sure whether to expand Maddy's family circle. Sunday dinner at the Barlow house, Luke knew, was a big deal. It was stepping into the Barlow world, with all the hugs and teasing and warmth.

"Sunday is Maddy's birthday," Peyton said.

Luke made a mental note. His daughter's birthday—a date that from this minute forward would be important in his life—in their lives. A date that he would never forget, or miss. And especially not this one.

"I'm gonna be four," Maddy said. "A big girl."

"Almost a whole hand," Della said, holding up four fingers. "Growing up right before my very eyes. I hope to see you again on Sunday, Miss Maddy."

Peyton looked unsure still. "We might be able to do that," she said. "As long as you don't mind more people at the family dinner table, Mrs. Barlow."

"There's always room for one more," Della said, then wrapped an arm around Peyton. "Or two."

"Thanks, Mom." Luke tossed the first stack of dirtied paper towels into the trash and tore off a bunch more from the roll. "I appreciate you bailing me out."

Della reached up and pressed a soft palm against her son's cheek. "Anytime. And I'm glad you're doing so well with her. It's time somebody in this room grew up."

"Hey, that's a lot to ask of a four-year-old."

Della just chuckled softly, then headed out the door. When she was gone, Peyton put Madelyne down and told her to go gather up her toys. Madelyne dashed out of the room, and Peyton set to work cleaning up the rest of the paint mess. "What did you mean, she bailed you out?"

"Me and the squirt there had a...difficult morning."

"Difficult? How?"

"She got upset when she realized you were gone. I tried to distract her, but I..." He ran a hand through his hair. "I sucked at it. I guess I thought I had more of a handle on this parenting thing than I do."

"It's tough, but not impossible. And even though I was surprised to see your mom here, I'm glad you called her. Maddy has been asking me about her other grandparents."

"Maybe we should tell her the truth."

"And maybe all of this is too soon. You said you worried about how good you are at the parenting thing, but..."

Peyton tore off another wad of paper towels, but Luke stopped her from attacking the table. "Sometimes I worry, too," she said softly. "That I'm making all the wrong decisions. I mean, look at how upset Maddy was today."

"She just missed you. You're amazing with her, while I'm still figuring out how to do this. It was no big deal."

She shook her head. "You should have called me immediately. I should have been here."

"Peyton," he said, lowering his voice in case Maddy was listening, "nothing went wrong. We hit a bump, and we got past it."

Maddy ran into the room, clutching one of her dolls. "Auntie P, did Luke show you the pitchers we made? And we played in the mud and swinged on the swing, and ate funny sammiches. I had fun, Auntie P. And candy."

Peyton glared at him. "You gave her candy?"

He shrugged. "A lollipop. A kid can have—"

"Madelyne is not allowed to have candy. Or to have lunch before noon. I have her on a schedule—"

"She was hungry, Peyton. So I fed her."

"It's not that simple. If lunch is early, then dinner is early and—"

He could hear the worry and stress in her voice and realized it had been as hard for her to leave Maddy this morning as it had been for him to take the reins today. Peyton had had a lot on her shoulders all these years—responsibilities that clearly hadn't been shared as they should have been by Susannah—and he could understand her need to maintain order and control. But in lightening up, Peyton might find a little happiness for herself, too. "The world doesn't fall apart," he said to her. "Trust me. Us boys ate constantly. My mom would tease us about padlocking the fridge, but truly, she didn't care. She always made sure there were cookies in the jar and muffins in the breadbox, for when we came in from playing in the sun, hungry enough to chew our own arms off. And we turned out just fine."

"We ate sammiches for second breakfast, Auntie P. It was good. I wanna have it again."

"Second breakfast?" Peyton asked.

"Most awesome meal of the day, isn't it, M-girl?" Luke bent down and gave Maddy a high five. "Right next to second dinner and second dessert."

"Maddy, go pack up your toys, please. Now."

"Are we leavin'? Cuz Luke said we could go 'sploring in the woods. I wanna catch a butterfly."

"Be sure you count your toys when you put them in the bag so you don't forget any," Peyton said. "You brought six toys, remember?"

"Okay," Maddy said. She trudged off to the living room.

Luke waited until his daughter was out of earshot before he spoke. "I thought we were going to have lunch together."

"I think it's best if we get going now. She's had a busy day here already."

"You're just a little stressed because things got off schedule. Lighten up, Peyton. She's a kid, and half the fun of being a kid is being spontaneous."

"You think I don't know that? I'm the one who's been raising her for the last four years. You don't have a right to come in here and tell me how to do that."

"Actually, I do," he said, moving closer, keeping his voice low. He met Peyton's hard stare head-on. In her eyes, he could see worry, fear, anger, a thousand protective emotions all centered around that little girl. He understood it, because a part of him felt the same way. Cautious and concerned, and wanting only the best for the child who had stolen his heart already. "I'm her father, and you brought her to me so I could be a part of her life. Let me do that, in my own way. So we have an extra meal today or get some paint on the floor. It's no big deal," he repeated. "And—" he gave her a grin "—I hear doctors say fun is good for you."

"I'm not against fun—"

"Then let's have some. You're here for a vacation, so take one. Don't worry about the schedules or the messes. I may not have four years of experience, but even I know kids make messes. They drop stuff and play in the mud and track dirt on the carpet. And that's totally cool. It's part of being a kid. And the fun part of being a grown-up is getting in the mud with the kid."

Peyton shook her head. "Growing up means not being messy, wild and uncontrollable."

"You talk like she's twenty, not four. Being messy, wild and uncontrollable is the best part of being young. Heck, all of us have a little of that in us." He moved into her space, the mess forgotten, the kitchen disappearing from his peripheral vision. He trailed a finger along the buttons of her dress. "Doesn't that side of you still exist, somewhere under the buttons and schedules?"

She held his gaze for a second, and it seemed a river of memories poured into the space between them. Then Peyton shook her head. "You don't understand, Luke. I have to be the grown-up. The constant—"

"Party pooper."

She scowled. "I am not. You don't understand, Luke. I grew up in chaos. Susannah loved that, loved the unpredictability of it, but I...I need to know when dinner is going to be on the table, and that we leave the house at eight on the dot, and that the moon is going to be in the sky every night. I need that structure because...because it makes me feel..."

"Safe," he finished for her. "I get that, Peyton, I really do. But if you let go a little, you might find that life is even sweeter that way."

"You're wrong, Luke." Peyton started to turn away. He grabbed her arm, the movement startling her, and she stumbled back and into his chest. Just as fast, Peyton jerked away. "I have to go."

"Wait. Not yet. Not like this."

"I have to get Madelyne back to the hotel. It's almost time for lunch."

"You have an hour until noon. Stay. I'll order a pizza. We can talk."

She hesitated, long enough for hope to bloom in his chest that she would say yes. "Talk about what, Luke?"

"The past. The present. The future." He gave her another grin. Always before, that grin would make Peyton's features soften, tease her into agreement. He'd watch an echoing smile curve across her face, and whatever had passed between them would be forgiven.

But this time, Peyton didn't smile. She just shook her head again. "You haven't changed a bit. I don't know why I keep thinking you have."

"Because you're refusing to see that there may be another way to be a grown-up, Peyton. Besides the one filled with rules and schedules."

Maddy came back into the kitchen, her half-filled bag of toys forgotten in the center of the living room floor. "Auntie P, are we goin' to get pizza? Cuz I wanna play with Charlie some more and Luke said I could afta Charlie took his nap."

Peyton bent down, greeting Madelyne with a big smile. "I thought we were going to the hotel pool after lunch."

Maddy pointed outside. "Luke has a pool. We can stay here. And I can play with Charlie some more."

Clearly, his kid was the smartest one in the world. He couldn't have said it better himself. "Brilliant idea, M-girl." He turned to Peyton. "Stay, have lunch and go swimming."

"I'm not dressed for it and I don't have Maddy's bathing suit and..."

"Meri left a suit here when she was over with Jack last weekend, so you can borrow that. And as for Maddy, heck, she's a kid, she won't care what she wears."

Peyton's gaze flicked between Maddy and Luke. "But I don't have her water wings."

"I'll be her water wings." He smiled again. "Problem solved."

"Can we stay, Auntie P? Please? Luke is really nice, and he likes playing dolls and he likes paintin' pitchers and he likes doggies."

Luke could see how much Peyton wanted to say yes. She kept glancing down at her niece's earnest face, then back up at Luke's. Just when he thought he'd won her internal battle, her features hardened.

"Let's go take a swim, Peyton," he tried again, before she could say no. He reached for the door handle that led to the pool. "Let's have fun."

"Don't you want to finish cleaning up this mess first?"

He glanced back at the paint, already drying on his table and floor. "It'll be there when we're done."

"But..."

"Live on the edge, Peyton. Leave a mess. Eat candy for lunch. And..." He swiped a glop of paint off the picture on the fridge and plopped it on her nose, if only because everything about her was too neat, too perfect, too buttoned-up. "Get dirty once in a while."

Chapter Eight

Maddy pouted for a solid hour. Peyton took her to Miss Viv's for lunch, but it was a waste of time. Maddy didn't want to eat and Peyton's appetite was just as uncooperative.

Peyton had been tempted, so tempted, to say yes to Luke. To stay for lunch and some pool time, especially if it meant seeing Luke's bare chest again. But just the fact that she wanted to stay, to loosen the reins on her life, let the mess rule the day and, most of all, see Luke half-naked again, all told her she should leave.

How was it that a man she had been infatuated with as a teen could still have such a hold over her emotions and thoughts? Had his kiss been that good?

Well, yeah. It had been amazing. Even better than she'd imagined in all those teenage dreams. And that was what scared her the most—that she wanted more. Not just more, not just a single kiss—

Everything.

A part of her did want to loosen those reins on her life, but she had seen where chaos got someone—and she'd always been the one left to clean up the mess and be the responsible—

Party pooper.

Was Luke right? Had she gotten so tied up in her schedules and order that she had left fun in the rear-view mirror?

After lunch, Maddy didn't want to go to the park, or to the pool, so in the end, they curled up onto one of the beds in Peyton's hotel room. Peyton found a children's movie on the television, and Maddy lined up her dolls to watch with her. Peyton got out her sketchpad, but barely scratched the white pages. Her mind wandered, and she found herself watching a movie about a prince rescuing a princess, and picturing Luke on a horse, sweeping her up to join him.

Riding off into the sunset?

No, that wasn't reality. Those fairy tales she read as a girl weren't going to come true here in Stone Gap with Luke Barlow, of all people. But her motivation to stick to that schedule and all those rules she loved so much was fraying like an old ribbon.

A second princess movie followed the first one, and as much as Peyton wanted to be up, working, doing something, she settled against the pillows with Maddy in her arms—and fell asleep.

"Auntie P?"

Peyton roused and found Maddy staring down at her. "Hey, monkey. Is the movie over?"

"Uh-huh. And somebody's knocking at the door, but I didn't answer it, cuz you told me not to."

"Good girl." Peyton pressed a quick kiss to Maddy's

temple, then swung her legs over the bed and rubbed the sleep out of her eyes. There was a second knock at the door, just as Peyton was crossing the room.

She peered through the peephole, and there, as if she'd conjured him up from her dreams, was Luke. He'd changed into blue plaid shorts and a plain white T-shirt. His hair was damp, as if he'd just stepped out of the shower. He looked good. Too good.

She took in a deep breath, then opened the door. "Luke, what are you doing here?"

"Since you couldn't stay for lunch, I took the liberty of bringing you dinner." He hoisted a pizza box in one hand, and a box of wine coolers in the other. A bag dangled from his wrist. "And apple juice for the squirt."

"Oh, we shouldn't—"

"You have to eat. I have food. Problem solved."

Despite her earlier resolve, she found herself caving in with a laugh. "You have all the answers, don't you?"

Maddy poked her head around Peyton's leg. "Luke!"

"Hey, Maddy." He bent down and held out the pizza box. "Would you like to have pizza with me?"

"I love pizza!"

"I know you do. And your favorite is pizza with little pieces of chicken on it, and lots of cheese. We had a long conversation about it."

Peyton blinked in surprise. Luke knew all that already? In just a couple of hours with Maddy? He'd clearly bonded with her, judging by how much she'd wanted to stay at his house, how she had pouted after they'd left and how she bounded up to him now.

"Can I have some?" Maddy asked.

He chuckled. "As much as you want, as long as you leave me a slice."

Before Peyton could utter a protest, Maddy was taking

the pizza box from Luke and leading him into the room. She slid the big box onto the tiny desk in the corner, then pointed at the bed. "You sit ova there, Luke. And, Auntie P, you sit ova there." She pointed at the corner of the same bed. "And I's gonna sit on this bed all by myself cuz I's a big girl."

"Somebody inherited someone's control-freak tendencies," Luke whispered to Peyton when they were sitting together on the end of the bed.

"I'm not a control freak."

"You, honey, are the biggest control freak I know. Except maybe Mac, who definitely needs to learn to relax once in a while."

"I just like things the way I like them."

He put out his hand as if to say, *See, exactly what I meant.*

"I's gonna give everyone their pizza," Maddy said. She opened the box, looked inside, then looked up at Peyton. "Auntie P? Where's the plates?"

Peyton shot him a glance. "That's one thing restaurants always have, which was why I was planning to go out to dinner. Just wait a minute, Maddy. I'll have to run down to the front desk and see if they have any. Or go to the store—"

"We don't need plates," Luke said. "We'll make our own."

"Make our own?"

"Just watch me." He tore the top off the pizza box, then divided the cardboard into three pieces. He handed the first one to Maddy. "Load her up, pardner."

Maddy giggled, then slid a piece of pizza onto the cardboard. Half the toppings ended up tumbling to the floor, but Luke didn't skip a beat. He thanked Maddy, handed the piece to Peyton, then repeated the action twice more. Maddy snuggled up on her bed and started watching a third movie.

"Come on, Peyton. Let's sit down at the American family dinner table." Luke gestured toward the pillows propped against the headboard. "And watch TV while we eat, like the best families do."

"The best families sit down at a table and converse while they eat. Or at least they do in Rockwell paintings." She grinned, not quite ready to admit yet that maybe Luke's version was more fun.

"We'll do that. Sunday at my mother's. Tonight, let's just overindulge in cheese and dough and watch…" he said, glancing at the TV, "some girl with fish legs sing."

Maddy giggled. "That's Ariel. She's a mermaid. She's pretty."

"Not half as pretty as the girls right here in this room."

Even though she was sure he wasn't flirting, Peyton felt her cheeks heat, and she dropped her gaze to her pizza. She listened as Maddy explained the plot of *The Little Mermaid* to Luke, and realized that for the second time in the space of two days, Maddy was…

Happy.

Her little face was animated, her eyes bright. She talked and laughed, and scrambled around on the bed, acting out Ursula's role and pretending to be the friendly seagull. She ate her pizza and drank her juice, and talked too loud, and in general, acted like an ordinary kid. It was a blessing, one so unbelievable, it nearly made Peyton cry.

As the movie drew to a close, Maddy's energy began to wane. She curled up against her pillow and, five minutes later, was fast asleep, in her own bed, with her trusty bear at her side. Peyton pulled the blankets up, turned off the TV and dimmed the lights.

"I think you wore her out today," Peyton said.

"*She* wore *me* out. That girl can talk faster than Jeff Gordon can lap at NASCAR."

Peyton laughed. "Well, she hasn't been talking like that or been that active and happy in a long, long time. I'm grateful that you got her to open up." She glanced at the bed and realized that continuing the conversation with Luke meant either standing at the end of the bed, or climbing back into the space beside him. And right now, with Maddy asleep and the room quiet, Peyton was all too aware of how much space two adults took up in a double bed, and how close she'd be to Luke. "Uh, you want to sit outside again?"

"Sure. And indulge in some adult beverages and conversation?"

"That sounds perfect."

He carried the remains of the pizza and the package of wine coolers out to the small balcony. Two nights ago, they had sat here in roughly the same situation. Except the dark and quiet night seemed ten times more intimate, with that kiss they'd shared hovering in the air, unspoken.

"Thank you for watching her today," Peyton said.

"My pleasure. And I mean that. Maddy's a great kid. You and Susannah did a wonderful job with her."

Peyton nodded and took a sip of her wine cooler. "Thank you."

They were quiet for a few minutes, sipping their drinks and listening to the sounds of the birds and insects settling in for the night. Luke twirled the bottle between his palms. "What kind of mother was Susannah?"

Peyton searched for the right words, the ones that would color the truth, shade it in a light that didn't make Susannah look bad. But the truth was, her sister had been a distracted, self-centered mother, one who rarely put her daughter ahead of partying and sleeping. "Susannah tried, but..." Peyton shrugged. "She was never really there. She loved Maddy, of course, but she was more of a friend than a parent."

"Maybe Susannah didn't feel ready," Luke said. His gaze went to something far beyond the hotel. "Or maybe she just was afraid of letting Maddy down. Screwing it up."

"Everybody's afraid of that when they have a child," Peyton said. "The first time I watched Maddy on my own, I was convinced I was going to drop her on her head or forget to feed her. But you figure it out and you do your best." She took a sip of wine cooler. "And read every book you can get your hands on."

"That's what I need." He chuckled. "A book for dummy dads."

"You're doing great."

"I'm trying. But there's always that fear that..." His voice trailed off.

"That what?"

"That you won't be there when it matters most." His voice was soft, and she got the feeling he wasn't talking about Madelyne.

"You do the best you can," she said again, and laid a hand on his. The touch was easy, as if she'd held his hand a thousand times before. "And cut yourself some slack. You're new at this."

His blue eyes met hers, and his thumb closed over her fingers, changing the simple touch to one layered with connection. There was warmth there, and honesty, and something more, something the two of them kept dancing around. Something that pushed as much as it pulled, and as much as she knew she should move, should tug her hand away from his, she didn't do either.

"I hope I can be even a tenth as amazing as you are

with her, and that I can build a relationship with her like you have. I'm trying, but its slow going," Luke said. "I've seen you with Maddy. You might as well be her mother. She's so close to you."

Another shrug. "I did what I had to do. I love her, and she's all the family I have now."

"But it should have been Susannah's job. And mine." He shook his head. "No wonder you were so angry with me. You probably resented me for not being involved, not helping out."

"She really never told you she was pregnant?"

"She never did. Believe me, Peyton, if I had known I had a child, I would have been there. I might not always be the best role model or be the most responsible Barlow, but I'm not the kind of self-centered jerk who would abandon my own child."

"I never said—"

"You didn't have to." He couldn't have blamed her, really. He hadn't exactly been Mr. Settle Down back when Peyton knew him. "It was all over your face when you showed up on my doorstep. I don't blame you. I would have thought the same thing if the roles had been reversed.

"I'm sorry you had to be there, to be the parent that Maddy needed, when you should have been living your own life."

"I didn't mind," Peyton said. But her voice trembled and her shoulders tensed.

Luke rose and came around in front of her. The narrow balcony put him inches away from her, and when he bent down to her level, he saw the tears in Peyton's eyes. They brimmed, but didn't fall, threatening to undo the careful control she held over her emotions. "I'm sorry," he said, softer again this time.

Then he raised his hand and caught a tear on the edge of his finger.

"It's okay," she said, but the last word whispered away when a second tear fell.

Luke cupped her jaw and met her gaze. "I'm sorry, Peyton. And I swear, you won't be alone in this going forward."

Her shoulders relaxed, and a third and fourth tear fell. But still she refused to yield to the emotions, to let them win. "It will be nice for Maddy to have you in her life. But truly, I have it under control—"

"Oh, honey, you don't. But that's totally okay."

It was the *honey* that did her in. Luke was blurry in her vision, but he was there, his hand against her cheek, solid and firm, and dependable. All the things she had sworn he could never be. And when he leaned in, she kissed him, because right at that moment, he'd become what she wanted, what she'd always wanted.

He hauled her against him, the kiss going from zero to sixty in a split second. His chest was solid, his touch was fire and she lost herself in his mouth, his hands. She tangled her fingers in his hair, and when he pulled her closer still, she straddled his lap and the two of them sank to the concrete floor.

His hand snaked under her shirt, sliding to the front to cup her breast through the lace of her bra. She gasped, her nipples puckered, desire erupted like a volcano. Between her legs, she could feel his growing erection, the promise there of a night she would never forget.

Oh, how she wanted that, wanted him, but there were three of them here, the third one asleep in the room just behind them. Maddy was why she was here in Stone Gap. Why she was returning to Baltimore at the end of the two weeks.

And on top of that, this was Susannah's boyfriend. Granted, that was years in the past, and Susannah was gone now, but the thought still put some brakes on the moment. Peyton pulled away from Luke and laid her head on his chest. His heart thudded beneath her cheek. "We can't do this. Not now. Not here."

"You're right. I wish you weren't, but you are."

"Plus, it's a little weird. I mean, you used to date my sister."

"I know what you mean. But I don't see you the way I did back then."

"I'm not the annoying nerdy little sister anymore?"

"Not at all." He pressed a kiss to her lips. "Not at all. And even though Susannah and I dated, and well…" He looked toward the bedroom where Maddy slept, then turned back to Peyton. "We were never serious. I never felt like this with her."

Like what? Peyton wanted to ask, but if she did, she knew she'd be opening a door to a path she wasn't sure she wanted to take.

He wrapped one arm around her. "Let's just sit here, like this, for a while. At least until I forget what I want to do to you."

She laughed, a chuckle that came from somewhere deep inside her, the kind of throaty laugh that was half flirt, half desire. *Doesn't that side of you still exist, somewhere under the buttons and schedules?* Maybe it did, because every time she was with Luke, another side of Peyton came to life. "Me, too."

"Sometime," he said, dropping another kiss on her lips, "you'll have to tell me what exactly it is that you want to do to me."

Sometime meant in the future. Sometime meant seeing him again, not because he wanted to be with Maddy, but because he wanted to be with Peyton. Sometime implied...more.

"Sometime I will," Peyton said, making a promise a part of her had made years and years ago. A promise she wasn't sure she could keep, but right now, she didn't want to think about that.

"I'll hold you to that, Peyton Reynolds." Then he sat back and they stared up at the stars. The conversation shifted to Orion and Scorpio, to the Big Dipper and the Little Dipper. She listened to his heartbeat while he spoke, and soaked up the warm night air, because tomorrow she would go back to focusing on her job and Maddy, and the reality that her life was far away in Maryland, and not here in Stone Gap on a concrete balcony under the stars.

On Wednesday morning, Luke headed into the garage early. There was a full schedule on tap today, and the earlier he got in to work, the earlier he could leave and the sooner he could see Peyton and Maddy again. Ever since Peyton's return, Luke's thoughts had revolved around two things—his daughter and the woman he had never noticed until now. Both added layers of complications and expectations to his life, two things he wasn't so sure he was ready for.

Even though his time with Maddy yesterday had gone well, the truth was he was upset that he'd needed to call his mother for help. He still worried about screwing up, about letting his daughter down, of doing what he had done four years ago.

Hurting someone he cared about.

Luke parked in the lot beside the garage. Two blocks down the street, where the business end of Main Street stopped with Sadie's Clip 'n Curl and the residential world began, Luke saw a familiar front porch. He wondered if the ratty old couch, missing the brown plaid fabric off one arm and held up by a chunk of concrete block to replace a missing leg, was still there. One hot summer, Luke, Ben and Jeremiah had seen the sofa on the side of the road, set out for the next day's trash pickup, probably after being replaced by a fancy leather recliner version. The three of them had hauled it down the street and up onto Jeremiah's front porch, partly because his house was the closest, and partly because Jeremiah's house was the destination they all flocked to after school. He had a good view of Main Street, a short walk to the ice cream parlor, and best of all, he lived next door to the Wallace twins, who often lay out in bikinis on the front lawn.

Luke hadn't sat on that sofa in years. After the accident—

Well, after that, a hell of a lot of things had changed.

Instead of walking down the street and seeing if the sofa was still there—if the past that had died years ago could be resurrected—Luke ducked into the dim interior of the garage. His father was already there, par for the course with Bobby Barlow, who'd spent almost every day of his adult life in this garage. All of Luke's memories of his father came wrapped in the smell of motor oil, and even now, whenever he inhaled the heavy, viscous scent, he thought of fishing trips with his father or long talks in the backyard while they tossed a ball. That was how a conversation with his dad worked—there was no sitting down at a table and pouring your heart out. There was tossing a ball or casting a line and letting the words fill the space between.

"Hey, Dad." Luke hung his car keys on the hook by the office door and grabbed a pale blue work shirt from the back of the chair, tugging it on and buttoning it up as he walked.

"Luke. Good to see you." His father poked his head out from under the hood of a Jeep that had seen better days. Bobby Barlow was a solid man, square in the shoulders, broad in the chest. The kind of man people called stout. Della had been trying for years to get Bobby to lose a few pounds, something his doctor harped on as much as his wife, but Bobby still sneaked out for a double cheeseburger at lunch or a beer at the end of the day. "Hand me that socket wrench, will you?"

Luke did as his father asked, then slipped into place beside Bobby, propping his hands on the metal frame and peering into the morass of wires and hoses snaking through the engine. The two of them talked about the problems the Jeep was having for a while, the male Barlow version of small talk.

"So your mother tells me you've got a daughter," Bobby said, as he bent down into the engine to tighten something.

"Didn't know I had a daughter until this week," Luke said. "Susannah never said a word."

Bobby put up a hand, which Luke filled with the new fan belt Bobby was installing. "So now you know. What are you going to do about it?"

"I'm still getting used to the idea, Dad. I haven't thought that far ahead."

Bobby straightened and reached for a rag for his hands. "If there's one thing having kids forces you to do, it's look ahead. From the minute Mac was born, that's all I've done is worry about the future. How to feed you guys, keep you in shoes and sports, and keep you from making stupid decisions that could hurt you. That don't stop when your kids are grown, you know. You still worry about them making the right decisions, and staying fed and clothed and warm."

Luke chuckled. "I'm doing fine, Dad. Roof over my head, and beer in my fridge."

"Yup, and I'm glad for that, but now that you're a father, you need more."

In that unspoken language of working together, Luke went around to the driver's side of the Jeep and waited for his father's nod before starting the engine. The engine hesitated a half second, then turned over, running smooth and easy. Luke turned it off, then dropped the keys into his father's palm. "I know. I need college savings plans and—"

"I'm not talking about that stuff. You'll always need that. What kids really need is love and attention. They need you to be there, to be the one they can depend on. Day after day, whether you're having a bad day or you just need a vacation or your damned knee is giving out." Bobby winced and gave his right knee a rub.

Worry spiked in Luke's chest. His father looked a little paler, a little older today. "Go sit down, Dad."

"I sit down, I might as well lie down in a coffin. I got stuff to do, Luke. Did you see the lot? There's five cars out there, all rush jobs for today."

"You need to get that other knee replaced. Call the doctor, schedule the operation."

"I can't afford the time off. Last one had me out for three weeks, then six weeks of rehab after that, slowing me down. I need to keep the doors open, keep food on the table. The knee can wait."

The unspoken question that had hung around all the conversations with his dad for the past year was when Luke was going to step into his father's shoes and make the garage a full-time job. For years, Luke had resisted.

Left the garage altogether for a couple of years, bouncing between jobs, trying to find where he fit. Jack had stepped in during Dad's last surgery, then left to begin his carpentry business when Bobby returned.

Luke had tried a hundred different jobs, but in the end, he always came back here, to the smell of motor oil and the place that felt more like his childhood than any other in Stone Gap. He had to admit he liked the heft of a tool in his hands, the sweet rush of success when a long-dead engine finally roared to life. He liked knowing his job made a difference in someone's life. Helped them get to work or drive their kids to school or visit grandma in the hospital.

He liked that. A lot.

Luke moved the Jeep out of the bay, switching it for a pickup truck with a sticky throttle. When he climbed out of the truck's cab, his father was already reaching for the hood. Luke put a hand on Bobby's. "Go home, Dad. I've got this."

"I'm fine. I'll just take a couple aspirin—"

"No, you won't. You'll go home, call your doctor and schedule your appointment. And you'll stay at home and recover until you're 100 percent. You won't worry about this garage or about anything to do with it, because I'm going to be here, every day." Luke leaned against the counter and thought it was past time. Time to leap into the future, time to position his future so he could pay for college educations and shoes and pizzas with little bits of chicken. "I want you to think about retiring."

"Retiring?" Bobby scoffed. "To do what? Sit around on the couch and watch reruns of *Oprah*?"

"Take Mama on a trip. Go to Italy or Greece or, hell, Savannah. You two have worked hard, and you deserve to spend the next forty years doing what you want to do, not what you have to do."

Bobby draped an arm over his middle son's shoulders. "Listen, don't feel like you have to take this over. I'll be fine. I just need a little rest and some aspirin."

"I don't *have* to take this over, Dad. I *want* to. I want…" His gaze traveled around the garage, over the tool chests that had once towered over Luke as a little boy, past the benches filled with parts and handprints and memories, past the office door that separated the boys from their dad's not-so-secret candy stash in his desk drawer. Luke had grown up here, in more ways than one, and now, he realized, he was ready to make that final leap. "I want to be all the things I need to be for my daughter. Dependable. Strong. Responsible."

Bobby's eyes softened and a smile warmed his face. "You're growing up."

"Took me a while." Luke shrugged. "But I'm trying."

Bobby gave his son's shoulders a squeeze. "I'm proud of you. And speaking of growing up, I want to meet this granddaughter of mine before she's heading off to college."

"You will. I promise. I don't know how I'm going to work this out in the future, with Peyton living in Maryland and me living here, but I'll think of something."

"Marry her." Bobby grinned. "That would solve everything."

Luke laughed, but it was a comfortable laugh, one that said maybe he was easing into more changes than he realized. "One big step at a time, Dad. Let's start with the garage. That's a commitment I can handle."

Chapter Nine

Peyton rose before dawn and spent the early part of the morning sending some emails back and forth with Catherine about the design. As soon as elements were approved by the client, Peyton started the ordering process, and scheduling the contractors. It felt good to get work done, to be back in the game. She copied her boss on the progress of the job and got a *you rock* email in response. Finally, her career was getting back on track, and the promotion she had worked so hard for seemed to be in reach again.

But then she glanced over at Maddy, curled up in the bed, wearing pink teddy bear pajamas, one foot out of the covers as always and her arm tucked around her stuffed bear. A wave of love hit Peyton like a tsunami, and at that moment, she didn't want to go back to Baltimore, didn't want to go back to work, didn't want to do anything but spend every spare moment with this angel who had been dropped into her life.

Maddy stretched, then rolled over and gifted Peyton with a smile. "Hi, Auntie P."

"Hi yourself, monkey. What do you want to do today?"

Maddy shrugged. "I dunno."

"It's Wednesday, and they have a festival in a town near here, so maybe we could go to that. There might be rides and things for kids to do."

Maddy sat up in bed, drew her bear onto her lap and shook her head. "It's ice cream day, Auntie P." Her voice dropped and she rested her chin on Bo's furry head. "Mommy liked ice cream day."

And then Peyton remembered. Wednesdays were the days that Susannah liked to celebrate. *Halfway to the weekend,* she would always say, and during the times when she did hold down a job for more than a few weeks, she would tell Peyton she needed a pick-me-up to help her last till Friday. When Maddy was born, that pick-me-up had evolved from beer to ice cream, a tradition that Susannah had kept up.

Peyton's older sister might have been a distracted, sometimes irresponsible mother, but she had done this one thing. Maybe because Maddy loved it so much, and maybe because it was an easy tradition to maintain. There was a little ice cream shop near the Baltimore condo, and every Wednesday after Maddy got home from day care, Susannah would walk her down there for a dinner made up of a hot fudge sundae. No matter how many times Peyton protested, citing the lack of nutritional value, Susannah had ignored her and taken Maddy.

After Susannah's death, ice cream Wednesdays had disappeared, too. At first because Peyton had been too overwhelmed to even think about what day it was, and later because she wasn't sure if sticking to the things

Susannah used to do would make it harder or easier on Maddy to accept her mother's death.

This was the first time Maddy had brought up Susannah since her mother had died. The psychologist had told Peyton that when Maddy was ready to talk about it, she'd be the one to introduce the topic. Pushing her too much, too fast, might make Maddy retreat again. But right now, there was a window open, and Peyton decided to nudge it just a tiny bit more.

Peyton took a seat on the end of the bed. "Ice cream day was really fun, wasn't it? I miss it."

Maddy clutched her bear tighter, her eyes wide and serious. "I wanna get ice cream for dinner. Like Mommy did."

"Then that's what we'll do," Peyton said.

Maddy brightened a bit. "Mommy loved ice cream. And unicorns. And purple things."

"And you," Peyton said. "She loved you, Maddy. And I bet she's missing you just as much as you're missing her."

Maddy looked away. "Can I play with my dolls now?" Her voice was teary, but strong.

"Sure." Peyton let Maddy go and let the conversation about Susannah drop. It was progress—not much, but something.

Luke had said he'd be working all day today, so Peyton and Maddy stayed busy with a trip to the mall for some more shorts for Maddy, then lunch at a restaurant with one of those indoor play places. Afterward they went back to the hotel so that Maddy could take a nap, and Peyton could do a little more work. Shortly before dinnertime, Peyton decided they would walk to downtown Stone Gap. If they were going to have ice cream for dinner, they could at least get a little exercise first.

As they rounded the corner onto Main Street, she saw

Luke heading away from the garage and toward them. As soon as he saw them, a smile filled his face, a smile Peyton echoed. Was he glad to see both of them? Or just Maddy? And why did she want to know that answer so badly?

Maddy started tugging on Peyton's hand. "It's Luke, Auntie P. Can he get ice cream with us?"

"Sure." Peyton told herself it was because she wanted Luke to spend more time with Maddy, not just because Peyton wanted to spend more time with Luke.

Maddy ran up ahead, and straight into Luke. She had her bear in her arms, and Bo tumbled to the ground with the collision. At the last second, Luke caught him and pressed Bo back into Maddy's arms. "Whoa there, cowgirl. Where are you off to in such a hurry?"

"Luke! Luke!" Maddy said. "We're getting ice cream for dinner and Auntie P says you can come, too!"

"Ice cream for dinner?" He smirked at Peyton. "Is someone stepping outside the boundaries of rules and schedules and filleruppers?"

"Just keeping a tradition that Susannah started." She ruffled Maddy's hair. "Right, monkey?"

Maddy nodded. "Are we going to get ice cream now?"

"Yup, but you need to hold my hand while we walk," Peyton said to Maddy, putting out her right palm.

"Luke, you hafta hold my other hand." Maddy put her left hand into Peyton's and her right into Luke's. "Now we all hafta walk together. Like a mommy and daddy."

Luke's eyes met Peyton's. Neither of them said anything about Maddy's pronouncement, but the message was there, in the unspoken trinity of two adults with a child between them. People in Stone Gap watched them pass, questions in their eyes, but Peyton kept on going, until they'd reached the little ice cream parlor that sat near the end of Main Street, a block away from Sadie's Clip 'n Curl. A bright pink-and-white awning hung in front of the little shop, over wide plate-glass windows and a cheery yellow interior.

Luke held the door for Peyton and Maddy. "You don't have to be a gentleman, you know," Peyton said. She passed by so close, she caught the tempting scent of his cologne, brushed the edge of his arm. Her heart stuttered.

"I know. But that doesn't mean I don't want to be one." He gave her a grin, then pulled out two chairs at a small table and gestured to Peyton and Maddy to sit. He tugged a napkin out of the dispenser on the table and draped it over his arm. "What would you like to order, mademoiselle?"

Maddy giggled at Luke's mangled French accent. Peyton stifled a laugh of her own. "I wanna sundae," Maddy said. "With chocolate ice cream. And sprinkles. And a cherry."

"And for madam?" He made a swooping gesture and bowed in Peyton's direction.

"Just a bowl of vanilla."

He arched a brow. "Madam, you are in the *premier* ice cream shop in Stone Gap, North Carolina. Where the cows that make the milk are happier than the cows in all of Paris."

She laughed. "And why is that?"

"Because here…" He made a swooping gesture with his arm, then his gaze came to rest on her face, saying, "They are surrounded by beauty."

Peyton's cheeks went hot as a furnace. He wasn't talking about her, couldn't possibly be talking about her. *Was* he talking about her?

"And yes, I'm talking about you," Luke said, as if reading her mind. "And my beautiful d—"

"Maddy," Peyton interrupted.

"Maddy," Luke finished, with a note of disappointment in his voice. He straightened and laid the napkin on the table. "I'll be back with your orders."

The flirty mood was gone, divided by the truth, the reality that she had yet to trust him fully, yet to believe he would be in Maddy's life for the long haul. Why? He'd been here thus far and had yet to let either of them down. Why was Peyton still waiting for the other shoe to drop?

She came to no answers before Luke returned, bearing a tray with three paper bowls. He affected the French waiter act again, laying the first bowl in front of Maddy. "Your sundae, mademoiselle."

Maddy giggled. "T'ank you."

Luke laid a second bowl in front of Peyton. "And for you, madam, the high school special," he said. "I think I got it right."

She stared down at a mound of mint chocolate chip ice cream, topped with a drizzle of chocolate syrup and a sprinkling of nuts. She hadn't seen a bowl like that in years. Five years, to be exact. "You remembered the kind of ice cream I like?"

"Only because the three of us came here, like, five times a week. I practically had the whole menu memorized when I was young."

"Thank you," she said softly. The part of her that still remembered the thrill of her infatuation with Luke was ridiculously flattered that he remembered something so small.

He slipped into the third seat, with a sundae of his own. He was just about to dig in when the door behind the counter of the shop opened and a six-foot-tall man in a teddy bear suit came lumbering out, wearing an oversize T-shirt with the shop's bright logo across the front.

The mascot waved at Maddy, his big head bouncing with the greeting.

Maddy shied away from the bear and pressed against the table.

"Maddy, he's just a mascot. There's a man inside the suit," Peyton explained, logically, calmly, "and he's just going outside to tell people they should come get ice cream. Would you like to say hello to him?"

Maddy shook her head, her eyes wide. "Nu-uh."

"It's just a costume, sweetie," Peyton explained. "In the back, there's a zipper for the suit and—"

"I don't wanna talk to him." She hunched over her bowl.

Luke picked up Maddy's bear, who had been propped up in the fourth seat. He put the bear to his ear. "What's that you say, Bo? Oh, my, I didn't know. Let me tell Maddy."

Maddy giggled. "Tell me what?"

"That Mr. Bo here thinks he's just seen his long-lost Uncle Jeb."

"Uncle Jeb?" Maddy asked. Her attention was on Luke now, not the bear mascot gathering up some flyers from the girl behind the counter.

"Yup. Did you know Mr. Bo here has a family just like you? He has a daddy and some uncles and even a grandpa. Bo said the big guy over there—" Luke lowered his voice and leaned in toward Maddy "—is his uncle Jeb, not seen since the great bear reunion of '82."

Peyton bit back a laugh. "Uncle Jeb? Really?"

"Hey, it's the South. It's possible." Luke winked, then turned back to Maddy. "So Uncle Jeb there might just like to see Bo, and meet him. They can *paws* for a minute, catch up on some bear stuff." He grinned at Peyton, and she rolled her eyes at his awful pun—but couldn't help smiling at how Maddy was losing her fear.

Maddy glanced over her shoulder at the mascot, then down at Bo. "Can you go wif me, Luke?"

"Sure, kid." As soon as Luke rose, Maddy followed and slipped her hand into Luke's again. They walked across the small shop together while Peyton stayed behind at the table, watching the whole exchange with amusement and a little wonder.

Her heart lurched, seeing six-foot-two Luke bending down beside his daughter, who was barely half his height. He was patient and sweet with her while they introduced her bear to the mascot and were given a free cookie by the young girl at the counter. Instead of shying away, as Maddy had always done before, she got up there and was talking to the mute mascot, who responded with exaggerated hand gestures and nods. Uncle Jeb made a big deal out of Bo, which delighted Maddy to no end. Luke stayed close, translating the mascot's head nods into a conversation between Bo and Maddy.

If Peyton had been asked to place a bet a week ago, she would have said Luke would maybe spend a couple of days with them, then be gone as quickly as a summer storm. But he was sticking around, getting involved, making a connection.

Becoming a father.

And that meant Peyton was going to have to make some tough decisions at the end of her two-week stay. What if, after the DNA results came back—results she had no doubt would prove what she knew in her heart—what if Luke asked for custody? As the remaining biological parent, he'd have a valid case. How could Peyton possibly let Maddy go?

Maddy came running back to the table, chattering

about Bo meeting his uncle Jeb, and how yummy the cookie was, and how she thought ice cream for dinner was the best idea ever. The three of them ate their sundaes, then headed outside into the perfect warm evening.

Peyton stood on the sidewalk beside Luke and a still-bubbly Maddy and decided she didn't want the evening to end, not yet. "I think I'm going to take Maddy to the playground. Let her burn off some of this energy and sugar, or I'll never get her to sleep tonight."

"Let's go to the new one Jack is building. He's got the swings installed, and the jungle gym."

"Swings?" Maddy jumped up and down. "I love swings!"

They headed down Main Street, toward a pair of shops, a bakery and a deli that sat beside the empty lot that was on its way to being the Eli Delacorte Memorial Playground. The equipment was bright blue, a nice contrast to the pale wood picnic tables and benches. Behind a roped-off area in the far corner sat a slide waiting to be installed and several ready-to-construct giant wooden puzzles, perfect for entertaining little minds. The rest was done and open for business, though.

"Eli was Meri's cousin," Luke explained. "He died in the war, serving with Jack. My brother really wanted a way to memorialize Eli, and he came up with this playground. I don't know if you remember, but Eli's parents own the bakery and the deli."

"Betty and George Delacorte?" Peyton asked, as Luke gestured toward a long wooden bench. She settled on the right end, draping an arm across the back, relaxing into the comfortable seat Jack had built. "I remember them. Every time I went in the bakery, Miss Betty would give me some kind of treat. She's a sweet woman."

"They're some of the most generous people in Stone Gap. Damned shame about losing Eli."

"He was a great guy," Peyton said. "I didn't know him well, but I heard lots of people talk about him. He was Jack's best friend, wasn't he?"

"Yup. Tough to lose your best friend." Luke's voice had a rough edge to it. He cleared his throat, but pain still lingered in his face.

Maddy had run ahead and was pushing Bo in one of the baby swings. She was singing her favorite song about the whale and the lemon. Another family came into the park, with a little boy about Maddy's age. Peyton watched, sure that Maddy would run back to her aunt's side, as she had done so many times in the past few weeks since her world had been rocked, but instead Maddy started talking to the little boy, and seconds later, the two of them were climbing on the jungle gym like a pair of chummy monkeys. The sight of Maddy playing with another child, a stranger at that, gave Peyton hope that maybe the Maddy she knew and loved was coming back to her.

"Want to talk about it?" Peyton said. With Maddy busy, it left her alone with Luke, and she realized that opportunity made her want to know more, to uncover some of the mysteries around a man she used to think she knew.

"Talk about what?"

"I've known you a long time, Luke," she began. "And when I came back to Stone Gap, I expected to find the exact same man I left behind. Irresponsible, uncommitted—"

"Gee, thanks."

She gave him an apologetic smile. "But you're not that man anymore. You've surprised me in a dozen different ways."

"Thank you. And I mean that one sincerely."

"But I get the sense that there's a reason for all that, a reason other than Maddy. Something changed you." Peyton didn't push any more. She was, after all, only an old friend, and his daughter's aunt. Despite the kisses they'd shared, she wouldn't call this…thing between them a relationship. She wasn't sure what she'd call it, but however they defined their connection, she wanted to be there for him if he wanted to open up, if he wanted help to erase the sadness that tinted the edges of his words.

He rested his elbows on his knees. His shoulders hunched, and he seemed to go to some place deep inside his soul. "Do you remember Jeremiah Thurber?"

She thought for a moment. "He was the one that released the chicken at the school assembly, wasn't he? He had everyone in stitches, but I thought the poor principal was going to have a heart attack." Jeremiah had been a well-liked kid, member of nearly every sports team at school, and one of those kids who made it onto every yearbook page because he seemed to be woven into the very fabric of their school. He'd also been one of Luke's best friends, part of the three-pack of Luke, Ben and Jeremiah, who were the toast of every party in town. "Great guy."

"Great guy—" Luke let out a breath "—who now spends his days locked in his room, playing video games."

That surprised her. Of all the people she'd known in Stone Gap, the busy, friendly, outgoing Jeremiah would be the last she'd picture that way. "Why?"

"Because of me." Luke cursed, then got to his feet and crossed to an old oak tree. He leaned against it, watching Maddy, but really, withdrawing into himself, away from her.

Peyton thought of the undefined parameters between them. She didn't have the right to push him, to find out what lay under those words, but that didn't stop her from getting up and joining him at the tree. Peyton put her hands behind her back and leaned against the rough bark, close enough to touch Luke, but far enough to give him the room he wanted. "What happened?"

He stood there awhile longer, while the happy sounds of playing children rang in the air like bells. Luke muttered another curse. "I *never* talk about it. But maybe I should. Don't all those experts say talking crap out makes it easier?"

"Like giving a wound some air to help it heal. That's how Maddy's psychologist describes it."

"She's seeing a psychologist?"

Peyton nodded. "I started taking her after Susannah died. She's had a hard time, and I needed...help."

A smile ghosted on his face. "Tough as hell for you to admit that, isn't it?"

She toed at the grass and avoided his gaze. "Of course it is. I've always been the poster child of self-sufficiency."

"You have indeed. I'm impressed." A wider smile filled his face now, and his gaze connected with hers. "I've always been impressed by you, Peyton."

That warmed her deep inside, in that empty place that had always thought Luke never noticed her. "Really?"

"You were always so studious," he said. "You got good grades, you read constantly and, even when we were kids, you were the one who worried about everyone getting home on time and having dinner."

"I had to. My mother was..." Peyton shrugged, as if the difficult childhood she'd had didn't impact her anymore. "More often than not, drunk or passed out. Susannah was the wild child, and she was never around, so that left me to be the one in charge."

His face softened with sympathy. Few people had

known about Peyton's mother, but many had suspected, and in Luke's features, she saw understanding, support. "How old were you when that started?"

"Old enough to know that it wasn't supposed to be my job." She looked at Maddy, who thankfully had none of that on her shoulders. She was a kid, in the best ways of being a kid, who played with her dolls and had ice cream for dinner once in a while, and didn't worry about adult things like empty cupboards and the electric company shutting off the power. "The only time I was really a kid were the weekends I went to my grandma Lucy's house. She'd bake cookies and teach me to sew, and tell me to go out and play. But when she was seventy-five, she got sick, and those weekends pretty much ended."

"Peyton, I'm sorry." He took her hand, his touch warm and comforting. "You have always had too much on your plate, too many expectations on your shoulders. You deserved a better childhood, more of those cookies and days outside."

She shrugged, as if it didn't matter. "It was what it was."

"But it doesn't have to always be that way. You can have more now, and you deserve more."

"Like what you have with your family?" A smile crossed her face. "I've always liked your family. I still do. They were like the…"

"What?" he nudged when she didn't finish. His fingers tightened on hers, and that touch encouraged her to say the rest, to admit the truth to herself.

"The family I dreamed I had. I used to pretend I…" Now she did stop talking and looked away, because there was no way in hell she was admitting the rest. *Pretend I married you and we had that family around us all the time.* "Pretend I lived somewhere like that."

"I had no idea you and your sister grew up like that," Luke said. "Susannah didn't talk about her home life much, and I was too, uh, busy being a teenage boy to ask."

She laughed and pointed at his chest. "Now, *that's* the Luke I remember."

"I'm not quite that bad anymore."

"Not quite." She grinned at him, and they shared a smile. They watched Maddy and her new friend play for a while, as the day drew to a close and the sun began to set. Peyton felt so much better, opening up to Luke, and realizing he supported her and understood. It was... nice. Very nice.

"If you ever want to talk about what happened with Jeremiah, I'm here, you know," she said softly. "That's what friends are for."

"Is that what we are? Friends?" His blue eyes were direct on hers, assessing, curious.

She sighed. "I don't know what we are, Luke."

"I don't, either, but I think it went beyond friends after that second kiss."

That sent a buzz through her, as if she was a teenager again and desperate for the handsome football captain to see beyond her glasses and her books. Goodness, she was hopeless. She needed to get back on track, to refocus their relationship into something she could define. And by define, she meant control, because if there was one thing Peyton didn't like, it was uncertainty.

The children had moved to the swings and were toeing off and drifting back and forth while they chattered about whatever topics four-year-olds chattered about.

"I'm the same as you, you know," Luke said after a while. "I don't like to ask for help. Or admit that I can't handle something on my own."

She let out a little laugh. He could have been describing her personal résumé. "I think that's part of human nature."

"Not always the smartest part." He plucked a leaf off the branch above their heads, shredded the green into tiny pieces, then tossed them on the ground. Then he let out a long breath, and his features turned somber. "I've made some pretty stupid decisions myself, the biggest of which was that night with Jeremiah."

They leaned against the tree, their heads close together as he talked. She could have reached out and taken his hand in her own, but she didn't. Instead, she stayed still and listened, watching the pain flicker in Luke's eyes.

"Four years ago, Jeremiah and I were at a party. One of those impromptu ones that spring up wherever there's an empty place and someone with a beer budget. Remember that factory outside town, the one that shut down back in the '80s?"

She nodded. She knew the place. It had gone from a bustling manufacturing plant to a ghost town, with half the buildings falling into disrepair. Years ago, the town had put up yellow caution tape and no-trespassing signs, but it did little to dissuade teenagers looking for a place far from prying eyes.

"Jeremiah's girlfriend had broken up with him that morning, so he asked me to be his wingman and designated driver. He wanted to forget her, know what I mean?"

She nodded. She knew how hard it could be to forget someone you were half in love with. Even now, standing a few inches away from Luke, every fiber in her being was attuned to his.

"But then I met some girl, a girl whose name I don't even remember now, and I left Jeremiah alone. He got it in his head that he wanted to leave, and he couldn't find me, so he..." Luke turned away and cursed. "He grabbed the first set of keys he saw and got behind the wheel. Hit a tree a quarter mile down the road."

Her breath caught. "Oh, Luke."

"Wasn't wearing a seat belt, and when he hit the steering wheel, he broke his back. Paralyzed from the waist down." Luke's voice became ragged, and a sob caught in his sentence. "He was *twenty-one*, Peyton. Just barely starting his life. And if I had been there, if I had stuck with him like I said I would—"

"You can't blame yourself for that. He's the one who got behind the wheel of the car, not you."

His eyes hardened and it made Peyton's heart break for Luke. "*I* was supposed to be watching him," he said. "I was supposed to be his friend."

"You weren't his guardian. He was a grown man, one who made one bad choice." Now she did take his hand in hers, but he remained stiff, unyielding. "You can't blame yourself, Luke."

"Yeah, well, I do. Every day." He pushed off from the tree and away from her. His shoulders were hunched, the lines in his face filled with regret and self-recrimination. "And if you want to know the truth, that's what I worry about every single day, hell, every single minute, since the day I found out I'm Maddy's father." His gaze shifted to his daughter now playing in a sandbox near the little boy's family. Luke's composure cracked. "I'm not father material, Peyton, no matter how many times I go out for ice cream and play at the park."

It all made sense. Luke's "irresponsibility" was about fear, not a character deficiency. She finally understood that, as well as she understood her own need to control everything so she wouldn't make a bad decision. Luke's regrets had clearly haunted him for a long, long time—and still did.

He started to leave, but she hurried after him, grabbing his arm and stopping him. "Maybe you're right, Luke, or maybe you're just scared as hell of screwing this up. I understand that, because I feel it every day myself. I worry all the time. What if I'm not the mom she needs? What if I make a decision that hurts her instead of helps her?"

"You're a great mom, Peyton. Maddy is lucky to have you."

"And she's lucky to have *you*." Peyton gave his arm a squeeze, and a smile flickered across his face. "Being with you these last few days has helped Maddy in ways I couldn't. All the ways she needed, ever since Susannah died. The man who made up that whole story about Uncle Jeb and helped a little girl feel safe when she was scared, *that* is the man who should be a father. And over there," Peyton said, pointing at Maddy, chattering with her new friend a mile a minute, "I see a little girl who needs that father, needs him more than maybe either you or she even realize. So, deal with your demons, and deal with them fast, because she needs you. Today, not ten years from now."

Peyton let Luke go and went back to Maddy. She waited, hoping that Luke would follow, but when she glanced over her shoulder a minute later, he was gone.

Chapter Ten

It was almost three full days before Luke could steal enough time to see Peyton and Maddy again. He was glad for the time and space, the comforting world of tools and grease and mechanical problems.

Working in the shop gave a man a lot of time to think. All day Thursday and Friday, and again on Saturday morning, Luke had thought about what it meant to be a father. About what Peyton had said about doing his best, about not blaming himself for the past and not letting that be the wall to the future. He'd always worried that he wouldn't live up to people's expectations—and truth be told, he probably hadn't done a good job of that at all—but with a child, those expectations weren't very high. Maybe he really had gotten through to Maddy, or maybe it had just been dumb luck that he connected so easily with his daughter. To Luke, it seemed as if all kids wanted was someone to listen to silly songs about whales and lemons, to hang up their messy paintings on the fridge and to just *be there*.

Peyton was right. As worried as Luke had been about screwing it up, so far, he hadn't. That made him wonder if maybe it wasn't too late to rebuild other relationships in his life. To start being there for the other people he had let down in the past. Today, not ten years from now.

After his lunch break on Saturday, he walked over to Jeremiah's house. He stood on the porch, where the old sofa still sat, faded by time and sun. Luke stood there a good long time, debating, then finally rang the bell. Jeremiah's mother gave Luke a surprised hug when she opened the door, then practically danced him down the hall to Jeremiah's room.

The dark room was caught in a time warp. Dusty trophies from middle school and high school crammed the shelves lining the space above Jeremiah's bed, now a hospital bed instead of the old battered twin he'd had as a kid. Pennants for sports teams arrowed across the blue painted walls, and a small army of old Lego toys crowded together on top of the dresser. The gray carpeting was gone, switched out for hardwood floors that wouldn't snag the wheelchair, and the doorway had been widened to accommodate the chair's width. But other than that, not much had changed. Jeremiah lay in his bed, a game controller on his lap, and some video game with aliens and soldiers played on the television, filling the room with the sounds of artificial gunfire.

Jeremiah sent Luke a nod. "Hey."

"Hey." The guilt slammed into Luke like a fresh, stinging slap across his face. He fought the urge to make small talk and then leave, as he'd done a hundred times before, back in the first years after the accident. Then it had gotten too hard to be here, and Luke's visits had trickled away to nothing. It had to have been almost nine months, maybe more, since he'd stood in this room. He took one look at Jeremiah's sallow skin and sunken eyes and decided being out of the cave he called a house would be good for his friend. "You want to come down to the garage this afternoon?"

Jeremiah twisted the controller right and slammed the buttons until the alien on the screen evaporated in a faux bloody cloud. "Nah. I'm good."

"Come on, come with me. I need someone to tell me what I'm doing wrong."

"Hell, I don't remember any of that stuff. It's been years since I worked for your dad."

"It's not like I'm going to ask you to change out a transmission. Just keep me company."

Jeremiah didn't answer. He kept on shooting.

This was when Luke usually left. The uncomfortable silence, the way Jeremiah ignored him, the way the trophies on the wall seemed to mock Luke—*if you hadn't been so distracted, there'd be more trophies, more life in this room*—but this time, he held his ground. He moved in front of the TV and blocked the game. "Let's go. This room is depressing as hell."

"No one's asking you to stay."

"And no one's chaining you to this bed, either. Get up and out the door, and get some sun before you turn into a vampire."

Jeremiah sighed and laid the controller to the side. "You are a total pain in the ass, you know that?"

"I hear that's my best quality." Luke grinned. He reached for Jeremiah's wheelchair and moved it beside the bed. "While you're at the garage, what do you say we put a 350 on this thing? Make it really hum?"

Jeremiah shook his head and a slight smile crossed his face. "My mother would kill you."

"Nah. She already told me she wants to adopt me. She likes my charming smile."

"She says that to every stray who walks in the door." But there was another smile at the corners of Jeremiah's mouth, and after a moment, he slid across the bed and into the chair. As he reached under his legs to lift them into place, Luke felt that slap of guilt again.

Your fault. You should have been paying attention. Should never have gone to that party.

Luke leaned forward. "Here, let me help—"

Jeremiah jerked away. "I got it." He shifted his weight in the seat, then gave the wheels a push and headed out of the room. Over Jeremiah's head, his mother whispered, "Thank you," to Luke, but at that moment, Luke didn't feel as though he'd done a damned thing worth anyone's gratitude.

The garage smelled of motor oil and gasoline. Dust motes floated in lazy streams across the room, but the space was clean, neat and organized. Tools lay in the chests and in designated drawers, and supplies stacked the shelves lining the walls.

"I don't think I've ever seen the place this clean," Jeremiah said. "Since when did your dad get so organized?"

"I did it." Luke shrugged. "I got tired of trying to find stuff, so I spent a weekend getting it all straightened out."

"You? Organized?"

Luke shrugged again. "It caters to my inner laziness. I spend less time looking for the impact wrench, and more time with the ladies."

Jeremiah laughed. "Now, that sounds like the Luke Barlow I know." He wheeled to a space beside the workbench and backed his chair against the wall. "So, how many are you dating at once now? Two? Ten?"

"None." Then Luke reconsidered the answer. After that kiss at the zoo… "One."

"One? You're slipping, Luke. I count on you for living vicariously."

"Nothing's stopping you from getting out there and dating."

"Nothing but this." He smacked the arms of the wheelchair. "It doesn't exactly scream *date me*."

"The right girl—"

"Doesn't live here." Jeremiah nodded toward the Mazda sitting in the bay. "What you working on here?"

"Joe's been having trouble starting it. I figure it's either the plugs or the ignition coil. If you want to help, you can hand me tools and tell me what to do."

Jeremiah shrugged, as if he didn't care one way or another. "I got nothing better to do."

As Luke got to work, Jeremiah began to ask questions, offer his advice on using this part over that part, replacing this over that. Jeremiah had always had an innate sense for what was wrong with a car, and as Luke tinkered with the engine, Jeremiah became more and more involved, even climbing out of his chair to slide under the car and give his two cents on the brakes. For a minute, it was like the old days when the two of them had worked in Gator's on weekends and during the summer. They finished up the Mazda, and Luke switched it out for a Chevy that needed a new muffler.

He was just finishing up the exhaust job when he saw a pair of familiar shoes enter his line of vision. They blinked little red lights, and that made Luke grin. He braced his hands against the underside of the car, then pushed, sending the wheeled creeper rolling out from under the Chevy.

Peyton stood just behind Maddy, a protective hand on her niece's shoulder. The two of them were the picture of late summer, with floral-print sundresses. Maddy's hair was swooped into a ponytail, but Peyton had left her blond locks long and curly around her shoulders. She had on simple white sandals, and he noticed a fresh coat of red polish on her toes. He wondered if she'd done that because she was going to see him, or if she always painted her toenails. His heart skipped a beat and he grabbed a rag from the bench to wipe the worst of the grease from his hands. "What brings you beautiful ladies into the garage?"

Peyton gave Maddy a little nudge. "Go ahead, sweetie. It was your idea."

"We wanna go on a picnic," Maddy said. "And we wanna ask you to go, too."

"A picnic?" He bent down to Maddy's level. "Is there gonna be fried chicken and potato salad?"

"I was going to pick up some healthier options," Peyton said. "Salads."

Jeremiah snorted. "Salads? What kind of picnic is that?"

Peyton gave him a smile. "Hey, Jeremiah. I haven't seen you in years."

"Nice to see you, too, Peyton." He nodded toward Maddy. "You have a kid?"

"She's Susannah's daughter. This is Maddy." Peyton bent down and waved toward Jeremiah. "Maddy, this is Jeremiah, Luke's friend."

"How's come you're sitting in a chair with wheels?" Maddy asked.

His brows rose in surprise, but he offered Maddy a good-natured smile. "My legs don't work anymore."

"How's come?"

Jeremiah shifted in his seat, and Luke braced himself for the answer. *Because my best friend stopped paying attention at the worst possible time. Because Luke let me down. Because—*

"Because I made some stupid choices." Jeremiah cleared his throat, his face pained, and the shadows that had been temporarily erased in the garage were back in place in his eyes. "Anyway, I better get home. See ya, Luke."

Before Luke could say anything, Jeremiah had wheeled out of the garage and down the sidewalk. Luke watched him go and felt that same stinging slap of guilt resonating in his chest.

"Luke, are you gonna come on our picnic?" Maddy asked, drawing his attention back to the little girl in front of him. To his daughter, who was asking him to leave work, and to go along with her on a picnic. Luke might not have a lot of experience being a dad, but he knew a lot of guys would give their right arm for a kid who wanted to spend time with them.

"Of course I want to go," Luke said, and he was rewarded with a thousand-watt smile from Maddy. His heart damned near burst.

"I can pick up the salads and meet you at the park," Peyton said.

Maddy made a face. Luke pinched up his nose and echoed Maddy, which made her giggle. "Salads are no fun for picnics," he said. "We need fried chicken and potato salad. And icebox cake."

"What's icebox cake?" Maddy asked.

"Something the ladies down at the Sip and Chew make

every single Thursday. They also make the best fried chicken in the county, so I think we need to zip on over there and pick up dinner. Then head on down to the lake for a picnic."

Peyton started to protest, but then Maddy started jumping up and down, and talking about cake and chicken and swimming. Peyton's protest died on her lips and turned into an indulgent smile. "Okay, we'll have fried chicken and cake. But just this once."

"I have to run home and change," Luke said, waving a hand at his grease-splattered shirt. "How about I pick up the food and then come get you two? Bring your swimsuits. The water at the lake is still warm."

He told himself he hadn't suggested the lake because he was hoping to see Peyton in a bikini again. Or that the thought of spreading out a blanket, then lying back with Peyton in his arms, seemed like the best way to close out the day.

"I was thinking we'd just picnic at the park," Peyton said. "Something easy, healthy and not too far away. It'll be bedtime before we know it, and the getting back from the lake can take some time."

"What's the worst that can happen? We stay too long and somebody falls asleep in the car?" He grinned. "Come on, Peyton, the lake will be awesome. And while we're there, we can tell the peanut," he replied, tapping Maddy's nose, "all the stories about how we hung out at the lake when we were kids."

Maddy turned and looked up at Peyton. "You used to go there, Auntie P?"

She smiled at her niece. "Yup. Me and your mom, when we were little girls."

"I wanna go," Maddy said softly. "Can we?"

"Okay," Peyton said. "Let's go get our swimsuits. I'll see you in…"

"Thirty minutes, tops," Luke said. "I'll call ahead to the diner, order the food and be over at the hotel in a little bit. You go back, chill for a while and let me do the heavy lifting."

Peyton laughed. "I don't chill, Luke. I'd have no idea how to do that."

Luke took a step forward and brushed a tendril of hair off her forehead. "Then let me show you. Starting tonight."

Chapter Eleven

Indulging.

It wasn't something Peyton did often. Heck, at all. But ever since she'd come to Stone Gap, she'd done exactly that. Indulging in a kiss with Luke—not once, but twice. Indulging in a lazy evening at the lake. Indulging in fried chicken.

And right back to indulging in Luke. Ever since they'd arrived at the lake and he'd taken off his shirt, her mind had gone blank. Despite promising to "chill," she'd intended to do some work while Maddy played with Charlie. But the notepad she'd tucked into her bag remained where it was, the design job far from her mind.

"Sure you want to stick to the all-grass diet?" Luke said, holding out a drumstick.

The spicy coating tempted her and seemed a hundred times better than the greens with balsamic vinaigrette that she'd insisted he pick up for her. "It does smell good."

"Then have a bite."

She put up a hand. "I shouldn't."

"One bite won't hurt you, I guarantee it." He grinned. "Take it from Dr. Luke."

That sent a little shiver through her, along with a mental flash of how exactly he could take her temperature. "Dr. Luke? Since when?"

"Since you could buy a degree on the internet."

That made her laugh. Her defenses lowered, and she leaned closer to Luke, wrapped up in those blue eyes, in the tempting honey of his voice. She took a bite of the fried chicken and nearly groaned. Her fingers went to her lips, as if she could hold the taste there. "Oh, my God, that is good."

"Told you so." He nudged the container toward her. "Here. Have a whole piece. Hell, have two pieces. Really live on the edge."

She picked out a wing, leaving the bigger pieces behind. Maddy had already eaten as quickly as possible, then run down to the edge of the lake to toss a stick for Charlie on the muddy shore. Luke had brought a blanket—surprising her because he'd covered all the details—and spread it out for him and Peyton to sit on. He'd set up the food, leaving the plastic container holding the icebox cake in the thick paper bag the diner had filled.

"I have to say, I'm impressed, Luke. You thought of everything," she said. "Plates, forks—"

"But not napkins. At least you had a stack of them in your purse."

She shrugged. "It's part of raising kids. You learn to have napkins and wipes on hand at all times." Peyton had figured that out pretty early on after Maddy was born. Susannah often left the house without a diaper bag, a change of clothes or even a bottle for Maddy. Peyton had become the de facto caretaker, the one who made sure to stash an extra set of everything in Susannah's car and kept more supplies in her own purse.

"I'll keep that in mind." He chuckled. "Of course, I don't have too many places to store extra wipes. Unless I get myself a murse."

"Murse?"

"The man-purse. Might make me stylish." He mocked draping a strap over his shoulder and gave her another grin.

She laid her chicken on a plate and leaned back on an elbow. Maddy ran back and forth along the shore, Charlie bounding along at her feet, waiting for her to toss the stick again. "I'm serious, Luke. You surprised me. I just didn't expect you to be so…"

"Responsible?" He chuckled. "I'm not, believe me. I just…"

"What?" she prompted when he didn't finish.

A sheepish grin filled his face. Of all the years Peyton had known Luke, she didn't think she had ever seen him embarrassed or shy. "After forgetting to bring that stuff when I got the pizza the other day, I wanted to make sure this time that I…I impressed you."

"Me? But why?"

"In case you haven't noticed," he said, leaning closer to her, lowering his voice, "I like you a lot."

She laughed, as if she hadn't noticed how her pulse sped up when he got close. How the whole world around them seemed to get smaller and tighter, more intimate. "What is this, high school?"

"Nah, if it was high school, I'd be the cocky football captain who was too full of himself to notice the beautiful girl a few grades behind him."

Her cheeks heated and her stomach did a little flip. In the distance, she heard the putt-putt of a boat motor, and some birds calling to each other. Now it was her turn to feel shy. "I wasn't beautiful in high school."

"You were always beautiful, Peyton. I just never noticed. I was clearly dating the wrong sister. And if I could go back and change that, I would."

"But then you wouldn't have Maddy."

"True. And that is something I wouldn't change." He brushed the hair off her forehead and let his touch linger on her cheek. "But now I want what I missed out on before. With you. Because you, Peyton, are the one who makes me want more. Makes me want to *be* more."

She caught his hand with her own. God, how she wanted to lean into that touch, to let it go wherever it would go, to fall down the rabbit hole with Luke Barlow. "Don't. Please."

"Why?"

"Because I'm not staying in Stone Gap. Because my priority is Maddy, and my job. Because I don't have time or room for one more thing in my life." Because she didn't want to get hurt, because she didn't want to screw all this up. Because this moment felt like a soap bubble, delicate, fragile, liable to burst with the slightest whisper.

"Because you're scared as hell to get involved with someone. With me."

"That's not true. It's just that I'm busy and overwhelmed and—"

"Scared as hell." He touched her face again. "I see it in your eyes, Peyton. I see it in the way you back away every time I get too close. And I see it because...because I feel the same way you do."

"You?" She snorted. "You were never afraid to date anyone."

"To date, no. But to get involved, to give someone my heart, and all that fall-in-love stuff, yes, I've always been afraid. Terrified, in fact. Men don't need haunted houses, they just need strong feelings to make them run for the hills."

Peyton chuckled. "Isn't that the truth."

He leaned back and propped his head on his hands. The touch was gone, the moment broken, and she told herself she was glad.

"Then it's settled," he said. "We'll both stay in our safe little corners and not get involved."

Maybe he was kidding. Maybe he was serious. Either way, a little ribbon of disappointment went through her. The fried chicken no longer looked appetizing, and the sight of her salad made her stomach turn. She wanted space and air, and room to think. To reorient herself on the smart course of not-falling-for-Luke-again. "I'm going to go check on Maddy."

She got up and walked down to the lake, pretending it didn't bother her that Luke hadn't pressed the issue. This was what she wanted—to not get involved, and not get involved with Luke Barlow, of all the men in the world. Whatever she might have felt as a lovesick teenager was dead now, and the adult Peyton knew better than to fall for a heartbreaker with a charming smile.

Except every day that she spent with Luke eroded her own arguments. He was no longer the irresponsible playboy she used to know. He was a man who remembered the plates, who showed up on time and, most of all, who made Maddy laugh.

That was when she wanted Luke the most. When she saw him bend down to Maddy's level to say or do something silly, something that coaxed a smile to her lips. When he'd stomped around the zoo with her, pretending to be an elephant, Peyton had been totally, utterly enchanted.

It hadn't been about the kiss, or the way he touched her, or how he made her heart skip a beat whenever he was in the same zip code. It was how he stomped his feet and made a mascot into a long-lost uncle and made a little girl giggle.

"Auntie P! Look at Charlie! He loves me!"

Peyton smiled at Maddy, who was sitting on the muddy bank with the dog, her arms wrapped around his furry body. He licked at her face, tail wagging, sending more mud flying over both of them. "You're getting all dirty. You're going to need a bath."

"Or a dip in the lake," Luke said.

His voice behind her sent a tremor through her veins. She wanted to turn around and turn into him, to finish what they had started with those kisses, to find out what being with Luke would really be like. But she didn't move, didn't turn around. "Maddy won't go swimming. I forgot her water wings and I know she won't even stick a toe in the water without them."

"You and your rules." He let out a low chuckle. "Learn to let go, live by the seat of your pants."

She gave him a grin. "I'm not wearing pants."

"I noticed, Peyton, I noticed." His voice was deeper now, the tease lighting his eyes. "Being at the lake is all about letting go. Which means you can…improvise."

"Improvise?" Peyton shook her head. "This is Maddy's biggest fear. I don't think improvising is going to work."

Luke watched Maddy, sitting on the bank beside Charlie. "Maybe, maybe not. Let me talk to her anyway, see what I can do."

"Good luck. I've tried every logical, reasonable argument I can think of," Peyton said, "but Maddy is firm on not wanting to swim."

"Maybe the key is to not be logical." He shrugged. "It's worth a shot."

She thought of the elephant steps and the finger painting and realized that she trusted Luke. A week ago, she hadn't, but after she had seen him with Maddy, and seen how, despite his fears, he had so effortlessly shifted into fatherhood, her feelings had begun to change. He might not be the strictest parent in the world, but he wasn't reckless with Maddy, and that was important. And he wanted to get closer to his daughter, which was the best thing for both of them. He couldn't do that if she didn't give him a chance to let the two of them bond more. Then maybe they would both tell Maddy the truth and give her the one thing she hadn't had in her life—a daddy. "Okay."

Luke loped down the hill and stopped beside Maddy. The mud covered her shirt and coated her legs, drying now into a crusty brown second skin. "Lord almighty, kid, you are muddy. How about we go swimming and get you cleaned up? You don't want to get into my car like that. By the time you get home, you'll have a garden growing on the floorboards."

Maddy shook her head. Charlie sidled up beside Maddy, and she bent down to give the dog a hug. "I don't wanna. I don't have my floaties."

"You don't need floaties. You have me."

She shook her head again and clutched Charlie tighter.

Peyton took a step forward, but Luke put a hand out, stopping her. He kicked off his shoes, then stepped into the water so he could bend down in front of Maddy. Charlie wiggled out of Maddy's grasp and came to stand beside his master. "You know, when I was a boy, I was scared of the water, too."

"You were?"

"Yup. My brothers and I came to this lake, and they all went swimming, but I always stayed on shore. I didn't want to go in, because I was afraid I'd sink like a stone. But you know who got me to go swimming?"

Maddy shook her head. Her fingers worked the edge of her shirt, something she did when she was scared. Peyton wanted so badly to go over there, scoop Maddy up and tell her not to worry, but she held her ground, waiting to give Luke a chance.

"Your mommy did," Luke said. "She used to come to the lake, too, in the summer, her and your aunt Peyton. Your mommy was my...my good friend."

"She was?"

"Yup. And she was one of the bravest girls I knew. Both your mommy and your aunt Peyton are really brave girls." Luke ran a hand down Charlie's neck. The dog's tail thwapped against the water, spraying a little bit on both of them. "Do you want me to tell you the story of how your mommy got me to swim?"

Maddy hesitated, then very slowly, she nodded.

Luke came out of the water and turned to settle onto the bank beside Maddy, heedless of the mud. Maddy dropped down into the space on Luke's right, the two of them looking out over the lake, while Charlie waited on Luke's left. Peyton stood just behind them, her heart in her throat.

"Your mom was one of those girls who would climb trees and ride bikes and do whatever the boys did," Luke said. "It was one of the things I liked best about her. She loved this lake, loved it more than any other place in Stone Gap."

"She did? How come?"

"Because she knew the legend behind the lake."

Legend behind the lake? Now even Peyton was entranced, and she took a few steps closer, settling onto an overturned log a few feet behind Maddy. Peyton had never heard any such legend, never heard Susannah tell a story like that.

"A long, long time ago, there used to be a fisherman who lived in a cabin on that tiny little island in the middle of the lake." Luke pointed to the small bump of land sitting in the distance. As far as Peyton knew, the island had been formed when the lake was dredged decades ago, to make it deeper. No one lived on it, not then, not now. "He loved his little cabin, loved how quiet it was, how the birds would sing to wake him up every morning, but one day, he realized he was lonely. So very lonely."

Even Charlie was wrapped in the story. The dog laid his head on his paws, pressing his shoulder against Luke's leg.

"The fisherman was in love with a beautiful woman named Annabelle, but she lived in town, here in Stone Gap. And that meant to see her, he had to leave his little island."

"Did he have a boat?" Maddy asked.

"He did, but it was broken."

"Did he tape it up? Cuz Auntie P always tapes up my toys when they break. 'Cept sometimes she has to glues them up."

From her perch behind them, Peyton smiled. Tape and glue and sometimes a quick trip to the store for a replacement for a favorite toy that an unsuspecting Maddy accepted as repaired.

"He couldn't tape it or glue it," Luke went on. "His boat was too broken for that. So he only had one choice if he wanted to see Annabelle. He had to swim. The only problem was—" Luke leaned in, lowering his voice "—the fisherman was scared to swim."

"Like me."

"Like you, and like me when I was little."

"What did he do?" Maddy's eyes were wide. The entire lake seemed to still, the water smooth as glass. The birds were quiet, the boat from before now long gone. Even the sun seemed to hold its position, waiting for the story to continue.

"Well, this fisherman had a dog, a goofy yellow dog." Maddy grinned. "Like Charlie?"

"A lot like Charlie. And this dog, he loved to swim, loved it like he loved playing fetch."

"Like Charlie?" Maddy asked again.

The dog's ears perked up, and his attention swiveled between Luke and Maddy. He clearly knew they were talking about him. Luke gave the dog a tender ear rub, then went on.

"*Exactly* like Charlie. So the fisherman sat his dog down and talked to him. He told the dog he was scared of swimming, but he really wanted to get across the lake to see Annabelle so he could marry her and they could live in that little cabin. He asked the dog to do something special for him."

Maddy was turned toward Luke now, her eyes wide, her attention on him and nothing else. "What?"

"He asked his dog if he would swim with him, so the fisherman wouldn't get scared. The dog wagged his tail and ran over to the water. So the fisherman took off his boots and got in the water." As Luke told the story, Peyton could almost see an imaginary fisherman standing in the water, filled with trepidation and desire and hope. "He was so scared, he was shaking, but his dog, that big goofy yellow dog, stayed right beside him. The fisherman walked as far as he could walk, then he stood there, not sure how to swim. The dog went out in the water ahead of him and showed him how to do it. Do you know how a doggy swims, Maddy?"

She nodded. "I see Charlie do it. He goes like this." She mocked a dog paddle.

"Exactly. That's how the fisherman did it, and he got all the way across the lake that day. He got out of the water, ran over to Annabelle's house and married her on the spot. They lived on that little island for a long, long time, with their goofy yellow dog, and they were very happy."

It was the perfect happy ending, Peyton thought. As wonderful as the ones she had read in the novels that were her best friends when she was a young girl.

Luke gave Charlie another ear rub, but kept on talking, his voice as calm as the lake lapping gently at their feet. "Your mom told me that story, and then she told me that if the fisherman could swim clear across this big lake, then I could swim out to the dock. She swam right beside me, and we swam just like the fisherman, all the way to the end of the dock." Luke pointed to the wooden pier, jutting twenty or so feet into the water.

"That's really far," Maddy said.

"How about you and me try swimming like Charlie? Just right here. We'll stay real close, so you can touch the bottom the whole time." Luke picked up the stick that Maddy had been tossing for the dog earlier. "Here, let's have Charlie show us how. Throw that in the water, Maddy, and Charlie will swim right out and get it for you."

Maddy got to her feet and stood at the very edge of the water. Charlie popped to his feet and stood beside her, his body tense with anticipation. "Charlie, you gotta swim real good, okay?"

The dog barked, and Maddy tossed the stick. It only went a few feet into the water, but Charlie charged after it all the same, switching to a dog paddle when his paws lost contact with the bottom of the lake. Then he turned, paddled back and climbed onto the bank to drop the stick at Maddy's feet.

"He did it!" Maddy squealed. "He's a smart doggy."

"He is indeed. Now let's take him with us, and we'll try to swim just like him." Luke put out his hand. And waited. Peyton could see the tension and hope in his face, how badly he wanted to bond with Maddy, to be her father. A father who taught his child how to swim. A father who helped his child overcome a fear. A father who was afraid of diving in, because he might sink.

Maddy looked at Luke's hand. She caught the hem of her shirt and bunched it into a tight ball, and kept on staring at his hand. Then she raised her gaze to Luke, a question in her eyes.

He smiled down at her. "Just like Charlie, Maddy. You can do it."

Her fist tightened around the fabric even more, and for a second, Peyton held her breath, waiting for Maddy to say no, for her to run back up the hill and far, far away from the water. But then her little hand opened, and the hem tumbled back into place. Maddy slid her palm into Luke's and took a step forward with him.

Another.

Charlie bounded ahead of them, his tail wagging encouragement. Luke made a gesture with his hand, and Charlie swam out into the lake.

Luke took another step. Maddy followed. Two more steps, three, the water rising to Maddy's waist, her chest.

Maddy's eyes grew wide, and Luke pivoted to take her other hand. "Now I'm just going to hold you here and you can lift your feet. You'll float, just like Charlie does."

Maddy's eyes were wide again, and Peyton strode down to the edge of the water, ready to go get her niece. She saw Maddy's hands whiten as she clutched Luke's tighter, but then, in a moment that made Peyton's heart stutter, Maddy kicked her feet behind her and then...

She was floating.

Not just floating, but laughing. Charlie was beside her, treading water, then he started paddling away, as if he sensed what Luke was trying to do. Maddy looked to Luke, a smile on her face.

"Let's swim like Charlie," Luke said gently. "Try one hand first, Maddy-girl."

Maddy hesitated again, her hands white, holding his so tight, she was probably cutting off the circulation. Wanting to trust. Needing to trust. Another heartbeat passed, and Peyton swore she stopped breathing in that time. Then Maddy let go of Luke's right hand and pawed at the water before her.

"Good job, Maddy." His voice was soft, encouraging. "Now try the other hand. Swim like Charlie does, and be sure to kick, too. And don't worry, Maddy, I'll hold on until you tell me to let go." He shifted until he was beside her, his hands under her belly, helping to keep her above water.

"You promise?" Maddy asked.

"I promise." He lowered his head until he was eye level with her. "I'll hold on, until you tell me to let go."

Maddy stared into his eyes, her face tense, anxious. She started dog-paddling, her legs scissoring at the water. She glanced over at him, her face alight with pride, then nodded. "Okay."

"Okay." Luke removed one hand, and Maddy dipped a bit, sputtered out some water, but then kept going. "You're doing it, kid, you're doing it," Luke said, pride swelling in his expression. "Now I'm going to let go, but don't worry. If you just keep swimming like Charlie, you'll be fine. I'll be right here, Maddy. I'll always be right here."

He pulled his other hand away, and Maddy gasped when she dipped down in the water again and swallowed another gulp of lake. She froze for a second, and Peyton rushed forward, knee-deep in the water now, but then Maddy recovered, sputtered for a moment and started paddling again. She powered forward, with Charlie keeping pace beside her, and Luke slowly treading water on the opposite side, never more than a few inches away. "I'm doing it, Luke! I's swimming!"

"You are indeed." His smile wobbled and his eyes glimmered. "And you are an awesome swimmer, Maddy. Awesome. I'm so proud of you."

Pride lit up Maddy's face, beamed like the sun in her smile. Beside her, Luke's smile was just as bright, his eyes just as full.

Peyton's heart clutched and tears welled in her eyes. "You're doing it," she whispered to Maddy, to Luke, to the amazing moment that was changing all of their lives. "You're doing it."

Chapter Twelve

"She's all tuckered out," Luke said an hour later. Maddy had been swimming with him most of that afternoon, motoring around the shoreline. As the sun began to set, Peyton had Maddy change her clothes and stay on the sand. They all gathered on the blanket and divvied up generous hunks of icebox cake. As soon as the dessert was finished, Maddy had curled up against Charlie, her head on the dog's back, and told him she was going to read him a story. Two pages into the picture book, Maddy fell asleep. Charlie took one look at the little girl draped across his spine, and he, too, settled down and went to sleep.

The sky was blurring pinks into purples, darkening along the edge of the lake where the sun was edging down. The fishermen had all parked their boats for the night, and the loons had winged their way home. The world around Stone Gap Lake had narrowed to just the three of them.

And, Luke had to admit, it was as close to perfect as the world could get.

If someone had come to him a week ago and said, *You're going to find out you have a daughter, and that will make you completely change your life in the space of a few days*, he would have said they were crazy. But here he was, going on picnics, spinning tall tales about the lake and watching a little girl sleep, thinking it was one of the most amazing things he'd ever seen.

He was getting soft. And maybe that wasn't a bad thing.

"I think all that swimming wore her out," Peyton said. "I should get her back to the hotel."

"My house is closer. Why don't we just go there? I have an extra bedroom for Maddy."

"And…?"

"And nothing more than I don't want the day to end." That was the truth. He was enjoying this new situation, the way it wrapped around him. It was like being home for Christmas, only better. Maybe he could handle this, after all. He wasn't sure where the future was going to go, or how he was going to work out custody with Peyton in Maryland and him in North Carolina, but that was something he'd worry about tomorrow.

Peyton's gaze lingered on her sleeping, happy niece. "Me, too."

Luke gathered up Maddy, hoisting her into his arms. Still asleep, she curled against him, and his chest filled. He stood there for a second, just holding her, holding the moment. "Tomorrow, I want to tell her," he said quietly to Peyton.

"But we don't have the DNA results back yet."

"Even if it says I'm not her natural father, I still…"

He glanced down again at Maddy. "I still want to be the father she needs."

Peyton hesitated, then nodded, a watery smile on her face. "I think it's time. But I think we should tell her together."

"Then maybe you should spend the night," he said, knowing the sentence would open another door. Take another step toward something with an uncertain future.

Instead of answering the unspoken question, Peyton changed the subject. "I'll, uh, put the picnic supplies in the car," she said. "You carry Maddy."

They trekked back to the car, buckling Maddy into her booster seat, then loading the leftovers and blanket into the trunk. It was only a few blocks from the lake to Luke's house, but the drive seemed to take ten times longer than usual. Maddy stayed asleep, and Peyton stayed quiet. Once they arrived at Luke's, Maddy roused a little, but fell asleep as soon as Luke crossed the threshold. He laid her in the guest bed, covered her with the light comforter—inordinately grateful that his mother had insisted on him having at least some real furniture and linens—then left the door ajar in case Maddy woke up and got scared. Charlie, as if sensing where he should be, curled up in the space at the foot of the bed and stayed with the little girl.

"Good boy," Luke whispered to the dog.

He found Peyton in the kitchen, stowing the leftovers in his refrigerator. Her hair was a little windblown from their day by the water, giving her a wild edge. She'd thrown shorts and a T-shirt over her bathing suit, but her feet were bare, her peach legs long and tempting. "I found a bottle of wine in your fridge. Do you want some?"

"Sure. I think I have an opener somewhere around here."

She laughed. "It's a screw top. We're good."

He grabbed two mismatched juice glasses from his cabinet, took the bottle from Peyton and poured them each a glass. She leaned back against the counter and raised hers. "Cheers."

He clinked with her and thought this toast was a hell of a lot better than any of the ones he'd shared with his buddies. "To a great day."

"It was a great day. Thank you."

"You don't need to thank me. I didn't do much beyond pick up the food."

"You taught Maddy how to swim. That was a huge deal, Luke." She smiled and shook her head in wonder. "I was so worried the whole time but you...you handled it perfectly."

He grinned. "Like a pro?"

"No." She paused and for a second his heart fell, then she lifted her gaze to his and he saw the sheen of tears in her green eyes. "Like Maddy's dad."

His heart swelled. He hadn't realized how much he needed—no, craved—hearing that stamp of approval from Peyton until just then. "It's the first time you've called me that. I like it. A lot."

"Then maybe you should get used to those words going forward."

"Maybe I should." They shared a smile in the dim light, then clinked glasses again, as if putting a seal on the promise.

"Was any of that story about the fisherman true?" Peyton asked.

"Bits and pieces. You know the South. There's a legend behind every strand of Spanish moss."

Peyton chuckled. "That's true. Did Susannah really make all that up?"

"Some of it, yeah. She had quite the imagination. I always thought she would grow up to be a writer or something."

"You know, when I was a teenager, I would have been jealous to hear you speak of my sister so fondly. But now…it's nice. Like we can share the memories of her."

"To Susannah," Luke said, and they clinked again. "And to the wonderful gift she gave us both."

"She did indeed," Peyton said softly. "I wish she had lived to see Maddy grow up. And to pursue some of her own dreams. Susannah just couldn't believe in herself, and I think that's what kept her from ever getting a decent job."

"You've done well for yourself, though." He tipped his glass toward her. "You took that creative Reynolds girl gene and made a hell of a name for yourself in interior design."

"How do you know that?"

He grinned. "Google."

"You looked me up on *Google*?" She laughed. "Why?"

He shifted into place beside her, hip to hip, parked against the counter. "Because when you can't stop thinking about a girl, you realize you want to know everything about her. And so you stay up late at night and check Google sometimes."

She blushed and dipped her head, then looked up at him through the curtain of her long blond hair. "Really?"

"Really." He brushed the hair off her face and tucked it behind one ear. "So what didn't the internet tell me?"

"There's not much to tell." Peyton wrapped her hands around the glass but didn't drink. "I lead a pretty boring life. Work, go home, go back to work."

He shifted in front of her. "What happened to the Peyton who used to go swimming in the lake when it was freezing out? Who used to tag along when I went trek-king through the woods or rescuing hurt dogs?"

"She grew up." Peyton shrugged. "I was never much for downtime, Luke. I was always busy trying to get good grades or get into college or get my career off the ground."

"Why? Why not stop and enjoy the picnics and skinny-dipping—"

"Skinny-dipping? *That*, I never, ever did."

"We will definitely have to find time to do that, then." He watched the way her breath sped up when he was near, and how she licked her lips, which made him want to do the same, to have her in his arms again. "What about lazy Sundays in bed, doing nothing more than reading the paper and making love?"

"I never, ever did that, either. Well, I've done the making-love part—" she blushed "—but not the lazy-Sunday part."

"Then that is another thing we should remedy some-day. And when we do, I'll make pancakes."

She smiled, as coquettish as a debutante. "You're as-suming I want to spend a long, lazy Sunday in bed with you."

The thought of her in bed with him, any day of the week, left him weak at the knees, made his brain short-circuit.

"Mighty presumptuous of me, but I think—" he reached forward, took her glass out of her hands and put it on the counter beside her, watching her pulse tick in her throat "—you've thought about it as much as I have."

"I've thought about a *lot* of things that involved you, Luke Barlow. I am, after all, a very creative girl." She blushed when she flirted with him, which was cute and endearing and sexy as hell. "You said so yourself."

Holy hell. That was a good thing. A damned good thing.

"As long as at least one of those creative thoughts revolved around a bed, I'm happy."

"In, around." She shrugged, and he thought it was the sexiest move he'd seen all day.

"You surprise me. Since when have you been thinking these 'in, around' thoughts?"

The blush again, and she glanced away. "For a long time. I used to…have a crush on you back in high school."

"You did? How could I have missed that?"

She shrugged. "I guess I was easy to miss, with all those books and those nerdy glasses."

He tipped her chin until she was looking at him. "You, Peyton, are impossible to miss. And I am glad to have this second chance with you."

A smile danced on her face. "Me, too."

"So, tell me," he said, leaning in closer. "Are you still infatuated with me?"

"Not at all," she said, then a tease lit her eyes. "What I'm feeling now is definitely much, much more grown-up."

"Hmm… I think I'm feeling the exact same thing. What is that they say about waiting? That it makes everything that much sweeter. And you are very, very sweet indeed."

His lips were centimeters away from hers, their breath mingling in the space between them. The tension that had been at the edge of every word today, every look, built like a pot finally coming to a boil. He leaned closer, tilting his head to the left, until his lips were brushing against hers and he could hear the rapid beat of her heart in the space between them. He wanted her, more than he could ever remember wanting anyone or anything. "I want to kiss you, Peyton."

Her eyes widened, but she turned her chin up toward his and laid a hand on his arm. "Then whatever are you waiting for?"

"You. To make the first move."

A smile curved up one side of her mouth. A sexy, seductive, amazing smile that danced in her eyes. "That's also something I've never done before."

"You have a very long list of firsts, Peyton Reynolds. I say we start working our way down them. Right…" He brushed against her velvety lips, and she leaned into him, but he pulled back, teasing her. "This…" He did it again, heard a little mew of disappointment when he pulled back again. "Very—"

Now Peyton surged into him, her hands tangling in his hair, crushing the distance between them. It was hard, it was fast, it was incredible, like a dam bursting. Just that quickly, she was kissing him and yanking his shirt out of his waistband. Desire surged through his veins, pounded in his head. He pressed her against the counter, his erection a hard length of need between them. She got his shirt off and tossed it to the side, and then her hands were on his skin, and whatever arousal he'd thought he was feeling before was nothing compared to the nuclear bomb her touch ignited. He tugged off her shirt, then fumbled with the clasp on her shorts.

Peyton pulled back, grinning. "I'll do it," she whispered, then flicked the clasp open and let the shorts drop to the floor, standing there in just her bikini and nothing else.

Now he slowed, because he wanted to enjoy her, enjoy this moment. He trailed kisses along her neck while his hands worked to untie the strings that held the top in place. The back came undone first, swinging the shiny green fabric forward, his hands following, cupping the warm, sweet globes of her breasts. His thumbs traced over her nipples and she gasped, arching against him. With one hand, she undid the strings, and the bikini top tumbled between them and onto the tiled floor.

He stepped back, letting the warm light above the sink bathe Peyton's skin with a soft gold glow. He plucked one of the strings against her hip and watched it unfurl. "You are beautiful."

She blushed, pale crimson filling her cheeks, flushing her chest.

"And desirable. And sexy as hell," he finished, then plucked the second string. When the bikini bottom dropped into the pile of clothes at their feet and Peyton stood before him, naked and inviting, he knew what he had been missing all his life. This...

Incredible, intoxicating, strong and amazing woman. Later, he vowed, later he would tell her that. But right now, all he wanted was to taste her and to know her. He started kissing her again, her neck, her breasts, her belly, every inch of her that he had never explored before, never known. And when he dropped to his knees before her and kissed her there, she gasped and her hands dug into his hair. Then she was moaning and calling his name and begging him, and he was scrambling in his wallet for a moment of common sense.

She took the condom from him, tore open the wrapper, let it, too, tumble to the floor with their forgotten clothes, then slid the condom on him with two hands. He nearly came undone at her touch, as if he was fifteen again.

He hoisted her up onto the counter and slid into place between her legs. She wrapped her thighs tight around him, and he thrust into her, one long, smooth glide, then another, another, another, until he was lost in the amazing world that was Peyton and she was calling his name in a soft, pleading voice. They came together in one long, glorious moment that seemed to stop Luke's heart. He held her there, until their hearts slowed and their breathing evened. But the magic, whatever amazing magic had just transpired, hung in the air, as if none of this would ever be the same again.

Eventually, he helped her down off the counter and handed her clothes back to her, though he would have preferred to stare at her amazing body for the next hundred years. "Stay," he whispered. "Stay with me tonight."

Peyton raised her green eyes to his. "There's nowhere else I'd rather be."

Chapter Thirteen

Sunday morning brought cheerful sunlight streaming through the windows of Luke's bedroom, warming the covers, and casting Luke in shades of gold. Peyton stretched and laid there for a long, long time, just watching him sleep. Last night had been...

Incredible. Everything she had dreamed of for years, and then some.

But as she reached for Luke, her hand hesitated. Last night had also added a complication she hadn't expected. Her life was in Baltimore, with her job, with Maddy. Not here in Stone Gap, with Luke. She hadn't come here with the intention of moving back here permanently, and the closer she got to Luke—too close already—the more her heart tempted her to stay. Her brain warned her to get out, to leave, before staying in bed with this man got too comfortable.

Reaching for the floor, she felt around and grabbed her shirt, pulled it on, then went downstairs to see if Luke had any coffee. In the kitchen, she saw the pile of mail he'd picked up on his way into the house yesterday, tossed on the counter and forgotten. On the corner of one envelope, she saw the return address for the DNA test center.

Her hand hesitated over that envelope, her heart in her throat. She knew the answer without opening the letter. Knew it in her heart.

Luke was Maddy's father, and always would be. Which meant she couldn't pretend any longer that she didn't have to figure out something regarding custody. She wanted to have a moment to breathe, to think.

She headed back upstairs, the unopened envelope in her hands. Moving quietly, Peyton rolled over and started gathering her clothes from the floor. Just as she was fumbling to tie her bikini top without taking her shirt off all the way, Luke reached for her, his fingers trailing a lazy path down her spine. Desire trilled along that line, but she pushed the feeling away.

"Good morning, beautiful," he said.

"I, uh, need to leave." She dropped her shirt over her head. "Lot to do today."

Luke drew back, then sat against the headboard, watching her twist her hair into a ponytail. "What do you mean, leave? I thought you were going to stay so we could tell Maddy that I am her father—that I want to be her father, regardless of what the test says, and then we can bring her to my mom's house for dinner and for her birthday. I'll need a few minutes to run to the store and get her a present, but other than that, I wanted to spend the day with both of you."

"The test already came back." She handed him the envelope. "It was on your counter this morning."

Luke tore open the envelope, scanned the sheet inside,

then broke into a wide grin. He flipped it so Peyton could read the words, too. *Probability of Paternity: 99.9%*

"So it's official," Luke said. "I'm really Maddy's father. That is...wonderful."

"Yup. Wonderful." But there was no excitement in her voice, just the deep dread with knowing that from this day forward, she was going to have to split Maddy between Maryland and Stone Gap.

Peyton wanted to stay here, in this warm bubble that came after making love. She wanted to believe this was forever, that they would all walk off into a sunset, happy forever. But Luke had made no such promises or declarations, and sitting here, waiting for a miracle, wasn't going to change anything.

"Peyton?" Luke asked. "What's up? Aren't we going to go tell Maddy?"

Peyton rose and pretended to be looking in her purse for something, just so she could avoid looking at Luke. Because if she looked at him, all comfortable in that bed with the sun glinting off his dark hair, she knew she'd lose her resolve. "I...I don't think that's a good idea. It's a lot to spring on Maddy, and I'm just not sure today is the right day to do that."

"What do you mean?" Luke swung his legs over the side of the bed, then pulled on a pair of shorts. "We talked about this, Peyton, and now that we know it for sure, I see no reason to wait another second."

She ran a hand through her hair, dislodging the ponytail. She yanked the rubber band out and flipped it around the hunk of hair again. Her hair was a mess, her life was a mess, but right now, she didn't care. She just wanted to leave before she said or did something she'd regret. "I just don't think it's a good time."

"Not a good time? Or..." he asked, reaching for his

shirt on the floor, discarded in their rush to get to the bed last night, "are you just scared?"

"I'm not scared of anything," she said. But she looked away when she said it. "I just have to go. I need to get Maddy some breakfast—"

"I have breakfast here. And if I don't have anything that you girls like, then we'll head down the street for breakfast." He pulled on his T-shirt, and even dressed, she realized, he looked just as tempting as he had undressed. "So let's get the munchkin up and grab some pancakes."

Every argument Peyton had, Luke had a counter. He was right, and she knew she had to tell Maddy soon that Luke was her father, but Peyton knew that once she did that, she'd be cementing a connection to Stone Gap. God, why hadn't she thought this through before she brought Luke into Maddy's life? Did she really want to keep coming back to this town, seeing this man, over and over?

This man who had made love to her, who had completely and totally captured her heart—

And had made her no promises. That was what bothered Peyton the most, what had her ready to hyperventilate. She was doing the one thing she warned her clients against—making rash, emotional decisions that would have long-lasting ramifications. *Think about it calmly, logically, with a clear plan for the future. Don't just think about today. Focus on tomorrow.*

And what had she done? Last night, she hadn't thought past that moment, about how much she wanted Luke. Not about what sleeping with him would do to her heart the next morning.

"We can do breakfast another day, Luke. I think it's best if I just get Maddy back on schedule."

"It's her birthday. Let the schedule go." He captured her hand and tugged her back down to sit beside him.

She wanted to curve into him, to tell him everything that was worrying her. But the truth was, Luke was the problem she wanted to talk about, and she sure as hell couldn't tell him that.

"What's really worrying you, Peyton?" Luke asked. "Because we need to talk about this. Talk about Maddy, and talk about the future." He gave her hand a squeeze. "I don't want you to worry, Peyton, because I want the same thing you do. What's best for my daughter."

Peyton let out a breath. "Good. I was worried…"

"Worried about what?" he prompted.

She swallowed hard and faced him. "Worried that you were going to do something crazy like ask for sole custody."

"Sole? No." He shook his head. "She loves you, that's clear, and you're her mother now. A good mother, I might add."

"I'm trying." She thought of how fragile Maddy still was, how the little girl was still stuffing her grief away. They'd made progress in the past few days, but they still had a way to go. She wished there was a guidebook for the road ahead, just so she could be sure every decision she made for Maddy was the right one.

"I don't want sole custody," Luke said, "but I do want joint custody."

The two words, words she had expected, but still, words she had hoped she'd never hear, hung in the air. "Joint? But…I live in Maryland. How would that work? She's only four. I can't just put her on a plane."

"So move back here. Let's raise Madelyne together." He took her hand in his and gave her the charming grin that had won her over a thousand times in the past. "I think we make a hell of a team."

"I can't move back. My career is in Baltimore—"

"I'm pretty sure we use interior designers in North Carolina."

"My condo is there—"

"And we have houses here. All kinds of them."

"Maddy's school is there—"

"Well, what do you know, we have schools here, too." He tipped her chin until she was looking at him. She was drowning in his blue eyes, in the temptations that lingered there. How easy it would be to fall for that again. Too easy. "What's your real argument, Peyton? Everything else we can work out. Work on."

She jerked to her feet. "I can't move here, Luke. I can't uproot my life, Maddy's life. I never expected you to get so involved with Maddy. When I came to Stone Gap, I thought you'd sign over custody to me and we'd be done."

"And you'd do what?" Frustration flashed in his eyes, set in his jaw. "Send me a photo once in a while, tucked inside a Christmas card? What about my parents? My brothers? You're not just denying me a relationship with my daughter, you're denying all of them one, too. And most of all, denying Maddy the very things she wants and needs. A father. Grandparents."

His words were sharp, harsh, cold, and Peyton wanted to take the entire conversation back, start over again. "Not just once in a while. I'd keep you in the loop on what was going on in her life." But saying that didn't make it any better. In fact, Peyton realized, admitting the truth made it worse, a lot worse.

"I want to be a part of my daughter's life, Peyton. And you can't take that away from me already, after I just found out I'm her father. I want more time, Peyton. I want time for the next gazillion years. I want to know her, watch her grow up, be there to open Christmas presents and see her off to school." He got to his feet and paced the room, cursing under his breath, running a hand through his hair. "I don't want a legal battle over this. I don't want a battle at all." He stopped pacing and faced her, anguish deepening the creases around his eyes. "Why won't you tell me what's really behind all this sudden need to leave? All day yesterday and last night, we were fine. Now you can't wait to get out of here and get back to Maryland?"

"I just...do better there."

"You did just fine here, you and Maddy. You told me yourself she's been happy here. Why would you want to change that?" He strode up to her, his blue eyes flashing with anger, then softening. He brushed an errant strand of hair off her forehead. "What is it, Peyton? Tell me."

It was the way he asked, those honeyed tones in his voice, that undid her. The truth came out in sentences that quaked, because Peyton had never admitted failure, never admitted she was overwhelmed or couldn't handle it all. "I'm scared, Luke. I'm scared of staying. I'm scared of leaving. I'm scared of screwing all of this up. But most of all—" her voice cracked "—I am so scared of relying on anyone besides myself. I know I can count on *me*. But there is *no* one else in my life that I can depend on, that I've *ever* been able to depend on. Just me."

And that, Peyton knew, was what drove everything she did. Why she worked so hard, moved so fast, stuck so religiously to a schedule. Because if she let up on the gas for even a second, let someone else pick up the slack, she was afraid they would let her down. As her mother had, time and time again. As Susannah had, every single day since Maddy had been born. And as Luke had, when she'd fallen in love with him and realized he never said he felt the same.

"Then let me help, Peyton," Luke said. "Let me be a part of Maddy's life."

Turn her life upside down. Rely on him. Trust him. That would be a monumental leap for Peyton, one she wasn't so sure she was ready to take. Before she answered him, Luke's cell phone rang. He answered it, then let out a curse.

"I'll be there in five minutes." Luke hung up the phone, tucked it in his shorts, then turned to Peyton. "Joe Miner got his pickup stuck in a ditch over on County Road 34. I need to get the tow truck and pull him out. Shouldn't take more than an hour, and when I get back, we'll finish this discussion, find a happy compromise, have breakfast and tell Maddy the truth. *Together*. Okay?"

She nodded, because she didn't trust herself to speak. Luke headed out the door and five minutes later, Peyton gathered up a sleepy Maddy and left.

The house was empty.

Luke cursed five ways to Sunday, but that didn't bring back Peyton or Maddy. He stood in his front hall, with a take-out bag from Miss Viv's in his hands, filled with warm chocolate chip pancakes and a birthday candle he'd bought at a convenience store on the way back, and knew he'd been a fool.

Charlie sat down beside him and started to whine.

"I don't suppose she told you where she went?" Luke asked the dog.

Charlie barked.

"Well, I'm not sure where *woof* is, but we're going to go get them anyway," Luke said. "Let's give Peyton a little time to cool down and think. In the meantime, I have one thing to do first. Something I should have done a long time ago. Sound like a plan, puppy?"

Charlie leaned his head against Luke's thigh and wagged his tail.

"Yup. Should have done it a long, long time ago," Luke said quietly, then he loaded Charlie in his car and headed for town. He made a pit stop at a toy store first, then drove to the other end of Main Street, to the quiet section of town. It was the Stone Gap he loved and remembered from his childhood, the one where kids climbed trees and wished on stars and thought nothing would ever cloud the future.

Luke pulled into Jeremiah's driveway, and as he turned off the car, he saw something that gave him hope.

Jeremiah. Sitting on the threadbare sofa on the porch. His wheelchair beside him, empty. Jeremiah sat on the far end of the couch, getting some sun on his face.

Luke loped up the walkway with Charlie at his heels. "Hey, you're in my spot."

Jeremiah chuckled. "This here sofa is on my front porch, which means I get first dibs."

It was a familiar joke, one from the old days when the three friends—Ben, Luke and Jeremiah—would wrestle over the best seat, meaning the one closest to the twins' house and providing the best view of their sunbathing bodies. Luke dropped onto the old cushions. It felt real good to be back here with his old friend while the sun danced off the white planks of the porch. "I came by to offer you a job."

"A job?" Jeremiah scoffed. "Doing what? Being a doorstop?"

Luke tried to hold back a laugh but it escaped him all the same. "You know, for a guy who can't walk, you're pretty funny."

"For a guy who can't catch a football, you're pretty ugly." Jeremiah grinned.

"I'm serious, buddy," Luke said. "I want you to come

work for me at Gator's Garage. My dad is retiring, and I'm taking over. I'm going to need an extra set of hands."

"How the hell can I do that?" Jeremiah gestured toward the metal wheelchair, never far away. "I'm stuck in a chair all day."

"I've been reading up on ways to make the garage more accessible. Lower counters, more things on wheels, and if I shave a few feet off the office, I can gain enough space to let you wrangle that chair around any car in the bay. Thankfully, I have a brother who loves to do construction, and I'm pretty sure I can get the family discount on the work." Luke grinned. "So, do you have any other arguments for why you shouldn't take the job and become a productive member of society again?"

Jeremiah looked at Luke for a good long time. They shared a history, with good memories and bad, promises made and promises broken. It seemed as if all that history filled the moments of silence while Jeremiah thought over Luke's offer. After a moment that seemed to stretch on forever, he nodded. "Only if you stock the fridge with Dr. Pepper."

"Sorry." Luke grinned. "I'm strictly a ginger-ale guy now. It's the drink of grown-ups everywhere."

Jeremiah laughed, long and hard, and the sound of it was music to Luke's ears. "I guess a man can learn to change."

"I guess he can," Luke said, and he sat back against the faded plaid sofa, thinking maybe if he could change this one thing, then maybe there was hope he could change the rest.

Chapter Fourteen

Peyton sat on the back deck of her friend Cassie's two-story house in Stone Gap and looked up at the sky. It was broad daylight, so there was nothing visible above her head but a few wispy clouds and a bright yellow sun. No stars to tell her which way she should go.

"The munchkin is watching a movie with a couple of my rug rats," Cassie said, joining Peyton and handing her a glass of ice water. "She's got her bear and a juice box, so that gives us a few minutes to talk. You want to tell me why you're packing up and leaving town before your two weeks are up?"

"I have a lot of work to do for one of my design projects and it would be easier if I was back in Baltimore to go over samples and—"

"Bull crap. You can hand that off to someone else. And your boss is expecting you to stay here the full two weeks." Cassie laid a caring hand on Peyton's shoulder. "So what's really running you out of here?"

Peyton sighed. "Luke."

"Did he screw up?" Cassie said. "Because if he broke that little girl's heart, I will kill him myself and stuff him like a Thanksgiving turkey."

"No, he didn't do anything wrong. And that's the problem." Peyton turned to her friend. Tears welled in her eyes, but Peyton refused to let them fall. "He was a wonderful dad. He taught her to swim and made her smile and laugh again and believe in…magic."

"Then what's the problem?"

"I'm leaving because…" Peyton shook her head and let out a gust. "He broke *my* heart."

"I'll still kill him and stuff him," Cassie muttered. "What did he do?"

"It's what *I* did." Peyton spun her glass and watched the ice cubes tumble over each other. "I fell in love with him and he…he doesn't feel the same."

Cassie put a fist on her hip. "Well, did you tell him how you felt?"

"Not in so many words. But don't you think he should have known?"

Cassie took both of Peyton's shoulders and turned her until they were facing each other. "Oh, girlfriend, you are one of the smartest, bravest people I know. You went after your career like an animal, left town right after graduation. You set up house for your sister and her new baby, taking on all those responsibilities that some people don't take on until they're thirty, hell, ever. But when it comes to love, you are the biggest scaredy-cat in the world." Cassie leaned in and lowered her voice. "You are too busy taking care of everyone else to see that you are giving yourself the short end of the stick."

"I'm not. I'm raising Maddy and working my job and—"

Cassie put out her hands. "See? Proves my point. Where on that list is Peyton?"

"It's hard for me, Cassie." Peyton shook her head. "You don't understand. I spent *years* taking care of everyone else. Somebody had to, or no one would get to school or eat or—"

Cassie placed her palms on Peyton's cheeks. Her hazel eyes softened. "You know what they say. Put the oxygen mask on you first, then everyone else. It's okay to fall in love. It's okay to decide you want to live here, near your best friend and the man who makes your heart sing, and it's okay to say *My life has changed and I no longer want the same things I did before.* That's not failure, that's taking a chance. Allowing yourself to want something else, something more."

"What do you mean?"

Cassie sighed. "Do you really want that promotion? The hours, the expectations? Or do you really want to be a mom to that little angel in the other room and run your own interior design business from home? Maybe buy one of those cute little Southern homes and turn it into the kind of place that makes other women green with envy, so they'll hire you on the spot."

Peyton turned away. She set her drink on the railing and looked out at the green expanse of Cassie's lawn. Bikes, balls and sundry toys littered the grass, as if a happy family life had burst in that space. "That's a whole lot of change, Cassie. I don't know."

"If there is one thing having five kids has taught me, it's that change is the only thing you can count on. And if you don't take the time to put yourself first when the opportunity arises, pretty soon you're going to get lost in the dinners and cleaning and homework." Cassie gave her friend a quick, strong hug. "So don't get lost, and don't be afraid to lean on the family you got right here in Stone Gap. We're not going anywhere. And neither should you."

After Cassie went inside, Peyton headed to the living room and snuggled on the couch with Maddy. The other kids had gone to the kitchen for snacks, leaving Peyton and Maddy alone. "What's happening in the movie, monkey?"

"The princess is going home wif the prince to tell her mommy and daddy that she's gonna get married."

"That's awesome."

Maddy nodded. She had her bear against her chest and the corner of an afghan fisted in one hand. On the screen, the cartoon princess started singing and dancing around the castle.

"So…" Peyton said, affecting a chipper tone, even though deep inside a painful fissure had been widening in her heart ever since she'd left Luke's house, "since today is your birthday, I thought we'd go to the store and buy whatever toy you wanted."

Maddy played with Bo's hair. "I don't wanna toy, Auntie P."

"Then what do you want for your birthday?"

Maddy turned and her blue eyes welled. "I want my mommy to come back."

Peyton's heart broke. She gathered Maddy to her chest and rested her chin on Maddy's head, to hide her own tears from her niece. Maddy climbed onto Peyton's lap, her thin arms wrapping tight around Peyton's waist.

"I want that, too, baby," Peyton said, "but she can't come back. Your mommy is up in heaven, with my mommy, and she can't visit or live here anymore. But she can watch you all the time."

"She's really not comin' back?" Maddy's voice cracked.

Peyton drew back and shook her head. The realization

hit Maddy and her face crumpled, then her tears became rivers running down her cheeks. Peyton's composure wobbled, then fractured, and her own tears brimmed over. This time, she didn't try to shield Maddy from her grief. For so long, Peyton had tried so hard to hold it together because she was afraid that if she cried, Maddy would fall apart, too. But maybe that was what Maddy needed most—to see that the other person who loved her mother was equally heartbroken by the loss. "No, sweetie. And I wish she was, because I miss her all the time."

"Me, too, Auntie P."

Peyton brushed Maddy's bangs off her forehead and pressed a tender kiss in that spot. "She loved you more than anything in the world, sweetie, and she wanted you to be happy. And I know she'd be proud as punch to see you turning four today. You're a great big, wonderful girl."

Maddy's smile trembled, but it held. "And do you think she saw me swimmin' wif Luke?"

"I bet she was up there, cheering and shouting, so excited that you were such a brave girl."

Maddy thought about that for a moment. She rested her head on Peyton's chest and Peyton held her tight, inhaling the sweet strawberry scent of Maddy's shampoo. "I like Luke a lot, Auntie P. Can we see him today? Cuz it's my birthday and he says I can play with Charlie."

See Luke. Tell him what she was feeling. And take a risk, make a change. Could she handle that?

Could she handle the regrets she would have if she didn't?

Peyton ruffled Maddy's curls. "Sure. I think that's a great idea." She was done running from what scared her. Heading back to Maryland wasn't going to change anything, and would only delay the big decisions she needed to make. Peyton needed to stay here and see this through to the end, no matter how things worked out with Luke. For Maddy's sake.

Peyton helped Maddy get dressed in the new clothes Cassie had bought her, putting a bright yellow sundress on her niece, then a floral headband in her hair. There were new light-up sandals from Peyton to complete the outfit, which made Maddy giggle. Along with a matching Barbie doll, and a teeny-tiny purse that Peyton had seen Maddy admire in a store earlier that week. Maddy delighted over every present, insisting on modeling with them in Cassie's bedroom mirror.

As they were leaving, Maddy lifted her blue eyes—Luke's eyes—to Peyton's. "Auntie P, am I gonna get a birthday cake today?"

"Sure you will, monkey."

"Good, cuz I wanna make a wish."

"You do, huh?" Peyton handed Maddy the new purse and doll. "And what are you going to wish for?"

Maddy clutched the doll to her chest with one arm, her bear with the other. "I'm gonna wish for a daddy just like the princess's. A daddy, and a grandma."

Above Maddy's head, Cassie gave Peyton a sad, understanding smile. Peyton looked back at Maddy and thought all she wanted was to see that look of happiness in Maddy's eyes forever. It was as fragile as a new ember, and Peyton knew exactly what she needed to do to fuel the fire going forward. "I know just where we can get both of those, sweetie."

Luke left three messages for Peyton. When she didn't return his calls, he swung by the hotel, but the front desk told him she had checked out already.

She was gone, and he had missed her.

How could he have been such a fool? He should have told her last night—before they'd made love—that he was utterly, completely in love with her. That he'd fallen in love with her sitting beside her on the balcony of the hotel, telling the story of Orion. That he couldn't imagine a day without her smile, her tender touch. And that he was going to do whatever it took to get her back.

He packed an overnight bag, then got back in his car and headed over to his mother's house. The driveway was filled with cars—both his parents' cars, as well as Jack and Meri's Jeep. Sunday dinner, a regular occurrence at Della and Bobby's house, and one of those traditions that Luke really liked. Maybe someday he'd do the same with his own wife and child. For a second, he allowed himself to picture that future, seeing Maddy grow up, them forming a life with—

No. That wasn't going to do him any good at all. Peyton had left town; she'd made her feelings crystal clear. He was just going to have to accept the idea that there was a very real chance he was going to end up a single dad, sharing custody across state lines. With his heart breaking every time he saw or talked to Peyton.

He got out of the car, gathering up Charlie's leash, dog food and bowl. The mutt followed along, as happy as a clam to be going to his second home—where Bobby would sneak him bites of chicken under the table. Luke opened the door and went inside. A football game was playing on the big-screen TV in the front room, where Bobby and Jack sat on the leather sofa, debating the last pass. He saw Meri in the kitchen, helping Della put the finishing touches on a platter of roast chicken.

As soon as she heard the door open, Della dropped what she was doing and ran up to him, then peered around his shoulders. "Where are Peyton and Maddy? I have a birthday cake all ready, and some sparkly candles that I'm sure she's going to love."

The sadness and disappointment hit Luke again like a wave. He never should have run out this morning to pull that truck out of the ditch. He should have called in a favor from Jack, then stayed and finished that conversation with Peyton.

"Peyton is going back to Maryland." Luke laid Charlie's stuff on the bench in the hallway. "I'm going after her, so I was hoping you could watch Charlie."

"Sure, sure," Della said. Her face softened, and she reached out to her son. "I'm so sorry, Luke."

"What's this I hear about a granddaughter coming for dinner?" Bobby's booming voice entered the hall before he did. His father was still hearty and strong, even though his painful knees caused him to limp a bit. He had on a bright orange shirt for his favorite team, the opposite color of what Jack was wearing, which meant the two of them were undoubtedly arguing over the best team in the NFL again.

"Uh, she's not coming," Luke said. Even saying it a second time didn't make it any easier to swallow. He'd screwed this up, but he was going to make it right before the end of the day. "I'm hoping—"

"What do you mean, not coming? Isn't that Peyton in the driveway right now?" Bobby pointed out the open front door.

Luke spun around, his heart leaping. He had to blink twice before he believed his eyes, but sure enough, there was Peyton, looking beautiful in an off-white sundress, flanked by Maddy, who was marching up the walk in a yellow dress and light-up sandals. She had her bear in one hand, a new Barbie in the other and a tiny purse dangling from one wrist.

Then Maddy raised her gaze to the porch and spied Luke. Her face broke into a wide smile, and a second later, she was running, her blond curls flying out behind her like wings.

Luke sprinted down the stairs and opened his arms to Maddy just as she sailed into his chest. It was just like the first time they'd met, except this time, Luke caught his daughter and held on tight. He closed his eyes, inhaled the sweet scent of her shampoo and counted his blessings. "Hey, kiddo. Happy birthday."

"T'ank you, Luke," Maddy said, stepping back, out of his embrace. "Auntie P said we were comin' to your house for my birthday and I was sooooo happy."

Peyton bent down beside them. Her eyes met his, and he saw a flicker of hurt in those green depths. There were clearly still things the two of them needed to talk about, but for now, she was here, with his daughter. Luke took that as a good sign.

Peyton turned to her niece. She drew in a deep breath, then waited a beat before she spoke. "Sweetie, I have something very important to tell you before we go inside. Something that's kind of a surprise." Peyton took Luke's hand in one of her own, and Maddy's in the other. "Luke is not just a friend of mine. He's also your…daddy."

"My…" Maddy looked at Luke. "Daddy?"

Luke wondered if it was possible for a man's heart to burst the first time he heard his child say that word. *Daddy.* Two syllables that made everything else in his life pale in comparison. "Remember how I told you I used to know your mommy? We were boyfriend and girlfriend for a long time, and that's when I became your daddy." That, he figured, was as technical as he wanted to get about the birds and the bees with a four-year-old.

Maddy looked from Luke to Peyton, her brows knitted in confusion. "But how's come you didn't tell me?"

"Because…" Peyton's voice trailed off, and in her face, he saw her wrestle with the truth. There was so much past history between Susannah, him and Peyton, past history that Maddy didn't need to know. He was ready to start with the here and now and let the past stay where it was.

"Because we thought it would be the most special birthday present ever," Luke said, and Peyton gave him a grateful nod. "So your Auntie P brought you here, so that you can meet my whole family today. You have a grandma and a grandpa, and two uncles, and an aunt, and—"

"I have a grandma?" Maddy said. Hope filled her voice, lit her eyes. "*And* a grandpa?"

Luke turned back to the house and saw his family, now emerging through the front door to assemble on the front porch. "And they already love you to pieces. Just like I do, kiddo." He put out his arms and Maddy stepped into his embrace. When her arms went around his neck, and her head nestled in the crook of his shoulder, he thought there was nothing better in the world than this moment. "Happy birthday, Maddy-girl. I love you."

"I love you, too, Daddy," she whispered.

No, *that*, Luke decided, that was the best thing in the world. Ever.

I love you, too, Daddy.

He wanted to hold on to this moment forever. To capture it in a shadow box and hang it on his heart. He closed his eyes and held tight for a long time. Then he hoisted his daughter in his arms, along with her bear and her doll and her purse, and put out his hand for Peyton. "Family dinner awaits."

She shook her head. "It's for family, so I really should—"

"Really should come, too. Because like it or not, you're part of this crazy family. For good." He took Peyton's hand and raised it to his lips.

"I've never had a Sunday family dinner," Peyton said. Tears shimmered in her eyes but his strong and stubborn Peyton didn't let them fall.

He thought of the young girl he used to know, the one who had made it her mission in life to care for all those around her because no one was caring for her. He couldn't undo the long road she'd taken to get here, but he could start paving a new path today.

"Then let's start right now, Peyton. With *our* family." He nodded to his parents, brother and sister-in-law-to-be. "The one you and our daughter just inherited."

"Okay," Peyton said, with a little hesitation and a lot of happiness in her voice. "But I didn't bring anything for dinner."

"You brought the only thing anyone wanted to see. One awesome four-year-old."

They strode up the walkway and into the house, where Maddy was immediately wrapped in the warm embrace of more family members than she could count. Charlie circled the laughing, talking group and let out little yips of approval, while Della bustled back and forth, adding streamers and a birthday tablecloth to the table. In seconds, it had gone from a typical family dinner to an all-out celebration.

Maddy was seated at the head of the table—Bobby giving up his customary seat to his first grandchild—and Peyton and Luke offered to bring in the platters from the kitchen. The busy hum of family conversation came in waves from the other room behind them. Maddy's birthday cake, a two-tiered pink-and-white confection with a quartet of sparkly pink candles, sat on the counter, waiting for the big moment.

"Before we go in there for dinner, I wanted to tell you something. After I left this morning, I did some thinking," Peyton said, "And I had a good conversation with Cassie. I ran out of your house because I was scared. I was afraid that if I told you how I felt, it would make me vulnerable to being hurt. To being let down. I decided that taking the leap is better than always wondering what if."

He couldn't blame Peyton for feeling that way. After all, he hadn't given her any reason to think that what was happening between them was going to last past her vacation.

"Before you leap anywhere, I have a confession of my own," Luke said. She started to protest but he put a finger over her lips. "I was an idiot last night. I screwed it all up, and I'm just going to chalk it up to a first time."

"First time? Surely you don't mean—"

He chuckled. "I don't mean sex. I mean first time falling in love. You are the first woman I have ever fallen in love with, and I want you to be the last."

"You're...you're in love with me?" She blinked.

"Totally and completely. In fact, I was about ready to hop in my car and chase after you. All the way to Maryland, if need be." He took her hands in his and held tight. "When you first showed up on my porch, I was scared as hell. I didn't know how to be a dad, how to be anything other than what I've been for the last few years, which wasn't much. And then seeing you with Maddy...that scared me even more."

"Why?"

"Because you are like mom of the year. You worry about the filleruppers and the schedules and everything I never even thought of." Peyton was an incredible woman, and if she ended up loving him even a tenth of how much he loved her, he was going to be one hell of a lucky guy. "And you...you take care. In such a wonderful way."

"It's just being a parent, Luke. You're going to be a great one, too."

"I'm going to try. But right this second, I want to be a great man. A man that you could fall in love with."

She drew in a breath and met his gaze. "I did that a long time ago, Luke Barlow, and I never stopped. For as long as I can remember, I dreamed of being with you, of being the one you looked at with love in your eyes. I even dreamed of being here, wrapped in this warm and wonderful Barlow family, and going to Sunday dinner."

"And now you're here." He grinned. He loved this woman, loved her stubbornness and her heart and the way she made him work harder for the things he desired most. "And I, for one, am damned glad. Especially because it saves me an eight-hour drive to do this." He dropped down on one knee and popped open a box. In it sat his high school class ring, a thick silver band with football players flanking either side of the center ruby. "If you'll have this slightly damaged bachelor, then I'd like to make an honest woman out of you, Peyton."

Her fingers fluttered to her mouth. "What...what are you saying, Luke?

"Marry me. Because I love you. There isn't another woman in the world I want to be with. I promise, we'll live wherever you want, as long as we live together."

Her gaze went around the kitchen, then out to the rowdy crowd seated at the dining room table. "But if we live here, we get to go to Sunday family dinners."

"You do indeed. Like it or not, my mom expects us every single Sunday. All of us."

"Speaking of Sunday dinner," Jack shouted from the other room, "when are we getting some?"

"Hold on a second," Luke called back. "I'm trying to propose to the woman I love here."

"Well, it's about damned time," Jack said. Della shushed him for cursing.

Luke laughed, then turned back to Peyton. "Will you marry me, Peyton? And before you say anything, I know it's not a real engagement ring, but it was the only one I had handy. Think of it as a temporary—"

"Yes," she said, taking the box from him, slipping the ring into place on her left hand. It was too big, and it spun on her finger, but Peyton didn't care. "This…this is perfect."

He got to his feet and drew her against his chest. He could feel her heartbeat, feel her every breath. Luke leaned in and kissed her, a tender, long kiss that held promises for later.

Then Jack started shouting from the dining room that the food wasn't getting any warmer while the family waited on the lovebirds, and the moment was broken. Luke and Peyton broke apart, laughing like two teenagers caught making out on the porch after curfew. Luke picked up a pair of platters and turned to Peyton. "Guess we better feed everybody before they start charging the kitchen."

They loaded up as much as they could carry and headed into the dining room. Just as Peyton was putting the chicken in front of Bobby, a low rumbling started outside, growing in volume until it became a roar. Just as quickly, the sound died.

"What the he—" Bobby's curse was cut off by a stern look of intervention from Della. "What? Who drives a

motorcycle that loud? Sounds like it was in our driveway, too."

"I told him to come," Della said, her eyes misty. "I
wasn't sure he would."

Then the front door opened and a familiar figure
dressed in black jeans and a dark leather jacket strode
through the door. He took off his helmet and grinned
the same grin that three other men in that house had. "I
heard one of you is getting married and I'm here to talk
you out of it."

Jack laughed and got to his feet. He clapped his brother
on the back. "Sorry, Mac, you're too late. I'm already
in love. Might want to talk to the other one. He just got
engaged five seconds ago." Jack nodded toward Luke.

Mac scoffed. "I go away for a few years and this is
the kind of craziness I come home to?"

Della wrapped her oldest son in a hug and drew him
toward the table. "It's the best kind of craziness, so hush
up and enjoy your family." She placed a kiss on his temple, as if he was five years old again. "It's good to have
you home."

Mac captured his mother's hand on his shoulder and
gave her a smile that seemed a little dimmer, as if whatever Mac had left behind was still haunting him on the
ride. "Good to be back, Mama."

Luke and Peyton went into the kitchen for the rest of
the dishes, and a place setting for Mac. Luke gathered
the basket of rolls and the glass butter dish his mother
used only on Sundays. He snuck a quick kiss on Peyton's
lips just as she was grabbing a plate. "So where are we
going to live, Mrs. Barlow-to-Be?"

Peyton looked around the homey kitchen, filled with
homemade bread and homemade memories. Who knew
that what she had been dreaming of, what she had been

seeking in all those books she'd read, was already right under her nose? She thought of Maddy's smiles, and how they seemed brighter here, surrounded by people who loved her. "Right here. In Stone Gap. That is, after all, where my heart is. Where it's always been."

Luke smiled, that charming grin that had won Peyton's heart a dozen years ago, and gave her one more kiss. "Mine, too, Peyton." His gaze went to his daughter, who gave him a wide, toothy smile, then circled back to the woman who had made his life complete. "Mine, too."

* * * * *

MILLS & BOON®

The Thirty List

At thirty, Rachel has slid down every ladder she has ever climbed. Jobless, broke and ditched by her husband, she has to move in with grumpy Patrick and his four-year-old son.

Patrick is also getting divorced, so to cheer themselves up the two decide to draw up bucket lists. Soon they are learning to tango, abseiling, trying stand-up comedy and more. But, as she gets closer to Patrick, Rachel wonders if their relationship is too good to be true...

**Order yours today at
www.millsandboon.co.uk/Thethirtylist**

0515_ST_13

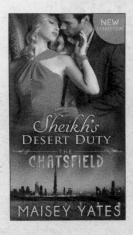

0615/23